Once the mighty Lazax Empire ⸻ galaxy from its capital planet of ⸻ treachery and war erased the Lazax from history, plunging a thousand star systems into conflict and uncertainty.

Millennia have passed. From the ashes of the Lazax Empire the Great Races begin to rise once again, looking to the stars beyond their systems, hungry for more.

It is a time of bold exploration and astonishing discoveries. Alliances must be forged, and fledgling adversaries crushed. These adventuring factions must be forever on their guard, for the shadows of the past are never far behind...

Intergalactic empires fall, but one faction will rise from the ashes to conquer the galaxy.

TWILIGHT IMPERIUM™

The
STARS
BEYOND

EDITED BY CHARLOTTE
LLEWELYN-WELLS

ACONYTE

First published by Aconyte Books in 2022

ISBN 978 1 83908 180 4

Ebook ISBN 978 1 83908 181 1

Cover art by Dominic Harman

Distributed in North America by Simon & Schuster Inc, New York, USA

Printed in the United States of America

9 8 7 6 5 4 3 2 1

ACONYTE BOOKS

An imprint of Asmodee Entertainment Ltd

Mercury House, Shipstones Business Centre

North Gate, Nottingham NG7 7FN, UK

aconytebooks.com // twitter.com/aconytebooks

CONTENTS

A GHOST OF A CHANCE

M DARUSHA WEHM

Captain Khu'Bin of the Mentak freighter *Entropic* stood on the bridge and glared at her navigator, even though Petty Officer Second Class zort-Zaibar had done nothing more than slither a little too loudly toward the communications station.

Khu'Bin kept her mandible closed – she was annoyed and frustrated by their recent run of bad luck; taking it out on her officers would only make things worse. When she'd first taken command of the *Entropic* she'd led a string of successful raids along the trading routes of the Coalition's enemies, but in the past month she had lost contact with three potential target cargo vessels. The latest sighting was over a week ago – an age for a privateer's ship. She was bleeding money on this run – covering fuel and supplies alone had put the ship's coffers deep in the hole – and this was her first captaincy. She had no guarantee of her continued command and no savings to cover a shortfall. While her crew worked only for shares of the spoils, they wouldn't be content with a big pile of nothing for long.

7

Those cargo haulers had to be somewhere. Space didn't just swallow ships whole and spit them out elsewhere. Not usually, anyway.

"Captain, we have a contact," zort-Zaibar called out.

Finally. "A ship?" Khu'Bin asked.

"No, sir. It's an object." zort-Zaibar's spoken voice did not allow for a great deal of inflection, but Khu'Bin could still hear the disappointment. "It appears to be nothing more than a big chunk of rock that's giving off some kind of magnetic signature."

Khu'Bin grinned hungrily. She'd seen that before, haulers slapping their most valuable loads with beacons that emitted false signatures in order to fool people like Khu'Bin. Well, not people just like Khu'Bin, since she wasn't fooled in the least.

"Things are not always what they appear to be. I bet you it's a cargo container in one of those dead drops," she said, confident. "Helm, put us on an intercept course."

"Uh, sir, can you take a look at this?"

Khu'Bin sighed. You'd think her crew would be a bit more eager to follow up on a possible "legitimate salvage" opportunity. Everyone aboard knew that this run had been a complete bust so far, even the intern.

"What is it, Gharri?" the captain demanded, then stopped short as she inspected the chart that Gharri had up on their screen. The contact was not far, only a short jump away from their current location. But that short jump was only possible by traversing Shaleri space. Astrogator Intern Phekda Gharri glanced at the captain with trepidation in their eyes, the fur on their face quivering slightly.

Shaleri space. The setting for stories pirate captains told their children about ships going missing, lost without a trace. Mysterious, deadly, haunted. People called it a lot of things, but to Khu'Bin it was one thing and one thing only: the fastest path between her ship and a potential cargo that would keep her crew happy and her ship in food and fuel for a long, long time.

"Chart a course, Gharri," she said, and her tone brooked no argument.

"Sir, yes, sir," came the intern's clipped response.

The *Entropic's* thrusters engaged, the faint vibration in the hull noticeable only to the few crew members whose physiologies could detect such slight disturbances. Khu'Bin's eyes darted between the star plotter on the main screen, showing the cartoonishly bulbous outline of the ship overlaid on a chart of the area, and the wide viewport at the bow of the bridge. The viewport showed nothing but the void of space, as usual, even as the animated icon of the ship on the plotter crept closer and closer to the line on the chart denoting the edge of Shaleri territory. It was labeled cleanly, with text in the common Mentak language, but to hear people talk you'd think it would read "here there be dragons" in glowing neon orange script.

The bridge was uncannily quiet as the icon on the screen which represented the *Entropic* drew nearer to the edge of Shaleri space, and Khu'Bin stared at the view outside the port with intensity. Even she held her breath as they crossed the line, invisible to any eye among her crew, about to be met by whatever it was that lay in wait on the other side.

Nothing happened. The light from distant stars continued to shine as steady pinpricks of brilliance in the eternal night of space, not twinkling as they appeared to from beneath the blanket of a planet's atmosphere. The ship continued on its ballistic trajectory, frictionless in the vacuum, just like it would on any other day in any other part of space.

Khu'Bin smiled and turned toward Gharri when a brilliant
bubble of light appeared in the distance in the port, then rapidly
expanded to encompass her ship, its interior illumination no
match for this intrusive glow.

"All stop!" the captain shouted, shielding her eyes from the
intensity of the photonic blast. To their credit, Phekda expertly
engaged the reverse thrusters, bringing the ship's velocity to near
zero in minutes. The light continued to bathe the bridge in its
cold illumination for a long moment before it unceremoniously
disappeared.

Khu'Bin had never encountered a phenomenon like this
before, but she didn't want to make her ignorance known to
the crew. She calmly waited while her eyes seemed to take
forever to adjust to the relative darkness, and when she began
to make out shapes again she saw that what had previously been
unassuming empty space before the ship was now distorted by
three silhouettes in the distance.

"zort-Zaibar?" she called out.

"Aye, captain," the response came, "I have three ships on the
short-range."

"Show me."

An image of the short-range scan appeared in place of the
viewport, and Khu'Bin could clearly discern three spherical
ships, their hulls glistening under the light of the stars. Her
nerves flared in equal measures of excitement and apprehension, but she forced her antennae to still.

"Where did they come from?" she demanded, although her
crew knew her well enough to know that she did not expect
an answer. She knew they wouldn't have one – there had
been no ships visible on their long-range scans, and no one
had technology that would allow them to simply materialize

in space out of nowhere. No one Khu'Bin knew of, at any rate.

"Evasive maneuvers?" Gharri asked.

There was nowhere for them to go that wouldn't take them further away from their quarry, and they needed that cargo. They had barely enough fuel on board to make it to the nearest star base. "No," Khu'Bin said. "zort-Zaibar, are you reading weapons signatures?"

"No, captain, but–"

"Hail them."

"Aye, aye." zort-Zaibar opened a channel on all known frequencies and sent the standard combined audio-video-text-pheromone greeting, but there was nothing in response, not even static. "They're not responding," the petty officer said.

"Yes, I am aware," Khu'Bin barked. "Helm, let's get back to it. Ahead, dead slow, show them our beam. Let's make it clear we're going to sail right past them. I don't want them to think we're *trying* to have a collision."

"Sir?" Phekda Gharri's mouth gaped open at the captain in disbelief, revealing a gleaming set of razor-sharp teeth.

Khu'Bin sighed. "All right, all right, this is above your pay grade, intern. I'll do it." She muscled Gharri out from behind the varnished old wooden wheel and spun it to port while pulling up the yoke. The wheel was a relic from a real Jordian sailing ship, the *Entropic*'s only interior concession to whimsy – its garishly painted hull being another matter entirely. The *Entropic*'s course clearly shifted to a trajectory that would easily pass the spheres at a respectful distance, en route to intercept the cargo on the other side of the passage.

"See," Khu'Bin said to no one in particular as they accelerated slowly toward the alien ships. "They can tell that we're no threat to them. They've just popped out to see who we are; it's nothing to be concerned about. Someone should get some pictures of those ships, though, they are pretty nea–"

Without warning, the farthest sphere erupted in a bright blue strobing glow while nearly instantaneously the *Entropic* was rocked by a blast. Khu'Bin brought the ship to a stop as damage reports began to bleat over the internal comms.

"Hull breach on the starboard quarter!"

"There's a fire in the cargo hold!"

"Casualties in decking. Three down, maybe four, ahhh!"

"They're firing again!"

Behind her a console exploded, and she turned to see her second in command fall to the deck, hands clutching his badly burned face.

"No!" she screamed, but another shock wracked the hull, and she was thrown into a bulkhead. Khu'Bin only had time to stare out the port to see all three spheres aglow before the universe exploded into blue light and then there was nothing more for her, for her ship, for her entire crew of one hundred and eight sapient beings.

Death was the end. The end of suffering, to be sure, but the end of everything else, as well. That was what Khu'Bin had always believed. But when she heard the teeth-grindingly annoying slurp of zort-Zaibar's tentacles on the decking, she doubted. Surely this was impossible. They'd all died, horribly. Hadn't they?

She awkwardly patted her own body, as if she expected to find herself turned into a specter, an incorporeal shade of her once living existence. But no. She felt only the familiar solidity of ridges of chitinous exoskeleton beneath the rough fabric of her uniform.

She scanned the bridge, and saw her crew going about their

tasks undisturbed amid a complete lack of scorch marks, hull breaches, or any sign of destruction whatsoever. She glanced again at the winking red lights on the tactical display, showing the position of the spheres. They were gone. There were no lights, no spheres. No sign that the past few minutes had ever occurred.

She'd known that command would be demanding. Perhaps she was more exhausted by the strain of this fruitless mission than she'd admitted to herself.

"Captain?" Her first mate, a handsome young human by the name of Alkalo, stared at her with concern in his large, dark eyes. He was unharmed, the smooth brown skin of his face showing no signs of injury.

Khu'Bin turned to check the star plotter – yes, they were approaching Shaleri space. Wait, only *approaching*? But hadn't they been well inside …

"Does this seem familiar to you, Alkalo?" she asked, keeping her voice low. She had no desire to alarm the rest of the crew.

He shrugged. "You know space all looks the same to me." There was a note of apprehension detectable in his voice, but Khu'Bin knew her second in command well enough to know that it was directed at her own skittish behavior, not the scenario they were facing.

"Of course," she replied evenly, allowing her forelimb to trail lightly down the sleeve of his uniform. She had watched him die, hadn't she? But here he was, solid as an asteroid. Whether it was a hallucination, a glimpse into a parallel universe, or just the effects of the weight of her responsibility, clearly what she'd seen was not real. She turned sharply to the viewport and stared out into the distance, at the space before them. No matter how long she stared, however, she could make out no spheres, no lights. Only the eerily empty black void of the universe.

She shook her head. Whatever strange experience had caused her to think they'd just been in a space battle, just horrendously *lost* a space battle, it was in the past. Her ability to accept changing situations and adjust to the unknown were what had made her an excellent naval crew member and what had led to her having command of her own privateer's ship at such a young age. There would be time to deal with hallucinations or prognostications at a later time. For now, there were cargoes to claim.

"Alkalo," she said, calmly and with a steady voice, "is the grapple crew ready for salvage?"

The first mate grinned. "Ready and very eager, sir."

"Then let's go give them something to do."

The ship's icon passed over the line into Shaleri space, and Khu'Bin's thoracic cavity vibrated. She tamped down the feeling – this was no time for irrational fear. She gazed out the viewport. There was still nothing to see: no deadly illuminated spheres, no uncanny light blinding their sensors. Only ordinary space and a straight shot at the plunder they'd been hunting for so long.

"Steady ahead."

Three vessels suddenly materialized before the *Entropic*. They were long, spindly things, with trunks of gleaming metal and wide plates of a crystalline substance. No. This couldn't be happening. Not again. Not… differently?

This time, Khu'Bin didn't hesitate.

"Helm, evasive maneuvers! Alkalo, get me firing solutions!" she shouted at her stunned first mate, who was already halfway off the bridge. He ran back to the weapons station and expertly brought the system online.

"Weapons hot."

"Fire!"

To Alkalo's credit, he made no comment about her orders, but immediately opened fire on the ships that had appeared before them. His well-aimed torpedoes streaked away from the ship and slammed into the enemy vessels. At the moment of impact, however, the alien ships shimmered like sunlight on moving water, then seemed to slip sideways through the space around them. The weapons melted into their shields, which appeared to ripple and absorb the energy with no ill effects to the ships. The alien ships made no immediate reaction, then they appeared to shrink into glowing balls. At the center of each ball, a dot of light blossomed, like a star going nova. It then began to spread toward the *Entropic*'s position like a stain, a great bloom of heat and pressure that hammered machine and flesh both in percussive waves.

The *Entropic*'s hull collapsed inward. Khu'Bin couldn't breathe. She couldn't move. She was dying. Her ship, her crew, her mission... gone.

Then even those thoughts were gone as the *Entropic* and all aboard disintegrated in a flash of blue light.

The third time it happened, Khu'Bin thought she surely must be dreaming.

She was in her quarters, gazing out the tiny viewport that could be seen from her bunk. There were no other ships in the area. No pirates, no smugglers, nothing but empty space. Ships should not be appearing out of thin air and shooting her to pieces. That sort of thing was usually relegated to bad holos and cheap entertainment. And nightmares.

"Bridge to Captain Khu'Bin," came a voice from the comlink. "Is everything all right?"

She stretched luxuriously before answering. "Everything is

fine, Alkalo," she said. "I'm just taking the opportunity for some relaxation." She dropped her voice. "You could join me, if you were so inclined."

Alkalo was her first mate in the crew, and something like her ninth mate in life. Tenth? It was easy to lose track. The *Entropic* wasn't a family ship by any means, but Khu'Bin had crewed with many of them since before she'd seized a command of her own. She knew the names and habits of every one of the hundred and eight people on board. Familiarity had bred fondness for quite a few of them.

"I'm afraid not, Koo," Alkalo said, with genuine regret. "In fact, you'd better get back to the bridge. We've finally got a possible cargo contact."

"Excellent," Khu'Bin said, levering herself out of the bunk. Then a shiver passed through her body. She shook off the feeling that it was all happening again. It wasn't like her to be so foolish. It had only been a dream. A terrible dream, to be certain, but nothing to be concerned about.

She strode onto the bridge and froze as she saw the star plotter, showing the now familiar outline of Shaleri space, with the tiny image of the *Entropic* sailing toward what she now knew deep in her antennae was their imminent destruction.

"Ready about," she barked, to surprised looks and questioning chitters from the crew. There was no doubt in her mind that none of them had any memory of the events she'd experienced, and she knew just as surely that it was her responsibility alone to prevent another catastrophe. "You heard me. Turn. This ship. Around."

"Aye, aye, sir!" Phekda Gharri stabbed at the console then reached out to spin the wheel.

Nothing happened.

"Helm!" Khu'Bin demanded.

"I'm giving it all I have, captain," Gharri said, and Khu'Bin saw her young officer visibly straining at the wheel, desperate to follow her orders, but as if it had a will of its own, the ship continued on its course directly toward Shaleri space.

"Captain?" Alkalo glanced at her sidelong. "Do you know something we don't?"

Khu'Bin looked around at her bridge crew, all engaged in trying to regain control of the helm, but otherwise unperturbed. It was not a dream. Somehow, she was living the same terrible moment again and again, different but the same. Why was this happening to her? And why was she the only one who knew that it was happening at all?

"I'm afraid I do," Khu'Bin said, as they passed over the invisible border and she braced for the inevitable.

This time the three ships were all different: one appeared to be nearly organic, with a vaguely reptilian shape, another had a large set of featherlike sails, and the third was an enormous floating mass of crystals, spikes, and other sharp and shiny appendages.

"What the hell are those?" Alkalo asked. "I've never seen anything like that before."

"They didn't show up on any of our sensors," said zort-Zaibar. "We're still not picking up their ion trails or their jump-space signature. It's like they just appeared out of nowhere."

"Could it be a projection?" Alkalo suggested. "Some kind of holoimage?"

Khu'Bin shook her head and said, coldly, "They're real." As she did, all three ships began to glow, a pulsing, throbbing kind of light that somehow hurt Khu'Bin's auditory receptors.

"Unggh..." she moaned, and then the light overwhelmed all of her senses, and then there was nothing.

•••

"Captain to the bridge. Captain to the bridge!"

Khu'Bin lay on her bunk, face down, with a pillow held tightly over her head, and waited for it to be over.

One hundred and seven other beings on this ship, and yet she was alone. Utterly and completely alone with the knowledge that they were doomed. There was nothing she could do about it; she'd tried and failed, and everyone had died. And then she'd had to do it all over again, and again, and again.

She envied the rest of the crew, their ignorance of their fate. Maybe it would be fine for them to live this moment over and over, not knowing. Space was a dangerous place, they all knew that. They all understood that any moment could be their last, so why not this one? If she couldn't change it, why not just let them have the end of their lives without her?

Shouts and klaxons sounded, fists pounded on the door to her cabin, but she doggedly ignored them all until the terrible blue light from those three ships intruded past her pillow and she felt something a little like relief.

The feeling evaporated when she came to on the bridge, alive again, her crew blissfully unaware that they were apparently trapped in an endless cycle of death.

Khu'Bin trudged back to her cabin, picked up her pillow, and lay down again.

She couldn't say how many times the loop had played out that way, with her hiding in her quarters, trying to simply avoid it all, but the number would have shamed her if she could remember. Not this time, though. She would put an end to this, once and for all.

Somehow, Khu'Bin was at the center of this situation. She was the only one who remembered each encounter, the only one who knew that they were trapped in some kind of deadly cycle. She was the one who had been so certain that it was a lucrative cargo masquerading as a worthless chunk of ore. And it had been she who had ordered the crew to enter Shaleri space, even knowing the stories about all those ships that had disappeared without even leaving behind debris. She'd thought they were only ghost stories, but obviously she'd been wrong. Were all those crews also here, perhaps in some other dimension, reliving their final moments over and over again for eternity?

The captain alone had made the decision that had led to this fate, and it was her responsibility to do whatever it took to end it. But this was no moment of heroic self-sacrifice. Khu'Bin was exhausted. It took her no willpower whatsoever to make this choice.

The glow had already begun as she walked down the main passage, shoving away the terrified and confused crewmembers who desperately failed to get her attention, and calmly stepped into the main airlock. She cycled the interior door, carefully following all safety procedures save for the most important one – ensuring that her vacuum suit was properly equipped. It was, in fact, not equipped at all when she cycled the exterior lock and stepped out into the void.

Her species could survive in vacuum longer than most others – the N'orr tolerance for cold was extreme, and her respiratory system coped with a lack of oxygen relatively well – but she knew that soon enough she'd lose consciousness and then, inevitably, die. In the meantime, she gazed at the naked splendor of space for the first time, drinking in the knowledge of her own insignificance as her body's systems slowed.

There was no revelation that death was the only way out of

this infinite loop, the only way to escape the trap her ship – her life – had become. There was no moment of clarity, no epiphany. She was simply dying, again, and experienced a sort of dull sedation as the effects of oxygen starvation slowly took their toll.

The stars were the same. The galaxy was the same. But there was something different about the universe now, something that made her tingle with a sense of wonder that she didn't experience when she glanced at the stars from within the safety of the ship.

It was the thought of her crew, her found brood. The ones who'd painted the faces of the bridge crew on the outside of the ship one day in drydock, flush with the spoils of a big haul and vast quantities of intoxicants. She gazed up at the mural now – at her own angular features, zort-Zaibar's bulbous grin, Phekda Gharri's sly wink, Alkalo's beauty – wondering what marvels her ship and her crew would experience if only they could get out of this terrible moment somehow. This moment that she alone was responsible for instigating.

And that's when she saw it, something so lovely, so luminescent and majestic, that she was compelled to focus her remaining consciousness on it.

It was just a slight flicker, a series of blips in the distance. Where the three enemy ships would be if her eyes had the advantage of the magnification of the *Entropic*'s sensors. Was this the final blue light of death? No, surely Khu'Bin would feel dread if that's what she was seeing, and she felt whatever the opposite of dread was. Euphoria, maybe. This was something different, something warm, something *personal*.

As she succumbed to unconsciousness she would have sworn she heard something, not aloud but in her mind. Surely it was only the echo of her subconscious – the voice, *voices*, saying, "You are not alone. We would know you."

Khu'Bin came back to herself in the midst of striding up the main passageway toward the bridge. She could tell that nothing untoward had happened yet – none of her crew were in the least concerned, and the ship was operating under ordinary running conditions. She increased her pace, wanting to get to the bridge before any sign of the three alien ships appeared.

She strode onto the bridge to find her crew at ease, calmly doing their jobs, as the *Entropic* passed across the border into Shaleri space.

"Captain," said zort-Zaibar. "We have complications."

"Complications?" Khu'Bin asked.

"Three ships' worth. They just popped up, out of nowhere."

"Show me." This time the ships she saw on the screen were gold and shaped oddly, like faceted gemstones. They looked as if they had each been hewn from a single crystal of metal, and their hulls gleamed luminously, but she knew they were the same three ships that had haunted her, that been at the heart of this waking, looping nightmare. But it had never been a dream. They hadn't flown into some kind of temporal anomaly. It was a lesson, an opportunity. She gazed at the ships, as if willing them to tell her what they wanted, then turned to face the crew.

"We need to try to make contact," she said.

"Hailing now," zort-Zaibar said, tentacles working the comms array at speed.

"They aren't going to respond."

"How do you know?" Alkalo asked, but Khu'Bin didn't answer. She needed to think. How else could she try to communicate with them, to make them *know* her?

"Captain," zort-Zaibar said, gesturing with a tentacle. "They're on the move." Khu'Bin turned to look at the sensor screen, where the image of the three ships was magnified, superimposed over their current position. They were a good distance from the alien ships, but their positions were getting closer even though the *Entropic* was at a full stop.

A full stop! As far as she could remember, the *Entropic* had been underway every time the encounter had turned bloody. Maybe that was it. Maybe she needed to let them come to her.

"Helm," she said, "I want this ship at a dead stop, no matter what happens. Understood?"

"Captain?" Gharri's voice trembled.

"What's going on here, Koo?" Alkalo asked quietly.

"No time to explain," Khu'Bin said, trying to insert an apology into her voice. She was their leader, and the only one with any knowledge of what had been happening. It was her responsibility, her burden to bear. If even one other member of her crew knew what she knew, at least she would have someone to talk to, another mind to set to the problem. But wishing things were different had never made them so, and she had to try to learn as much as she could before it all started again. Before they all died, again.

The three alien ships approached slowly, but their movements made distinctly indirect paths toward the *Entropic*'s position. It was almost as if the ships were dancing. Starlight glinted off their golden hulls in strobing patterns that did not appear entirely random as they stopped, then turned in place. The dance began again, the three ships now rotating and burst-accelerating around each other in complex maneuvers. Khu'Bin remembered that in none of the encounters had any particle beams, any torpedoes, been fired by the aliens, and she began to question whether this had ever really been a battle at all.

As a naval cadet and, later, a privateer, she'd been taught to be wary of encounters with unknown entities. Even allies could be dangerous in the wrong conditions. But her experience had been that most individuals would prefer to avoid a fight, that more citizens of the galaxy were seeking connection than conflict. What if these aliens had actually been trying to welcome them, the killing light a misguided attempt to communicate?

While the *Entropic* hung motionless in space, the alien ships came about, facing each other, then angled toward the *Entropic*. Khu'Bin saw that each ship was a pyramid of gold, with a smaller golden pyramid at the point, and the beauty of them struck her.

"Captain," Alkalo said. "What are they doing?"

"They're trying to talk to us," Khu'Bin said.

"How could you possibly know that?" Gharri blurted, the first time the young intern had ever spoken out of turn. Good. It was about time they showed a little confidence.

Khu'Bin didn't have time to explain, and she didn't know how she would even go about trying to make sense of what had happened even if she'd had all the time in the universe.

"I'm going to need you to trust me. They're trying to communicate, I'm sure of it. And we need to find a way to communicate back." She racked her brain. Hadn't her ancient ancestors communicated by body movements? Before they'd evolved the ability to imitate the spoken language of mammals?

"Helm, are you with me?" she asked, as kindly as possible.

"Sir, yes sir," Gharri replied.

"Good. I want you to mirror what the lead ship does. If it turns thirty degrees starboard, you go thirty degrees port. Got it?"

"Yes, Captain." Having an instruction seemed to shock Gharri back into action, and the intern punched buttons and jogged the helm, skillfully following the movements of the lead ship. The alien ships matched their leader's movements, the four vessels maneuvering around each other like dancers on a stage, albeit awkward ones. Gharri matched the lead ship well, but the *Entropic*'s thrusters were not designed to create the fluid movements of the alien ships, and after a few moments they lost synchronization. The gold pyramids came to a stop, then began to emit a blue glow.

"What's that weird light?" Alkalo asked.

"Oh no," Khu'Bin said, as the wave of illumination intensified in the space outside. "No, not yet–"

The blue light flashed, and Khu'Bin found herself once again back at the beginning of the encounter, the alien ships already appearing on a fast-moving approach. She roughly shoved Phekda Gharri out of their seat and took the helm herself, to the great confusion of the bridge crew, and rotated the *Entropic* hard, adding a burst of speed as she pulled the ship around. The alien vessels responded in kind, and reflective designs on their now matte gray hulls caught the light and threw it back in thousands of speckles. The four craft jogged around each other like the biscuits Alkalo liked to make, shaken in a hot buttered pan.

As the dance continued, Khu'Bin found herself thinking about how beautiful the mirrored patterns on the hulls of the other ships were, how in every configuration they'd presented themselves, they'd gleamed in the starlight. She remembered those warm flashes of light she'd seen when she'd been floating in the vacuum, so near to death and yet serene.

And now, again the ships caught the light and made the whole encounter more than movement, like a complex performance that was missing only music. She'd come to think of the alien ships as graceful, exquisite even, and her own sturdy but clunky ship as some flotsam that merely caught their attention. She remembered her time as a youth visiting the seaside on Gargin, so different from her desert home on Quinarra. She'd spent hours watching the sea, listening to the squawking of the seabirds on the shore as they fought for scraps, and was suddenly struck again by the fact that the alien ships had never once emitted anything other than light. No sound, no projectiles. Only strobes of light that had been reflected as they moved in the darkness, before the terrible blue death.

"What are they trying to tell us?" she murmured aloud.

"Captain?" Alkalo's voice startled her. He sounded concerned, and she couldn't blame him. Taking the helm with no explanation just to lurch the ship around randomly and dangerously, muttering to herself. From his perspective, she must look like she'd utterly lost her grip on reality.

"Do you believe those ships are attempting to communicate?" he asked, and Khu'Bin realized, finally, that even if she was the only one who knew about the time loops, she wasn't the only one aboard who could help to decipher the aliens' actions.

"I think so," she said, "but I can't figure out how."

"I have an idea," zort-Zaibar said, who was staring out the viewport, carefully observing the ships as they turned and dipped. "Look at the way the light flashes as they move. It's not random. There must be some kind of pattern there."

"Analyzing," Phekda Gharri said, working the ship's computer with great speed. "I'm cross-checking all the databases. It might take a while."

"We don't have a while," Khu'Bin said.

"What do you mean?" Alkalo asked, with no sense of urgency in his usual casual demeanor.

Khu'Bin glanced out the viewport as the alien ships still bobbed and weaved. How long did they have before they gave up on this iteration and sent her alone back to the beginning, to try again?

"There's more going on here than it appears," she said, wishing she could explain but knowing there was no time. She watched as the computer worked, willing the analysis to go faster, to finish before that blue light intensified and it was once more too late.

"Captain, I have something," Gharri's voice came to her as if in a dream. "zort-Zaibar was right, there is a pattern. It's a series of eleven prime numbers, in an uncommon trinary notation."

"Trinary!" zort-Zaibar said. "No wonder it looked familiar. I took a class on ancient Piltdar trinary numeration when I was still in the larva cloud."

"What's trinary numeration?" Alkalo asked, but Khu'Bin interrupted him.

"No time for that now. We need to send a return communication immediately. Using light. Any ideas?"

"How about the ship's forward spotlight?" Gharri suggested.

"Yes!" Khu'Bin said, clapping the intern on the shoulder with a forelimb. "Alkalo, make that happen."

Without a word, the first mate complied. Remarkable, reliable Alkalo, always willing to act first and ask questions later. She hoped she'd finally be able to answer those inevitable questions, but first they had to break out of this loop, to learn this lesson.

"Thank the stars," she murmured as soon as the *Entropic's* light beam began to flash. Almost immediately the alien ships' movements came to a complete halt, then they re-formed into an orderly grouping a good distance away from the *Entropic*. They still glowed, but subtly, warmly.

"So, Captain. I don't suppose you'd like to share what's going on here with the rest of us?" Alkalo asked, and Khu'Bin began to laugh.

"I would indeed," she said. "You have no idea how much I'd like to share."

She described the repeated encounters she'd had with the various forms of the alien vessels that none of the others had any memory of, glossing over the many, many versions where she'd abandoned both her post and all hope. Even the abridged story was hard to take, and the stunned faces of her crew stared back at her – shock, horror, and confusion competing for predominance among their reactions. But before any of the bridge crew could ask one of the many questions they surely had, the ship's warning tone sounded. A small vessel had been launched from the lead alien ship and was making its way toward their position.

"Is this it?" Alkalo asked, a tremor in his otherwise normally calm and collected voice. "Are we all about to die? Again?"

"I don't think so," Khu'Bin said, willing her antennae to stop twitching. "Nothing like this has ever happened before."

She closed her eyes, trying to still her nervousness. She wanted to say that she knew it was over, that whatever these aliens might have in store for them it couldn't be worse than what she had encountered before. She wanted to say that, but she couldn't. She wasn't going to lie to them, not with her crew looking to her for answers and reassurance and knowing that she had no idea what to expect.

The small alien vessel was shaped like a miniature

battlecruiser, but without any visible weapons. Its hull was matte gray metalwork like the three main vessels, and it was also covered in some kind of intricate mirrored design which she couldn't make out at a distance.

The shuttle glided in to hover a good distance abeam of the *Entropic*, then, with a sudden burst of speed, it shot forward toward the bridge. As it turned to face the main viewport, the design on the vessel's hull changed from an abstract scrawl to legible runes. Khu'Bin had never seen anything like them before, and yet they felt intimately familiar.

Like in a dream, the runes came into focus, and Khu'Bin felt a thrill of excitement pass through her as she was somehow able to understand them. She couldn't read them, not exactly, but she knew what they represented. *Knowledge.*

"This is it," she said.

"What?" Alkalo asked, breathless.

"Something completely new."

We are of Creuss. The voice sounded close, like it was coming from someone standing on the bridge, but Khu'Bin knew it originated from the vessel. There was no distortion or interference, no indication that it had been sent through the communications system, but she heard it clearly. She glanced at her bridge crew and could see on their faces that they had heard it too.

"We are the ones who always have been and always will be. We come from beyond the gate, from a world of plasma and light. We are of Creuss, and we would know you."

The shuttle began to glow, and Khu'Bin had a moment of panic until she saw that the light that emanated from the shuttle was a brilliant, pure yellow. It filled the bridge and reminded

Khu'Bin of images Alkalo had shown her of midday on Jord. It was intensely bright, yet somehow it was not painful, not terrifying. None of the other crew were shielding their eyes, either.

An aperture on the shuttle opened, and a figure emerged into the vacuum of space between it and the *Entropic*, floating gracefully toward them. It was a formless shape that appeared to be entirely and solely made of light and energy. Its features were indistinct and hard to discern. It appeared as folds of light which shimmered into complex patterns, emitting different shades at varying intervals, as if they were layered pieces of stained glass which glimmered with all of the colors that Khu'Bin could sense: gold and purple, ultraviolet, green. But above all, blue.

"What is this?" Alkalo said, his jaw hanging open at this incredible sight. Before he could finish, the light shimmered, disappeared, and then a form reappeared, now apparently encased in intricately patterned metal armor. There was no hint of the energy inside. It approached the airlock and waited patiently for admittance.

"Captain, are you sure–?" Gharri asked, nervously, as Khu'Bin strode toward the passage.

"Of course I'm not sure," Khu'Bin said gently. "But we have the opportunity to make history here. To meet with something – with *someone?* – no one has ever encountered before. And if I've learned one thing from all those times we died, it's that as long as we're still living, we have a chance to do something remarkable. So let's take it! Alkalo, you're with me."

They marched to the chamber which connected the relative safety of the ship and its many systems required to keep them all alive with the cold, dispassionate vacuum beyond the hull. Khu'Bin stared through the armor glass port on the ship-side door and, remembering with chagrin the last time she'd stood at this airlock, engaged the cycle.

The exterior door opened with a clang, and the metal-covered figure hovered in the space just outside, turned about thirty degrees off vertical from the artificial gravity of the ship. It rotated to match the cant of the *Entropic* then floated into the lock and settled on to the "floor". It was roughly humanoid in shape, with two arms, two legs, and a head, but completely covered by the decorated metal armor – even the helmet was entirely opaque.

The outer door cycled closed, and a moment later the one on the ship side opened. The object stood in the lock, apparently waiting for an invitation to board. Khu'Bin extended her forelimb to the visitor, who took it gently in its own metal gauntlet. It was flexible, like chainmail, but smooth and solid to the touch.

There was nothing inside the glove. No bones or tendons or chitin, no flesh or muscle. No blood, no skin. It didn't feel alive in any way that Khu'Bin understood. But the "hand" of the metal suit was strange to her touch, with an almost mammalian warmth to it that belied its apparently inorganic composition.

"I greet you from the other side of the gate," came a voice from inside the armor, in a blandly unaccented version of the common Mentak language, the timbre lilting like a song. "I am called Sei Hiamaeli. We are of Creuss." Was that mass of energy a living being inside that armor? The stranger gestured vaguely to the space beyond where the three alien ships maintained their positions.

"My name is Khu'Bin. I am the captain of this ship, the *Entropic*. We are… of the Mentak Coalition." Khu'Bin had never been involved in a diplomatic mission before, but she'd seen this sort of thing done in entertainment vids. She bowed stiffly. "We are honored to make your acquaintance."

"The honor should be mine," Sei Hiamaeli replied. "To us, you appear as phantoms, shadows of the energy that exists in our realm. But I see that you are as alive as I or any of my kind. We have so much to learn from ones such as yourselves. May I enter your vessel?"

They'd been standing in the airlock this entire time, and Khu'Bin stepped back quickly to make room for this... what were they? An emissary of some empire called Creuss? Or was that their species?

Sei Hiameali's armor looked like it ought to mass at least fifty kilograms, and the *Entropic's* gravity would have given it significant weight, but the newcomer's steps were light, and their footfalls were nearly soundless as they walked into the passage.

"You thought *we* were ghosts?" Khu'Bin said. "Why?"

"You are not of Creuss," Sei Hiamaeli replied. "Such a thing is not possible and yet – here you are."

"Is that why you ..." Khu'Bin tried to find a delicate way to ask why they had murdered her entire crew over and over again. "Is that why you were manipulating time? Why we kept repeating the same encounter?"

The representative of the Creuss was silent for long enough that Khu'Bin wondered if she had failed badly, and said something so deeply offensive that she'd ruined any effort in making an alliance with these aliens. Then, finally, Sei Hiamaeli said, "*Time*. For you this is a concept referring to the progressive evolutionary development of the universe, including all its constituent parts. A causal chain of events. The linear passage of moments."

"Yes, I suppose you could define it like that," Khu'Bin said. "Do your people experience time differently?"

"No, not differently. We do not experience it at all in our universe. Time is not of Creuss."

Khu'Bin didn't know what to make of that. A life without time? How was that even possible?

"So, did you even know what you were doing?" Alkalo asked, emotion creeping into his voice. "Forcing the captain to relive those… events over and over again?"

"The manner in which experiences unfold here is new to us," Sei Hiamaeli said, as if that were an explanation.

Khu'Bin put a limb on Alkalo's arm. "It's all right," she said.

Sei Hiamaeli did not seem to understand the significance of Khu'Bin and Alkalo's conversation, and instead looked around as if inspecting every small thing about the passageway, which was frankly not very interesting. But to the Creuss, even the simplest objects appeared fascinating.

"Your universe is most unusual," they said as they drew a metal finger gently down the bulkhead. "So… solid."

"Yes," Khu'Bin said. "Is it true that where you come from, things are different?"

"Very different. We have none of this… matter in our universe." Sei Hiamaeli spread the fingers of their glove and pressed their hand to the bulkhead as if testing that its solidity was real.

"I don't understand," Alkalo said. "Where you come from, there is nothing solid?"

"Nothing solid, nothing liquid, nothing gaseous. We are of energy. We are of Creuss."

"So this metalwork." Khu'Bin reached out and just stopped herself from running the tip of her forelimb along the runes of the intricately decorated armor. "It does not come from your world?"

"No. There is no contact between our realms. We do not know that there is any reality other than our own. Then material begins to appear from the gate, artifacts from your universe. We collect it, learn to shape it, learn how to make it bend to the natural laws of your universe. We find that we can use it to contain our forms so we can traverse the gate that separates our people. So that we may know you."

"Oh," Khu'Bin said, not really understanding how this could work, but fascinated by the prospect of a passage to another reality. What treasures might be found in a universe of light? "Could we traverse this gate as you have done? Visit your world?"

"It is not possible."

"Why not?"

Sei Hiamaeli clasped their gloved hands with finality. "It is not possible. We have no such matter with which to construct armor for you. My suit, our ships, they are all of your world. Strange particles that appear on our side of the gate. This is what remains of the lost souls from your universe that touch our domain."

The missing ships. All those stories told in the dark of the void about Shaleri space, that it was haunted, cursed. Was that where they had gone? Through the gate? How dangerous was this part of space after all?

"But in this moment we know you," Sei Hiamaeli said. "We can protect your matter from the energy of our gate, allow your solid forms safe passage through this space on your side of the passage. And now we can visit your universe, learn from your universe." They spread their arms wide as if to show off the armor.

"I see," Alkalo said. "Does that mean that these suits protect you from our world?"

"Yes, just as they protect your world from us. We cannot be separated from them in this universe for long. If we were, we would soon cease to be. And you, as well." Khu'Bin remembered the faint blue glow of the figure they'd seen before the suit enveloped them, how it reminded her of that terrible light that had ended everything so many times.

Sei Hiamaeli gestured at Khu'Bin, extending a metal glove toward her.

"This is of the material we collect from your universe, shaped and prepared in our universe, connected by the energy of the gate. The suits are of us, and they are of you. The substance of both universes must join together for us to be able to interact."

Khu'Bin smiled. "Then let us show you our world."

Khu'Bin led the emissary of Creuss on a thorough tour of the *Entropic*, where they spent most of the time touching as many objects as they could get a gloved hand upon. Once they had met every crew member and walked upon every deck, Sei Hiamaeli returned to their small shuttle, then escorted the *Entropic* safely past the invisible but deadly gate, toward the magnetic signature which had drawn them into Shaleri space and this unprecedented meeting. As Khu'Bin had guessed, it was not a rock but was indeed a large multipart cargo container with a masking beacon affixed to its side. Almost certainly some black-market hauler had dropped it there for their contact to collect at a later time, but it was, technically speaking, abandoned. Legitimate salvage, and her crew were more than ready to see what its many crates contained.

When the *Entropic* had successfully hauled the container into the ship's hold, Alkalo joined the salvage crew busily opening up each individual crate with glee, and Khu'Bin signaled the crew's thanks to Sei Hiamaeli with the forward spotlight. The shuttle flashed back once, then returned to the three main Creuss ships and docked at the largest of the vessels. The ships powered up, emitting a pale yellow glow, and turned away from the *Entropic*. Then with a shimmer of incandescence that seemed to come from a point in space itself, they disappeared. Back through the gate to their own strange universe of light and energy, Khu'Bin supposed.

In exchange for a few public star charts, the emissary offered safe passage past the anomaly for any "material vessel". Eventually, the Creuss would use more of the matter they'd acquired to create a demarcation zone marking the edges of the gate to keep ships from this universe from getting caught in its vortex. In the meantime, Phekda Gharri prepared a record of the waypoints they'd used to bypass the gate safely while piloted by Sei Hiamaeli. zort-Zaibar sent the coordinates to the nearest Mentak Coalition outpost to be shared with the rest of the privateer fleet. Soon enough the word that clear passage had been found in this part of the quadrant would make its way beyond the Coalition, and vessels from many worlds would begin to pass through this corridor. The Ghosts of Creuss would surely be back to visit this world, and no one knew what their presence would mean for any of them. But as of this day, Shaleri space was haunted no longer.

Khu'Bin settled into the captain's chair and watched the salvage tally on her screen, progress bars for fuel and supplies ticking up nicely while valuable trade goods were added steadily to the inventory. It was a lucrative haul, finally. Her crew should be proud.

She wondered exactly how much of her experience she would share with the Mentak Coalition when they returned to local space. She'd be sure to describe their meeting with Sei Hiamaeli, and the little she could make of their strange domain on the other side of the Creuss Gate. But she knew she'd never share the full story. No one would believe it, and besides, a pirate captain always keeps a few choice items from the spoils for herself – and her crew. After all, without her crew, a captain is nothing.

THE FIFTH STAGE

ALEX ACKS

Mibu no Kyona had forgotten how different the air of a Mentak Coalition ship smelled. It had all of the ordinary ship-scents that she'd become reacquainted with during the journey: the faint, metallic tang that always came with recycled air; the salty undercurrent of whatever food had been most recently made; the musk of bodies not washed as frequently as they might be a downside due to resource restrictions. But the subtle differences were inescapable, the new spices involved in cooking, the scents native to a non-human people with a different diet than what they were used to on Jord. A valuable reminder of foreignness, perhaps, when it was at times very easy to mistake members of the Mentak Coalition for fellow humans of the Federation of Sol.

Through the airlock, which Kyona had mentally dubbed "no-frills" out of a surfeit of politeness, she spotted her sometimes-colleague and sometimes-adversary, Rull Mallak, captain of the *Irascible*. He had the characteristic long face and bluish complexion characteristic of someone from the Barony of Letnev, but his ancestors had been exiles to Moll Primus. The broad smile he offered her as soon as the door slid open was not, in her experience, at all characteristic citizens of the Barony either.

"Kyona!"

Neither was his tendency toward informality.

"Rull." She smiled and stepped through to take his offered hands. "It's been too long."

"Too long, indeed," he echoed. "When was the last time we met face-to-face?"

She pretended to think about it. This was part of their little dance of greeting, comforting in its own way. The utter normalcy of Rull was a balm to her nerves, severely unsettled by both the space travel – something that had never agreed with her – and the prospect of what was to come. "The trade summit on Tantalus Station, wasn't it? When you spilled that horrible, bright red drink all down the sleeve of my dress?"

"You wound me by implying such intent. I was pushed." His eyes twinkled. "Though it was a very nice dress, and I don't blame you for still mourning its loss."

For all its obvious intention as light banter, there was much in that statement that struck like a blow. *Mourning.* And *that dress.* Because of course, Chioma had given her that dress. Five years later, and she was still stumbling into unmarked voids in her life. She held gamely onto her smile, not wanting the conversation to divert off course into awkward sympathies. "Has my memory betrayed me, then?"

Rull tucked her hand in the crook of his elbow and led her down the narrow corridor of his ship, a feat only possible because he was tall but exceedingly lanky, and she'd always been quite small for a human, something that was an inconvenience when she wanted to reach things down from cabinets without using the grav step, and otherwise an asset in the way it encouraged others to underestimate her. "No, you remember that unfortunate incident correctly. However, that wasn't the most recent time we've met."

"Oh my, I must have gotten my dates mixed up. You'll have to forgive me."

"It was far less memorable since no one's clothing got destroyed," he drawled. "But remember that music exhibition Beraan Iq Fersah threw?"

The sly look he shot her was easy enough to read. "Dreadful," she agreed. "No wonder I'd wiped it from my memory." Four years ago, her first trip off world after the *Dies Opulen* had been officially declared lost at the end of a year of fruitless searching. She remembered little from that time. "We're a long way from that kind of venue, now." A mild observation, a prompting toward the point of her visit. She'd always preferred to remain oblique, to leave silences for others to fill, because their choice of words was always so informative.

He patted her hand, a gesture of enthusiasm rather than conciliation. "Indeed we are! We've moved into a far more rarefied space."

"So you've done it?"

"I thought you were chasing nebula ghost stories when you first contacted me, but I pulled every string that was mine and chased down every rumor and whisper." Rull grinned. "And yes. I've gotten you a meeting with these so-called Arborec."

The guest quarters on the *Irascible* were only slightly larger than a closet; considering the size of the ship, that made it positively palatial. Kyona tucked her small chest in the cabinet obviously intended for that purpose, which doubled as a desk by day and a bed by night.

By the standards of career spacers, Kyona traveled with an unconscionable amount of luggage. Chioma had teased her to no end about it, the few times their schedules had synchronized enough to allow them to travel off world together. By the standards of other diplomats of her tier, Kyona's luggage was horrifyingly spartan, a tiny wardrobe that was inflexible to surprise events.

There was an art to dressing that Kyona had mastered when she was a girl who had no ambitions beyond an eclectic history degree that focused on fashion. She had adopted the ancient tradition of the kimono, because the true key was the accessories. The garments themselves were so unfamiliar to even many other humans that their perceptions of her intended message were easy to manipulate. Where it became truly interesting was in crafting her unspoken messages to the eyes of those completely alien to Jord – in this case, alien eyes that she had no solid data on.

She unpacked her secure communicator – not that she assumed anything to be truly secure when she was on Rull's ship, and she knew that he knew that; it was all part of the game – and sorted the messages she hadn't wanted to deal with while deeply nauseated by interstellar travel. The subject of the first made her smile: *Unauthorized Pursuit of Fairy Stories.* The contents were no less charming, a thinly veiled threat by the vice-secretary of the outbound diplomatic corps that, for her flagrant misuse of her less-than generous government expense fund and utilization of non-Federation intelligence personnel, she would find herself in need of a job... if this turned out to be nothing.

A success always redounded upward, a failure rolling swiftly into the gravity well. The message could have been summed up far more efficiently as the old command: *With your shield or on it.*

Kyona had never been the one interested in taking risks. She was no wartime negotiator, nor a person who preferred the stakes to be high and the discussions to be filled with hidden knives. She'd always been determinately boring, much to Chioma's despair.

But that was why she was out here, wasn't it? Leaning on the shoulder of her strangest friend, ready to burn her professional bridges. On paper, a new species was a chance for the Federation to add to its too-small roster of allies after the Twilight War, a possible source for trade that could get Jord new technology or access to novel biological entities that could be sources for food and medicines in the future. It would be a personal coup for her as well, after she had been shunted into humiliatingly minor roles for the last several years – a thing she could not even fault her superiors for, considering the understandably poor performance that had led her to such a place.

But... the truth was, these "fairy stories" she would soon be speaking to were from deep within the unknown reaches of space. Intellectually, Kyona knew that a single lost ship in the vast black was less than a single grain of sand on the beach. Yet some part of her still thought if she flung herself out far enough, there was a beloved voice she might find again.

"I'm so glad you were feeling well enough to join me," Rull said, offering over a plate of fresh flatbread.

"I would never forgive myself for missing a single meal while taking advantage of your hospitality," Kyona said, as truthful a statement as she ever uttered. The *Irascible* might be small and generally cramped, but Kyona well knew that was because the lion's share of the interior space not necessary for the ship's operation was taken up with a shockingly opulent pair of rooms – reception and dining – and a galaxy-class kitchen.

That was another thing she'd counted on when she'd opened her negotiation with him about this trip. Traveling on her own, with no retinue and no support, she would be wholly dependent upon venues she did not control. Rull, at least, she could trust to want to make himself look good.

They exchanged more generic chatter, catching up on their gossip through a delicious cold soup and into something that Kyona could almost convince herself was fish, though she knew it to be generated protein. "While you were chasing my ghost stories out on the edge of known space, I don't suppose you learned more details of our specters?"

"I was about to ask you the same." He eyed her over the rim of his glass – water, not wine. He was deliberately not trying to loosen her up, a gesture she appreciated. And, he had once told her, the Mentak valued fresh, clear water as much if not more than any number of vintages, because it had been such a vanishingly rare resource on their home world. Prisons didn't tend to sport many pleasant lakes or rivers. "Since I certainly hope your own spies have been hard at work."

"Would that were the case, though I'll be happy to share what little I received before the resources were allocated elsewhere." It was no more than she'd already told him, just the bare hints of a presence, a new civilization, in a sector previously lost to all contact. A pattern of derelict ship disappearances, which was what had caught her interest. "I'll send you all the files I have when I go back to my quarters."

His expression told her that he wasn't impressed, but he looked resigned to what little she had to offer. "I can tell you that they were able to communicate appropriately in return to the messages I sent. So they've figured out at least some of our various languages, assuming they're not some lost branch of one of our peoples. The linguistic patterns were sufficiently strange to indicate several centuries of drift."

"An interesting theory," Kyona remarked. "One I suppose we'll test quite soon."

Rull snorted. "I've got a long-range scan of one of their ships, too." He took a small holoprojector from his pocket and set it on the table. The image it cast was bulbous and unlike any ship design she had ever seen.

"I have a difficult time imagining that a human built that," Kyona observed.

"What readings we received from it were odd as well. But at that distance... difficult to say." He turned the projector off. "Sorry to be sending you in so ill-prepared."

"You've already done me a greater favor than I can repay by arranging this meeting to begin with," Kyona said, well aware that, like her superiors, Rull had positioned himself well to reap the rewards of any success she had while easily washing his hands of any failure. "I don't suppose they gave you any indication of who I might be dealing with?" Even a name was a start; knowing how to properly greet someone was a shockingly important first step.

"'The Dirzuga' is all I have for that," Rull said. "But I couldn't tell you if that is a name or a title."

"*Dirzuga*," Kyona repeated, copying Rull's pronunciation with easy precision. "It is something, at least."

Rull smiled, raising his water glass as if to offer a toast. "That it is."

•••

They rendezvoused with the Arborec ship the next day, after Kyona had spent a fitful night trying to sleep in the tiny but comfortable bunk of her cabin. She dressed herself carefully in a black kimono, on which the traditional family mon had been replaced by the crest of the Federation of Sol, and an obi richly embroidered with golden swallows and stalks of bamboo. With little to go on culturally, but knowing first impressions were important, she tried to find a medium between elegance and conspicuous opulence, choosing her most ostentatious hair ornaments, brilliant gold with a delicate array of flowers in all vibrant examples of all six colors of jade, but keeping her makeup fairly simple and, by human standards, modern. After her first read on her counterpart, she would know better how to dress herself in subsequent meetings.

Rull's long distance scan, as strange as it had been, did not do justice to the ship that wove itself into existence out in the black. Its immensity was breathtaking. Kyona had seen ships of that size before, but only in military revues either as the flagships of fleets set forth as unsubtle intimidation or the immense freighters that could carry entire space stations across interstellar distances, mobile mountains of welded alloy that the mind could not truly comprehend. What she had read before as an incoherent collection of bulbous projections resolved now into the imperfect radial symmetry of an organism, something grown rather than built, like the shelves of mushrooms circling tree trunks in a forest.

"No," she breathed. "Definitely not human."

"They're hailing us," Rull said, his tone strangely laconic. He cocked an eyebrow at her. "Do you want to do the honors?"

Kyona shook her head. "It's your ship, and we will both be your guests. That part of the negotiation is best left to you."

Rull offered her an ironic little bow, a gesture that was

definitely not standard for the Mentak, but very him. He opened the comm channel with a gesture. "Arborec ship, we hear you. This is Rull Mallak, captain of the *Irascible*. The Mentak Coalition welcomes you, and I will be delighted to be your host."

There was a long pause, strange in an era when transmission times were nonexistent. The voice that answered was flat and without affect. Kyona had never heard any sort of artificial intelligence or universal translator sound so emotionless. "*Irascible* Mentak Coalition Rull Mallak I sing greeting. I will myself send to your ship."

Rull glanced at Kyona, who shrugged. This was not the first time either of them had encountered a bad translation issue. Rull said, "Of course. We are ready to receive your shuttle at your convenience. I will send you our atmospheric specifics shortly. Am I speaking to the Dirzuga?"

"Dirzuga is also me."

Another glance from Rull; Kyona made an open-handed gesture in return. His guess was as good as hers.

"I am pleased to make your acquaintance, then, Dirzuga. We look forward to many fruitful discussions."

"Respirate the same air we will," the voice intoned. "Sing." The channel cut off.

Rull signaled to one of his people to send over the package of technical data he and Kyona had previously prepared. "I think that went well."

"Can't say I've had a first greeting quite like that, before," Kyona remarked. Though she was beginning to worry that she would require more linguistic support than either she or Rull had on hand.

"I know. We're both on the cutting edge now." Rull smiled. A soft chime echoed through the bridge, and he checked his display. "Well, they wasted no time. They've sent what I must assume is a shuttle, based on mass if not design, and it'll be docking shortly. You'd best prepare, my friend."

Kyona tucked her hands into the sleeves of her kimono, finally feeling the first stirring of both anticipation and trepidation. Though she knew it was best not to speculate, she wondered what the Arborec would look like, what they would sound like without a comm channel or a potentially dodgy translator as an intermediary.

The displays around the airlock lit up; the shuttle had docked. Colored spirals and characters in three languages displayed the progress of the pressure normalization and air cycling. "And here we go," Rull murmured.

Kyona did not answer him, but fixed a politely blank expression on her face as the airlock door rolled open. The air that flowed through from the shuttle was humid and curled with water vapor; what reached them smelled green and alive in a way that Kyona associated with the more tropical areas of the botanical gardens near her home. A lone figure emerged, the steam tearing around them.

Something about the profile alone hit Kyona like a blow – the set of the shoulders, perhaps, the gait, something was familiar and *wrong* – and then she walked across the threshold. About two meters tall – 203.5 centimeters exactly, Kyona *knew* – clad in a shapeless, matte black garment of strange material that hid most of her body, head once shaved spacer-bald now covered with what looked like a headdress of plants, ebony skin that shone with residual moisture, and lacings of what looked like yellow-green rootlets – but the refined shape of the face was unchanged, one that Kyona knew as well as her own.

Dimly, Kyona understood that she was clutching Rull's jacket tightly enough that one of the seams began to part with a snarl. He had an arm around her. He was saying something, but she couldn't understand the words when her mind was so wholly taken by the sight in front of her.

"Chioma," she whispered. She felt as if she could not breathe. "Chioma!" Her fiancé, missing for five years and dead as far as every government body, every family member, everyone who had known her was concerned – everyone but Kyona.

And those deep, beautiful brown eyes that had once been so warm, had once held so much laughter and affection, gazed on Kyona and showed... nothing. "I am Dirzuga Nephele," she said, her voice, too, betraying no recognition, nothing but perhaps a mild curiosity as she looked at Kyona and Rull. "I am the voice of the Symphony that will sing in negotiation."

"Chioma?" Kyona asked once more, the sudden surge of hope she'd felt shattering like glass. There had to be an explanation for this, she thought frantically. Chioma, rescued by these Arborec, working as a diplomat for them in repayment for their aid, perhaps. But even as she spun these stories in her mind, that beloved face tilted toward her and betrayed no recognition yet again.

Kyona shoved herself away from Rull, tearing from his grasp. Part of her knew the foolishness of her actions; she was, without a doubt, a moving diplomatic incident as she staggered forward. The woman who called herself Dirzuga Nephele regarded her with mild curiosity as she covered the distance between them, as Kyona grabbed the strange, slick fabric of her garment. "Chioma, it's me," she said, desperately. "Please, my love."

"I am not acquainted with your greeting," Nephele said, though she made no move to pry Kyona's hands away.

The blankness in her eyes was too much. "Why don't you know me?" Kyona whispered, and then Rull had her by the shoulders, and *he* was the one who peeled her fingers away.

"It's a very nontraditional greeting for first meetings," Rull said, his arms fully around Kyona. He pulled her back several steps. "We apologize for any confusion it might have caused."

Kyona heard all of this as if at a distance. She hadn't quite gone limp against Rull, but no longer had the will to fight. "Get me out of here," she whispered. If her legs had any strength, she would have fled on her own. The only sign Rull gave of having heard her was one of his hands tightening on her arm.

"I understand your meaning," Dirzuga Nephele said. She gestured back toward the airlock. "With words I can only convey that I am curious at our meeting, and wish to learn more. Including of the trade you have proposed."

"Thank you," Rull said. "If you'd follow my second in command, there–" he nodded toward the woman who had been waiting patiently to the side "–she'll take you to the meeting room. We shall join you there shortly."

The moment the door had shut behind Nephele and his officer, Rull turned his attention to Kyona. "Are you all right?"

"I don't understand what's happening," she whispered, bewildered.

He stared down at her for a moment, then all but force-marched her back to the dining room, which was half set up for the formal meal planned to follow the first meeting. He put her in one of the chairs, disappeared for a moment, and came back with a bottle of poison green liquid. The alcohol esters radiating from the small glass he poured from it were enough to make her eyes water. "Drink," he commanded.

Kyona drank. It burned the entire way down; the utter

unpleasantness of the experience certainly had a focusing effect on her mind. She put her face in her hands the moment she could abandon the glass on the table. "That was Chioma. You saw it, didn't you?"

"That did look very much like Chioma," Rull said. He sat down next to her and pulled up a small data display, scrolling rapidly through it. "A clone, perhaps?"

"But *how*?"

"The *Dies Opulen* has been missing for years now," Rull said gently. "Depending on the circumstances of its disappearance and the behavior of the basic AI autopilot it had on board... it could have ended up nearly anywhere."

"That name she told us," Kyona said into her hands.

"Hm?"

"'Nephele' is the brand name of a soap," Kyona said. "One of Chioma's favorites. She must remember something, then, right?"

"Or there was some of that on the ship with her," Rull pointed out. He shook his head. "A strange detail to get hung up on, Kyona. But... darling, I don't think you're being rational about this."

"How the hell am I supposed to be rational right now?" Kyona demanded.

"Just so," Rull agreed. "The circumstances are quite strange. For an agent with Chioma's face to show up specifically when you are the negotiator is... too much of a coincidence for my liking."

A chill ran through Kyona's body. "Do you think this is some kind of... *tactic*?"

"I wouldn't necessarily go that far," Rull said. "Since that would imply I understand what they're trying to do. But this whole thing smells of a bad air filter if you ask me."

Conspiracy or coincidence? In the moment, Kyona found she did not care. She hurt too much, an almost physical pain echoing through her body every time she thought of Chioma's blank face. Even as she recovered her ability to think after that initial, terrible shock, all that came with it were more questions. Was it a threat? A deadly insult? And what was this woman, who wore the face of her long-lost beloved? A clone, as Rull had suggested? The true Chioma, her mind hollowed out with techno-viruses or brutally reconfigured with five years of ceaseless conditioning? Each thought was more horrifying than the last.

Rull had continued to talk as Kyona's thoughts scattered in a hundred directions at once. What caught her attention back at last was him saying, "The turn-around for your ship should be fast. I can cover for you."

"You think I should leave?"

Rull offered her a sympathetic smile. "I certainly wouldn't blame you if you wanted to! This is not a good way to begin negotiations for the Federation is it, with you ..." He seemed to be searching for a more diplomatic word than what was on his tongue before saying, "... caught off guard."

"Compromised," Kyona said, a tad harshly. "That was the word you were reaching past, was it not?"

Rull shrugged, hands opened helplessly. "It's really no business of mine, darling. This is not even an official Coalition mission. In this, I speak only as your friend who has seen you go through an unimaginable shock. You really ought to see to yourself first."

Kyona shook her head. She had not seen Chioma since she'd boarded the shuttle that would take her to the *Dies Opulen*. Everyone else had given up, while Kyona had not. And now, it seemed, her patience and steady belief had paid off. Chioma lived, even if Kyona did not understand how that came to be, or what transformation she had undergone to make her forget even her own name. The idea of fleeing had never crossed her mind, and the offer coming from Rull felt repulsive. "No," she said firmly. "For five years, I've had no answer on what happened to my fiancé. This… this is the first hope I've been offered."

"*Hope*," Rull said.

Kyona stared at him. "When you have been adrift in the void as long as I have, even to be cut by blowing dust promises there is land somewhere to be reached."

There was a long pause as Rull seemed to process this, his expression changing in a way she wasn't certain how to read, a hint of calculation to his gaze that, any other time, she might have found alarming. Now, she was simply glad that he was here, and that he was, however badly, trying to look out for her.

"I will send all the sensor data I have back to the Coalition and see what they might be able to come up with. I'll help you find your answer. Though I hope it will be one you like."

Kyona closed her eyes for a moment, trying to find a new position to settle her reawakened pain. "Any answer at all will be better than none."

Rull insisted that she drink water, and eat a bit of glucose paste that tasted of artificial fruit. It bought her enough mental distance that she was able to fix her makeup, correct her clothing, and refocus. It felt like an unseemly amount of time had passed before they once more stood outside the door to the main meeting room. Rull's second in command, a woman Kyona only knew in the vaguest of senses, greeted the both of them.

"Been watching the monitors while we waited," she said. "She ain't moved so much as a hair. Don't even know if she's been blinking, truth be told."

Kyona ignored Rull's glance. Her hold on herself felt too fragile now to admit to any outward sign of worry. "I'm grateful for her patience," she said, her tone harsh. "Let me in."

Nephele stood in the center of the room, looking curiously up toward the ceiling when the door opened. She turned to face Kyona, her expression not changing, and said, "Chioma."

Hearing the name in that familiar voice, even if the inflection was entirely wrong, felt like a punch to the gut. Kyona held onto her cool expression through an act of sheer will, though she reflexively closed her eyes. "That's …"

"Stated to be an unusual greeting, but I will return it." Nephele's head tilted slightly again.

Kyona bit back a flare of anger, wondering if she was being mocked. It would be a very political thing for someone to do, to set their opponent off balance by finding what emotional levers they had. If these Arborec were not so isolated as they seemed, it would be a trivial matter for anyone with access to Jord's public networks to dredge up the ghost of Chioma. In a way, the paranoid thinking was a relief. She could attempt to tackle this as a problem to be solved, a mystery, another game of strategy during negotiation.

Kyona closed her eyes and took a deep breath against a feeling of sudden nausea. "A more standard greeting would be traditional now," she said firmly. Then she bowed. "Like so."

Nephele looked at her, head tilted in an almost birdlike angle, then followed suit. "Gesture rather than words. Interesting."

"The people of Jord are many and varied," Kyona said. It was a standard conversational piece that she hauled out frequently, words she had uttered so many times that they had nearly stopped having meaning to her.

"Of many minds, yes?"

Kyona could almost have relaxed into this line of questioning; she heard it so often, from certain other cultures who liked to use the perceived fractiousness of the humans as a bargaining chit. "I assure you that when the High Minister speaks, it is with our unified voice. We govern via consensus, and in that we find strength."

"You do not govern all humans?"

"No. I represent only the Federation of Sol. We are the largest human government by an order of magnitude." She wondered what would be next, the implied threat that the Arborec would take their negotiations to some nebulous other faction of humans. Yet she could not quite relax into the steps of this oft-practiced dance because of who was saying these familiar words – or at least the face they wore. *You know all of these things, Chioma,* she wailed in the confines of her own mind. *You helped me perfect these answers.*

"I find this fascinating," Nephele said, which was a distinct deviation from the normal course of this kind of conversation. "Will these other humans return to you?"

This, too, she had a diplomatic answer for. "The Federation of Sol respects the independence of the other human governments, but we are of course always eager to welcome our fellows home."

"To be so separated," Nephele said, shaking her head.

"Ambassador Nephele," Kyona said. Making the name pass her lips was far more difficult than she could have thought. "I can negotiate only on behalf of the Federation of Sol. I hope you were not given the impression it was to be otherwise."

"No impressions," Nephele said. "I wish only to understand the way of your species in this."

But you are *part of my species.* Kyona made herself smile. She should, she knew, inquire after the Arborec and their ways, to try to understand why they found humanity – which really, in the grand scheme of social systems, was no outlier – so puzzling. She found she did not have the strength. She could not stand to look at Chioma's face any longer and see a stranger looking back at her. "I have several cultural brochures prepared about the Federation of Sol and our homeworld, if you would like to read them?"

"Yes. That would be of much use."

"I will have those transmitted to your ship, then." Kyona rose to her feet. Nephele watched her curiously but made no move. "Our initial greeting has gone well, and I thank you for it. We shall resume talks tomorrow in one standard Sol day, if that's agreeable to you."

It was a load of engine wash; anyone who had been involved in the intergalactic game of diplomacy would have been appalled by Kyona ending a meeting so abruptly, let alone without gracefully redirecting the time to some kind of state meal like the one that had been nominally planned for the afternoon. Kyona did not care; she felt like the very air was choking her. Either the Arborec ambassador would not understand anything was amiss, or she would be compelled to tip her hand and admit that she understood more than she claimed.

Nephele nodded. "Do you wish for me to return to my ship in the meantime?"

"Do you not wish to take rest in your own quarters?"

"That is unnecessary. If you will give me your brochures, I shall absorb them while I wait."

No, Kyona absolutely did not want this strange ghost to be on the same ship as her. She had no good way to refuse such a request, however. "Of course, it will be our pleasure to have you as our guest." Another standard phrase, recited by rote.

"Thank you, Kyona," Nephele said.

Kyona offered her a bow and all but fled from the room. Rull waited outside; he tried to speak with her, and she simply brushed past him.

It was only in the privacy of her own room, after she had screamed into her pillow and then cried, that she realized two very strange things – the way Nephele had said her name, and that the Arborec ambassador, who had claimed such lack of familiarity with all things human-related, would agree without question to a pause of a Sol standard day.

Unasked questions all but hovered around Rull like a swarm of flies when Kyona informed him – after calming herself, drinking a bit of tea so her voice wasn't rough, and putting a cool cloth on her eyes – of Nephele's continued presence and her own abrupt adjournment. He did not, to his credit, give any of them voice. Rather, he shrugged and said, "This'll give us more of a chance to passively observe the Arborec ambassador, at least. And more closely examine her shuttle."

"Will you let me know if you find out anything... relevant?" She knew better than to expect a full sharing of intelligence. In a way, that was also the coin that paid for her presence here. She was giving Rull – and through him the Coalition – presumably the closest look anyone would have of the Arborec any time soon, and with her as a distraction besides.

"I promise that I will." He reached out to lay a hand on her shoulder. "I know for us, 'friendship' doesn't quite mean the same as it does for other people... but I still have no desire to see you left dangling out into the void."

It was perilously close to sentiment on his part. Kyona offered him a grateful smile. "I will be certain to buy you quite a bit of time."

Kyona steeled herself as best she could in the morning to face Nephele again. She dressed with the same deliberation as a soldier putting on body armor, though her purposes this day were different than for those she normally crafted her outfits. Rather than trying to make a statement about the Federation of Sol's position or subtly manipulate her opposite, this time she carefully dressed herself in every item she had brought with her that she knew Chioma would be familiar with.

The kimono was one that Chioma had seen her in countless times, though it was an unremarkable and unrelieved formal black. The obi patterned with peacocks and peonies was one Chioma had given her as an anniversary gift, something Kyona normally found too painful to wear even now, but she was glad at whatever impulse had driven her to pack it. The hair pins she wore were the ones Chioma had once declared her second favorite, faux tortoiseshell replicas of a museum piece that aesthetically did not match the rest of her outfit in the slightest. Aesthetic harmony was the least of Kyona's concerns, though were Nephele to find her wardrobe choices repugnant, that would also be quite valuable information in its own right.

But when she sat down across the table from Nephele, all of her logical considerations fled, and she felt only the return of an old anguish – and a new, growing anger that sat hot in her gut.

"A good morning to you, Ambassador Nephele," Kyona said. She made herself smile, an expression that felt practiced and forced even from within. "That is our common and standard greeting, by the way."

"Dirzuga Nephele is correct," Nephele said.

"Is *Dirzuga* your word for ambassador? It isn't translating properly."

Nephele shook her head. "Dirzuga is Dirzuga. Descendent of Arzuga."

"And Arzuga is…?"

Nephele seemed to freeze for a moment, head tilted. It was almost like watching an AI suffer a fatal error, disturbing in her flat, unblinking expression. Just as Kyona was about to ask if she was well, she said, "The grower of life from death."

It was remarkable, how much of someone's face was built by the animating personality within; in that still moment, Kyona had truly seen the face of a stranger.

Arzuga must be a god of some sort, Kyona thought. She considered if she should push for further information, but generally speaking, gods were a cultural minefield. She had no doubt Rull was listening in with keen interest, and she would consult with him on the matter later. "I will address you properly going forward. I hope I have given no offense."

"Why would there be offense?" Nephele asked. "There is only the truth."

"I understand," Kyona said with a polite smile, though she most definitely did not. "Did you find the cultural pamphlets useful, by the way?"

"Yes." Nephele tilted her head. "Confusing, but useful."

"How were they confusing, if I might ask?"

"Variation," Nephele said, as if that word alone was all that was needed. "I noted that you changed your appearance today. Is that significant?"

Kyona felt her heart sink. "It's a matter of individuality," she said, a bit weakly.

"I observed this in the pamphlets. An experimental imperative?"

She couldn't even guess what was meant by that. "No. A personal preference. Such adornments can have great significance or none beyond the part they play in the aesthetics. Yet all send a message, conscious or not."

"What is the meaning of yours?"

Kyona's face felt stiff as she made herself smile once more. "A desire for harmony and welcoming, the blossoming of new friendship."

Nephele's head tilted. "The color of the decoration in your hair is... striking."

Kyona felt as if the woman had grabbed her by the throat from across the broad expanse of the table; she could barely breathe. "It's copied from a much more ancient original. Do you like it?"

"I do not like nor dislike," Nephele said. "I merely observe."

"If you will excuse me, Dirzuga Nephele, I must take a short recess," Kyona said.

"For what purpose?"

"For biological function," Kyona said firmly. She left the room to find Rull waiting for her in the hallway, a steaming cup in his hand, which she accepted gratefully. The tea scalded her tongue, but even that familiar pain calmed her.

"I take it you've been watching," she said.

"Of course." He looked toward the closed doors. "Fun thing that we've noticed. In addition to not blinking, Nephele seems to not have any... biological functions, as you put it."

Kyona took another scorching mouthful. "I think... I feel she is mocking me." She touched the hairpins. "And yet..."

"Too many correlations, not enough causes," Rull said. He took the cup when she shoved it back at him, still half full. "Will you be adjourning early again today?"

Her throat still burned, as did her stomach – as did the knot at the center of her chest, something composed entirely of emotion. "No. I need more information just as much as you do." With that, she straightened her back and walked back toward the room, trying to find the serene outward pace that would let her pretend everything was all right.

Dirzuga Nephele waited inside as if she had not moved – and at this point Kyona very much doubted that she had. "A rapid biological function," Nephele observed.

"Indeed." Kyona sat, her hands folded in her lap and hidden by the sleeves of her kimono so that the trembling of her fingers was obscured. "As we have concluded our greetings, I believe it is time we started negotiating terms between our people."

"For what?" Nephele asked.

"For trade," Kyona said firmly. "Of both knowledge and goods."

"What I seek first is knowledge," Nephele said. "That is my mission."

"It is mine as well," Kyona agreed. "But knowledge is only the first bridge." Another rote phrase, one that she settled on like a comforting old friend. "Let us cross it together."

Kyona had long since learned her job was to not actually forge agreements or commit the legal details of treaties to paper; she did not have that sort of power. It was for diplomats like her to establish the channels, to offer the temptation of material goods that her opposite lacked, but to never actually promise anything she was not already specifically allowed. The legal scholars and political attachés would follow later, and they were the ones who would craft vacuum-tight agreements that the judicial traditions of two different cultures could agree upon.

And in this, her unauthorized venture, she had even less range to work than normal. There was nothing she had been authorized to give away beyond the most general of information about the Federation of Sol that was public knowledge in most places. She could make vague declarations of more to come if the Arborec were to wish to come to a more solid agreement with her government in a round of more formalized negotiation, but no more than that.

In a way, Nephele as her opposite made that portion of her work easier over the next few days – and also infinitely more frustrating. Kyona soon learned that Nephele – and presumably the masters who held her leash on the Arborec homeworld – were not at all focused on trade. Their aims seemed to be entirely about gathering knowledge, and not just of the Federation of Sol. Perhaps if her people, too, had languished in complete galactic obscurity with no outside contact before now, their drives would be different as well. But Kyona found it intensely strange as she offered the Dirzuga data packet after data packet to fill a potentially endless appetite for reading, which she did rather than sleeping, eating, or blinking it seemed.

Kyona had attempted a couple of diplomatic dinners. Watching Nephele, through Chioma's face, regard the food as if it was all a foreign riddle was more than she could bear. After the first meal, during which Nephele did not eat at all, Kyona had furnished her with chemical scans of all the food, in case some biological conflict was the issue. At the second meal, Nephele had taken one of the spiced flatbreads that were the specialty of Rull's cook and simply held it in her hand the entire time.

They did not share a third meal together. Nothing was being accomplished by them but the continual weathering of Kyona's soul.

Kyona's heart quailed every time she looked at Chioma, a fresh wash of black, awful grief coming over her in waves. She had been told, when she'd sought counseling after a months-long struggle with her grief, that such pain came less frequently with time, that it ebbed and swelled like the tide. After five years, she'd reached the point where she could go months without feeling that raw clutch of sorrow at her throat.

And now, it was as if none of that time had passed. Part of her always exulted at seeing Chioma's face again; she couldn't help but think of the many nights she'd prayed to whatever god she thought might listen that she would give anything – anything – to see her just once more. But there was something not quite right about her eyes, her expressions, not that she was an imperfect copy, but as if she was being animated by a spirit not hers. In its own way, that feeling was a compounding of her loss, a wrongness on top of grief.

During the breaks throughout the meetings, that Kyona called because she could no longer stand to look at Nephele's face, and in the ship-time evening, Kyona consulted with Rull in the room they had designated, by mutual unspoken agreement, as their shared office. He brought her tea during the day and more of his terrible liquor – a foul thing called Chantir – at night, which she gratefully accepted.

"She must be in communication with her ship in some way," Kyona remarked after the third day. "I'm certain of it. The data I requested regarding their biological engineering arrived while we were still in the meeting, precisely to specification." She rubbed her temples. "And yet she has never left that room. But I've seen those pauses she makes in conversation – and you have, too, Rull? Please tell me you have."

"Oh, I have." He raised his glass. "Don't entirely know what to make of it, but it's like watching an AI access a remote databank through a slow connection."

Kyona finished her drink and then held her glass out to him. It was foolish of her to have even one when she should be on her guard, but stress had already gnawed her ragged. She needed something to relax the tension of her shoulders. "She's still in there, Rull. I believe it. I think I see her, sometimes, in the way she forms her vowels, or stands, or seems to almost recognize me. Like she wants to wake up and cannot." It was perhaps a paranoid fantasy she had built. Part of her hoped that Rull would tell her she was a fool and pry her fingers loose from this razor-edge straw she grasped.

"If you're right about this remote communication – and I believe you are from my own observations – then ..." Rull frowned and refilled his own glass, which he then turned delicately in his hand. "Darling, I do think it's a possibility that you are correct, and there is a mechanism remotely controlling her."

Kyona emptied her glass in a single, painful gulp. "That's ... that's *horrible*."

"What a torment that would be, controlled like a puppet on strings, unable to call out for help ..." He shuddered. "I certainly hope that I'm wrong."

"Should I hope so as well?" Kyona asked. "There must be a way to break this spell."

"That is the positive side to it," Rull said. "I will do what I can, I promise. I've already sent what information we have back to the Coalition."

"Should I try to draw things out a bit more to buy time?" Kyona asked. It was an easier prospect than it sounded. Nephele still seemed to harbor no understanding of how normal business was conducted and was in no hurry. Technically, Kyona's leave from her position would run out soon, but that felt like a hopelessly mundane concern.

"It couldn't hurt," Rull said. "The longer things go, the more information we have. And, if she leaves…" He shrugged expansively, the liquor in his still-full glass not quite sloshing out.

Kyona emptied her small glass once again in a burning gulp. If this fever dream masquerading as a diplomatic meeting ended, would she ever see this Dirzuga Nephele again? Would Chioma once more vanish into the void, this time to never reemerge? "I will hope your people work quickly."

Her hopes were answered far more swiftly than she could have imagined. After a morning spent on such inane topics as flower arranging and Jord's music, both of which Nephele seemed to find both fascinating and baffling, the Dirzuga had said, "You turn all things to art."

Kyona had recognized it instantly as a line from one of Chioma's favorite songs, one her fiancé had drunkenly serenaded her with early in their relationship. Momentarily overwhelmed with sorrow and anger, she abruptly adjourned for lunch, even though the hour for breakfast had only just passed. It had become clear that Nephele still did not comprehend these subtleties, perhaps because she never seemed to eat.

Rull found Kyona in their office and wordlessly handed her a cup of tea. "You're looking rather shattered, darling."

"No more so than normal." Kyona was at least not in such

a state this time that she could not blow on the tea to cool it before taking a soothing sip. It was sad that she could joke about this constant, background level of emotional pain.

"I may have something that will bring you a bit of hope in this darkness," Rull said.

"Oh?"

"Regarding our conversation yesterday…" With a little flourish, he drew a small, cylindrical device from his sleeve and offered it to her.

Still holding her teacup, Kyona took the cylinder with her other hand. It was shockingly heavy; she nearly dropped it. "What is this?"

"Freshly synthesized. I don't really understand the particulars of it," Rull said with an apologetic smile, "But our tech fellows believe this will at least temporarily cut off the communication between this Dirzuga person and her ship, and then we shall see who she really is, hey?"

Kyona turned the device in her fingers. "How temporarily?"

"It's some sort of aerosol, so however long it stays in the air. Five minutes, perhaps, with our filtration systems? Long enough to be able to learn what you need to know."

Kyona curled her hand into a fist, the device in her palm. It was shocking how quickly Rull had been given this solution, but he had been constantly sending information back to his command. Perhaps this project was being given a higher priority than she had assumed. "Tell me how to use it."

Though Nephele still seemed uncomprehending of human body language, Kyona was careful to keep her expression smooth, her gait practiced as she returned from the so-called lunch break to resume. The device Rull had given her sat heavy in the sleeve of her kimono. Looking across the table at the strange non-expression on Nephele's face, she felt no hesitation over what she had decided to do.

"What were we speaking of, before the break?" Kyona asked.

"Your music," Nephele said.

"Ah, yes, I remember. Do your people have music as well?"

Nephele tilted her head. "To me, everything is music. The world is a harmony."

It was a strange verbal tic that Kyona had noticed; when she asked Nephele a general question about the Arborec as a people, she always answered in a way that spoke only of herself. She wondered if it was a translation issue, or perhaps one of simple culture. The unwillingness to speak in any kind of generalities was strange. But in this moment, she also did not care. As Nephele continued to talk, Kyona slipped her hand into her sleeve, extracted the device, twisted it in half as Rull had told her to do, and then set it on the table.

Nephele stopped midsentence. "What is that?"

"Nothing important." Kyona folded her hands back into her sleeves. "Please, continue."

As Nephele began to speak again, the device emitted a soft puff of vapor that might have almost looked like water, but there was something more metallic about its sheen. For a moment, nothing further happened, but then what looked like a wave of tiny sparks spread through the air, a spray of some kind of glitter that twinkled briefly and then vanished.

Nephele stopped talking again. She looked left, then right, tilted her head as if listening. It was this behavior that had first given her the idea that Nephele must somehow be receiving communication from her ship through unconventional means.

"Is something wrong?" Kyona asked.

"It has gone silent," Nephele said.

"What has?"

"The Symphony." Nephele frowned, which was the most recognizably human expression Kyona had yet seen on her face.

"I have heard no music," Kyona said. "Are you certain?"

"The Symphony is ever-present. That flash in the air," Nephele said. "What was it?"

"Just a simple aerosol," Kyona answered. She wasn't going to deny that truth entirely. "To clear the air of the room. Are you feeling all right, Nephele?"

"It's quiet." And there, too, recognizable uncertainty. So like Chioma it made Kyona's heart seize.

She rose to her feet, stepping around the table. "Chioma?"

Nephele frowned. "Why your non-standard greeting now?"

Kyona ignored her. "Chioma, can you hear me? Are you there?"

Nephele slammed her hand down on the table; the sharp sound made Kyona jump. "What is this Chioma? How have you silenced the Symphony?"

Perhaps it was the built-up strain of so many days of having to maintain her peace, or perhaps it truly did seem foolish to continue the prevarication when *something* had obviously happened, and at Kyona's hand. "Chioma is the woman whose face you wear!" Kyona cried. "Whose life you have stolen. And I will have her back!"

In a righteous world, such a dramatic declaration would have had the desired effect – or any effect at all.

"Explain!" Nephele shouted, sounding more human than she ever had – and furious.

Kyona, not at all rational herself, shouted in return, "Give her back!" She half stepped around the table, seized by a mad, despairing urge to throw herself at Nephele and shake her until

Chioma, who she knew must be underneath it all, emerged.

Nephele gripped the massive table, picked it up, and threw it. Kyona screamed and ducked to the side; the corner of the table still caught her shoulder and knocked her to the floor, and then it smashed against the wall with a deafening crash. The lights in the room flickered, sparks cascading down the wall from the half-shattered decorative wall covering. When Kyona staggered to her feet, her wild glance at Nephele showed nothing familiar in those features, nothing human in her expression. She ran for the door, thinking she could open it, slip out, and slam it closed somehow.

The door, when she hit the panel with her palm, did not open. The display flashed with orange starbursts that Kyona vaguely knew to be Mentak Coalition emergency symbols. She slapped the panel again, frantically.

Nephele grabbed her by the shoulders. Kyona screamed, knowing that it was pointless, as the Dirzuga pressed her face-first into the unmoving door.

Kyona frantically beat her hand against the door, wildly staring at the emergency symbols. It took several long, terrifying seconds for her to realize what they meant: *Depressurization emergency. Take shelter.*

There would be no help forthcoming for her from Rull. She might very well die in this room even if she survived Nephele's sudden rage – though that was the much more immediate problem. Kyona forced herself to breathe, no mean feat with Nephele's weight against her back and her face pressed against the wall. Whatever incident she'd set off with Rull's device, she had to face up to it now.

"Chioma was my fiancé," Kyona wheezed, and the *was* of that statement hurt with a fresh pain.

"I do not know *fiancé*," Nephele snarled.

"Let me go and I'll explain. I promise." If anything Nephele's grip tightened more. Kyona gasped. "You're hurting me."

"Symphony first," Nephele said. "Then fiancé."

"Agreed," Kyona gasped. Nephele let her go so abruptly that she reeled backward and fell, landing hip-first on the deck. It hurt, another bruise to add to the collection of the last minute, but Kyona didn't care. She was busy taking in as much air as she could. Nephele loomed over her, and she raised a hand in what she hoped would be understood as a placating gesture. "Please tell me what this 'Symphony' is, so I can understand what's happened. Then I'll be able to answer."

"The Symphony is *me*," Nephele said. "The… music that connects all of the parts of *me*."

"Music," Kyona repeated.

"The music is the network. The Flaah… spores weave it together."

Kyona put her face in her hands. Her head hurt; it was also easier to try to make sense of this when she wasn't looking at Nephele's face. "You have a communication network that is composed of spores?"

"I am the network. I exist across Nestphar, across space. Near-infinite parts of one whole."

Why had she not asked these questions before? Much of what Nephele was saying now had been pieced out in their earlier discussions, and she simply had not put it together, had not listened, had not *asked*. She had been too busy trying to see Chioma behind every phrase instead of trying to understand the message beneath it.

"You are one entity," she said slowly, because as a concept it was still a bizarre one. "In many bodies."

"Yes."

"Why *that* body?" Kyona had wanted to demand this answer; it came out more as a despairing wail.

"Tell me what you have done with the Symphony."

"I don't know," Kyona admitted. She pushed herself to her feet and cast around, looking for the device Rull had given her; she found it in the wreckage left behind by the table. She offered it to Nephele. "We surmised that you must have some constant communication back to your ship. Rull didn't tell me that he knew it was spores." She frowned. "Though he must have known, for whatever this is to have worked. Spores are… very different from the communication modes we normally deal with." Why hadn't he told her, in that case? And he had claimed that the Coalition scientists had developed this in less than a day, which seemed impossible in that light. There was always self-interest in the game the two of them played, but they had always been collegial equals before, and now she felt suspiciously and resentfully like she had been used as an unwitting pawn. "And that–" she pointed at the door panel "– indicates there's some sort of depressurization emergency, so this room has been completely sealed off from ship air. Would that keep out your spores?"

"Yes," Nephele said. She looked down at the device in her palm, and then tucked it away in her garment, though Kyona had noticed no pockets in it. "Now, explain *fiancé*."

Kyona squeezed her eyes tightly shut. "You understand that each of us is an individual, correct? Not… like you, I suppose."

"I find it strange, but I grasp it. Each, a private symphony that never returns to the whole."

"That person you are in… is someone I once knew. She was very important to me." Kyona hoped to leave it at that. She did not want to have to clinically describe love or relationships or any of the things that were necessary to truly explain the concept of "fiancé".

"An individual can be of particular import to another individual," Nephele said.

"Yes. That is part of individuality. We have preferences for... and against each other." Kyona made herself breathe deeply. "How did you come to have that body?"

"A ship drifted into my space. All beings on board were deceased. Some sort of virus, I concluded. But they were biological material like I had yet to encounter. I took them into my laboratories and found they made a home for a particular type of spore, and that spore that made the new being created a part of the Symphony." She tilted her head. "I knew, from examining this ship, that these beings were unlike me, that they had concepts I lacked, terminology for and ways of communicating I lacked. This–" she gestured to her body "– allows me to speak with you in a way you can understand, and allows me to interpret your many methods of communication in ways that translate to me. This has a name."

"Oh," Kyona breathed. It was too much information at once. She knew what had to be most important was what Nephele said about communication, about the creation of her as a Dirzuga. But what sat in the front of her mind, what was simultaneously knife and balm to her heart was knowing, five years later, of Chioma's fate. The entire crew of the *Dies Opulen*, dead of some kind of plague. The ship adrift. All these years she had kept her hope alive, when she should have accepted what everyone else had known to be the truth. She sat abruptly.

"Why do you seat yourself on the floor?"

Kyona shook her head. "I need a moment to... to understand

the world as it is. You've told me that Chioma – the person whose body you are using – has been dead for five years."

"That is correct."

Kyona put her face in her hands. She did not cry; the tears would not come. "Would you – would you give her body back?"

"Why?"

"So that I can see her properly buried!"

Nephele gave her another of those uncomprehending looks she was coming to despise. "If I understand the meaning of your individual, that person is dead when their biological function ceases. They are only matter, returned into the cycle so that new life may grow."

"Yes, but–"

"New life has grown in dead matter. Nothing of this individual you seek remains. This is part of me. There is no reason to cast it off."

"But she is mine to mourn!" Kyona burst out.

Nephele's head tilted in the other direction, the movement strangely birdlike for a moment. "She is gone. The possession of dead matter does not change that."

Kyona clutched her hands around her middle, sick and angry. She wanted to continue to fight, but saw no empathy, no understanding from the Dirzuga. And why would there be, when she barely understood what it meant for so many individuals to exist? She could fight this, she could demand, but would the ultimate cost of that conflict, to both herself and possibly the Federation of Sol be worth it? What closure would Chioma's body lying in the soil of Jord provide her that knowing her fate didn't already? The idea of this Arborec occupying her was viscerally repugnant yet... knowing Chioma, knowing how she felt about being on-world, Kyona had to admit with sick humor that she might have preferred this fate.

She pressed her fingers against her eyelids for a moment and made herself say, "We have to hope that whatever emergency has hit Rull's ship, he will fix it and rescue us."

"Do you think he will fix it?" Nephele asked. Something in her tone made Kyona look up. The Dirzuga had not emoted terribly well at the beginning, but she had developed subtleties over the few days they had been in close contact. In her expression, Kyona read a particular kind of doubt.

"Do you think he would not?"

"Individuals act on their own purposes," Nephele said. "The odds of such an emergency occurring just as you sought to cut me from the Symphony are vanishingly small. Particularly when there was no sign of attack or impact."

In some ways, it was the most human she had yet sounded. It was, simultaneously, the least like Chioma she had ever sounded as well. Even the stilted, confusing speech of someone not quite habituated to Federation standard had been closer to Chioma's manner. This coldly scientific recitation belonged to someone else entirely.

Because this wasn't Chioma. And had never been.

Kyona licked her lips, which were suddenly very dry. "I have… similar doubts." *A betrayal.* Another knife in her heart, but Rull was her friend in the same sense as any nominally allied diplomat she had worked with was. She might like him, but she could never forget that he first served his own interests and that of the Mentak Coalition. Though she might have hoped, at least, that he'd treasure their friendship enough to give her a running start if he was planning to stab her in the back. She certainly would for him. Yet she thought now, of how eager Rull had been to tell her to give up on the negotiation, then how he'd gently tried to encourage her to see it as an insult, how he'd adroitly encouraged certain courses of action at every turn, so subtle that he could retreat into concern whenever she pushed back.

That hurt did not matter. She had once thought herself an expert at boxing up such feelings and putting them away. She did her best to do that again, now, before continuing: "It could very well be that the Mentak Coalition would much prefer we not ally."

Keep the Federation of Sol weak and sectioned off and foster more dependence upon the Coalition, perhaps. Put themselves into a greater bargaining position with the Arborec by keeping them isolated as well – or even open them up to conquest, if they were already experimenting on such countermeasures. They must have already had encounters with the Arborec for such a weapon to even be in development – another thing Rull had plainly lied to her about.

"They have now proven they hold a successful weapon against me," Nephele said.

Hell, it might not even be the whole Coalition. They all served the same general aim, but Kyona knew well that individual captains tended to act independently. That speculation did not help now.

"He may also be monitoring us," Kyona said.

"If that is the case, we will find out soon enough." Nephele walked over to the panel and examined it. "Do you have an interface for this?"

"Yes, of a sort." Kyona took her small communication screen from her sleeve and offered it to Nephele.

Nephele seemed to pluck tools directly from the garment she wore, small, organic shapes growing out to meet her fingers.

She set to work on the panel. "What will you do, if this Rull individual has betrayed you?" Nephele asked.

"Most likely nothing, if he has a good enough story. I cannot prove anything, and we are on his ship." Curious, Kyona asked, "What will you do?"

"I do not attack other ships," Nephele said, though Kyona thought she felt an unspoken *yet*. "I only harvest what I find adrift." She did something with one of her tools, and the alarm lights abruptly went out.

"Did you just turn them off?" Kyona asked.

"The room beyond this door was at vacuum. One of the airlocks was open. I caused it to close. Atmosphere has returned."

"Is there a reason for an airlock to simply be open?" Kyona asked, knowing already what the answer was.

"If it was told to be open." Nephele offered her the communicator back, and then melded her tools back into her garment.

"Perhaps a malfunction," Kyona said.

"Perhaps." Nephele tapped the panel, and the door opened. She walked boldly out into the next room – a lack of caution, Kyona supposed, that came with knowing the death of that body would not in any way kill the entity that moved it. Kyona followed her, half-expecting to find the room beyond a fire-blackened wreck due to a malfunction. Instead, it looked precisely as it always did. The airlock to Nephele's ship was open, and the Dirzuga stood near it, head bowed for a moment.

"Are you all right?"

"I have returned to the Symphony," Nephele said. "All is well. I was not permanently impaired."

"I'm glad to hear that." Kyona glanced toward the door that led to the crew's portion of the ship. "I'm going to look in on

Rull. You may want to be prepared to leave, should something untoward happen."

Nephele inclined her head slightly. "I will wait here."

Kyona walked boldly down the hallway to the "office" and entered, to find Rull inside. He was drinking more of his horrible green liquor, and he choked on it when he looked at her. The expression on his face told Kyona that he had not expected her to live through being trapped with the angry Dirzuga... and that either he had been too much of a coward to watch her death in real time, or Nephele throwing the table had damaged the room's surveillance. She found she did not care which of the options it was. Both fueled her cold anger as she offered him a polite smile. "Well, that was quite nerve-racking, wasn't it, Rull?"

He coughed to clear his throat. "Kyona! Oh, I've been so worried, darling. My engineer has been working on the bad circuit that caused the depressurization of the airlock. I'm glad to know they fixed it... though I'll have their ears for not calling it to me faster."

"I'm certain they're very busy," Kyona said.

"Is the Arborec ambassador well?"

"Yes. I'm sorry to say that your device did not work." If he could smile impenetrably and lie to her, she had all the skill she needed to do the same to him. She wondered, now, how far his deception went. Had he known about the Dirzuga? He must have; otherwise how would he have been able to get that device so quickly? Had he known the Dirzuga wore Chioma's body? How much cruelty did he hide behind that smile?

"Ah, damn. Sorry to hear that."

"It's all right," Kyona said. "It feels strange to say now, but... I found what I needed."

•••

The negotiations concluded the next day; Kyona would have liked for them to finish immediately but judged too abrupt an end would seem suspicious to Rull. It took time for Kyona to recall her own ship, as well; she still had several hours between politely seeing Nephele off and her own departure. The Dirzuga's leaving had been far less dramatic than her arrival, simply an exchange of polite nods, the acknowledgment of work already accomplished. Kyona had taken her last look at Nephele's face and gotten to offer the goodbye that had been denied to her for five years.

The *I love you*, she kept unspoken; she knew Chioma was not there to hear.

Rull treated her with the care of the guilty, his solicitude greater than it had ever been, as if he were silently apologizing for having put her in such danger. Kyona pretended not to notice, though she was happy to use it to her advantage, requesting logs from him that would keep him busy while his crew prepared for her departure.

Alone for what she had claimed would be a short walk around the ship prior to her departure, she took her communications screen from her sleeve and looked over once more at the message Nephele had placed there.

She believed the Arborec when she said that Chioma was gone; there had been nothing of her personality left. But looking at this message, Kyona suspected – though she knew she could not prove – that something of Chioma's brilliance and knowledge lived on. Her fiancé had been a ship's engineer of no small skill. How else would the Arborec had known how to bypass the *Irascible*'s systems so handily during the faked malfunction? And how else could Nephele have left her such clear and concise instructions, tailored for a non-expert, on how to utilize a conduit on the other end of the ship from the engine to introduce a resonance into the system that would, in eight hours, cause the full shutdown of the ship's power core, undetected until it was far too late?

Kyona finished the last of the programming sequences from the instructions and carefully closed up the conduit, wiping away all traces of her presence. She felt sick unto her soul, thinking of the *Irascible* floating dead in the black the way the *Dies Opulens* once had. Yet this, in cold fury, she owed to Rull, his crew, and the Coalition for what they had tried to do to the Federation – and to her. This, she also owed to Nephele for giving her the incalculable gift of the truth of Chioma's fate, no matter how difficult it had been to hear at the time – and because to give the Arborec the key to a weapon that had been used against them was an incalculable gift that would not be soon forgotten.

She met Rull at the airlock where her ship waited. He offered her an unctuous smile. "Got a bit rough in places, but you accomplished great things, eh?"

"Indeed. You were a greater help than you'll ever know." Kyona made herself pat him lightly on the arm. "It was good to see you, my friend. Perhaps our paths will cross again." *Though I doubt it.*

"Of course they will," Rull said. "And I look forward to it."

SIX MONTHS LATER

Kyona sat at the center of the Federation of Sol's negotiation team, a position that she still felt utterly unused to even after her un-looked-for promotion five months ago. She had brought the initial agreement – not even formal enough to be called a treaty – with the Arborec back to Sol as a gift to her own people and perhaps even something of a self-righteous gesture of her own rectitude. She had thought, then, to return to her former low position in the diplomatic corps; that was all she had wanted, truly.

Instead, she had, quite unthinkingly, made herself the only expert in the Federation of Sol on communication with the Arborec. Not a bad consequence of her action, but one she still reeled from.

The junior attaché next to her shifted nervously. "Is it true that the Arborec speak through dead people?" she asked.

"In a sense, though that isn't how they think of it, and you must keep that in mind. However the person who sits before us might look, they are one small part of the Arborec being, the mouth they have sent to speak with us." Kyona took a small sip of tea.

"And is it true they rob graves?" the young woman whispered.

"We might view it like that, but they do not, and you must remember that too." She heard the soft chime that indicated the door was about to open. "Welcoming smiles and no more questions. They are our allies."

"Kyona from Federation of Sol. It is good to see you again," the Arborec said, entering the room.

Kyona sucked in a quick, shocked breath, though she gamely held on to her polite smile. "Dirzuga … I don't suppose this one is also named Nephele?"

"Chantir."

Chantir. The name of a particularly vile green liquor favored in the Mentak Coalition. "Dirzuga Chantir, then," Kyona said. "The Federation of Sol welcomes you in friendship."

"Ah, the standard greeting. I am happy to accept."

Across the table from her, the Arborec smiled at her using the face of a man once named Rull.

SHIELD OF THE REEF

ROBBIE MacNIVEN

PART ONE

There had been times when Lyra had wondered if she would ever see his face again.

Even in that moment, standing at the final compression checkpoint of the docking spur, she was unsure about what lay beyond. Would he be waiting? Would she be ready if he was? Would she be ready if he *wasn't*?

She watched the light above the checkpoint's blast hatch. All around, the mass of passengers chattered or waited silently as Reef Wardens moved among them, conducting final travel log and ident checks, a random search to supplement the automated scans already completed when the *Arkut* had docked at Sevenport, in orbit above the foremost planet of the Soldar Reef. So far, it seemed the wardens had discovered nothing untoward. Most of the transportees were humans doing the

short hop from Redhaven or the Tamar system, but there
were a few Saars and Kazaranids, and a small group of Xxcha
who managed to negotiate on behalf of a human family whose
excessive food allowance caught the ire of Sevenport's officials.
There was even a Hacan trade delegation near the back,
slumming it with a public system hop.

More concerning was the one rogue-looking Letnev with
the energy beam scars and the duo of humans she was certain
she recognized from her last hit job on Holdmire. They hadn't
made her, thankfully, or she was just mistaken about their
identity. Nevertheless, she kept her hood up and her back
to the rest of the passengers whenever possible, her eyes
instinctively scanning those nearby, constantly evaluating their
threat potential and what her responses would be when things
went down.

If things went down, she corrected herself. She had to stop
doing that. Fitting people up for a weapon, or a bodysuit. That
was all behind her now. Hopefully.

The light above the hatch pinged to green, and the heavy
entranceway concertinaed open with a hiss. Lyra slung her
rucksack over one shoulder and pushed forward into the rush
of bodies, eager to be out of the checkpoint and away from the
unfamiliar crowd. She wanted to confront the fear that had been
twisting in her gut. She always preferred to face these sorts of
things head on.

Sevenport's arrival terminal lay before her, a sprawl of
shopping kiosks, information points, food hubs, and a plethora
of scrolling markers that pointed the way to onward travel. The
space was circular, cavernous, with multiple gantries ringing it
all the way up to a glassplex dome that showed the distant stars
and the winking running lights of interstellar vessels docking

at the orbital station. It was buzzing with activity, a hundred different species and a thousand different languages and dialects vying.

The glories of the Soldar Reef, a small corner of the galaxy that owed no allegiances to any external empire.

Lyra's heart was racing as she scanned the crowd that had amassed for the *Arkut*'s arrival. Despite the bustle she felt isolated, exposed. It was the same feeling she had whenever she found herself caught out in the open during a gunfight. It made her skin prickle and sent ice up her spine.

Calm down, she told herself. Take a breath.

She did so, smelling the stale, recycled air of the space station and the dry tang of ever-laboring gravitational regulators. As she settled herself, she felt a buzz in her thigh pocket.

She pulled out her savant and woke up the screen with a flick of her thumb. It had just logged two new messages. One was an automated welcome to Sevenport and the Soldar Reef. The other was from the one she had been looking for, Zanth Keen.

"Come upstairs," it read.

Lyra looked up. The nearest gantries were just as busy as the main deck, and it was impossible to discern a single figure. She glanced back at her savant again, then returned it to her pocket and made her way to the nearest escalator.

That only made her feel more uncomfortable. She was being watched. She tried to shake off her unease, but all she wanted to do now was get onboard one of the outbound shuttles, get back onto the *Arkut*, and get off-world again. She'd been in a lot of scrapes in the past few years, but she couldn't recall being as afraid as she was now.

In the end, she didn't have to hunt through the upper gantries for him – he was waiting for her at the top of the first escalator.

She stopped dead, oblivious to the people having to push past her.

There he stood, tall and straight-backed. His dark hair was edged with silver now, slicked away from his forehead, and his lined, scarred face remained impassive. The only thing missing from her foremost memories of him was the white and gold of his immaculate Reef Defense Fleet uniform. Today he was wearing simple black and gray office garb.

For a second that felt like a lifetime, Lyra stood still. Zanth held her gaze, and it seemed as though all the chaos of the station went on pause. Then he smiled, and Lyra felt a rush of relief.

It was still the same smile.

She threw herself into his arms. The embrace was difficult, Zanth's old auto-prosthetic left limb not responding easily. He held her tightly as the busy hubbub around them resumed, swallowing them back up.

"Lyra," Zanth murmured, unmoved in the midst of it all, safe and dependable.

"Father," Lyra said.

It was a short shuttle ride from the orbital station down to Kerees, capital city of Andeara, the largest inhabited world of the Soldar Reef. Lyra spent the whole journey talking animatedly. The fear and uncertainty were gone, replaced by joy. Despite a decade apart, and everything that had happened in those long years, her father still loved her, and had still welcomed her. For a while, talking about old friends, the state of the Reef Defense Fleet, and the antics of their home's cleaning drones made it feel as if she had never left. As if she was still twenty-one years old and all the bloodshed and death in between had never happened.

"Where's Ma'?" she asked as the automated shuttle service slid into their home's berthing strut. Zanth had already told her prior to her arrival, but she wanted to hear it again. She wanted to know for sure that her mother was just as happy with her homecoming as her father.

"She should have just finished her speech in the Parliament," Zanth said, disengaging the safety restraints and leaning over to slot his cred bar into the unmanned shuttle's pay unit. "She might be home already."

Lyra shucked her rucksack onto her back again as she stepped out onto the strut that extended before her family home. She took a moment to gaze about, taking in the sight of the place she had grown up in, and the city that sprawled above and below it.

Like all major habitation points on Andeara, Kerees was built layer upon layer, tiered along the sides of the towering Mount Kerees. Much of the planet's surface was covered in inhospitable marshland and continent-sized swamps – anyone who survived the local wildlife and gasses would struggle to find a square of soil firm enough to sink a foundation into. Thankfully for the first marooned settlers, great mounds of bedrock jutted up from the marshland across Andeara's southern hemisphere. Geological activity, the specifics of which Lyra had labored through during her school days, provided a safe base for the cities that had steadily sprung up since the arrival of intelligent life. Mount Kerees was the largest.

The Keen household was part of a block that stood upon a rocky bluff on the eastern face of the great mound, not far from the flattened peak that was home to the government quarter. The larger part of the slope-city sprawled beyond the spar on which Lyra was standing, a jagged descent from the spires of the EastFlank housing projects to the chimney stacks and monolith-like refineries of the industrial belt that circled the foot of the mount, bordering the marshlands.

It was early evening, and the air was hazy and heavy, filled with smog that melded with the sky hanging low overhead. It created a layered effect over the hundreds of spires and chimneys stretching out below, and was pierced by thousands upon thousands of lights, from living block windows to the illuminator stab-beams of the funicular trains and the fly-lanes.

The wind that knifed around the city's bristling crown snatched at her, making her black hair stream and tugging at the raised collar of her yellow leather jacket. It brought with it the smells of the city – exhaust fumes, refined marsh gas, and the bitter, metallic aftertaste of an industrial hub approaching the pinnacle of productivity. For all its hardness, it was a welcome world away from the sterilized stillness of a space-traversing cockpit or the musty stench of a packed system-hopper cargo hold. The city was alive and bustling and spread out all around her, and it made her spirit soar.

"Did you miss it?" Zanth asked, as he noticed how she lingered.

"I did," she said, surprising herself. For years she had dreamed of getting away from this place, from its smog and gas-stink, from its buzzing fly-lanes and crammed tiers of high-rises, one structure atop another, one life upon another. Now though, it felt like what it had always been – home.

Zanth opened the block's front door as the shuttle buzzed away, and Lyra dragged herself from the view to follow him inside. Like all but the wealthiest properties, the Keens' home was small and mostly vertical, a series of modular habitation units built into the side of a domestic block. Lyra had once struggled with its confined nature. Not anymore though – compared to the berths of an interstellar long-hauler or the slum shacks outside Last Hope, the place she had grown up in was a sprawling mansion.

The house was entirely familiar – warm, tidy, and clean. The walls were white modular panels that could be slid back to expose computator terminals, biosphere controls, and storage space. The floor was a soft gray carpet, layered with intricately embroidered red and gold rugs that mirrored those in the Reef Parliament.

The front entrance led to a short corridor with doors on either side and steep stairs at the end. As Lyra entered, she could hear a whirr from the kitchen as the home's automated systems – a trio of basic cleaning drone-robots that as a child she had named Topsy, Turvy and Wurvy – prepared dinner. She was headed toward the kitchen when a figure emerged from a door to her right, so sudden she instinctively dropped her hand to a sidearm that was no longer there.

"Maker be thanked," Amara exclaimed, and threw her arms around her daughter, oblivious to her surprise. She hugged even harder than Zanth, and when she finally broke the embrace, she kissed Lyra on the brow.

"I've prayed for this," she said. "Almost every night."

"It was definitely every night." Zanth laughed, holding his hands up defensively when Amara cast him a look – he had never subscribed to the religion of the Makers, so popular among the humans living in Reef space.

Lyra's mother was like her – tall, sharp-featured, but with smile lines that Lyra didn't yet have. There was more white among her raven hair than Lyra remembered, but otherwise she was unchanged, her scent and the warmth of her embrace immediately bringing back memories. She was still wearing the formal black and yellow gown of a member of the Reef Parliament, having clearly just arrived before Lyra and Zanth.

Like most politicians on Andeara, she worked tirelessly to maintain the Soldar Reef's self-governing status, independent from the conflicting factions throughout the galaxy. The Reef was an independent system, tucked away near the edge of the Sol Federation, and its politicians worked hard to keep it that way.

"Prayers or not, you have been brought back to us," she said to Lyra. "You must be hungry!"

"You make it sound like I haven't eaten since I left," Lyra said, grinning as her mother tutted.

"It feels like you haven't! Let me change, and I'll deactivate the drones and make you something myself. Grazer soup? We've got fresh bogboar and vineweave as well."

"Grasp this opportunity with both hands," Zanth said. "Normally I'm the one who makes food when the drones are down."

"I have missed your vineweave," Lyra admitted, causing her mother to clap her hands.

"Then vineweave you shall have!"

"Is my room still upstairs?" Lyra asked, continuing along the corridor. The door at the top of the stairs slid open automatically, its sensors recognizing her.

"More or less," Zanth said, following her up. "It's housed more than a few visitors over the years, but your mother would only let them in if they promised not to touch anything."

Standing on the threshold of her old bedroom, Lyra realized that Zanth wasn't joking. The space looked almost exactly the same. Star charts were plastered across the walls, and the shelves were heavy with books and story-slates – adventure tales mostly, often involving legendary, far-off Mecatol Rex. There were more tangible volumes too, concerning the Reef and its independence from the neighboring Sol Federation. The fold-down bed was fully made beneath a shuttered window hatch. She knew that opening it would reveal the block's fly-lane outside – she could feel the thrum of grav engines coming faintly through the glassplex.

She'd been twenty-one when she had last stood in this room. The weight of what had happened since threatened to overwhelm her, until she felt Zanth's hand on her shoulder. It was like an anchor, holding her steady while the sudden tide of emotion raged.

"I'll give you a moment," Zanth said. "I'm going to help your mother. Take a shower if you like. I assume you remember where it is?"

Lyra nodded, too choked up to respond properly to the quip. She stepped fully into the room, letting the door slide shut, leaving her alone with her thoughts.

It was surreal. For years now she'd wanted to come back. The realities of her contracts and the cost of getting to the Reef had ensured that had been impossible until now. It threw her old life into such stark contrast.

Ten years as a hired gun, a bounty hunter operating in Sol Federation space and the Contested Zones – the sharpest life lesson anyone could hope for. She had become a fighter at best, a killer at worst, someone who no longer dreamed about exploring the galaxy.

Could she really leave that darkness behind? She'd come home with blood on her hands, and she was worried she was going to stain everything around her, everything that remained pristine and untouched. It felt unnatural to be back amongst things that bordered onto her childhood when she was a child no longer.

That didn't have to be the case, Lyra told herself. She had made the choice to break with the past. She'd destroyed her weapons and false identities. She had come here to give herself space to think, and time to make sure that the past couldn't catch up with her.

One step at a time.

She placed her rucksack at the foot of the bed, pulled off her jacket, and opened the shutters. Outside, darkness was falling, an ochre sunset fading to black, the shadows growing deeper and the lights brighter. Rain was falling, streaking down the glassplex and making the running illuminators and tail beams from the passing traffic glitter and distort.

The water made her realize that she did actually want a shower. The *Arkut* had only had public wash blocks, which she'd used as infrequently as possible. Warm water and a decent pressure might let her untangle her thoughts and add emotional distance to the light years she had put between herself and her past.

She stood and headed for the stairs.

Washing left her head feeling a little clearer, and the scents of cooking that reached the fold-out washroom cubicle on the stairway reminded her how hungry she was.

Her parents were waiting for her at the table. Despite its ugly name, the bogboar ribs were delicious, and the fiery pot of stewed and steaming vineweave fibers had been done to perfection. All memories of the freeze-food and reheated void cartons that had been her lot during the system hop dissolved with the first bite.

They talked for a while about family and old acquaintances, rehashing much of what Lyra and Zanth had discussed on their way down from Sevenport. Eventually, Amara asked the question Lyra knew had been simmering longer than the boar.

"What made you come back?"

Lyra set her fork down. She tried to find the right words, but instead met only memories. The stink of sweat, the sticky residue of blood on her hands that wouldn't come off. The smell of burned flesh, smoke rising from cauterized energy beam wounds. A hundred faces, pale, gaunt, streaked in grime, looking up at her with abject fear from the crushing confines of the hold where they'd been rammed like cattle.

"I was tired," Lyra said.

She caught the look that passed between her parents. Amara's was one of uncertainty, Zanth's a warning shot. Don't ask.

"Well, you're home now," Amara said, reaching out and squeezing Lyra's hand, masking her doubt with a smile.

"How did the speech go today?" Zanth said, making a gallant effort to change the subject.

"What was it about?" Lyra added, eager to escape the memories that had briefly threatened to rise up and consume her.

"It was a vote of thanks," Amara said. "For Delan Gurrow."

"Did he save the First Minister again?" Lyra asked, twisting another knot of vineweave around her fork.

"No, he's retiring."

Lyra paused and tried to do some quick mental math, gauging the age of Gurrow. The Rokha warrior had been acting as the bodyguard to the First Minister and, through that, been a figurehead for the independence and strength of the Soldar Reef for as long as she could remember.

"He can't be that old," she said. "Even if it's a decade since I was last here. Besides, Rokha live longer."

"It's nothing to do with his age, or capability," Amara said with a hint of bitterness.

"Your mother doesn't like to delve into the sticky business of the current regime's politics, even at the dinner table," Zanth said, but Amara waved her hand.

"The current First Minister is not an honest person," she declared.

"Of course he isn't, he's in the Reef People's Coalition," Lyra said. The democratic rulers of the Reef typically rotated between the three main political parties on Andeara, the People's Coalition, Brightstar, and the New Reef Collective. Amara was just the latest in a long line of Collective politicians. She rarely had a good word to say about her party's main opposition, the isolationist Reef First.

She laughed humorlessly at Lyra's words. "Even for the Coalition, this First Minister is a rotten one. There are all manner of irregularities happening behind the scenes. Jettisoning Gurrow is just the latest. Apparently he was too close to what Karrow has been doing and didn't approve. I said as much during my address."

"And what did Karrow say to that?" Zanth asked, referring to the current First Minister and ruler of the Reef Parliament.

"Just what you'd expect," Amara said. "That I was trying to make political capital out of something innocuous and that we should be celebrating Gurrow's lengthy service instead of point-scoring."

"So, the position of Shield is now vacant?" Lyra wondered.

"It is," Amara said, looking at her sharply for a moment.

"Hirlow is acting in the role as captain of the Parliamentary Guard, but it's only temporary."

"I doubt anyone will be able to live up to Gurrow's legacy," Lyra said. The Rokha felid had been Shield of the Reef since before she'd been born, the guardian of eleven successive First Ministers and the symbolic protector of the disparate peoples that called the Reef home. Something truly bad had to be bubbling away for him to step down.

"You've come back at an interesting time," Zanth admitted. "Gas processor strikes, new tariffs on sub-stellar trade, the news last week about Qualid going rogue. There are even rumors of the Sol Federation sniffing around for the first time in centuries. Thankfully I'm no longer a part of it all. I retired from the RDF last month."

"I hope they gave you a speech in Parliament too," Lyra teased. Her father snorted, but said nothing. Zanth had worked as a military advisor to the Reef Defense Fleet. With help from Amara in Parliament, he had been steadily improving its defensive capabilities. Both the Reef's constitution and the attitude of the many peoples that called it home forbade expansionism, but the warships and system monitors that guarded the small enclave's independence were now capable, thanks to Zanth's years of service.

"Karrow has already started the application process for the next Shield," Amara said. "He'll want someone he can control better than Gurrow." Lyra gave a little shrug as she continued to eat. For a society that considered itself pacifistic by nature, Reef politics were as cutthroat and dirty as any she had encountered in the wider galaxy.

They finished dinner and talked for a while longer before Lyra excused herself. A sudden, heavy weariness had descended on her, not helped by the fact that her body was still struggling to adjust to the time-jump. Most system hoppers slowly amended their day and night cycles to match that of the target destination, but the *Arkut* was a scabby interstellar lugger that offered no basic luxuries, meaning she was still strung-out on the wrong hours.

She slumped down on her bed and closed her eyes, trying to stop worrying. Surely she was safe now. She had to start thinking about setting the weights she had been carrying down, hopefully forever.

As she slipped in between the bedsheets, she made herself imagine that no time had passed since she had last slept here, that everything that had happened in between had been a dream. She entertained that for as long as she could while drifting off, knowing that it wouldn't last.

If she was lucky, she'd wake up in the morning and remember the truth. If she was unlucky, her nightmares would remind her before then.

She knew she was dreaming, but that didn't make it any less terrible. It was like a memory on repeat, twisted and distorted. She had flashes of sensation, so potent her mind told her they were real. The stench. The blood. The hold, packed with bodies, except now when they looked up at her, it was not the starved faces she had seen, but the features of those she knew on Andeara – old friends, her mother and father. All of them racked by pain and fear. All of them screaming.

Lyra twitched awake. Her room was silent and dark. Nothing moved. For a second, she had forgotten where she was.

Had she screamed too, or had it only been in the dream? She lay still, heart pounding, wondering if she'd woken her parents. Could she hear movement?

No, voices. She rubbed her eyes. It was late enough to be early. She pulled back the sheets, the horror of the nightmare melting as curiosity took hold.

She slipped from the bed and padded silently downstairs, feeling like a child again. When her parents argued it was never with raised voices. The tone always ran low and fierce. That was what she was hearing right now. They were still in the kitchen. She sat on the bottom step, listening.

"We should just be thankful that she's back," Zanth said. "After the first few years I thought we'd never see her again."

"I'm as relieved as you are," Amara replied. "But what's to stop her from leaving again? She'll get bored."

"Maybe she's gotten all that out of her system. She's seen some bad things. Maybe done them too. I've seen those looks, before I came to the Reef."

"That's exactly why I don't want her to leave again. That lifestyle, it fractures the soul. Always running, always killing. We should never have let her go in the first place."

"There'll be plenty of killing if she becomes the Shield. Not that it's even a guarantee she'd pass the selection process."

Lyra felt her pulse quicken. She'd thought her parents had simply been arguing over whether they could convince her to stay on Andeara or not. Now she realized that Amara had suggested more than that. And what had Zanth meant when he had spoken of a time before he came to the Reef?

"It's been a century since a Shield died protecting the First Minister," Amara said. "It's considerably safer than running bounties beyond the Reef!"

"Times change," Zanth replied. "You know things are deteriorating. I mean, Qualid alone? When was the last time a captain went rogue? I'm still locked into the RDF intelligence system, I've seen the reports. He's been attacking shipping on the edgeward lines. And that's only the most pressing issue. Do you really wanted her to be sworn to protect slime like Karrow?"

"It isn't about the First Minister in power. It's about service to the wider whole. If we've got anything to say about it, Karrow will be out come the next election cycle. I want to keep her here, properly this time. That means giving her purpose. She's just the same as I was. I found an outlet in politics. She chose… a different path.

"A deadlier one, if only marginally," Zanth said.

"Do you think we'll ever know what she did out there?"

"No. And I'm not sure I want to. I knew the day she left the daughter we knew would never come back."

Lyra didn't want to hear any more. She stood up and walked silently through to the living room, the lights blinking on. Most of the furniture and the electronics had been slotted away into the wall panels for the night, but one object still occupied the far corner, next to the shuttered window hatch. Its presence surprised her.

It was a torso mannequin draped in a fleet uniform jacket. She had always assumed it was one of the first RDF ones her father had worn. It was sky-blue, double-breasted, with silver shoulder bars and a stiff, raised collar. On the left of the chest were two large silver badges, one a blazing comet, the other a planet and its orbiting moon. Though washed and pressed, it was badly damaged – the left arm was little more than a length of hanging rags, and a series of holes perforated the fabric, below the medals. Stains were visible around the damage, darker patches that Lyra knew to be blood.

She had only seen the uniform once before. As a child she'd

discovered it in her father's wardrobe. When he'd found her, it was the angriest Lyra had ever seen him. Afterward Amara had hugged her tight and told her that it wasn't her fault – sometimes Da' didn't want to remember he had the jacket. When Lyra had asked why he didn't throw it out, she had said, with the endless mysteriousness of an adult, that sometimes he didn't want to forget either.

Over the years Lyra had tried to piece together why. She knew her father had fought in a great naval action against pirates just beyond the borders of the Reef, at Outer Tarst. It had been an ambush, and his fleet had been wrecked. Amara had rescued him, and that was how they had met.

Lyra approached the uniform, hesitant, as though the damaged garment might lash out. She reached out and lightly touched one of the medals, the comet. Not for the first time, she wondered what it meant and how her father had earned it.

Amara had told her how she had saved her father's life. After becoming a member of the Reef Parliament it was customary for a minister to devote time to charitable work, and Amara had registered as a medic with the salvage fleet. She had found Zanth lying on the floating remains of one of his flagship's survival rafts.

The closest Zanth had ever come to telling her the same story was when he had taken her to the Museum of Galactic History. It still housed the survival raft he had been found on, which had been donated to the museum's collection. Holding Lyra's hand, Zanth had stood within the old shuttle and spoken briefly of Outer Tarst, and of a friend he once had in the fleet, Captain Temetz. He seemed to miss him badly. Lyra assumed he had been killed.

Besides that one visit Zanth never spoke of the battle.

"I was thinking about getting rid of it."

Lyra turned, startled. Zanth was in the doorway, his expression unreadable. Lyra was momentarily lost for words.

Her father stepped into the living room, and she realized he was looking at the uniform.

"I should have destroyed it," he said. "I left it out, because I knew seeing it every day would spur me to act. I would break the cycle of forgetting and remembering, over and over."

"Why now?" Lyra asked, curiosity overcoming her concern. "After all these years?"

"I'm not sure," Zanth admitted, moving to stand beside her. "Just a feeling. Things in the Reef… they're not as simple anymore. There are bad times ahead."

"And burning your past would change that?"

"Maybe. I don't believe in any gods. But perhaps there's some sort of cosmic balance. Perhaps I should have destroyed it years ago, when your mother found me. When I found peace."

"No one knows what the future holds," Lyra said. "I learned that not long after I left here."

"I regret not stopping you," Zanth said, his tone heartfelt. "I should have been firmer. I failed you, as a father."

"You couldn't have, and you didn't," Lyra replied, burdened by her thoughts. "I'm not a child anymore, and I wasn't when I left. I had to go. Cosmic balance, or whatever."

"More like the headstrong determination of youth."

"That's the one."

They lapsed into silence together, the torn and scarred uniform seeming to judge them.

"A part of me still sees myself in it," Zanth said. "After all, we suffered in the same fashion."

He reached out with his prosthetic, the artificial digits

clicking faintly as they brushed against the shredded cuff of the jacket's left sleeve.

"Sometimes it reminds me that I survived. I should be thankful of all I now have."

He was silent again, before looking at Lyra, his voice finding focus.

"How much did you hear earlier?"

"Enough, I think," Lyra said. "Enough to know you're refighting the same battles. Ma' wants me to stay, and you don't think I can be made to."

"Yes," Zanth said. "But with an important difference."

"The Shield." She still hadn't had a chance to order her thoughts, to take in the idea that Amara thought she could become the foremost guardian of the Reef's rulers.

"She's right to think you'd be capable," Zanth said. "You and I may not have spoken often during your absence, but there was enough contact for me to work out some of what you were doing. What you went through. I suspect I'm no longer the only Keen with weapon-scars on my body."

"You're not," Lyra said, her tone growing harder. She didn't want to have this conversation. She never wanted to have this conversation.

"The Reef doesn't produce good warriors," Zanth said. "But you're a warrior now Lyra, whether you want to be or not. You could be the next Shield. I'm sure the process is a difficult one, but I'm also sure you would be a contender. But that doesn't mean you *should* be."

"I'm done with fighting," Lyra said. "I've cut all ties to that life. That person is dead."

"But she lived in a different plane of existence from the one the Shield would inhabit," Zanth said.

"You're the one who said the Reef Stars were becoming more dangerous."

"They are," Zanth replied. "I'm arguing your mother's case, but I disagree with her. You know how her family have always been. Tied to duty, to the Reef. Serving its people. She sees an opportunity to mold you. You were never going to be a politician, but you can still serve. She doesn't fully realize it, but that's what she wants for you."

"There's nothing wrong with serving the common good," Lyra said, turning defensive. "That isn't what worries me."

"It's what you might have to do during that service," Zanth said. "I understand. I told her, and I'll tell her again – we cannot demand you bind yourself to this little corner of the galaxy. Your life is your own. Live it."

Lyra said nothing, thinking. She had been afraid of discovering rejection and change here, but she was starting to realize things had grown more complex. A part of her had indulged the thought of staying, but she struggled to imagine that life. She no longer wished to live the hair-trigger existence of a contract hunter, a star-stalker, but that didn't mean she could settle into politics, or education, or law, or any other respectable Reef profession. She was certain anything like that would push her over the edge. Perhaps the Shield was the compromise.

"I have decisions to make," she said eventually. "I came here hoping for a refuge, but I knew I'd have to make choices eventually. It just seems like I'll be doing it sooner rather than later."

"You should still rest," Zanth said. "Set all this aside for a while. You're safe here. This will always be your home."

Lyra embraced her father, and he returned it.

"I missed you," she told him. "I missed both of you, so much."

"And so did we," Zanth said. "If that cosmic balance is worth anything, we won't be parted again."

Lyra tried not to think about any of it for the next few weeks. She settled back into old routines, tinkering with the drones, helping them and her father maintain the house, and talking to her mother about Parliament. Amara wasn't home often – a flurry of votes combined with committee meetings and EastFlank surgeries kept her busy. Zanth admitted that while Amara was always working – it was what she enjoyed – lately it had been demanding more and more of her. Things had rarely been this heated. There were talks of strikes and civil unrest.

Lyra did her best to remain oblivious to it all. She struggled to accept that the place she had grown up, where she had always felt safe and accepted, was no longer a haven. Perhaps it had never been. Why would the role of Shield exist if the Soldar Reef was so peaceable? There had been assassination attempts on past First Ministers, and minor uprisings like the TaBek Gas Strikes or the WestFlank Resolution. Throughout it all, the Shield had remained a visible symbol of strength and stability, a sign that the Reef's pacifism was defended by the necessity of force.

It was a juxtaposition Lyra had never truly appreciated before, but which she found herself pondering now.

Neither Zanth nor Amara had mentioned the Shield since that first night. Lyra was too young to remember the last time there had been a selection process. Just how a Shield was actually chosen was shrouded in mystery, but stories abounded.

A combination of physical and mental trials were sure to form part of the selection – the Shield was expected to be the complete warrior, competent with a plethora of weapons and experienced in a range of tactical situations. They had to be level-headed, and able to solve problems rapidly, ensuring that they were never outwitted or caught short.

Perhaps most difficult of all, they had to be of indelible character, immune to corruption or factionalism. They stood above the Reef's politics, in defense of the whole.

How far that felt from the life Lyra had led. Comparing herself to the old exploits of the Reef's Shields made her angry. This was a role she could handle. She did her best to overcome that self-doubt, but it was difficult.

Her nightmares continued, the memories of an ex-bounty hunter refusing to lie quiet and still. She started awake most nights, sweating, reaching for a weapon that wasn't there, seeing snarl-drones or bug-eyed strike troopers breaking in through her door or window hatch. When she went outside, for morning jogs along the slope or to take the funicular down to buy groceries, she saw the faces of targets she'd been assigned.

She had never taken a job that wasn't honest, and that was what she kept telling herself.

For most of her career she had worked with the Sol Defense Assistance Initiative, a department of the Federation's intelligence branch that offered a legal framework for those willing to hire themselves out as mercenaries. The work was, supposedly, legitimate, cracking down on illicit smugglers or bringing in dangerous fugitives beyond Sol space, jobs that would be costly in terms of procedure and finance if Jord tried to undertake them with its own personnel. Hirelings were cheaper to employ, easily replaced, and easy to cut loose if something went wrong.

At first Lyra had enjoyed the thrill of it, but things had soon started going wrong. One of her bounty partners had been killed in a firefight with kex smugglers off the Yarin Spiral, and another who she'd almost counted as a friend, a Saar named Pelt, had left her to die when they'd been cornered by gangland brutes on the edge of Mentak space. The losses and betrayals quickly mounted up, and Lyra had realized that she had entered into a dirty and desperate business.

It had taken time to amass the funds for a route back to the Reef, not to mention the courage necessary to break the spiral and turn down contracts, but one last job had done it.

That had been the worst. It was the one that still haunted her.

One evening, unbidden, she almost found herself opening up about it to her mother. She faltered, and Amara just hugged her until the darkness receded. Afterward she admitted to Lyra that Zanth had told her she had overhead their discussion about the Shield. She promised it wasn't her intention to push her into anything, but Lyra had told her she wasn't. Service was in her mother's nature, after all, which meant it was in hers as well.

A month after her return, Lyra looked up from the dinner table and spoke.

"I'm going to do it," she said.

Until that moment, she hadn't been sure of her decision, but the words solidified the intent. Amara was the first to respond.

"The deadline for applicants is tomorrow."

"Then I'll apply tonight," Lyra said. "The main line to the government quarter is still running at this time."

Zanth began to speak as well, but Lyra kept going.

"I know what you think, Da', in fact I know what you both think. You haven't forced me into this. It's what I want to do.

I came back here to find solace, but I have to decide what the future holds. I don't want to leave the Reef again, but I do need a purpose. Something truly worthwhile. There's no greater satisfaction than protecting others. I think that's the best way to give back, after what I've taken. So tonight, I'm going to try to become the next Shield of the Reef."

PART TWO

A week later, a black shuttle with Reef Parliament markings pulled up to the block's strut.

Amara was in a committee meeting, so only Zanth saw her off.

"Do you know how many others normally make it to this stage?" Lyra asked, trying to mask her sudden nervousness. She knew that only a small number of candidates were chosen for the in-person assessments and was surprised to have received a response so quickly.

"It won't be many." He took her hand in both of his. "Relax. Whatever happens, we're always here."

She hugged him before stepping aboard the ominous shuttle. Like most conveyers in Kerees it was unmanned, and its doors hissed shut as soon as she was seated. She waved to her father but realized that the windows were tinted.

The vehicle slid away, its high-end grav motors making barely a purr. Like the bodywork, the upholstery was black. Lyra felt like she was being taken to report to one of her handlers from the Assistance Initiative.

To make matters worse, she realized it wasn't taking her uphill toward the government quarter. It was gliding down, deeper into the city. She had expected a briefing area close to the Parliament. Where she was actually headed, she had no idea.

The panel above the computator cockpit was a monitor, she realized as it abruptly lit up, displaying the interior of what she recognized to be the office of the First Minister.

Karrow was there, a Kazaranid in parliamentary black and yellow, the colors well suited to his glittering black and ochre carapace. The Kazaranid were an insectoid people, six-limbed and with mandibles, antennae, and large multi-segmented eyes. They communicated with other peoples via a translation vocalizer worn around their spiny throat.

"Good afternoon, candidates," the First Minister said, his words buzzing hard and soulless from the vocalizer. "This is Karrow addressing you. At this point, each of you are making your way to the Lower Kerees Defense Force armory, where you will equip yourselves for the task ahead."

Lyra frowned. She had anticipated a string of interviews followed by simulations and tests. Combat runs, pressure scenarios, problem solving, not to mention interviews.

"Instruction dockets will be provided upon your arrival," Karrow continued, clasping both sets of hands. "In order to assist speedy induction, please remove the keycard from beneath the monitor panel to show security. I look forward to greeting the future Shield of the Reef in person."

The monitor turned off.

"Is that it?" Lyra demanded, but the screen remained silent. For a role so intrinsically linked to the ongoing survival and independence of the Soldar Reef, surely the selection process would take some time? Lyra had been braced for days, if not weeks, of grueling mental and physical challenges. But from the way the First Minister had spoken it seemed like it would all be over in a matter of hours.

Lyra's sense of discomfort grew. She knew exactly what all this reminded her of. A terse familiarization briefing prior to the assignment of a bounty.

She reached under the monitor and located the keycard before settling back in her seat, watching the slope streets glide by, trying to fathom exactly what she had gotten herself into.

She wanted to make a difference. Her father was right, she had burned her need for adventure down to nothing, but it had been replaced by something else. The last job she had done, the one that had come close to breaking her and disturbed her every night since, had also convinced her there was still some purpose to life. She could do good. She could protect. That, Lyra told herself, was why she had come home.

She tried to believe it.

It was better than the realization that maybe she had no purpose at all.

The armory was a stark block of plastone and steel sitting squat on the lower-mid slope of Mount Kerees's northern face. The shuttle released Lyra onto its docking strut, to be welcomed by six people in Defense Force combat gear. It had started raining – the north face often took the brunt of inclement weather when it came in off the marshes. Heavy droplets drooled through the mesh decking of the strut and made the sheer, cliff-like building before her glisten. The guards were wrapped in drenched capes with raised hoods, but their weapons were unshrouded and live.

One of them approached, combat boots ringing on the decking.

"You're one of the candidates?" the man asked. Wordlessly, Lyra handed him the keycard. He passed it to another guard, who scanned it against the armory's entrance terminal and entered a series of codes.

There was a *thunk* as the blast hatch disengaged.

"Welcome to the armory, Lyra Keen," the first guard said, returning her card before motioning her to follow him. She stayed silent as she stepped out of the seething downpour.

Despite the building's size, the entrance corridor was narrow and tunnel-like. The guard took her into a cage-like space where her keycard was scanned by a gray-uniformed attendant sitting behind a table next to a set of lockers.

"If you have any weapons, declare them now," the attendant said.

"I don't," Lyra replied. The attendant gave her a disbelieving look, and she shrugged.

"If I had weapons, you wouldn't need to bring me here."

The attendant was unmoved, speaking again.

"Please place your savant in the tray and take the identity chit. It'll be returned when you leave."

She hesitated, unwilling to surrender her last link to the outside, but decided she probably wouldn't get signal in the armory's depths anyway. She handed over her savant and was provided with a heavy-looking docket filled with papers and printed images.

"Briefing," the attendant said simply.

"All paper, very old-school," Lyra commented dryly, surprised they were using something so rare on Andeara.

"More secure," the guard who'd admitted her said. "Come on, let's move."

He took her out the other side of the cage and through another set of doors, then down an open-sided elevator that made a harsh buzzing sound as it moved.

Abruptly, Lyra found herself wishing she did have a weapon after all.

The armory's core was as military-industrial as its exterior. A multi-leveled hangar housed rack upon rack of weaponry, from RemTek pistols all the way up to quad blasters and Executor anti-aerial launchers. There was defensive kit too, helmets and flak vests, bug-eyed gas masks, and full digital interface goggles. It all came in a variety of shapes and sizes, modular weapons and protection systems catering for the fact that just under half of the Soldar Reef's population were non-human.

Being amongst so much weaponry left Lyra feeling cold. She had been in plenty of places like this. It always preceded something bad.

The guard paused in the center of the hangar. Lyra saw another figure in Defense Force fatigues approaching with a digital slate, a Rokha. She was a tall, feline-like anthromorph with a glossy black pelt that shimmered beneath the harsh lighting.

"Candidate Two," she said. Lyra didn't respond to the impersonal greeting, though she found herself wondering how many others had been summoned. She had expected many, but could see none. Surely there were more than two people competing?

"My name is Captain Sanay of the Intelligence Division," the Rokha said, her green felid eyes holding Lyra's. "The First Minister has asked me to field any questions you have."

"I see," Lyra said. She had plenty of questions already, but she wanted to find out what the briefing docket contained. Sanay motioned her over to a metal table beneath one of the weapon gantries, and Lyra spread the docket's contents across it.

It rapidly became clear that her fears were correct. This wasn't a selection process. It was a hit.

The information concerned a Captain Qualid, a Kazaranid

formerly of the Reef Defense Fleet. Lyra recalled her parents mentioning him. He had been wealthy and powerful, first-spawned from the largest Kazaranid clan-nest in the Reef. But apparently the stories were true. For unclear reasons, Qualid had gone rogue and, with his frigate *Relentless*, had started raiding traders on the edge of Reef space.

Karrow wanted him killed or captured. It was there, bluntly stated on the page. Whoever completed the assignment would be instated as Shield of the Reef. Lyra could hardly believe it. They were being used. A part of her wanted to walk away immediately, but she was angry. She should have seen something like this coming.

She turned to Sanay, but before she could speak she saw movement on the gantry behind the Rokha. A figure was emerging from between two of the weapon shelves, carrying a blaster casually over one broad shoulder.

Lyra stared. She recognized him, though she wished she didn't. He in turn paused at the edge of the gantry, gazing down, looking amused.

"Maker be cursed," Lyra said, feeling her anger rise to a dark fury.

The figure's name was Pelt. He was a hulking brute of a Saar, a furred, canid-like creature who had once competed alongside Lyra as a bounty hunter. He had left her for dead on Rondo. They had encountered each other only once since, on the Jura job. Seeing him here was like being haunted by an ugly specter, dragged up from the foul depths of her past.

"I wondered if I'd find you here," Pelt said from his vantage point. "I remembered you were a Reef girl."

"Same can't be said of you," Lyra said. "What are you doing here, Pelt? This isn't your home."

"Home is where I plant my feet, Sharp," Pelt said. Sharp had been one of her old aliases, just as she was sure Pelt was one of his.

"He can't be applying to be the Shield," Lyra said to Sanay, trying to channel her anger. "It's only for Reef citizens."

"But I am a citizen, as of today," Pelt said, giving her an ugly grin. "Fast tracked, courtesy of First Minister Karrow."

"This is a farce," Lyra snarled, turning away. "I'm leaving."

"Not immediately," Sanay said, moving to block her. "If you refuse the test assignment, you are to be held here until one of the other candidates completes it, for security reasons."

"Firstly, this isn't a *test assignment*, it's an assassination order," Lyra snapped, squaring up to the Rokha. "Secondly, there's no legal authority by which you can detain me. I've done nothing wrong."

"You signed up to remain seconded to the Defense Force for the duration of the test," Sanay said. "That's regardless of whether or not you decide to participate. You won't be allowed to leave."

Lyra bit back a retort. She was furious, and the fact that she could sense Pelt enjoying it only made it worse.

"What do you think is going on here?" she asked Sanay, hoping the captain might see sense. "This isn't how the Shield is chosen. Karrow is using us as free fixers. He's making a mockery of the title!"

"I have my orders," Sanay said, unashamedly. "As do you, Candidate Two. There is a shuttle waiting to take you to the orbital at Clear Point. You may requisition whatever arms and armor you wish here. If you refuse, you will be held until word of the operation's success or failure is ascertained."

"Feel free to sit this one out, Sharp," Pelt taunted. "You know I'm always first to the kill."

Lyra turned back to him, doing her best not to lash out. Her anger was close to boiling over. This was not what she had come home for.

"You know all about killing, Pelt, I grant you that," she said icily. "But being the Shield isn't about killing, it's about saving. There's no way I'm letting you become the next protector of the Reef."

Pelt laughed, but Lyra ignored him and looked back at Sanay. "Show me to the energy rifles," she said.

Only one other candidate had been chosen for the test. She arrived not long before the shuttle departed, a human, kitted out with parliamentary guard flak and a Aj5 kinetic blaster. She wore her bleached hair cropped short, and seemed far too young to Lyra, though she was probably the same age as when she'd first set out as a bounty hunter.

She introduced herself as Anleth. Lyra could tell from her accent that, unlike Pelt, she was native to the Reef. Maker-alone knew how she'd ended up in this mess.

Nothing was said as they were ferried up to Clear Point. The tension between Lyra and Pelt was practically an electrical charge, lancing across the transport cabin. She hated his arrogant smile. He represented everything she'd come to detest about her old profession.

She tried to hone her thoughts, to zero in on what lay ahead. This wasn't just a test. It was going to be a live operation. She had to rediscover that edge she'd deliberately tried to blunt over the past month. It was going to be painful.

She had chosen a Martel K5 energy rifle and a hand-blaster. They were reliable, but didn't pack enough power to punch through walls or bulkheads – she always tried to avoid collateral casualties. Lyra had no idea if there'd be any of those where they were headed. The briefing had implied that Qualid's whole crew was with him, but it had only spoken about killing the captain. Capture certainly seemed impossible.

Pelt engaged Anleth in small talk as the shuttle docked at Clear Point. Lyra was fairly sure he did it to annoy her, but she resisted the need to tell him to shut up – some information could be useful. It turned out that Anleth was a member of the Parliamentary Guard, and hoped for more than just securing the government quarter and participating in the yearly opening ceremonies. Lyra wanted to tell her that she'd made a mistake, that she should go back to her duties and avoid people like Pelt.

She killed the impulse. Right now, she couldn't afford any sort of attachment, especially to the competition.

They docked at Clear Point and boarded *Vigilant*, a small scout vessel tasked with taking them to the edge of the Reef system. It would be three day-cycles before they reached the last known location of Qualid's frigate, *Relentless*, and it would probably take longer for the scouter's powerful locator systems to pinpoint just where it was hiding.

Lyra made a promise to herself that she wouldn't try to kill Pelt in that time.

Thankfully, it didn't take the *Vigilant* long to locate its prey.

The *Relentless* was pinpointed on the edge of an asteroid cluster near the border of the system's edgeward trade lanes. Insertion into the target vessel was via raft dart. *Vigilant's* were single-manned, which was perfect. None of the trio wanted to share their plans.

Lyra locked herself in and set the coordinates she'd memorized from the dossier. After the small dart left *Vigilant* she went through a weapons check; strapped on her flak vest, kneepads, and elbow pads; and zeroed in her ocular monocle. She did so with cold efficiency, her mind devoted to practicalities. This was what a fellow hunter had called "the zone", that dark place removed from worry and compassion.

It was the place soldiers entered to survive. Some spent so much time there they eventually couldn't leave again.

Relentless appeared on the dart's small display, sensors rendering it as a three-dimensional holo. The only positive aspect of Qualid's treachery was that the RDF still had a log of his ship's schematics, providing the sort of intel that made all the difference. Lyra scanned it. Her intention was to hit the prow directional thrusters, trigger a meltdown, and use the service vents to infiltrate the bridge blister. She assumed that with the engines disabled Qualid would head to the bridge to take control. Lyra would take him out in the confusion and exfiltrate using one of *Relentless*'s forward emergency rafts.

The fact that there were three of them all going after the same prize complicated things. She had tried to predict how the others would make their move. Pelt was always direct, but she couldn't imagine being more direct than hitting the prow thrusters. She knew there was a high chance she would run into him, in which case she fully intended to treat him as hostile. Anleth was more difficult to judge – while she looked young and inexperienced, Lyra had detected a steeliness about her.

Ultimately, she didn't know how it would play out. Plans would unravel and unforeseen problems would spring up. It would come down to sharpness and adaptability.

The dart locked in on the section of *Relentless* Lyra had highlighted, and began to accelerate, its speed and small size enough to ensure it went unnoticed on the frigate's sensors.

Relentless yawed into view on the raft dart's visualization monitor. Starting as a glimmer, it rapidly materialized into a sleek, powerful-looking warship, its armored flanks and prow glittering in the starlight, running lights winking along its sides. Lyra killed all the dart's systems bar navigation, plunging herself into darkness. The dart made for the frigate's directional thrusters, and Lyra held her breath as the tiny craft entered the ship's in-close defensive range.

There was no hail of energy beams or bursts of chaff. *Relentless* lay still, seemingly dormant. Its sheer flank rushed up to greet the dart, and Lyra strapped herself in before the retrogrades popped, decelerating the craft and allowing it to settle against the frigate's hull.

The external magnetic seal locked into place before the energy cutters activated, starting to sear into the frigate. Lyra brought her targeting monocle fully online and smacked a power cell into her Martel energy rifle, feeling the weapon thrum as she set it to maximum output. Kill-switch.

The cutters slowly worked through *Relentless*'s protective plating, the exterior of the dart rotating as it bored inside. It cauterized the entry wound as it went, sealing the dart's prow from the inimical void beyond. Lyra waited in the cramped cockpit, clearing her mind the way she always did at the start of a mission, trying to settle her pulse and find that dreadful calm that best facilitated acts of violence.

There was a red light above the cockpit's prow hatch. She watched it, hearing the dull whine of the energy cutters finishing their work, remembering the wait at Sevenport's checkpoint before arriving on Andeara. She had dared to hope that all this was behind her.

She realized now that she had been wrong.

Her punishment was not yet done.

Silently, the light winked green. She yanked down the hatch lever and ducked out as it fell open, bringing her Martel up and sweeping left to right.

Her dart had delivered her into a service corridor above the ship's prow directionals. It was a narrow space, the walls lined with corroded pipes, the deck underneath a metal latticework covering more. They were pressure distributors for firing the directional thrusters that allowed *Relentless*, like all Reef frigates, to adjust its course with alacrity. The air was cold, and Lyra's breath started to frost. Corridors like these were kept on minimal power, existing to allow the engineering crew to access and monitor the systems.

She lowered her rifle and began to advance, the reticule on her monocle constantly roving, hunting for a target-lock.

There were none. She reached a stairwell and felt the ship becoming more alive around her. The temperature rose as she left its exoskeleton and moved down to growing ticks and murmurs of vitality, from the rattle of the pipes to the louder buzz and stronger illumination of the light strips. The bare, grimy walls became enclosed in white paneling, and the deck became solid flag-plates.

Despite her best efforts, her nerves rose the deeper she went. She had to make contact soon, even if it was just some system-checker heading off duty. Lyra knew only in that moment, and not before, she'd find out if she still wanted to do this.

Yet there was no one.

She reached the control berth for the directional thrusters. It was abandoned, its two entrance hatches sliding open upon her arrival. She stalked between the control panels and the empty chairs, her thoughts churning.

What if Qualid had abandoned ship? But *Vigilant* had scanned for lifeforms and reported returns. What if there just weren't enough crew members to work the directionals continuously? That seemed likely, especially when a ship was anchored, but surely there'd at least be a deck monitor?

What if there was some sort of infection or quarantine? Or a mutiny? What if someone else had seized the vessel?

What if it was a trap?

Lyra felt herself starting to panic. She hesitated, looking around the directional berth, realizing that her guard was shot and if something went down, she'd be easy prey. Make a decision, she told herself. A mission-call.

She was still going to the bridge, but she'd take the direct route. If there was no resistance, the danger that the other candidates would do the same and get there before her was too high. She had to resolve such uncertainty as quickly as possible.

Taking a moment to steel herself, Lyra locked her monocle's uplink back to her rifle's muzzle, and set off, deeper into *Relentless*.

Anleth rounded the corner, her Aj5 kinetic raised and primed. She was met by nothing.

It had been the same with every corridor she had passed through. She'd hoped that infiltrating the frigate via the waste dispensary would ensure minimal contact, but not to this extent.

She was starting to think this was a mistake. Her nerves were frayed. She had wanted to prove herself to the Parliamentary Guard, especially Lieutenant Sorren. He had always come down on her hardest, always seemed primed to catch her out. When she'd seen the Shield vacancy and resigned from the Guard, Sorren had laughed at her. It had only hardened her resolve.

All that seemed like a long time ago. Now she was alone on a frigate full of traitors near the edge of Reef space with two hardened killers. It had been a terrible, impulsive idea. She hadn't even told her parents.

The woman, Lyra, had seemed almost approachable, but Anleth suspected it was a veneer, an effort to get her to lower her guard or divulge her plans. There was a hardness about her that switched to barely restrained fury whenever she interacted with the Saar, Pelt. As for him, he was mocking and arrogant. Clearly the pair had a less-than-cordial history. Anleth tried not to think about how many bounties they'd completed between them. They both had killer's eyes.

None of those thoughts helped as she explored the seemingly abandoned frigate. Here she was, kinetic rifle in hand, and no one to shoot at. She didn't know if that was worse than ending up in a firefight.

Anleth reached the elevator that would take her to the bridge blister. She had initially scanned Qualid's own quarters, hoping to catch the Kazaranid alone, but there had been no sign of him. She didn't know what to do besides go deeper into the ship.

That was when the corridor started to move. She froze before realizing what was happening – a series of small lights had turned on, multicolored and shifting. She spotted the emitters along the edges of the decking plates. She frowned, confused.

More activated. The passageway became a kaleidoscope of colors, oscillating constantly. Anleth looked down its length, and immediately regretted it.

Her vision swayed. She felt as though the whole corridor was moving, the deck sliding out from under her, the walls spinning. She dropped her weapon and screwed her eyes shut, throwing out a hand to steady herself. She heard a clattering sound and tried to look, but the dazzling lights had turned her vision end over end. She was aware of figures emerging from concealed wall panels at both ends of the corridor. She fell, crying out.

They were on her before she could get back up again.

So far this had been even easier than Pelt had anticipated. Ever since contacts had put him onto the fact that the Reef was looking for a new Shield, it seemed as though the stars themselves were aligning for him. The idiot ruler, Karrow, had taken a liking to him, impressed by the brutal litany of successful operations he'd conducted. The First Minister certainly didn't seem to share the insular views that normally held true for Reef folk.

As far as Pelt was concerned, the Reef peoples were cowards who didn't have the guts to defend themselves. His people had learned what became of those who didn't look out for their own. Perhaps he would change that. But right now, the most important thing was securing the position of Shield and guaranteeing himself a heavy salary for a couple of years while he kept a low profile after the botched job on Cyrene.

He advanced down the service corridor, quad cannon clicking softly as he kept its barrels rotating. He'd decided to circle the ship and insert from the other side, hitting the port flank of *Relentless's* prow, just above the directional thrusters. It seemed the precaution had been unnecessary because he hadn't encountered a single soul. It appeared the fearsome rogue crew were sleeping on the job.

The reappearance of Sharp had been a complication, but nothing major. She was easily riled. In all honestly, Pelt didn't mind her – she had too many morals but was dependable enough with a blaster. He hadn't abandoned her out of spite on Rondo, just convenience. Poor little human seemed to have taken it to heart. He chuckled as he recalled the outrage when she had realized he was in on this job too.

He paused, scenting the air, hunting for signs that he'd been detected. Perhaps this was too easy? But no, when had anyone from the Reef, rogue or not, proven a capable adversary? It was all according to plan.

Then, things abruptly stopped going to plan.

With a stomach-turning sense of dislocation, he felt the floor simply disappear from under him as the decking plate he'd been standing on shifted to one side. Before he could do anything he was falling.

It wasn't a long drop. With a splash and a grunt he hit something warm and viscous.

He tried to rise but failed. This was no cooling duct or a waste chute – whatever substance he had fallen into, it didn't want to let him get up. It clung on, black and tarry.

Pelt snarled and fought against it, but it only dragged him down harder. It wasn't particularly deep since his feet had hit the bottom, but he was in up to his waist, and could barely right himself, let alone pull himself up.

Not that there was anything to pull up with. The space he had fallen into was essentially a small, open-topped box. There were no pipes, no handholds, no means of climbing, even if he could extricate himself from the slurry now matting his fur.

Too late, Pelt realized the obvious. He had walked into a trap.

The bridge lay ahead, its blast doors open. Lyra stopped. Too easy. Way too easy. If she hadn't been sure of it before, now she was certain. They were expected.

Her instincts started screaming at her. She turned back down the corridor she had been advancing along, intending to head straight for the emergency raft. Get off the frigate, hail *Vigilant*, and give up on this before something truly bad happened.

Too late. A keening noise erupted, an achingly sharp pitch that assaulted her hearing. She hissed in pain, unable to avoid dropping her rifle as she clapped her hands to her ears.

Her world shrank until there was nothing but the maddening whine. She dropped to her knees, teeth gritted. A shadow fell over her. She made herself look up. There was a figure emerging from a panel that had been pushed away from the wall, a Hacan in ship's crew overalls. He was carrying a crowbar.

He swung for her.

Reflexes overcame the pain. She snatched the Hacan's wrist, turning the force of the blow into a twist. She saw the gold-furred felid's muzzle open, but couldn't hear him cry out. There was no sound but the hellish ringing.

She sensed another presence behind her, human this time, in the same uniform as the Hacan. She snarled, cornered, lashing out with a foot. He went down almost on top of her, and she wrestled him onto his back, managing to pin his throat. She realized he was wearing bulky ear protectors, his eyes wide as she grasped him in a chokehold.

Clearly, they hadn't been expecting this much resistance.

The Hacan was back on her. He'd dropped the crowbar and grabbed his remaining good hand. Lyra tried to throw him off without losing her grip on the other assailant. The pain in her skull was almost too much now. She could barely think as her survival instincts kicked in. She wasn't going down, not like this.

The Hacan managed to get his working arm wrapped around her waist, physically lifting her off his shipmate. He stumbled, and Lyra landed on her feet as his grip abruptly disappeared.

A monster appeared to have tackled the felid from behind. It was a massive, stinking beast, matted from head to toe in foul black slime. It bellowed loud enough for Lyra to hear as it hauled the Hacan down and delivered a brutal punch. The Hacan was big but already injured and clearly hadn't anticipated being attacked by what seemed to be a beast dredged up from nightmare. The felid stayed down.

Lyra feared she was next, but only when she made eye contact with the oozing monstrosity did she understand what – or who – it was.

Pelt. At some point he'd been drenched in sludge. Judging from the look in his eyes, he was furious.

"What in the seventh dimension are you doing, Sharp?" he demanded, bellowing loud enough for Lyra to hear. He seemed to be totally unaffected by the noise.

She didn't try to reply. The human she'd been struggling with was getting back up. She snatched at his ear protectors and ripped them off. The man immediately cried out and clapped his hands against his head, face screwed up in pain as he dropped to his haunches.

Lyra tried to put on the ear protectors, but staggered, and had to be caught by one of Pelt's slimy hands. Her vision was graying out.

Then, finally, blessedly, the noise ended. Lyra didn't realize at first, as the ringing in her ears continued. But it was no longer as intense. With Pelt's help she steadied herself, blinking back the pain as it settled down to a dull throb.

The relief was only brief. Pelt drew her gaze down the corridor toward the bridge blast doors. The space was now filled with a motley array of what could only be the crew of *Relentless*.

Most were humans, but there were Saar, a Letnev, Hacan, all in a mixture of shipboard overalls and fatigues. All were properly armed and the hum of charged energy weapons reverberated along the corridor.

"Knew I should've just left you," Pelt growled, shifting slightly so Lyra was between him and the crew.

"Did you fall into the ship's waste chute or something?" she asked. She was trying to come up with a plan that didn't involve risking her life sprinting along the corridor in the opposite direction while dodging energy beams. She suspected Pelt would try to trip her anyway.

Even that slender hope disintegrated as she realized there were more crew members blocking off the opposite end of the passage. They were well and truly cornered.

"Stand easy," rasped a soulless, metallic voice. It came from the direction of the bridge. The crew parted, and an individual in the white uniform of a Reef Defense Fleet captain limped forward.

He was a Kazaranid, five-limbed with a prosthetic lower leg that clumped on the deck. His mandibles twitched. He was missing an antenna. Lyra recognized him immediately from the briefing docket. It was Captain Qualid.

"Welcome aboard *Relentless*," the arachnoid said, his voice sounding just like First Minister Karrow's, grating through the vocalizer unit that his kind used to communicate. "This isn't normally how I greet people on my ship."

"Who tipped you off?" Pelt asked. "Karrow?"

The vocalizer made a grating sound that, combined with the twitching of Qualid's mandibles, Lyra took to be laughter.

"Rather unlikely, I'm afraid," the captain said.

"But this is a setup," Pelt continued. "You knew we were coming."

"I was hoping someone was," Qualid clarified. "Exactly who, or when, I wasn't sure, but we have been ready for a while."

The captain made a terse gesture, and more space was made around him. A crewmember hauled a struggling figure forward. It was Anleth. Her hands had been bound in front of her, and she looked equal parts angry and ashamed. She stopped fighting when she caught sight of Lyra and Pelt, realizing that Qualid's victory was complete.

"That makes three," he said. "Which, I suspect, is the full complement of assassins onboard."

"We're not assassins," Lyra said tersely. Her ears still ached. She was trying to figure a way out of this, but so far keeping Qualid talking seemed like the best bet. She knew she didn't have to negotiate well, she just had to negotiate better than Pelt. They'd been in this sort of situation before, and he had been the one to walk out and leave her stranded. That wouldn't happen again.

"Why are you doing this?" Lyra demanded.

"Before I can explain, you need to understand that nobody on this ship will harm you," the captain rasped. "Not without my orders. Your freedom will come sooner if you cooperate."

"Where have I heard that before?" Lyra said, recalling Sanay's threats.

"I think it's best if we discuss this somewhere more cordial," Qualid said. Lyra exchanged a glance with Pelt, who shrugged.

"You're the one with the guns, captain," he said to Qualid. "For now, anyway. Lead on."

The three of them were brought into the captain's cabin, to the rear of the bridge blister. As befitted a Kazaranid, it had shelves and storage stacked vertically, almost to the ceiling, along with a web-bunk stretched out between two corners. A desk sat before a semi-circular porthole showing the sprawl of a nearby asteroid belt and, beyond, a field of glimmering stars.

Swivel seats were produced from the bridge. Lyra, Anleth, and Pelt sat, while Qualid took his place behind the desk, settling with a crackle of limb-hairs and the clicking of his carapace. Several crew members, still armed, took post on either side.

"So, Karrow sent you," the captain declared. "I had hoped for more, but you three may be enough."

"Before you say anything more, you'll unshackle Anleth," Lyra told the Kazaranid bluntly. The third bounty hunter's hands were still bound, and she looked utterly miserable as she sat next to Lyra.

"She keeps trying to assault my crew," Qualid said.

"Understandably," Lyra responded. "Remove the restraints or you can put them on both of us and throw us in your brig."

Qualid considered her with his unnerving insectoid eyes, then tapped a claw on the desk. One of the guards unshackled Anleth.

"Stay calm," Lyra told her as the restrains were removed, maintaining steady eye contact. "We won't abandon you."

"I might," Pelt grunted. Lyra shot him a glare. Thankfully, Anleth didn't make any sudden movements, just rubbed her chafed wrists.

"So, are you going to explain yourself or not, captain?" Pelt asked, shifting himself in his chair. It creaked dangerously. The Saar was still dripping with sludge.

"I am considering my words carefully, Pelt," Qualid said.

"You know our names?" Lyra demanded. She was still trying to piece together how they'd ended up in their current situation. She had feared the worst in the corridor, but everything since had shown that Qualid wanted to talk. Why, she couldn't fathom. They were at his mercy.

"I still have friends back on Andeara," the captain said, steepling two sets of hands.

"Like I said, a setup," Pelt growled.

"Only partly. I know you came here to kill me, but I've no intention of punishing you. In fact, the opposite. I need your help. Two of you hail from the Soldar Reef. Even with Lyra's extended absence, you both must know that these are troubled times for our little corner of the galaxy."

"Spare us," Pelt said. "What do you want help with?"

"Exposing First Minister Karrow as a traitor to the Reef, its constitution, and its peoples," Qualid said.

All three Shield candidates remained silent. Qualid continued.

"Some time ago I uncovered evidence that the current First Minister has been making contact with elements from outside of Reef space, specifically agents of the Sol Federation. Parliament is wholly unaware. I believe Karrow is conducting unauthorized negotiations that would harm our future independence."

Lyra took a moment to process Qualid's claim. She had heard nothing good about Karrow since arriving back on Andeara, but Qualid had shown no evidence to back his accusations. It seemed farfetched to believe that even someone as devious as Karrow would betray the Reef in such a way.

"If that's true, why are you skulking out here instead of doing something about it?" Pelt asked.

"Easier said than done," Qualid answered. "Karrow suppresses information and installs his puppets in positions of authority. He's been building his power base for several election cycles now. I believe this is his endgame – cede the Reef to the Federation in exchange for the position of First Minister for life. I knew Karrow would seek to silence me when I discovered what was happening. So, I did what any good frigate commander does, and took the initiative. I informed my crew of the situation. They backed me. We broke dock at Sevenport and have been hunting the trade lanes ever since."

"That doesn't sound like the actions of someone seeking to expose corruption," Lyra pointed out, still not trusting Qualid's claims. "It sounds like the work of a pirate. Trust me, I've known enough over the years."

"A sorry necessity," Qualid said, spreading his bristling limbs. "But my raiding has been exaggerated in official reports – reports that pass through Karrow's desk. I have harmed no one, and have taken only token payments. I wish to steal nothing, but there is strategy at play. I must make myself seem like a threat to Karrow, but not one great enough to warrant unleashing the rest of the fleet on."

"Your goal was to make Karrow try to eliminate you covertly?" Anleth asked, picking up the questioning.

"My goal was to acquire reinforcements," Qualid said. "My crew is not suited to clandestine operations. I am the inheritor of one of the most powerful Kazaranid families in the Reef, but out here I have few resources."

To Lyra's surprise, Pelt began to laugh, a deep, nasty chuckle.

"You're a bold one," the bounty hunter said. "I understand now. You need assassins, so you got your rival to recruit them, then snagged them for your own use. What are you going to offer to turn the tables, huh?"

Qualid's mandibles twitched, which Lyra took to be a sign of disapproval.

"Firstly, Karrow is not a rival," he said, his synthesized

voice giving no indication of his displeasure. "He may be from a different nest-clan, but this is not nest politics. He is deceitful, and he means to shatter the society that I swore to protect. Secondly, you were the ones who claimed you were not assassins, and I do not intend to employ you as such. But I did deliberately set out to capture you, and yes, I need your assistance."

"Easier to ask when you've got us at gunpoint," Lyra pointed out, glancing at the crew members.

"Insurance," Qualid said. "You would do the same, at least until we have established trust."

"What do you want from us, then?" Anleth asked.

"Help exposing Karrow," Qualid said. "I need to return to Andeara and conduct further investigation, as well as contact potential allies. The links between the First Minister and the Sol Federation must be fully exposed before Parliament if he is to be stopped."

"Where's the evidence?" Lyra pressed, still unsure of the Kazaranid. He seemed sincere, but it was difficult to gauge the insectoid. Maybe he had made his claims up and was just the latest schemer intent on manipulating her for the skills she had acquired beyond the Reef. She refused to let that happen. Yet, if what he claimed was true, it was imperative that someone act to stop Karrow.

Lyra had spent enough time with the Sol Federation to know that some coveted the nearby Reef and its small string of habitable planets. Thus far the human empire had failed to stir itself over the system, their attentions elsewhere, but threat of colonization was a familiar fear among Reef citizens. The fact that there was now a real danger put Lyra even more on edge. It wasn't the sort of accusation that could be safely discarded.

"I have prepared all the evidence into packets for each of you," Qualid said. "I recommend you review them at your own leisure. The ship is about to enter its night cycle, and I suspect you are tired. Rest, and tomorrow we will speak again."

"Where are we sleeping, the brig?" Pelt demanded humorlessly.

"You may choose a berth together, though I suspect you would rather have individual cabins," Qualid said. "That can be arranged, though I am afraid if you wish to leave your accommodation, you will be accompanied by a crew member. I must maintain the security of my vessel. I'm sure you understand."

"Seems we don't have much choice in the matter," Pelt said. He made to rise, a look of surprise giving way to frustration as he discovered the sludge had welded him to the seat.

"I can only apologize for the techniques used to restrain you," Qualid said. "The ship was filled with traps in anticipation of Karrow sending hirelings. Just how did you escape the pit anyway?"

"You underestimated a Saar's claws," Pelt snarled and, with a bellow, ripped himself free, almost snapping the armrests.

"This better wash out." He looked from his matted fur to Qualid as Lyra fought the sudden urge to laugh. "I'm not shaving myself!"

Lyra was admitted to a berth on the frigate's starboard aft, beneath the engine mounts. It was swelteringly hot, and she could feel the vibrations of the ship's power source through the metal around her. She could only assume it was better than the brig.

A crew member dropped off a data stick before informing her

that he would be outside. She pressed the stick into one of the ports of the berth's computator. It caused the monitor screen above her sleeping cot to activate.

She touch-scrolled through the data. Qualid had separated it into tiers, from what he considered lesser evidence up to the most damning. Much of the former was unassuming or circumstantial. Karrow had a habit of pulling out of meetings or not taking minutes. He enjoyed extended breaks at the First Minister's residency at Far Rock, an estate perched upon one of the smaller geological spurs, deep in the southern marshlands. There were financial irregularities, spelled out by Qualid's margin text.

Among the better indictments was surveillance footage. Most of it showed two men and one woman at various locations around Kerees and – the critical link – a brief, soundless meeting between Karrow and one of the three. Lyra replayed it several times. The three sure didn't look much like Reef citizens. Their hairstyles were well out of date and their dress was drab, as though they had deliberately chosen what they thought was the most unassuming clothing possible. None of that was proof that they were Sol infiltrators, but they certainly came across as outsiders or recent arrivals.

There were docking manifests showing that the three had arrived several months before, supposedly on a short system hop from Tarval 9. She didn't recognize the names.

Lyra barely slept as she tried to digest it all. Something untoward was definitely happening, but little pointed to Sol infiltration. It seemed almost unthinkable that the Federation would be making a play for the Reef.

On the other hand, from what she had seen and heard about Karrow, she could well imagine that he would sell himself to the highest bidder. If the Federation did want to bring the Reef under indirect control, he would be the ideal puppet. And what of Qualid? The Kazaranid intended to use them to his own ends, but were those ends really the protection of the Reef, or was there more at play?

The next day, after a breakfast of vac-packed ship's rations, they were summoned back to the captain's cabin. Anleth played her hand first.

"Something has to be done," she said to Qualid. "You must have a plan?"

"I do, but without you it will be difficult to implement."

"What is it?" Lyra asked.

"I believe my allies have located where the three persons in the footage are staying, in Kerees," Qualid said. "We will capture them. Doing so could blow the entire plot apart. At the same time, I hope to present this evidence before Parliament. Obviously, they will not allow me to speak in an official capacity, so getting in front of an audience may prove difficult."

"So, what, we're the muscle?" Pelt asked. He'd failed to wash all the black muck from his fur. Lyra dreaded to think what the frigate's shower block looked like.

"More than just that," Qualid said. "Anleth, you have a presence in the Parliamentary Guard, and if I'm not mistaken Lyra your parents are an advisor to the RDF and a sitting minister of Parliament. As for you, Pelt, your lack of contacts here renders you less susceptible to Karrow's influence."

Pelt let out a brief laugh. "So I'll just naturally work for the highest bidder?"

"From what I know of you, you've taken one job too many in Sol space," Qualid replied. "If the Federation seized the Reef, this would no longer be a safe haven. That, and the fact that I have considerable personal wealth with which to reward you, should be incentive enough."

Pelt only shrugged.

"How do you know it's the Federation?" Lyra asked, trying to get to the root of her concerns. "If they are Federation agents, they should be better at hiding it. I worked with Sol intelligence. They're good at what they do. If a team had been deployed to Andeara, they wouldn't be walking about in lockstep wearing the grayest clothing in Kerees."

"I have traced the features of one on *Relentless*'s own archives," Qualid said. "His name is Guth, a junior officer with the Federation's warfleet. Just why he is being used rather than a trained agent, I do not know."

Lyra's thoughts started to race. Suddenly the awkwardness of the humans caught by surveillance made sense. Perhaps Sol intel wasn't involved after all. Maybe this was a fleet initiative. Volunteer crew wouldn't be cut out for this line of work. But why them?

Abruptly, she felt a surge of concern for her parents. Members of the Federation fleet were in Kerees, and they were unaware. Both were senior figures in the Reef's political and military hierarchy. What if they were targets? She had to warn them.

"You can count me in," she told Qualid. "But we have to leave soon. Whatever they're planning could be enacted any day now."

"I agree," Anleth said, clearly angry at the idea that a First Minister, a being she had sworn to protect in the Parliamentary Guard, seemed to be on the cusp of betraying the Reef.

Qualid nodded, then turned his compound gaze on Pelt. The Saar gave another nonchalant shrug.

"I'm guessing if I don't go along I'll be enjoying an indefinite stay here," he said. "Alternatively, just how much were you planning to reward the soon-to-be-saviors of the Soldar Reef with?"

"As a base pay, one hundred thousand credits," Qualid said.

"Don't suppose you'll put that in writing?" Pelt asked.

"No."

"Didn't think so. It'll do, for now."

"How are you getting us back to Andeara?" Anleth asked. "You can't break in-system with *Relentless*, the Defense Fleet will take you."

"If you give me the coordinates of the scout vessel I assume dropped you here, I will open fire and scare it off," Qualid said. "They will assume you have been eliminated. It should buy us time to return to Andeara aboard one of my frigate's rafts. It will be small enough to make planetfall without detection, though we will have to touch down in the marshlands. Hopefully we can still stop the Reef from being drawn into yet another game of empire-building."

The return to Andeara was slow and unpleasant. The raft belonging to *Relentless* was larger than the darts used by *Vigilant*, but it still struggled to provide living space for four persons. Lyra did her best to review the evidence that Qualid had supplied.

"How did you end up scurrying back here anyway?" Pelt asked Lyra, close to the final approach to Andeara. "You just went off the grid."

The last thing Lyra wanted to do was talk about it with Pelt, but she knew he would keep persisting if he sensed it annoyed her.

"I was with the team that hit *Severast*," was all she said. Pelt did his best to mask his surprise.

"Gods be," he cursed softly. He didn't ask her again.

They made planetfall southeast of Kerees, near one of the raised highways that linked the city-mounts.

The raft had to be abandoned – it had barely touched down before it began to subside into the dark, popping morass. They had landed next to one of the Kerees-Southspire highway entrances though and were able to clamber onto the grav-supported concrete without becoming completely drenched.

"You said we'd be getting picked up?" Pelt asked. Qualid had claimed he had a contact who would collect them after they'd touched down and triggered the raft's sensor beacon.

"Let's hope they find us before the Defense Force investigates," Anleth said.

Thankfully, the wait was brief. An eight-wheeled land hauler with slatted sides pulled up to the edge of the highway. It was a logistics vehicle, and the driver was a Kazaranid with the same patterns on his carapace as Qualid.

"In the back," Qualid told them. They climbed aboard, finding spaces among the pallets.

"I have a safehouse in Kerees," Qualid said as the vehicle set off, his body bisected light-and-dark by the hauler's slatted flanks. "We can use it as a base, but we need to act quickly. My nest kin have located the suspected hideout of the Sol infiltrators. It's in a hostel block near Slopetown."

"Pelt and Anleth should be enough for a strike on them," Lyra said, perching on the edge of one of the pallets. "I need to deliver this evidence to my parents."

"It is unwise to spread news of our return, even to those you trust," Qualid said.

"I know, but they have to hear this. My father is a senior

Defense Fleet advisor, and my mother is a minister of Parliament in opposition to Karrow. She may have further evidence we're unaware of."

"Giving up already then, Sharp?" Pelt said. She gave him a hard look in the half-dark, but refused to rise to the bait.

"If I'm right about this, it could be the breakthrough Qualid needs," she said. "Or are you not big enough to take down three humans yourself, Pelt?"

"You know I am," Pelt said testily. Lyra looked at Anleth, whose expression implied she was less than thrilled at the prospect of staying with the Saar.

"Always let him go through doorways first," she told her. "I'll be back as soon as I've made contact."

PART THREE

"Stand aside," Pelt said, patting Anleth on the shoulder.

He had seemed like an unpleasant being when she had first met him, and that had turned out to be a high point in their relationship. She shifted from the doorway, scowling as he hunched over the locking pad.

The residence housing the Sol agents was a rent-a-pod hostel just off Slopetown, one of the main shopping hubs in Kerees. It was a grimy area, constantly bustling, and the cheap accommodation and large numbers of new arrivals made it a good place for off-worlders to blend in. As she waited Anleth crossed her arms and leaned against the wall, making hard eyes at anyone passing on the slope-street. This wasn't the sort of place where you wanted to get involved in other people's trouble.

The locking pad beeped. Pelt growled in frustration. Anleth pursed her lips, but said nothing.

"Old-fashioned way then," Pelt said, taking a step back.

"Ladies first," he added, looking at her with a grin.

"Not a chance."

"Some team we're shaping up to be," Pelt grumbled, before hitting max charge on his blaster and kicking the door in.

Pelt stormed in, blaster raised, and discovered two of the three targets sitting around a table, apparently deep into a game of Nightfall Empire. The pieces – along with the table – were hurled to one side as they dived for cover.

They were supposed to be taking prisoners, but Pelt always liked to introduce himself first, and that generally involved a lot of shooting. He let rip on full auto, searing energy bolts through the table, a ratty old couch, blowing out a viz-block and ricocheting off a stack of pots and pans.

One of the two humans pulled a snub-nosed pistol. Her shots went wild as she threw herself to one side to avoid Pelt's barrage. The other one was already bounding up a flight of stairs at the back.

Pelt was about to nail the one who'd shot at him, but Anleth knocked his weapon to one side.

"Prisoners," she said.

"You catch them then," Pelt barked angrily. The second Sol agent was already scrambling after the first.

Anleth ran after them.

"Stop," Anleth shouted, but the pair paid no heed. The stairs in the dingy block were steep, and even at full lunge she struggled. She fired a warning shot with her RemTek, immediately regretting it as she half deafened herself and blew a chunk of plaster out of the ceiling.

The first agent had reached the next floor and was struggling with the door. His compatriot, the one with the pistol, put a charge through the lock. The door opened, but Anleth had gained ground. She threw herself into the one with the gun, sending them both sprawling into a second dilapidated hostel pod.

The gun clattered across the carpet as Anleth managed to slam a fist into the woman's gut. She wheezed and snatched at Anleth's short hair, wrenching it viciously. Anleth cried out as she was thrown to one side, just as the man rushed at her.

It was badly timed on his part. On her back, she kicked up and away, catching him hard on the knee with the sole of her combat boot. He went tumbling over her, slamming his head off the doorframe.

The other one was going for her gun. Anleth threw herself at it as well. She missed, but knocked the other woman's hand and caused the sidearm to skitter away beneath a derelict couch.

"Traitor," the woman snarled as they grappled.

"I've never betrayed anyone," Anleth spat back.

"You're human," she said, trying to get a grip on her throat, trying to choke her. "You've betrayed Jord!"

Anleth clawed her wrist and managed to bend back two fingers until there was an ugly crack. She squealed and let go, giving Anleth the leverage to get up.

"Not every human is part of your damned Federation," she snapped as she kicked her once, twice, her body flushed with adrenaline, the fury of combat making her forget herself.

The Sol agent managed to knock back an elbow and cause her third kick to miss. The attacker used the opportunity to get to her feet, swinging with her good arm, her eyes full of rage and pain. Anleth blocked, every second of guard combat training coming in useful, but was forced to give ground, driven back toward the room's window.

Abandoning all poise, the woman charged her. Anleth took advantage of the broken fingers by going for that side, but couldn't stop her from locking an arm around her throat. She began to panic.

"All humans come from Jord," the woman snarled. "You should know your place in this galaxy."

Anleth was too busy struggling to retort, desperately ramming an elbow back. She felt the grip suddenly relinquish and managed to turn just as the Sol agent threw herself at her again.

She sidestepped, and kicked out at the same time. The combination of the blow and momentum carried the surprised agent on, straight through the apartment window. There was a crash of glassplex, and the woman disappeared with a scream into the space beyond it.

Anleth stumbled to the opening and looked out. Unwisely, she realized. Though they had entered from the ground floor and only gone up one flight, they had done so from up-slope, which meant the other side of the block was a good five stories off the down-slope street.

She leaned back from the window, panting, coming down hard off the adrenaline spike. She heard movement, and turned, expecting to find the second agent rising, but he was unconscious. Pelt had finally made it up the stairs, panting unhealthily.

"Took you long enough," Anleth admonished.

"Saars weren't made to run up stairs," Pelt responded, wheezing. "Besides, we've got one." He gestured to the man slumped against the doorframe.

"You can carry him," Anleth said. "And if anyone stops us, I'll answer the questions."

Lyra saw her father's face go from delight to concern when he found his daughter standing at the front door.

"Lyra, what's happened? Why are you here?"

"Where's Ma'?" Lyra demanded.

"She's giving a speech about the education reforms."

"Call her, or her aide, and tell her she needs to get home."

Someone else might have demanded an explanation, but Zanth was a military man who knew an order when he received one. He made the call as Lyra came inside and checked the locks.

"You may be in danger," she said. "There are infiltrators from the Sol warfleet in Kerees, right now."

"How do you know?"

Lyra showed him. Zanth froze the image of the three figures on the monitor and looked at it for a long time.

"I know one of them," he said quietly.

Lyra frowned. "How?"

Zanth remained silent for a while, clearly battling with a decision he had long delayed. Eventually he looked her in the eye, and spoke.

"I know one of them because his name is Temetz. Captain Temetz, at least when we served together. In those days, I was an admiral in the Sol Federation's warfleet."

Lyra stared. How could that be true? How had they hidden something like that from her?

"I don't believe you," she said. Zanth sighed.

"It's true, Lyra. I was born on Jord. I served until the battle of Outer Tarst, when pirates decimated my fleet, and your mother saved me. After that day, I never looked back. I became a citizen of the Reef. That's what I am now, and what I'll be until my dying day."

Lyra sat heavily on one of the wall-chairs beside the monitor. Somehow, it all made sense. The mysterious old uniform, his reluctance to talk about it. She had always assumed it was due to the horrors he had experienced, and while that was undoubtedly the case, it was clear there was much more to it.

"Did you have a family back there?" she asked, the sudden thought looming large. "On Jord?"

"No," Zanth said. "My parents died when I was young. I joined the fleet hoping to get away. I didn't realize just how literal that intention was."

"And you didn't tell me?" Lyra demanded, with a hint of anger now. "Why not?"

"Your mother and I discussed it many times. It always seemed as though there would be… a better time. I never felt truly free from my past. With good reason."

His gaze returned to the monitor. Lyra frowned, her confused emotions sharpening to a single, pointed question.

"Why are they here?"

"I was hoping you could tell me," Zanth replied. "Temetz was my subordinate in the Federation fleet, and one of the few who made it back to Jord after Tarst. I hoped he believed me dead."

"You think he's hunting you?"

"I don't know. But if he's here…"

"The warfleet may not be far behind." Lyra finished the thought. It filled her with dread. But surely the Federation would not exert such force just to chase down a long-lost fleet officer?

There was a knock at the door. Lyra's hand went down to her hip – she was relieved this time to feel a sidearm there. They looked at each other.

Zanth nodded, once. Lyra stood and moved into the hallway, stopping at the door hatch. She pulled up the external scanner, which produced a small holo image of Amara, standing outside.

Lyra unlocked the door and ushered her quickly inside.

"We wanted to tell you," Amara said. "But it was your father's story. He didn't feel ready."

Lyra had been struggling not only to come to terms with her father's past, but to see how it fit into the present. Were the Federation really here to punish Zanth? Or was Temetz acting on his own initiative? Where Zanth had reacted with silent surprise as Lyra had laid the conspiracy out before him, Amara answered with fury.

"Karrow is a treacherous beast," she snapped, smacking a palm on the living room table. "I knew he was devious and ambitious, but this is something else. The greatest scandal in Reef history!"

"We can still stop it," Lyra said.

"You'll need more evidence," Amara said. "I can access parliamentary files. Transfer what you've shown to me."

"It'll be dangerous," Lyra pointed out as she began doing so. "Karrow won't be acting alone."

"It wouldn't surprise me if he's paid off the whole of the Coalition," Amara said bitterly. "But I won't let this stand."

Lyra knew there was no hope of stopping her mother. That, in a way was reassuring. She no longer felt alone with the burden, or uncertain of what she should do. The time for action had overtaken all other considerations. Regardless of her father's past, she realized they had to carry on with the plan.

"We need to get evidence before Parliament," she said. "The first meeting after the end of recess. That's what Qualid is hoping. The others are currently trying to capture the infiltrators. They're the ultimate evidence."

"Is that wise?" Zanth asked. "It'll tip Karrow off. And I doubt Temetz will be easily caught. He's a good tactician."

"Has he come back for you?" Amara asked. Lyra looked at her father, watching the struggle play out as he considered his answer.

"I don't know," he replied. "Even before our ships were taken out of action at Tarst, he blamed me for not predicting the ambush."

Amara put her arm around her husband's shoulders. "What happened was not your fault. Do not refight it again, all these years on."

"Whether or not he is here at the Federation's behest, I have to assume he's hunting me," Zanth said. "This house is no longer safe."

"We should go to the reserve zone," Amara said.

"What's that?" Lyra asked, momentarily confused.

"A place your mother and I have in case something like this ever happened," Zanth explained. "A safehouse."

"You've been planning for this for years," Lyra said with a sense of realization. She felt like a fool for not working it out sooner.

"A good strategist is always prepared," Zanth said. "How long do you think you'll need to collect more evidence at Parliament, Amara?"

"I can't take more than a day," she said. "It reopens tomorrow."

Lyra hurried upstairs and retrieved an old savant from her drawer, taking the charger with her.

"Send me the coordinates of where you're going to be," she said. "I should get back to the others. Like you said, if they've managed to hit Temetz, and Karrow realizes we're onto him, he will probably act within the next day."

"Understood," Amara said, pausing to hug her briefly. "Stay safe."

"And you." Lyra felt a pang of sorrow at the fact she had brought this on her family. She suppressed it. This was the middle of an operation, and that was never a good time for emotion.

The fate of the Reef was about to be decided.

"His name is Guth," Pelt said, cracking his knuckles. "But we already knew that, didn't we, Guth?"

The question was addressed to the man seated in the center of the room, bound to a chair by thick, glistening strands of Kazaranid webbing. Qualid was off to one side, silent, four arms crossed, while Anleth stayed by the window, looking out onto the street below. The block, near the base of EastFlank and the industrial refineries, was derelict. Judging by the old webbing and musty smell, it had been Kazaranid clan accommodation once. Presumably the property belonged to Qualid or his nest kin.

"Tell your fellow human what you told us," Pelt growled at Guth. He looked rough, and far from defiant. Lyra's expression remained stony. Pelt patted his shoulder.

"Who are you?" he urged.

"Guth Svelson," the man said, not meeting Lyra's gaze.

"And what are you?"

"Second Lieutenant on board *Imperious*."

"A Sol frigate," Qualid rasped, the emotionless voice making Guth wince.

"So, it really is the warfleet," Lyra said, feeling her determination redouble.

"And why are members of the Sol Federation's armed forces on Andeara unannounced?" Pelt asked.

"The iridium," Guth said. Lyra frowned and looked at Anleth, who glanced back from the window and shrugged.

"From what we can gather," Qualid said slowly, "the Federation elements here believe the worlds of the Reef contain large quantities of raw, unmined iridium."

"But they don't," Lyra said, stating the obvious. She had never heard such a claim before.

"Then someone needs to tell him," Pelt said, looking at Guth, whose eyes were on the floor.

"This doesn't make any sense," Lyra said.

"It does if you have one of the largest warfleets in the galaxy and require iridium for thousands of kilometers-worth of framework and armor plating," Qualid pointed out. "Elements of said fleet are currently poised on the fringes of Sol space, ready to make the hop."

"You think the Federation has been misled about resources in the Reef?" Lyra asked, still trying to see how this new piece fit into the wider puzzle.

"I think there are multiple duplicities at work here, and we are peeling them back, layer by layer," Qualid said. He carried on, speaking to Guth. "Tell my friend how you ended up on the Reef."

"We weren't given much intel," Guth said, his tone surly but beaten. "Only that Temetz is in charge. It was work for the intelligence branch, but rumors were the fleet had gotten the scoop and wanted to secure it for ourselves. We came to help the captain with a handover of iridium, with more to come. We were told because of the politics in the Reef, we had to keep our identities a secret."

"But there is no iridium," Lyra reiterated. "So what is Karrow really trying to sell? Does Temetz know?"

"I suspect we'll need to locate Temetz to find out," Qualid said.

"I told you, he didn't say where he was going," Guth protested.

"He must be planning something for tomorrow," Lyra said. "During the reopening of Parliament. My mother is sure of it."

"Did you warn her?" Qualid asked.

"Yes. She'll help us. She's gathering more evidence."

She didn't mention Zanth or his past. Now wasn't the time to share that kind of knowledge – the last thing she wanted was to run the risk of being cut from the operation. She would have to work out the connection between her father and the Sol presence alone, and fast.

"We will need it, and her," Qualid continued. "My influence doesn't currently extend into the government sector. All the Kazaranids there are from Karrow's clan. If we're going to make it into Parliament, we'll need both your mother and Anleth's contacts in the Guard."

"And a plan. That might help," Pelt grumbled. "Preferably one that doesn't involve any more slopes, stairs, or insurmountable heights. My thighs are killing me."

"There are always more of those in Kerees I'm afraid," Qualid said.

That night, Lyra brought her parents to meet the others. She did so only after much thought. It was difficult, to involve them in all this, to drag them into the same sort of danger that had left her with so many nightmares. She tried to tell herself that this wasn't her fault, that the Federation would be here whether she had come home or not. Still, it felt as though trouble followed her.

There was no choice. They had been flung together into the

heart of a conspiracy that threatened to unmake everything they held dear. Zanth seemed wearied by it all, haunted by the reemergence of his old life, but Amara was fired with determination, resolved to defend the place she called home. Lyra took strength from that.

Together, they laid their plans.

"I don't want to stay," Zanth said, as he watched Lyra finishing reassembling her RemTek on the apartment's kitchen table.

"Someone has to warn the Defense Fleet when we're at Parliament," she replied, smacking in a magazine. "And there's no one better placed to do that than you."

"What if Temetz isn't at the Parliament today?"

"He's powerless if we expose Karrow and mobilize the Reef," Lyra said.

"You're trying to keep me out of danger," Zanth said, a rare hint of anger in his voice. "You want me to stay here in this safe house while the rest of my family put their lives on the line."

"With all due respect, Da', I've been putting my life on deadlier lines for years now," Lyra answered, deciding to meet her father's accusation head on. "I know what I'm doing. And the Parliament is Ma's turf. Someone has to get in touch with the Reef fleet, though, and not before the rest of the plan kicks off, or Karrow might find out. If you don't convince Fleet Command to scramble ships, all this could be over before it begins. We could have the whole Sol warfleet in-system. It's not a sideline task. It's vital."

Zanth looked at her, his expression hard, but then, to her surprise, he offered a wry smile.

"You would have made a good officer," he said. "And you'll make an even better Shield when this is all over."

Lyra scoffed, holstering the pistol. She'd barely thought about the role of Shield since she'd met Qualid. Now it felt like nothing but a sham, a distraction. There was no Shield to protect the Reef. It was down to her family, and her friends. And Pelt.

"The Shield is an icon; without someone strong to hold it up, it's meaningless," she said. "And you don't need to be the Shield to do the right thing. I've learned that the hard way."

Zanth's expression turned thoughtful. "What happened out there, Lyra? What made you come back?"

The question caught her off guard, so much so that she found herself beginning to answer it.

"A ship, called *Severast*... The job was a hit on the Jakaxi Cartel. They'd been people-smuggling through the Contested Zones. The Federation finally decided to do something about it, and we were the ones they hired."

Zanth said nothing, letting her speak at her own pace. She allowed herself to continue.

"We intercepted the *Severast*. It wasn't a hard job. But what we found onboard..."

Memories assailed her. Hundreds of starved faces looking up at her, eyes blank, souls fled, and bodies broken.

"They treated them worse than animals," she said, tears stinging her. "Nothing should be treated like that. No one."

"But you saved them," Zanth said, laying a hand on her shoulder.

"As many as I could," Lyra said, voice wavering. "Which will never seem like enough. Never."

Zanth hugged his daughter close.

"Sometimes we fail," he murmured. "All peoples do. It's what we do after that counts. Even when your path strayed, you never stopped trying to protect. You're the best of your mother and I.

You're just the sort of person these worlds need. And tomorrow, we're going to prove that."

For the first time in over a month, the Greater House of the Parliament of the Reef was nearly full.

The chamber itself was circular and tiered, the individual seats arranged around a central dais occupied by the Speaker, with the First Minister and cabinet on one side and the opposition on the other. The ceiling rose to a dome, featuring a great fresco that showed moments in the history of the Reef, from the landing of the first marooned settlers to the founding of the mount cities on Andeara and the first expedition to the neighboring ice-world of Tarst. A third of the dome was still blank stone and plaster – history yet to be written.

Amara gazed up at it all. She had been visiting the chamber regularly all her life. As a junior minister she had been in awe of that ceiling, yet now she rarely looked up. Perhaps there was a metaphor in there. She was too busy down in the dirt, fighting the hard fight on floor's tiers to remember that there was color and beauty spread out above her.

The chamber was filling rapidly, the space echoing with footsteps and swelling chatter. It was hard not to wonder whether the events about to play out would one day be recorded upon that ceiling. As the ministers arrived for Karrow's first speech of the new cycle, she had greeted colleagues and engaged in small talk about the parliamentary break. It was a struggle not to seem on edge. She looked up now, deliberately, and wondered how posterity would remember her and her family, if at all.

It was preferable to staring at Karrow. He and his entourage had arrived moments earlier, taking their seats on the central dais. His carapace was dressed in the heavy yellow and black robes of his formal office, his antenna ringed by golden clasps. It made Amara silently furious. She focused that rage, channeling it into appearing calm.

Her eyes were drawn to the window ports that ringed the walls. They were observation booths for those who had permission to sit in on sessions, as well as spaces for the press corps. They would be full too. One port was the control room where the lighting and security measures, as well as the content on each minister's podium screen, was monitored. She watched that window for a while.

The last of the Reef's politicians were taking their seats. Conversations were dying. That was when a voice rang through the cavernous space, echoing back from the painted scenes above.

"Out of my way!"

Amara looked right. She felt her heart beginning to race. Perhaps the plan was a bad one? Perhaps that fresco wouldn't record any of them, because they would fail, and their efforts would amount to nothing. The Soldar Reef would fall, and the dome would be left forever unfinished.

She caught sight of her daughter. She had a RemTek in one hand, and was hauling along another figure in another. It was Qualid.

"Move aside," Lyra barked. "Make way for the Shield of the Reef!" As she got further into the chamber, she shouted up at the dais, voice defiant.

"I've captured him! I've captured the traitor, Qualid!"

Lyra kept a firm grip beneath Qualid's under-right arm as she hauled him along the main aisle to the Greater House's central platform. The Kazaranid's four limbs had been bound together by a locking bar, and his head was bowed. Lyra had her

RemTek in her other hand, and kept it pointed upward as she manhandled her prisoner past the shocked ministers.

With Anleth's help she had managed to get past the parliamentary guard outside. Those within the chamber moved to stop her, but hesitated. Everyone recognized Qualid.

"Stand aside," Lyra shouted again, as the shocked muttering of the politicians rose. "I'm here to see the First Minister!"

She locked eyes on Karrow, who had risen from behind his podium, his mandibles flicking furiously.

"What is the meaning of this?" he buzzed.

"What does it look like?" Lyra demanded, stopping at the foot of the dais and tugging at Qualid so that he looked up at the crowd. "My name is Lyra Keen, and I'm here with the fugitive Captain Qualid. That's what you directed, First Minister Karrow. And I believe that makes me the new Shield of the Reef."

The voices rose in uproar. She resisted the urge to search the crowd for her mother, keeping her eyes on Karrow and Captain Hirlow, commander of the Parliamentary Guard, who had mounted the dais alongside him.

"This is an outrageous breach of protocol," Karrow began to say, but Lyra wasn't paying attention to his words. So far, so good. Unseen under Qualid's arm, she activated the savant in her hand, and spoke.

"Now."

Pelt grinned to himself, rolled his shoulders, and settled in alongside the Sliver Rocket Launcher. It was as heavy duty as could be, practically small-scale artillery, and when Qualid had supplied it, Pelt had known he wouldn't be able to resist the chance to use it.

Today was his lucky day. He'd taken up position on the rooftop of the Reef Financial and Economic Center, directly east of the Parliament building. It was the third-tallest structure in the government quarter, after the Parliament itself and the Shrine of the Maker, and it offered him an angle on the Parliament's central dome. The security for the opening ceremony had set up to protect the entrances and exits, creating a cordon that would keep the ministers safe. But Pelt wasn't going after the ministers.

The savant he'd laid on the rooftop beside him crackled with Sharp's voice. Go time. He wasn't sure if he was currently involved in a coup, or preventing one, or maybe both, but he had realized one thing – he was enjoying himself. It had been years since he'd gotten his paws on a proper Sliver Launcher. His supposedly quiet sojourn in the Reef had turned out to be quite violent, and he wasn't complaining.

He slammed home a synthetic diamond charge into the Sliver Launcher, then pushed in ear-protector nubs and settled in, cranking down the weapon's elevation. He only needed a second to aim. It wasn't like he was going to miss that target.

Relaxing, he pulled the firing lever.

Anleth bent over the locking pad, forcing herself to slow down. She punched the code in, digit by digit, silently praying the security clearance for the Greater House's control room hadn't been changed.

The pad made a thudding sound, and showed red. She cursed under her breath. No access.

"What in the name of the Maker are you doing?" demanded Lieutenant Sorren as he strode along the corridor toward her, seeing only a woman in the uniform of the Parliamentary Guard.

Anleth looked up slowly, and saw recognition dawn in her old commander's eyes.

"Anleth," he said. "You're supposed to be—"

She punched him, with the butt of her pistol, in his face.

"That's been a long time coming," she said, as he squealed and clutched his bloody nose. "Door codes, now!"

"Just what do you think you're doing?" Sorren repeated, eyes watering.

Anleth fired just past his head. The blast blew a chunk out of one of the corridor pillars at Sorren's back, and the ferocity of the discharge made him jump, spattering blood from his nose down the front of his ceremonial uniform.

She had hoped to keep things quiet until she was inside the control room, but she no longer had that luxury.

"Codes," she repeated firmly.

Stuttering, Sorren gave her the updated numbers. Anleth ordered him to turn around and get his hands up while she entered them.

"You're mad," Sorren said. "Whatever you're planning, it won't work."

"It's already working," Anleth responded as the door slid open. The room beyond was a dark space lit by the angry glow of a dozen monitor screens and control boards. Two operators stared up at her in shock from their seats.

"Out," Anleth ordered, waving her pistol. They scrambled to comply.

She shut the door behind them and re-entered the code on the interior locking pad before hitting the scrambler, sealing it. As she did so, she felt the savant in her pocket buzz. She was almost out of time.

Almost, but not quite.

•••

A hole appeared in the domed fresco of the Greater House, a small shaft of light streaming through.

It was followed a heartbeat later by a dozen more. Shattered plaster and stone rained down on the dignitaries below as bursts of hyper-fast synthetic diamond ripped through the structure above, cutting up figures of the Reef's past.

Screams and shouts filled the chamber. Ministers dived to the floor or rose, jostling as they tried to get out from behind their podiums. In the midst of it all, few noticed Lyra unlock Qualid's restraints.

More were aware when she leapt onto the central dais. Hirlow pushed Karrow down protectively and raised his stave, the ceremonial weapon of the Captain of the Parliamentary Guard.

"Get away from the First Minister," Lyra shouted, but Hirlow remained defiantly between her and Karrow.

Lyra hesitated. She had been afraid of this. Afraid that to stop Karrow she'd have to kill. She'd done enough of that already. But the First Minister had to be captured.

In the end she was spared the struggle of shooting Hirlow down. One of Karrow's ministers flung herself at Lyra. She smashed the butt of her pistol against the attacker's head as she sidestepped, avoiding her grappling but ending up closer to Hirlow. The captain lashed out.

The stave missed, shattering the screen on top of one of the podiums. Hirlow didn't have the space to recover, but he stepped in even closer so he could force Lyra's pistol to one side.

She delivered a stinging blow to Hirlow's cheek, sending him reeling, but the distraction allowed Karrow to leap down from the dais and scuttle for the doors.

"Qualid!" Lyra shouted as she tried to pursue, only for Hirlow to snatch her by the shoulder and slam her against another podium. Qualid had skirted round the base of the dais in an attempt to cut Karrow off, and managed to snag one of the First Minister's lower limbs, sending him sprawling. Qualid was on top of him in a moment, mandibles snapping as they grappled.

Lyra snarled at Hirlow, blocking a strike toward her face, returning with a wicked jab. He stayed in close so she couldn't use the RemTek, his expression grim. Lyra knew that, as far as he was concerned, she was an assassin.

Hirlow again managed to pin her wrist to one side and slam her back onto a podium, intent on breaking her over it. She twisted but found herself unable to free herself from his grip.

Lyra heard her name being shouted, and saw her mother mount the dais carrying a podium's detached screen. She tossed it to Lyra, who grabbed it with her free hand and smashed it over Hirlow's head. The captain dropped like a lodestone.

"Don't you dare touch my daughter," Amara growled, as Lyra tossed aside the shattered screen. Hirlow stayed down, his scalp bloody.

"Karrow," Lyra managed, no time for thanks as she looked past her mother. Qualid had lost his grip on the First Minister, who was now closing on the crowded main doors, his robes shredded, cradling what looked like a broken upper limb.

"Have the podiums been activated?" Lyra demanded as she leapt down from the dais, pausing to look back at her mother.

"Not yet," Amara said. "Either way, I need to get to the speaker's chair, and you need to get out before the Parliament's energy shield is triggered."

"Get out? Why?" Lyra asked, confusion cutting through the adrenaline, making her hesitate. This wasn't part of the plan.

"I track-locked your father's savant. It's left the block on EastFlank. He's going somewhere."

"Why?" Lyra asked, growing frantic. Everything was poised on the brink of success or failure. She couldn't wait.

"I don't know for sure," Amara said. "But look around. There's no sign of Temetz. I don't think he's here. I think he's going after your father."

"Come on," Anleth hissed, stabbing the data stick into the control room's main computator port and desperately screen-clicking through the necessary permissions. Beyond the port she could hear pandemonium in the main chamber.

Even worse, Lieutenant Sorren's furious voice had been replaced by multiple, shuddering impacts against the door. It wouldn't be long before the guard brought up something powerful enough to break through. She had reconciled herself to that. What mattered was whether she could fulfill her part of the plan first.

Her hands danced across the primary monitor as she transferred the stick's data and sent it to the podiums arrayed around the Greater House. She clenched her fists, watching the loading bar, feeling sick with tension.

A terrible, ear-aching shriek filled the control room. It sounded like Sorren had managed to get a steel-carver lugged upstairs. They were cutting through the lock.

She looked back at the screen. It was taking agonizingly long. She gazed past it, through the glassplex port at the chamber beyond. Chaos reigned there. Would anyone even notice what she was uploading? Right now, it didn't seem like it.

The sound of the saw rose to an aching intensity. Part of it began to bite through the door, spitting fat sparks. She closed her eyes, silently praying.

There was a chiming sound, barely audible. Her eyes snapped

open to be greeted by the most welcome monitor message she had ever seen. Data transferred. She punched the activation button. In the chamber beyond, the screens on each podium lit up.

At the same time, the saw cut off, leaving her ears ringing.

Anleth turned in her swivel chair toward the door, then slipped the cell out of her hand-blaster and laid both the gun and the power source down on the floor in front of her. Then she knelt and clasped her hands behind her head.

The door slid open. Smoke filled the control room, followed by the pounding of boots and the stabbing beams of target locks. She stayed still as a dozen parliamentary guards rushed in, weapons primed, blast visors lowered. Sorren was amongst them, his nose caked in dry blood, his eyes murderous.

"I surrender," Anleth said.

"Come on," Pelt growled, sending another salvo of diamond shards whipping into the exterior of the Parliament's dome. He'd lacerated it, but so far it hadn't had the desired effect.

The Sliver Rocket Launcher was smoking and vibrating with every shot. Finally, as Pelt eased off after another volley, there was a crack like a lightning strike.

A film of glossy purple energy burst into being, encasing the central dome in a shimmering sphere. It was a defensive shield, and he had expected someone would activate it as soon as shots had started tearing through the building.

He shifted onto his knees and abandoned his ear-nubs and the launcher in favor of a compact, bullpup kinetic carbine. The Parliament was no longer his concern. More pressing was the sound of slamming doors and boots pounding on stair rungs below. They'd pinpointed his location.

"I'm about to have more company than I'm comfortable with, Sharp," he said into his savant. "So you better win some hearts and minds in there soon, and by soon I mean, right now!"

Lyra didn't receive Pelt's message. She was too busy running. The decision seemed like an impossible one – abandon the plan and her mother, and run the risk of total failure in an effort to save her father. In the end Amara had almost made the choice for her. She had given Lyra a ministerial keycard that provided access to the Parliament's undercroft, offering a safe way out of the pandemonium in the Greater House. They had planned to use it as an escape route if things went wrong. Now she took it out onto the slope-street and down to the nearest funicular, the one that would take her to the Museum of Galactic History.

That was where the tracker showed Zanth had stopped. She tried calling him but received no response. She was drenched in sweat, panting, her sidearm holstered as she took the transport down to the museum. No one tried to stop her.

She raced up the long stairs to the building's front doors. Remaining at home and contacting the fleet had seemed like the safest option for her father, but that had been assuming Temetz would be at the same location as Karrow. Lyra feared something terrible had happened, or was about to.

"Please don't run in the corridors," snapped a museum attendant who froze when he caught sight of Lyra's sidearm. She ignored him, trying to remember where the downed raft shuttle was. She now realized it was an old Federation craft, a fact she hadn't appreciated when she had visited as a child. That was what connected Zanth's past to his present. That had to be where he'd gone to confront Temetz.

She spotted a graphic of the shuttle under a "Cultures of the Quadrant" sign. West Wing. She raced toward it, darting between surprised museum-goers.

As she went, a sound boomed through the hushed space, sending icy dread through her.

Two gunshots.

"Speaker, I'm afraid I must make use of your chair," Amara said, having to shout to be heard.

"This is all most irregular," the Speaker, an elderly, craggy-skinned Xxcha, stammered.

"Your broadcaster then," Amara snapped, snatching the microphone stalk protruding from the lectern and turning it toward her.

"My fellow ministers, listen to me," she barked, her voice booming through the speakers. "Please find your decorum. The blast shield has been activated. No one is able to get in to harm us, and no one is able to leave!"

The words had little effect on the panicked politicians. She could see Qualid, having been hauled away from Karrow, now pinned to the floor by three parliamentary guards. Karrow himself was still trying to fight his way toward the door, now sealed by the newly activated blast shield.

"In the name of your Maker, look at the screens!" Amara shouted, voice so loud it caused the speakers to whine painfully.

Amara had already seen the individual podium tops light up with the data transferred by Anleth from the control room. It was Qualid's evidence, and more besides, collected by Amara over the past day. Incontrovertible proof that Karrow was in league with forces hostile to the Soldar Reef.

"We have a traitor in our midst," Amara pressed on, her voice becoming vehement. "What you see before you proves it. Our ruler, the being elected to serve the peoples of the Reef, has been making deals behind the back of every honest minister in this chamber!"

The attention was finally shifting to her, and the screens. She slammed her palm against the side of the lectern for emphasis.

"I am this moment lodging a motion to have Karrow stripped of the title of First Minister. I am also calling upon the Parliamentary Guard to arrest him, on charges pertaining to conspiring with enemies of the Reef!"

If anything, the uproar that followed was even greater than it had been when Lyra had stormed the dais. Some of it was directed at Amara, but even more was channeled toward Karrow. Those nearest to him edged away like they'd just discovered he was infectious. On the podium screens, images showing him meeting with the Sol agents played alongside a confession being given by the captured Guth.

"You are a treasonous slime-farmer," Amara said, venting all her anger and adrenaline at the First Minister. "A disgrace to your office, and us all!"

Karrow was trying to reply, but his voice was easily drowned by Amara's booming oratory. She noticed that Captain Hirlow had recovered from the blow her daughter had administered and regained his feet, one hand holding the back of his head as he looked from Amara to Karrow.

"Captain, I call upon you to arrest him," Amara said, pointing at Karrow.

"On your word only?" Hirlow demanded.

"On the evidence before you all," Amara said. "Take your time, review it. We're not going anywhere, not until all of you are familiar with the sordid web our treacherous First Minister has woven."

Zanth had always suspected it would end like this. That was the real reason he hadn't destroyed his old uniform. It seemed fitting it would be the one he wore now.

After contacting the RDF, he had traveled up-slope, to the Museum of Galactic History. The whole way he worried about Lyra and Amara. The plan they had hatched was bold but should have allowed them to create a captive audience to view the evidence of Karrow's wrongdoing. That was, if everything went to plan.

For his own part, all Zanth had to do was let the fleet know the dangers of a potential Sol incursion. They thought he was in more danger than the others, but they didn't know Federation protocols like he did. And they didn't know Captain Temetz.

Zanth ignored the messages on his savant. He stood in the remnants of the Federation shuttle that had borne him after the battle of Outer Tarst, wearing his old, torn Sol warfleet uniform. It still fit. Wearing it, and standing in the shuttle's burned, preserved remains, left him feeling numb. It was how it had to be though. The part of him that had served the Federation had never really died. It was time it did, and if it took the rest of him with it, then that was the price he had to pay. One way or another, he would never wear the uniform again.

It was almost a relief when he heard quiet footsteps behind him. He turned to see Temetz duck through the shuttle's hatch, dressed in his own captain's uniform. He looked much older than Zanth remembered him.

The two locked eyes, sharing the silence. Temetz's expression was hard, cold. Zanth tried to imagine what was running through his thoughts.

"I'm glad you came here," Temetz said eventually. "I hoped you would."

"It seemed fitting," Zanth replied calmly. "How did you know I was still alive?"

"You want to distract me while help arrives?" Temetz pulled a Federation naval service pistol from his pocket. "That won't work I'm afraid."

"No help is coming," Zanth said. "I've told no one I'm here."

Temetz seemed to consider that for a moment, before speaking.

"Call it an instinct. You were always lucky. Even when your ship took a pounding and most of your bridge crew lay dead, you'd walk away without a scratch."

"I got more than a scratch that time." Zanth raised his prosthetic arm. The accusations kindled his anger, but he fought to keep it under control. He wanted to understand why Temetz had come all this way before the end.

"You deserved more for how you mishandled the fleet that day," Temetz said. "The certainty that you were still out there has haunted me. I couldn't find proof, and I couldn't find a way to get to the Reef with the resources I needed. But I've managed it at last, with a little help from your corrupt politicians and the Sol warfleet's greed. Now I can finally restore the balance."

"How did you get leave approved to come here? I can't imagine the admiralty looking kindly on a private vendetta into neutral space."

"They don't know about this part," Temetz said. "I told the fleet that idiot Karrow wanted to strike a deal for Reef iridium."

"The Reef has no iridium."

"But they didn't know that, and Karrow was happy to falsify evidence. I convinced the fleet to send a covert team ahead to lay the groundwork. It was cover enough for this."

"You'll be dismissed after this," Zanth said. "At best."

"It's worth the risk," Temetz said icily. "After all these years. This is for all the ones you killed that day."

"I killed none of them." Despite his resignation, Zanth felt his anger rising. "The intelligence was wrong. No one could have predicted that ambush. It took me years to accept that, but it's the truth. I know that now."

"Well, you can ask the opinion of my crew and yours when you see them," Temetz said.

He raised his gun, and shot Zanth twice in the chest.

Lyra burst into the remains of the shuttle, her ears still ringing from the gunshots.

Her father was on the deck, and a man – Temetz – was standing over him with a Federation service sidearm. He turned as she entered. Perhaps he recognized the likeness. Perhaps he just saw a woman with a RemTek. Either way, he raised his pistol.

An old naval captain versus a bounty hunter. There was no contest. Lyra shot him before she had even fully realized it, her reflexes raw and whip-fast. Temetz froze and stared down in shock at the hole in his abdomen. His light blue Sol uniform, almost identical to the one Zanth was wearing, flushed crimson. He dropped.

The RemTek fell too. Lyra threw herself down at Zanth's side, clutching his shoulder, looking for the wounds, filled with horror and despair.

Her father's eyes caught her own. He was still conscious. Wordlessly, he raised his metallic left arm. Two holes had punched through it, corresponding with two dented medals on his chest.

Zanth began to laugh. Lyra did too, head bowed over him, panic giving way to a shocking flood of relief.

The bullets had struck Zanth's prosthetic arm as he'd instinctively brought it across his chest. They had punched through, but had lost enough force that when they struck Zanth's chest they had dented the silver and bruised the former admiral, but hadn't penetrated.

"Cosmic balance," Lyra said, allowing herself to slump back against the side of the old shuttle.

It was over.

It was nearly five months before Lyra returned to the Greater House. The ministers were arrayed around where she sat on the central dais. Peoples of every kind, united in governance of the Reef.

She glanced at her mother, sitting beside her. Amara now occupied the First Minister's chair. She was currently looking up, seemingly ignoring the activity of the chamber around her.

Lyra followed her gaze. Above, the dome soared away, its once-spectacular fresco marred by scars and fresh, blank stonework.

"What's left of the Coalition is proposing we make Pelt pay for the repairs," Amara said.

"If he knew that he'd already be on a transport out-system." Lyra laughed, looking to where Pelt and Anleth were seated, talking to one another in the back row of the dais's government section. All of them were present as guests, invited by the newly elected First Minister of the Soldar Reef, Amara Keen.

The past months had been almost as chaotic as the clash in Parliament. In the immediate aftermath Anleth and Pelt had been released, but all of them had been ordered to remain in Kerees while the evidence put forward about Karrow was assessed. Karrow himself had been arrested and, along with the Sol agent Guth, had been questioned. Karrow still wasn't admitting anything, but Guth had been more than happy to elaborate. After reaching out to the Federation, the surviving fleet officer had been returned to them. The entire incident was a shocking embarrassment to warfleet command, and an envoy was expected from Jord any day, bearing a formal apology and reparations.

Lyra regretted killing Temetz, but she refused to let the pain of that action take root. It was done. That was the sort of mindset she knew she had to become comfortable with if she was to stop the past from unraveling her future.

The evidence had been sufficient for the ministers. The People's Coalition had been purged of Karrow's cronies, and their public ratings had nosedived. There had been a snap election which had seen Amara of the EastFlank elected as acting First Minister for the remainder of the cycle. Amara's delight had been tempered by her usual drive. There was more than enough work for her to throw herself into, but Lyra and Zanth had celebrated for her.

And now they had all come to Amara's opening speech.

Lyra was surprised Pelt hadn't disappeared off-world yet, but he seemed intent on sticking around. The situation had been almost cordial between them. Almost.

One person who had left was Qualid. He had returned to his frigate, which had docked at Sevenport. Both Zanth and the Kazaranid had alluded to the complexities of fleet politics – despite playing a leading role in exposing Karrow, his defection and supposed piracy had left him out in the cold as far as promotion was concerned. Seemingly he was thinking of resigning and heading out-system. Lyra hoped he stayed. The Reef needed good peoples if it was to prosper.

The Speaker called the House to order, and Amara was invited up to take the place where she had first exposed Karrow's treachery.

Lyra felt a fierce sense of pride as she listened to her mother's speech. What she hadn't anticipated was the moment Amara called her, Pelt, and Anleth forward.

"Without these three, it is unlikely any of us would be in this chamber today as free representatives," Amara announced once the applause had died away. "Therefore, I intend to propose more than a vote of thanks. All three began this undertaking because they wished to become the next Shield of the Reef. They put themselves forward selflessly, to defend the democracy of the Reef."

Lyra glanced sideways at Pelt, but he wasn't making eye contact. Anleth was beaming though.

"We are still in need of a Shield," Amara continued. "And all three here proved themselves equal to the role. I am therefore proposing, in my first act of Parliament, that the position be expanded from one to three. I am calling for all to be raised to the title of *Shields* of the Reef!"

The acclamation of the Greater House rang from the scarred dome. Lyra felt shock, but also an unexpected delight. Suddenly, for the first time in years, it felt as though the future lay before her, clear and uncontested. She looked over at the others, uncertain how they would react. Anleth was close to tears, and Pelt was clearly trying to mask his happiness.

"Looks like I'm staying after all," he said.

•••

That night, Zanth burned his Sol uniform on the roof of their habitation block. Lyra was with him. It was evening, and the sun was setting amidst the city smog, slowly impaling itself onto Kerees's lower spires. As the shadows grew, the fire remained a flickering constant.

They watched in silence for a while. It didn't take long for the jacket to be consumed. The proud blue fabric and its bloodstains blackened and disintegrated, turned to black ash.

"I'm glad you came back," Zanth said to Lyra, not taking his eyes off the flames.

"I'm glad too." She watched as the medals that had saved her father's life slowly started to melt. She reached out and grasped his hand, the metallic one. "I had to, after… After *Severast*."

As she spoke the name, she surprised herself. This time – for perhaps the first time – it did not come with a jolt of pain. She allowed herself to keep speaking, not thinking about it, no longer hesitating, allowing the hypnotic flames to draw out the poison as they ate away the last of the uniform.

"I think it's over," she said, with growing conviction. "That part of my life. A new part is beginning. At least, I hope it is."

"Hope," Zanth said, looking across the fire at his daughter, the flickering light undercutting his features. He looked proud, she realized, proud and calm. He had discovered the same peace she had.

"You're a Shield of the Reef, Lyra," he said. "And for us, you'll always be the very embodiment of hope."

FIRST IMPRESSIONS

SARAH CAWKWELL

SOMEWHERE IN SPACE
EN ROUTE TO ARCHON REN
HACAN TRADING SHIP "BOUNDLESS
OPPORTUNITY"

"There is expectation, and then there is reality."

The young Hacan trader moved away from the viewport and began to pace the length of his small, but well-furnished cabin. "Take interstellar travel, for example. On the one hand, what a *triumph* of science and technology. What a *marvel* and what a privilege to be able to travel from one sector of the galaxy to another with comparative alacrity. How unquestionably miraculous it is to wake up on one world and be thousands of light years away before late afternoon." He thought a moment before continuing wryly. "Relatively speaking, of course."

Reeth appreciated the technology that drove their vessels. He did not *understand* it, nor did he particularly want to, but it was most certainly a convenience. It afforded so much opportunity.

"Yet for all its wonder…" Reeth paused in his oration for a moment and considered his next words. He was recording his personal log prior to the final leg of their journey, and his father had encouraged him to be as honest as he could be. It would serve him well in the years to come. *Record everything*, said his father. *Then, you can look back on your earliest endeavors and remember them fondly*.

Apparently.

His father had given him a lot of advice through the years, not all of it wise, but all of it extremely heartfelt and filled with love and affection. Reeth wondered, for a few short moments, what his father would say if he were here right now, and that still-fresh ache of grief clutched at his heart and threatened to take hold. He marshaled his feelings – another of his father's more relevant teachings – and focused on the here and now.

"Yet for all its wonder," he repeated, determinedly continuing the task, "interstellar travel has one extremely specific, but significant drawback. It is *immensely* boring. It's quite unlike planet-side transit. There at least you have scenery, terrain, the unexpected vistas of an environment. There, you can appreciate the world around you. Out here, in the aching loneliness of deep space…" He shifted his view to the inky void beyond the thin pane of plasticon that separated him from freezing oblivion. "Out here, there is *nothing*. And plenty of it. Anything you *do* see is so far away as to be almost incomprehensible."

The plenty of nothing allowed him to catch sight of his own reflection in the viewport, and Reeth tugged restlessly at his mane below his jaw. Several days of travel had left him looking decidedly shaggy, and for a moment, he indulged in a little vanity. Physically he was in his absolute prime, a picture of impeccable health, but cosmetically he should really consider engaging in personal grooming before they arrived at their planned destination. Subtle movement in the reflection caught his attention, and he glanced over his shoulder, setting down the recorder and turning to afford his visitor the courtesy of her station.

The Hacan who entered was tall for a female of their species, although still only reaching his shoulder. She was statuesque and elegant, and her movements were accentuated with an easy, languid grace that oozed confidence. A smattering of gray in the dark fur around her eyes, and the sandy yellow of her muzzle was all that hinted at her age. She tipped her head to one side and for a few moments kept her silence as she studied the younger Hacan with an intensity that he found a little uncomfortable.

When she finally spoke, it was in an even tone that could command an entire room to silence with a single, cutting syllable. He had seen his father's sister do that on many occasions.

"So tell me, Reeth. Are you fully prepared for this meeting?"

As she spoke there was a fractional bow of the head and lowering of the tail that acknowledged the authority of his position, a posture that came as naturally to her as breathing. Reeth instinctively straightened, baring his teeth in the correct and formal response to her gesture of respect.

"I have always been ready, Genthii," he replied. His voice was mellifluous and had a lyrical quality to it. Several members of a delegation from Sem-Lor who had spent time in Reeth's company had expressed the belief that he was singing to them. "You should question whether the Xxcha are fully prepared for this meeting." He tugged again at his mane and treated Genthii to a smile, his fangs bared in affection. From his earliest days, his aunt had been the closest thing to a mother he had known among the clan. The youngest of his family, Reeth had only the faintest memories of his clan-mother. Genthii had been the female mentor in his life, and while the rest of the family had also had their part in raising him, he owed her much.

"It is strange to think of you in command of the clan. Your older siblings have given you no trouble, have they?"

"They're content to let me take our father's place. They have their own interests and investments, and if I keep our fortunes favorable as Father did, they will not question his choice of successor. My bonds and dividends far outstrip theirs." It was no idle boast. From a young age, he had negotiated contracts and won over hard sells more effectively than traders twice his age. Reeth's success was second only to his confidence. "When this opportunity arose, I would have been a fool to let it pass by. Father always expressed an interest in a bond with the Xxcha Kingdom, after all."

"Your father was always keen to venture where others walked with caution. You are more like him than you think." When his posture shifted to one of pride, his shoulders straightening, Genthii stopped him short. "That was not necessarily a compliment. Your father was a fine broker. Perhaps even one of the best I've ever known. But even *he* was prone to recklessness at times. Think before you act, Reeth. That is all the clan asks of you. That is all *I* ask of you." Her hackles half rose in unconscious challenge.

"You question my authority and the success of my station?" The admonishment was lighthearted and punctuated with a gesture of exaggerated submission.

She snorted softly, her ruffled fur settling. "I've known you since you were a kit. Old habits die hard."

"Still." He spread his paws, continuing the charade of

supplication. "If you want me to be taken seriously, perhaps you could start by doing so yourself." His nose twitched slightly in amusement, and despite herself Genthii's posture softened to one of tolerant acceptance, and she rolled her eyes theatrically.

"I suppose I may just about be able to manage that, Reeth."

"Thank you. Now then. Let's hear it. Why are you truly here? I appreciate that the obviously delightful pleasure of my company is almost irresistible, but there's something else, isn't there?"

Genthii smoothed her paw down the front of her russet robe and moved to take a seat beside the table at the viewport. Reeth, resigned to giving up on his personal log, took the seat opposite her. She pushed the cowl of the robe back, and the facade of regal grace fell away. The Hacan referred to it as "showing their second face", the exposure of vulnerability that was considered seemly only among clan-kin.

Reeth was struck, suddenly, not just by the white that peppered her muzzle, but by how tired she appeared. Genthii had been a part of Reeth's life for so long that he had always simply assumed that she would be there forever. But then, he had thought that about his father as well.

That discomfort at the recall of loss returned, but he pushed it back. Now was a time for business, for focus. Reeth was many things to many of the Hacan. The surprisingly astute young scion of a wealthy and well-respected clan, still viewed by the elders as a stripling. He was a son, a brother, a nephew, and a friend and, so it was said, could sell sand on Arretze. He was given to charm and had the ubiquitous silver tongue that so many of his clan possessed, and that was one of several reasons his petition to pursue their current interest had succeeded.

"I wished only to have words with our illustrious delegation leader before we enter Xxcha space. The Kingdom may prove to be harder to win over than any bond you have forged with our own kind, Reeth." Her voice carried a low growl of warning, and his sense prickled at it, partly through annoyance. She saw his reaction and relented wearily. "I know that you have studied, done your research, and that is truly commendable. I am proud of you. But some of the others have expressed doubts."

"Doubting what, precisely? My leadership? Because of my youth and relative inexperience with out-worlders? All the things that the clan whisper behind my back?" There was a fierce snarl of open challenge behind the words, and Genthii simply kept her golden eyes locked on his until he settled again.

"Always so quick to assume the worst of your clan. No, Reeth. We all trust to you to represent our interests well on Archon Ren. There are absolutely no concerns in that area. The doubts are over whether this trip will yield anything of actual value or simply open old wounds – intentionally or not. We must tread carefully, son of my brother."

"I intend to be cautious," he said. He sensed her unease and quelled his own, not wanting to give her further cause for concern. He had his hesitations and doubts – of course he did – but he had chosen this path, and he must continue to walk it. He gently moderated his tone and manner in the hope that it would offer up reassurance in his confidence. "I wouldn't have embarked on this undertaking if I didn't wholly believe that we will be able to establish a profitable relationship with the Xxcha." He leaned forward on the polished white stone of the table, his eyes glinting with earnest certainty. "There is much we have to offer them, and the fact that they accepted our petition of negotiations is a good sign."

"After our shared history?" Genthii pondered for a moment and turned her head to stare out at the silver-scattered velvet darkness beyond. "The Xxcha had every reason to refuse our overtures. The fact they are prepared to receive us now may indicate a softening of stance by the Kingdom, or it may be something potentially dangerous. They are not Hacan, and friendly overtures notwithstanding, they should not be easily trusted." She looked back at her nephew who was now leaning back in his seat, his posture one of easy confidence.

"I believe we are more than capable of moving past our shared history," he asserted. "And if not, then at least we may be instrumental in laying the foundations of reparation." Genthii tipped her head to one side and watched him as he spoke. He was filled with the dynamic passion of youth, a casual certainty of his own skills and efficacy. He knew that as blood-kin, she felt affection for him, but it was not the way of their people to be demonstrative.

"I hope your optimism is rewarded," she said. "Because if we can leave Archon Ren with a bond, or fortunes-willing a warrant of trade, it will be lucrative indeed – and not just financially. Credits may make the worlds go round, Reeth…" She got to her feet, and so did he – the gesture silently offering her his respect. "But reputation is the hardest of all currencies."

She pulled up the hood, resuming the manner of the inscrutable matriarch. She inclined her head graciously and swept from Reeth's cabin. He watched her leave and stared at the space where she had been moments before. Her words had given him much to consider, and what she had added at the end about respect woke an old hunger in him: the need to be recognized and respected for what he was.

After a short time, he reached for the voice recorder and picked up where he had left off before his aunt's arrival.

•••

IN ORBIT AROUND ARCHON REN – XXCHA HOME WORLD

They had been in orbit around Archon Ren for hours now, and Reeth's patience was stretched to its absolute limit. Words were exchanged between Genthii and some unknown representative of the Xxcha down on the planet's surface, and she reassured him that all was in order. There was due process to be followed before they would be allowed to land, just as it was with all visitors to the Hacan worlds.

It was nothing like the smooth, economic efficiency of Kenara where vessels were processed and admitted – or on occasion, detained – with relative alacrity. He tempered his irritation by studying the view of the planet below.

Grudgingly, he acknowledged that it was a beautiful sight: a globe of white, blue – so much blue – and green that drew the eye and painted an image of a world quite unlike the arid home of the Hacan. His clan hailed from Arretze, one of the three planets orbiting the Kenara star, a vast expanse of wind-blown desert where water was one of the most precious commodities imaginable. Reeth stared at the planet below and tried to imagine what it would look like on the surface.

One of the bridge crew looked up from her station and caught his attention with a swish of her tail and a flash of her green eyes. He fixed a level gaze on her and allowed her to speak.

"Our arrival has been noted and our credentials duly logged. Permission has been received to proceed." As if in answer to his thoughts, she delivered the words he had been waiting for.

"We may commence landing at our leisure." The Hacan finished her report, and Reeth turned from viewing their destination and forced down his exasperation.

"Finally! Tell the delegation to meet me in the auditorium in five minutes for a final review of our strategy ahead of first contact." He stalked from the command deck, down the corridors toward the large hall in the belly of the vessel. Most Hacan vessels, great and small, had an auditorium. It was a place where all could be considered equals in diplomacy, commerce, and strategy. It was also where Reeth had assembled the four other Hacan who would accompany him to the world below.

The chamber had no seating, encouraging delegates to pace and mingle freely and, for the Hacan, to read form and posture more easily. A table in the form of a single block of deep, rich, reddish wood occupied the center. This was a family relic, an heirloom of the clan that had been gifted to Reeth's father following his first successful deal with a powerful Semanoran faction on Sem-Lor.

Reeth ran his paw across its smooth, lacquered surface, allowing his mind to briefly indulge in the pleasure of contact with a priceless piece of his clan history. Perhaps it was foolish to have such love for an inanimate object, but this table had borne witness to the success of his clan. It was *his* job to ensure that legacy continued.

He was glad that he was the first to arrive; it allowed him the time he wanted to compose his posturing in a way that would lend a sense of presence. He paced, considering whether conveying authority, determination, or tranquility would serve him best among his peers. He settled on phlegmatic. It was an unconscious mimicking of the composure his father had always adopted and was noted as such by the four Hacan who entered the room shortly after him. Two of them arrived together, the others independently.

Genthii was not a part of the delegation bound for the surface.

It had been a mutual decision: Reeth had initially wanted his aunt's support, but she had deftly steered her nephew away from a potential dependency on her presence. He had been left with the faintest feeling that he had not made the decision to leave her in charge on the ship while he descended to Archon Ren, but that *she* had made it for him

Oh, she was *good*.

The group traveling with him ranged in age from those who were close to his own, right through to Kurruq, an experienced gray-mane, who regarded him coolly from beneath grizzled brows. Reeth silently endured their scrutiny as they approached. It was not a challenge, not as such, but a test to see whether he was truly worthy of taking his father's mantle. It was, after all, unusual for a trader to name a younger offspring as their heir. In this break from tradition, Reeth had to clamber the immediate hurdle of the unexpected. He may not have been the proven trader that his father had been, but neither was he his older brother, an impetuous, free spirit of a Hacan. Reeth had the brains, the conviction, and more than anything, the *desire* to succeed. His older siblings had been more than content for him to take the reins – now he had to convince those who still doubted.

A fierce determination surged through him, but he controlled the urge to snap at them. He was *more* than worthy, and he would show them all *just* how worthy.

"My friends," he said, when they were gathered. He circled the chamber before pausing to lean upon the table. His eyes considered each face in turn. "Thank you for coming. I'm sure you all appreciate the importance of this historic meeting with the people of Archon Ren. The Xxcha have remained closed to us ever since the loss of Archon Tau, but *we* have been chosen to represent the Emirates in this, and it may be the most extraordinary opportunity our clan has been granted in our lifetimes."

It was a nice little speech, and he was proud of it. Four sets of eyes were locked on him as he spoke, and he could discern, without looking directly at any of them, that they nodded in what he hoped was approval.

"Where Reeth leads, we follow," said Hecuus, an older male Hacan who inclined his head graciously at Reeth. "So lead us."

"Oh, I will." Reeth grinned at him. "Trust me."

ARCHON REN – PLANET-SIDE

The spaceport of Kklaj was astonishing in its natural beauty, and as Reeth stepped from the shuttle, he was struck by the sheer scale and aesthetic of it all. Given the relative hostility of the environment, permanent structures on Arretze tended toward the functional, with little thought given to external ornamentation or ostentation. The edifice he found himself in was unlike anything he had ever seen.

Stone pillars laced with intricate carvings arched toward a high, vaulted ceiling and in turn supported a canopy of glass panels, some colored startling shades of deep reds and greens in flowing, organic patterns. The sunlight shone through these panels, casting dancing motes of scintillating light on the concourse.

The sweeping vista offered by the open roof space drew his eyes upward, and they fixed on the proximity in the pale sky of the planet Archon Tau. In shocking contrast to the jeweled marble Archon Ren had looked to be from orbit, its sister world was a devastated chunk of gray and brown rock that, while distant, seemed to radiate a sense of sadness and loss. Reeth tore his eyes away from the sight, wary of being caught staring.

Every facet of the architecture here was undeniably fascinating, but Reeth steeled himself against it. He would *not* allow his delight to distract him from his duty. Nearby movement pulled him from his reverie, and he turned his attention immediately to the small group who had arrived at the end of their concourse and who were patiently waiting to receive them.

Reeth drew himself up to his full height and straightened his robe, a heavy fabric of dark, bottle green that draped over his slender frame loosely, hiding the bunched muscles of his feline build beneath its folds. Each member of his delegation wore robes in the same color, each with a flash of contrasting thread embroidering the clan symbol on the right shoulder.

Reeth's own heraldic crest was worked in glittering silver thread, his right as the head of the clan. It was a clear indication of his position to other Hacan; to the Xxcha, he suspected, it would merely mark him as an individual of note. He glanced at his companions and nodded.

He moved with an easy, confident lope that ate up the distance between the shuttle and the waiting Xxcha. He slowed just a little as he approached them, momentarily taken aback by the unexpected scale of the reptilian natives of this pristine world. At his full height, Reeth was almost two meters tall, and he was considered a little short among his clan. The Xxcha matched his height, but their bulk was impressive. Every aspect of the planet's inhabitants exuded gravitas. They were physically intimidating – despite their mild reputation – and Reeth's confidence shrank for a few seconds.

He rallied quickly as the distance between them closed,

allowing the practiced veneer of diplomacy to slide effortlessly over the doubts that suddenly needled at his conviction. His amber eyes swept over the party that waited for them. There were three Xxcha there to greet them, all clad in loose, gray robes that concealed much of their bodies. Other than their necks and faces, very little flesh was visible but what could be seen ranged in color and tone from a light gray on one Xxcha through to a deeper, darker mushroom tone on another. The skin at the necks was folded and wrinkled, looking to Reeth's eyes to be dry and leathery. The hands raised in greeting ended in claws that were not visibly sharp and quick as were those of the Hacan, but no less a potential weapon for that.

Reeth glimpsed discreet vocalizers in the necklines that would facilitate communication. There were individual touches in the form of different colored trim, but there was nothing Reeth could see to differentiate male from female. He supposed the Hacan may seem equally androgynous to the Xxcha.

"Esteemed visitors of the Emirates of Hacan to this, the Xxcha Kingdom, I offer you most sincere greetings." The Xxcha who spoke had thick, craggy features that suggested they might be an elder of the species. The rumbling pitch of the voice suggested the Xxcha was female, but Reeth had traveled far and wide enough – and had done enough research of his own – to appreciate that among many of the species in the known worlds, gender was little more than a construct, used for convenience and nothing more.

They dropped their head in a low, respectful bow, and the Xxcha on either side followed suit. The first Xxcha raised their head and studied Reeth with eyes that shone with curiosity and wisdom. Reeth could also sense something else shining behind those eyes: something akin to kindness. He had not really given a lot of thought to the personalities of the Xxcha, and while the warmth was welcoming, there was no surprise. He focused on the speaker again.

"My name is Aaxac and it is my great honor to represent my people while you and your…" There was a pause, a fraction of a heartbeat. "…your clan visit our world."

The deduction was simpler than it seemed; they all wore the clan crest, but Reeth was impressed despite himself. With a low, well-practiced bow of his own, so deep that the long tail of fur that he wore at the nape of his neck nearly touched the ground, he responded in kind.

"And it is the honor of the Emirates of Hacan to be allowed to set foot upon Archon Ren, Aaxac. My name is Reeth of Clan Haghura, and it is my pleasure to bring with me the opportunity for our nations to open diplomatic and commercial channels."

"At least to discuss the possibility of such," interjected Kurruq. Reeth shot him a look that, had they been daggers, would have pierced his cousin to the quick. They had barely set foot on the planet, and already his authority was being undermined. He had to take control sooner rather than later. *Don't leave them an opening,* Genthii had advised him before they had left the ship. *If they perceive a weakness, they will seek to take advantage of it.* He realized now that she may not have been talking about the Xxcha. He was still under scrutiny in his new position as leader. Rather than deter him, this sudden epiphany stirred a deeper determination to succeed and prove himself.

"As my cousin says," continued Reeth, so smoothly that it barely seemed to have been an interruption at all, "the chance to negotiate with the esteemed Xxcha is an exciting opportunity for my people, and I – that is to say, *we,* look forward to it."

A series of formal introductions followed on both sides

with the easy familiarity of most diplomatic prologues. So far, thought Reeth, so good.

After they had made their way through the necessary pleasantries, Aaxac gestured to the large doors through which the Xxcha had entered. "We have arranged secure accommodation for you while you are with us. You may wish to begin by inspecting them so that we can be sure they are up to the exacting standards of the Hacan?"

Reeth sought the mockery in the words but found none. He was fascinated by Aaxac. The vocalizer translated their rumbling language with a gentle accent, drawing out the syllables in a melodic, faintly hypnotic way. It was not slow, and neither did it labor in its expression, but conveyed a deliberation in every word. By contrast, the Hacan's physiology meant that as much was conveyed by posture and body language as by spoken word. Reeth found himself slowing his own pace to match that of Aaxac.

The group moved out into the daylight of Archon Ren. Having spent a long journey incarcerated in a ship and forced to exist on recycled air, the Hacan inhaled long and deep and were rewarded with the natural scents of their arboreal surroundings. The air was balmy and humid, quite unlike the dry heat of Arretze. There was moisture in that warmth, the suggestion of recent rain, and the faint saline tang of a nearby ocean – all swept into his olfactory senses by a light, caressing breeze.

Aaxac swung their huge head to the side, watching the reaction of the Hacan with interest. "I understand this to be a very different climate to that which you are used to," they observed, and Reeth nodded.

"This is the first time I have been on a planet with so much water in the atmosphere," he confirmed, and he let his eyes close, enjoying the warmth of the sun on his face. It was refreshing and exceptionally welcome after the trip.

"I am told that it can be oppressive to those unused to the humidity."

"It is different, but not so far from what we are used to," said Reeth. "Arretze, while comfortable to us, can be cruel to those unused to desert habitats. It is in our differences that we find value, don't you think?" He thought himself canny in his choice of words and was rewarded with what he took to be a nod of approval. "And perhaps it will be those very differences that we can harness to reach an accord."

"We can talk more of this later. We will be within the residentiary shortly. You should find it comfortable within, and it has a most excellent view of the valley." Aaxac indicated the discreet structure of glass and wood that lay ahead. "We have many of these hub villages across the planet, serving as habitats, political centers, and sites of contemplation and reflection."

The Xxcha continued to describe what could be found within: traders rubbing shoulders with politicians, poets, and engineers, all sharing the same living space. As they passed through the entry arch, the air temperature gradually cooled from sticky and humid to pleasantly temperate. The interior was quite beautiful: what had appeared deceptively small from the outside contained a broad, open space strewn with vibrant, flowering plant life. The same floral aromas that Reeth had detected outside were redolent here as well, threaded through with more herbal scents.

For a moment, he felt a pang of homesickness. The hot winds of the desert, the dry scent of sunbaked sand and cracked earth... air that hurt the lungs if you breathed too deeply and which would bleach color from even the hardiest fabric. The giant Kinuu trees that clustered in the shady polar vales, the colossal starflowers that only bloomed during the equinox but which painted the valleys for a few, short days with a riot of color... and the ever-present hum of busy and equally dazzling insects as they went about their frenetic work...

It felt so far away right now.

"We grow much of our own produce," Aaxac explained as the party walked down an ornamental stone pathway winding through trailing fronds of vegetation as though they were passing through a jungle. Moments later, they exited into another airy plaza with Xxcha activity continuing its normal routine. There were colorfully decorated stalls where sales of fruit and vegetables were occurring. There was a large fountain in the center of the plaza, an abstract design that trickled water into a crystalline pool, and several small Xxcha, who could be children, were playing by the side of it.

"We have brought spices with us," said Reeth, enthusiastically, but Aaxac just shook their head again.

"Business later, Reeth, if you would."

Fine.

There was every kind of life imaginable here, the Xxcha living and breathing beside the flora and fauna of their home, and despite the hustle and bustle of it all, there was a sense of languid ease to the entire scene.

Hecuus leaned into Reeth, his voice low and audible only to the Hacan for who the words were intended. "Take note. See how relaxed everything is? They display their wares openly. There is no guile here, no artifice. They weaken their own negotiating position!"

Reeth shot a sideways glance at Hecuus and raised his right shoulder in a barely perceptible shrug, a gesture of acknowledgment but also one of dismissal. *I can make my own decisions,* the gesture could have said. *I don't know what you mean,* perhaps. Or even, *Thank you for your observations, I will take them under advisement.* Either way, the message was understood, and Hecuus stepped back into line. The tip of Reeth's tail swished lightly in satisfaction. He had been aiming to dismiss Hecuus, and his effort had played out to perfection.

"Your party will be housed within these chambers of the residentiary." Their meanderings had brought them to a beautifully carved wooden door. "There are rooms enough for each of you. Location maps have been provided to help you find your way to the Dusk Chamber of a Thousand Voices where we will meet. Please – take your time to refresh yourselves with the food and drink we have provided. We are keen to begin our deliberations, but we are equally concerned with your comfort while you are our guests. It would be a poor foundation for our future relationship to begin without the correct degree of courtesy. There is a Xxcha saying…"

Aaxac paused, then the wrinkled face split in a smile. "Forgive me. It has been a long time since I have entertained visitors, let alone those from another world. Shall we say… meet in the Dusk Chamber in an hour's time?"

"That seems more than reasonable," said Reeth. Aaxac inclined their head graciously and indicated the door in front of them.

"Then here are your rooms. Please, once again accept our hospitality while you are with us."

Reeth kept up his formal stance until all the Xxcha had exited and, his whiskers quivering with curiosity, explored the suite of rooms with great interest. They turned out to be more expansive than he had been expecting and, while simple at first glance, were actually far more advanced in their facility than they appeared. There was *wealth* here, and Reeth imagined he could taste it.

He was *pleased* by these accommodations, in a very true sense of the word. After a brief respite for each of the Hacan to claim their own space, they reconvened in what Reeth had designated to be his suite. There was a table there around which they could gather.

"This could be easier than we thought," was the first suggestion put to the group, Hecuus repeating what he had said to Reeth. "The entire world is so sedate it's practically asleep. I'd wager we will be done within a day and be on our way home with a writ of commerce."

"Do I look like I was blown in with the last sandstorm, Hecuus?" Reeth's lip curled a little and he snorted. "I'm not taking that bet. But I *am* inclined to agree. The Xxcha have a reputation for shrewd negotiation. I was expecting a more formal welcome. Even belligerence."

"Is it possible that this is a ruse?" Kurruq posed the question that was at the front of Reeth's own mind, and he stroked at his mane thoughtfully as he pondered his response.

"I think," he said, after a couple of moments, "that our best course of action is to eat and drink and then have our opening discussions. There's no way to accurately assess their intentions until we start to talk and hear what they have to say. Eventually, it will become clear whether our shared history is going to cast any sort of shadow over the proceedings."

At his words, the other Hacan shifted uncomfortably, and Reeth narrowed his eyes at them. "You know we may have to broach the subject. If, and when it happens, I trust you to exercise caution and discretion. I still don't understand exactly why our petition was accepted when so many before us were so firmly refused."

"I think you may be right," said Hecuus, after a few moments had passed without any further comment from Reeth's trade delegation. He clasped Reeth's shoulder. "We should relax a while. Refresh ourselves. Then we can talk to the Xxcha. Reeth has spoken well."

After his companions had retreated to their own suites, Reeth picked up his personal recorder. He tentatively tasted from the basket of unfamiliar fruit, initially without appetite, but that soon changed at the discovery that the fruits were individually delicious. He had not expected such warmth from these people.

He was no fool. Young, certainly, but he was also sharp, insightful, and a student of history. Curiosity as to why the Xxcha were finally opening up their space to the Hacan after years of polite but firm refusals gnawed at him. Reeth knew his history, or at least as much of the histories that had survived. He knew about the old wars, the Quann crisis and the conflict that had followed. What he did *not* know was how Xxcha history recorded these events.

This entire enterprise had been Reeth's idea. It had been his ambition and his initiative that had led him to approach the Xxcha, fully aware of the previous failures and rejections. He emphasized his fascination with the history of the galaxy, of how he was maturing into a new era that was filled with endless opportunity. How he had no expectations and promised nothing, but that he *hoped,* how he very *sincerely* hoped, that the Xxcha may, one day soon, extend an invitation to the Hacan.

He had not pursued the issue when no immediate reply was forthcoming, but within a few short months a formally worded invitation had arrived addressed to Reeth, inviting the young trader and a delegation of his clan to Archon Ren. Everyone – other than Reeth – had been suspicious of this unexpected response. The Xxcha had been insular for decades, quietly keeping to their core systems with friendly but firm disregard for their galactic neighbors. Some whispered that the allegedly peaceful Xxcha were silently building their military into a planet-killing force following the years of warfare. Most dismissed such raw gossip as highly unlikely.

"It can't be understated how hospitable the Xxcha have been since our arrival," Reeth began as he looked out of the window of his suite. It overlooked the busy central hab-dome, and he watched as the locals went about their daily business. It was lively and colorful, and the muted babble of voices floated up through the plants and shrubbery that graced the dome's interior.

"We have been welcomed into their culture with open arms. We have been given exceptional accommodation. Aaxac seems interested and open to conversation. On the surface at least, everything appears to be going as planned. Everything is just fine."

He moved away from the window and sat on the huge and comfortable bed that was evidently designed with the Xxcha physique in mind. Given the exceptional circumstances, Reeth now had an almost unlimited mandate for negotiation on behalf of his clan. They had brought with them samples of Hacan herbs, fabrics, smelted ore, and other commodities from Kenara. There was also the possibility that the Xxcha might be interested in the trade of information. It sat at the back of Reeth's mind.

"All my reading and study has led me to believe that the

Xxcha are a purely peaceful kingdom," he said, continuing his musing. "Certainly, there are defensive system monitors and fighter patrols, but everything that I have seen since our arrival reinforces that supposition. They would appear to be a people at peace and with few desires, which raises questions around what, exactly, we are going to get out of this meeting."

Reeth rose to his feet, prowling the room as he spoke. "Time, as always, will tell," he concluded and set down the recorder. He stopped again at the window and drank in the living, natural beauty of it all. The Xxcha may well have retreated from the galactic stage, but they had certainly not allowed that to in any way affect their thriving culture or population.

"Time will tell," he murmured aloud.

The Dusk Chamber was a cool, vaulted hall located in the lower levels of the structure. Heavy, crimson folds of fabric obscured the windows. The Hacan arrived and were collectively grateful for the ongoing respite from the humidity – but the gloom of the chamber was puzzling. Seeing the obvious curiosity of their visitors, one of the Xxcha, bigger than most of the others, discreetly toggled a control and the curtains retracted onto slim rails, allowing the warm afternoon sun to stream in. Dust motes danced in the beams, hinting strongly at the fact that this chamber had not been opened for some considerable time. Reeth's nose, always sensitive to such things, could pick up that dry, musty scent of old air and a space that has been absent of life.

"Thank you," he said sincerely when the chamber was once more lit. "You'll forgive us our curiosity, I hope?"

"There is nothing, in this instance, to forgive," came the ponderous reply, and the Hacan took their seats opposite their reptilian hosts, Reeth sliding into his chair last. He let his eyes roam across the assembled Xxcha, and once again, he was struck by the apparent diversity represented in such a small number.

"Honored guests of the Emirates of Hacan, we bid you a formal welcome to Archon Ren, seat of the Xxcha Kingdom. We hope that the accommodation is to your satisfaction, that you have thus far found our welcome to be warm and hospitable, and that you are prepared to discuss our mutual futures in good faith."

"Noble Xxcha," replied Reeth, noting with a sense of satisfaction that the alien who had opened the blinds looked up with a start at the honorific, "on behalf of the Emirates of Hacan, we thank you for your gracious welcome and for granting us the rare opportunity to visit your throne world. We have come in good faith on behalf of the Quieron and clan Haghura."

There was visible surprise at Reeth's choice of wording. The Xxcha, who hitherto had demonstrated amiable good nature toward their guests stiffened fractionally – even if only momentarily. To the Hacan, used to reading fractional shifts in body language and posture, it was as obvious as a wounded howl. Aaxac looked from left to right and then inclined their head easily.

"The greetings from your Quieron are noted."

This made Hecuus visibly uncomfortable as he perceived – rightly or wrongly – some veiled disdain in that curt response. He leaned forward with his paws flat on the table, pressing down hard. It was an aggressive stance, and it did not go unnoticed.

"Hecuus, peace." Reeth could feel annoyance and irritation at his cousin's instinctive reaction, and while he could perhaps acknowledge a level of understanding, it was important to keep face in this situation. As such, when he responded, he kept his tone mild. "Yes, Aaxac. I met with the current head of all the clans prior to our journey here for the official sanction on our negotiations. As the First Trader of my clan, I have a certain element of autonomy, but I respect their oversight in all things, particularly when it comes to an exchange with a foreign power."

Aaxac put a claw on the table and sketched absent designs in the thin layer of dust on its surface. It was little more than an idle, meditative movement, but the tension in the Xxcha dissipated like morning mist. Whatever it was that they did was enough to rebalance the discussion, and Reeth was grateful for it. "Have I caused offense? This was not my intent."

"Now it is *my* turn to ask forgiveness." Aaxac's blunt face cracked a small smile. "Our people and yours have shared history. We are a long-lived people with equally long memories, and it is the way of the older generation to cling to the past. Alas, this is sometimes at the expense of the future. It has not escaped our attention that you are a young one, Reeth – which is not your fault. Perhaps you are *too* young to fully appreciate…"

"You offer insult?" The retort from Khadi was sharp, and Reeth's head snapped round to look at her. It was clear to them all that the Xxcha were assessing them, attempting to get their measure, but warning bells sounded at the back of Reeth's mind. Khadi's tone was needlessly abrasive. She was the only one of the delegation not of his bloodline but had married in from another clan some years previously. Her personality was an unknown variable, but her letters of recommendation had been impressive.

Acutely aware of his rather selfish need to appear fully in control, Reeth considered interrupting, but an instinct suggested he wait. It proved to be a mostly wise decision. "Yes, Reeth *is* young, but he is proven. Do not presume to underestimate…"

"Enough, Khadi," said Reeth, flashing her a quick and easy smile that he sincerely hoped conveyed the gratitude for the compliment, but also reminded her that he was, in fact, in charge. "You don't speak for me, and I reassure the Xxcha that no offense is taken." Khadi met his gaze briefly, and a silent contest of wills ensued. After a few seconds, Khadi lowered her eyes deferentially, and he knew he had won her over with his easy assertiveness.

"Again, forgive me if I have chosen my words poorly." Aaxac's eyes glittered with something that might well have been amusement.

Reeth cleared his throat and reached up to straighten an imaginary crease in the collar of his robes. "You are forgiven, Aaxac. Your assumptions about my youth are not wrong, but don't mistake youth for ignorance. I know more of our shared history than you might appreciate."

"Then you know why it is that the sanction of your Quieron might draw an unfavorable response?"

This was the moment that Reeth had suspected would come, but that he had hoped to avoid. He was both startled and relieved that it had happened during the opening exchanges, rather than potentially souring things later – but he would have given *anything* for it not to have happened at all. The history and distance between the two civilizations suddenly weighed heavily on him, and he felt a tremor of uncertainty that he was not robust enough for this confrontation.

There was only one way to find out, and that was to adopt his father's methodology. Approach the situation head on, and deal with the consequences as they came.

The memory rose, unbidden.

Arretze. Air... hot and dry. Walls of painted sandstone bedecked with clan banners and honorifics. The stillness of the mostly empty chamber that swallowed sound hungrily. The low, sonorous growl of the Quieron.

"Your initiative has done you credit, Reeth, but tread with care. Should you succeed, then the profits of this venture will rightly swell the coffers of clan Haghura. But to have sanction for this enterprise, I will extract a promise which you will make on the name of your clan. Regardless of the outcome, you will be representing our – and by extension all Hacan – interests on Archon Ren. It is vital that you understand the possibility that nothing may come of this, a passing curiosity of the Kingdom, perhaps. Regardless, you will be our voice in a forum long closed to us and for reasons tangled by war and loss. You must swear that your account of our nation is the best you can give."

And then, they had given him the full truth of it. It was wrapped in reason and presented through the rose-tinted lens of commerce, but still, it was ugly.

What Reeth had learned in the privacy of that meeting had shocked – but not truly surprised him. It explained why it was that every previous overture to the Kingdom had been met with cool, polite but emphatic rebuttal. He thought on those facts now, as he sat opposite the dark-eyed Xxcha. He could feel every pair of eyes in the room on him; those of his own people and those of their hosts.

The silence stretched out. The Quieron had demanded his discretion in this matter, trusting to his judgment to represent the Hacan's best interests. His family had counseled him against probing old wounds out of a deep-seated fear of the harm it could do to negotiations. Yet the Xxcha had carefully challenged him to acknowledge the issues, and the choice now was here in front of him. Two clear paths lay ahead. One called for dissembling. Caution. Tact.

Reeth chose the other.

"Yes," he said, and his eyes locked with those of Aaxac. He did not break the connection but concentrated on injecting every shred of honesty into that single word. When he was sure he had Aaxac's full attention – and *only* then – did he allow himself to continue.

"Yes," he repeated. "I am aware of the shared history of our nations. I can fully appreciate why you might react unfavorably to an…" He paused, selecting his words with care. "An official sanction."

He became aware of several subtle changes in poise from his companions and knew that they were discomfited by the direction he had chosen to take. Khadi signaled for his attention, and when she spoke, she did so in their own language.

"Reeth, remember what we discussed. Discretion."

"The time for discretion has passed. There is more danger in choosing to avoid the specters of the past than in directly challenging them." He laid a paw on hers in a reassuring gesture. The tension remained, but she released him and allowed him to continue along this forthright, potentially dangerous path without further objection. Reeth returned his attention fully back to the Xxcha and allowed his eyes to move from one representative to the next. They were all regarding him silently and strangely; he found it encouraging rather than intimidating.

"It is my desire to reestablish a relationship between the Hacan and the Xxcha," he said. "Nominally, with the view to establishing fresh commerce – but all of us gathered here know that there is far more to a partnership than simple transaction and that more can be gained than simple goods and services. I will ask for your guidance in this, my friends. For I know only what I have learned from my own people."

"Reeth." Hecuus's tone held a tense note of warning. Reeth chose to ignore it. He had begun this journey now. To not see it through to its conclusion would be a show of weakness and one that could prove costly later. The fact that his chosen path could also prove costly in the more immediate future also did not escape his notice – but he resolved to boldly stride forward or forever lose face.

"Aaxac, before we can *truly* begin to move forward, I must ask you to share how the Xxcha perceive our relationship. Not the history as I understand it, but *yours*." He looked back down the line of delegates and felt a shiver of anticipation. His words had clearly sparked interest; it showed in all those dark eyes that were locked on him. "I ask not out of idle curiosity or some perverse desire to revisit unhappy antiquity, but because understanding the past is the only way either of us can work together to create a better future."

It was not as hard as it might have been to smother his pride. Aaxac had been nothing but open, and Reeth felt confident in leading this conversation down a potentially dark path. It might have unforeseen consequences, but as his father had once said *if one does not take the path less traveled, how will you ever discover anything new?*

As spontaneous addresses went, it was startlingly eloquent. Was he satisfied with his choice of words? Yes. Would he congratulate himself? Maybe he might, later. But he knew that the next step was likely to be the most perilous – the one that could make or break this nascent relationship.

Another metaphorical crossroads opened in front of him. There was still time. He could still opt for the more conventional approach. They could discuss the wares they had brought with them and what the Xxcha had to offer in return, but now that he had taken the other route, he had the distinct impression that his direct approach had earned him some approval.

The path less traveled.

The dark smudge of Archon Ren's sister world hung low in the evening sky beyond the windows, clearly visible against the lambent orange of the coming dusk. Reeth let his eyes trail to study its ominous form, and then he spoke the words that had been on his lips since they had left home to come here.

"Tell me about the occupation. Tell me about Archon Tau."

He had experienced silences over his years of negotiation. Awkward silences. Those that were uncomfortable. Anger, sometimes. But this was *new*. The four Xxcha were virtually impossible to read, but Reeth could discern curiosity, anticipation, and trepidation in that long, frozen moment. Then, just as suddenly as it had ceased, time unstuck, and the future began to tumble out.

"An excellent question, Reeth," said Aaxac, and their voice held, much to Reeth's surprise, an element of respect. "And before I continue, I think I speak for all of us here present when I say that I admire your candor." Around them, the other Xxcha rumbled their assent. Reeth inclined his head in acknowledgment and hoped that the gesture in no way gave away how hard his heart was pounding in his chest.

"Archon Tau was not always as it appears now. It was not always an irradiated wasteland. There was a time when our people inhabited both worlds, and both were as beautiful and filled with life as the Archon Ren that you have seen. I will spare my colleagues a retelling of the Federation of Sol's *pragmatic* approach to liberation. Its results are quite plain for any with eyes to see."

This much, Reeth knew. This much, he had learned for

himself through simply asking questions and studying the war archives during the journey to Xxlak.

"I understand that it was the Barony of Letnev who took Archon Tau from you originally?" He asked the question carefully and gently, still acutely aware that he was stepping in dangerous territory.

"You are mostly correct, Reeth, although it is a little inaccurate to say the Letnev took Archon Tau from us. Alas for the perpetuation of half-truths. Allow me to elucidate. We ceded the world to their expansionism in a move to retain some autonomy. Complete domination, annihilation, or enslavement was not an attractive prospect, and thus did we negotiate." A second Xxcha who had been introduced as Rha'cexx picked up the thread and unfolded from the seat, beginning a slow lumbering pace up and down his side of the table. "Peace was never going to be an option with the Barony of Letnev, their greed too great, their ambitions too militant. Despite ceding Archon Tau, it would have been only a matter of time before they returned to complete their subjugation."

"It was a bitter compromise," said Aaxac, nodding their great head. Reeth felt, more than saw, the terrible grief in the words. "A bitter compromise. They brought their vast fleets, and had it not been for those who negotiated for the Xxcha, the conquest would surely have been complete. It is a vanity to say that the negotiations were brilliant, but they *were*. And thus, we were able to retain a little freedom. Archon Tau was lost, but only for a brief time. The Barony settled there, fortified, and installed their own regime. The Xxcha who remained on the world..."

"Do not continue if you do not wish to." The words came from Khadi, and it surprised Reeth. He had not thought her to be so sensitive to their hosts. He shot a sideways glance at her trying to gauge her mood or intent, but he could not. Her expression was stoic and impassive.

"I do not wish to," said Aaxac. "But I must, now that it has begun. You understand?"

Khadi paused for a moment, and then she nodded.

"Our people who remained on Archon Tau were less fortunate than we might have hoped. They were second-class citizens, existing at the whims of the Barony. No further terms were offered. It was the darkest period in the Kingdom's history – and it was not only the persecution of our people. There was more. So much more."

Reeth remained silent as the Xxcha spoke. There was a conflict going on within his soul. On the one side there was the need to sate his curiosity about these people, about their history, about learning what was unspoken. On the other side, a need to remember the boundaries of respect that should be afforded to all new trading partners. After an unspoken exchange with their colleagues, Aaxac stood, and the Hacan delegation respectfully followed suit.

"Reeth, would you walk with me? Your companions may remain here. I assure you that they will be well attended and want for nothing." It was an unusual request during what were, at face value, official proceedings. But it was also of the moment, and Reeth had not risen to his position through a life dictated by indecision.

"It would be my pleasure, Aaxac," he said. "I have asked for clarity. It is imperative that I now hear your truth, however uncomfortable. Before we leave, I would ask one thing of you, if you would indulge me?"

"Speak."

"I require reassurance that I have not offended you."

Later, he could not have said why that reassurance was so necessary, just that it was important at the time.

Four sets of glossy, reptilian eyes fixed on him with cool regard, and he felt their assessment like a forensic evaluation. They probed for flaws, even a weakness that could be exploited. What they saw – or perhaps, what they had heard – was satisfactory. Aaxac shook their great, blunt head, and a small, enigmatic smile crossed their leathery features.

"You have not."

There was an unspoken "yet" that resonated through the chamber. Everyone heard it. Reeth's hackles rose just a little, but he kept his expression neutral. There was a cultural subtlety at play here that he keenly wished to understand. If that meant moving away from the formality of the Chamber and into the company of a single emissary, then so be it.

"Then I will endeavor to keep it that way," he said. The smile remained on Aaxac's face, and they beckoned for Reeth to follow.

They moved out of the chamber and onto a high balcony that hugged the arboreal exterior. The sun was a fiery disc of orange on the horizon, and the cool breeze of the evening had stolen much of the humidity of the day. Ribbons of mist drifted lazily from the canopy below, heady with the scents of sap, resin, and fecundity. Reeth breathed it in, more comfortable now that the damp heat had diminished. The early nocturnal chorus of avian life warred with the growl and churr of unseen creatures waking from their rest.

"Your hospitality has been without question," he said, after they had walked in silence for a while. There was nothing awkward or uncomfortable about the peace; in fact it was entirely companionable. "And yet I cannot shake the idea that I have broached a subject that I would have been wiser to avoid."

"For better or worse, history is the fire that serves to forge us into the people we are today. The history of the Xxcha, the history of the Hacan – both are littered with events and decisions that have shaped us – and so they will continue to do. As a nation, as individuals, as players on the galactic stage." Aaxac looked down at Reeth, and he was struck, once again, by the size of his counterpart. For all their cumbersome nature, for all their mild eloquence, he was acutely aware that should they ever be spurred to violence, the Xxcha's greater size and strength would make them formidable foes.

Reeth was no warrior, but he knew how to defend himself. In a galaxy filled with dangers, he considered himself fortunate to have never needed to employ those skills, and the prospect of ever having to defend himself against one of these gentle giants was daunting. Fortunately, he was not able to dwell on it any further, as Aaxac had resumed their narrative.

"We said before that the loss of Archon Tau represented the darkest period of Xxcha history. You will have surmised by now that we are a Kingdom of peace. We have ever advocated compromise and mutual understanding over the aggression of so many nations. There have been many times where the intervention of our diplomats and ambassadors were able to prevent unnecessary bloodshed. Tragically, there have been an equal number where our words have gone unheeded, and opposing forces – you may wish to take in this view."

The sudden interruption of the conversation caught Reeth by surprise, and he realized that he had barely noticed the path they had taken. Aaxac had led them around the balcony and onto a bridge that linked the residentiary to another structure.

The overpass was wide enough to accommodate three Xxcha and hung dizzyingly high above a suburb of Kklaj City.

Softly lit avenues snaked lazily between the trees below, flanked by bulbous individual habitats that blended comfortably with the natural environs. Vibrant sprays of ornamental flowers fed by meandering streams seemed to attend every property. Amongst it all, the Xxcha bustled – in as much as their vast bulk allowed – about their business and beyond the suburbs, Reeth spied several other expansive arboreal residentiaries, their own balconies and bridges affording an unparalleled view of the city.

"With the shadow of subjugation looming and the atrocities taking place on Archon Tau, a decision was made that broke our king's heart, but without which we could not survive. Our people, peaceful, quiet, meditative, and progressive, began to develop our own soldiers and weapons." Aaxac's voice was soft and reflective, and Reeth did not know what to say or what to think. His own people favored negotiation over war, but a few hours on Archon Ren and he could barely imagine what it must have been like for the peaceful nation to surrender a part of themselves to violence.

He leaned on the bridge and stared out over the slice of Xxcha life as it washed over his senses. When Aaxac began speaking again, it stopped simply being one individual sharing words with another, and he was able to picture the scene clearly.

Imagine, if you will…

The Federation of Sol Phoenix fleet appeared in the skies above Archon Tau on a bright, spring morning. Their arrival was heralded by contrails of fire and debris above the planetary exosphere as they engaged the Letnev picket ships and orbital defense platforms left to defend the occupied world. Outnumbered, and already in retreat, the Letnev forces broke in a matter of hours. Burning wreckage scored the atmosphere and rained down onto the surface below, littering the jungle with the bones of dead vessels.

The Federation of Sol's reasoning was simple: they were not prepared to allow the Barony of Letnev to maintain what had become a fortified stronghold on another world. While on the surface it seemed that they had come to aid the Xxcha, there was no intention of such. They were here to serve what they arrogantly believed to be the best interests of the galaxy – and themselves – at large.

It was only the first of what was to become many bombardments.

While the Letnev and their subjects were shielded from much of the devastation, Archon Tau had already begun to die as millions of indigenous creatures that called the forests home were wiped out. Dust plumes blossomed high into the clear, blue skies, and radiation from ruptured drive coils and fuel chambers leaked into the soil, poisoning the air and water.

It was only the beginning.

Secreted in hardened batteries across the planet, the Barony retaliated with punishing volleys of macro-artillery fire. The massive guns hurled shells the size of buildings into orbit, filling near-space with a storm of hypersonic shrapnel capable of perforating the hull of anything smaller than a super-dreadnought. Built without consideration for the local ecosystem, the guns did as much damage to the planet as they did to the Federation. Titanic vents expelled gales of toxic propulsion vapor, and punishing waves of recoil overpressure flattened the nearby jungle.

But while the opening moves of the siege inflicted terrible harm to Archon Tau, the impact and consequences on the Xxcha population were many times worse. The subjugated people of Archon Tau begged the Letnev to seek terms with the Federation, but their pleas were ignored. The Barony would cede nothing and resolved to make the Federation pay in blood for every inch of ground.

Imagine, if you will…

"Dissidents will not be tolerated," the Barony decreed. "To speak of surrender during a time of war is sedition punishable by the harshest censure. Any citizens identified in open support of negotiation with the enemy are to be reported to local sector enforcement immediately."

Used to careful contemplation and measured dialogue, many Xxcha were quickly incarcerated for voicing their belief in the need for peace. As the siege of Archon Tau ground on from days into weeks, imprisonment turned into forced labor as the Barony's need to keep the war machine fueled and supplied consumed lives at a terrifying rate.

Heavier Federation ships weathered the planetary defenses and systematically targeted the artillery silos with orbital bombardment. Killing beams of plasma-fire sliced through fortified magazines and triggered detonations that buried hundreds beneath tons of collapsing rock and burning jungle. Continental wildfires raged out of control, creating thermal hurricanes that ripped up and incinerated even the largest and hardiest trees and rendered them to ash. Pulverized rock dust from the blasts choked the rivers and streams, slaughtered the aquatic life, and turned many of the lakes into rancid bowls of viscous sludge.

Once the orbital defenses were broken, the Federation started the surface campaign in earnest. It was branded a *liberation* in as much as they were freeing the world from the grip of the Letnev, but it was clear that the preservation of Archon Tau was secondary to the expulsion of the Barony. The Phoenix fleet would not leave a fortified position at its back from which an enemy could strike.

Advancing platoons of Federation spec ops forces employed industrial defoliants ahead of their advance to flush the elite Barony troops out of hidden positions. Heavily outnumbered, and with their backs to the wall, the Letnev extracted a heavy toll for every step the Sol forces took, every position taken, every fortress broken.

Throughout it all, the peaceful Xxcha were caught in between. Yearning for freedom from the Barony but horrified at the cost as they watched their world die around them.

Reeth could picture it all so very clearly. Every image that Aaxac's quiet retelling painted in his imagination was as vivid as though he were standing to one side watching the exchanges take place. What a horror it must have been to sit by and watch the death of your own world and to be helpless to stop it.

Helpless? The next thought came through unbidden, and it was harsh and uncompromising. Or hopeless? Peace had its place in the galaxy, certainly. But to be so unprepared to defend yourself, to allow such appalling things to happen to your world? To your people?

Imagine, if you will…

Reeth snapped his attention back to Aaxac's painfully gentle recounting of the terrible fate that had befallen Archon Tau. How the horrors went on and on, and in the skies above Archon Ren, the sister world transformed from a beautiful twin to a mutilated shadow.

"And so it went on for two, terrible years," said Aaxac. "We still have holo-records of what it was like before the Barony and the Federation came. Clear blue skies, soft ribbons of cloud, warm, pink dawn-light on distant horizons."

The last days of Archon Tau were lit only by flames, and the flickering electrical discharge of atmospheric ash cyclones hundreds of miles across.

What had been a tropical paradise had instead become a wasteland consumed by artificial winter. What remained of the lakes and oceans froze, and the thin air filled with flurries of toxic dust that would take centuries to disperse. In the wake of the Federation's victory, Archon Tau had become a dead world. Free, but dead.

"It was considered necessary, you see Reeth. The Barony would not concede, and the Sol forces could not ignore them. The Federation shattered our world to save human lives. A pragmatic approach, but a cruel one." Aaxac heaved a great sigh of grief, and Reeth was genuinely moved to sympathy. "In the end, nothing survived. The Xxcha of Archon Tau were silenced for once and all time."

Aaxac turned their large, wise eyes on the young Hacan, and Reeth read deep sorrow and pain therein. "The Federation of Sol were the youngest of the spacefaring races and the Xxcha counseled strongly against provision of weapons to further their ambitions. The Hacan would not listen to our warnings, driven by the scent of profit. Your people's greed played into not only the destruction of our people, but the annihilation of an entire planet. Such a legacy is hard to forgive, young trader. The wound is still raw and bleeding, but a time comes when the world must move forward and cease looking backward."

"I am ... sorry," said Reeth. He was. He was more than sorry, and the word seemed highly inadequate to express what it was that he was feeling. "Don't think I'm unsympathetic to the plight of your people, Aaxac, because I am."

He took a long, slow breath and looked around once again to try to reconcile the description of barren Archon Tau with the thriving life around him. Even as he did so, he became acutely aware that around a dozen figures were approaching from the other end of the bridge. He had been so caught up in the retelling of the fate of Archon Tau that he had never even noticed the doors open to allow a platoon of heavily armored Xxcha onto the span.

A chill ran down his spine in response to the sight. Every one of the adult Xxcha with whom he had come into contact, already tall and broad, was intimidating in a ponderous sort of way. But the hulking troops approaching across the bridge were nothing short of terrifying. Aaxac was watching Reeth's reaction to the sight with undisguised interest.

"We are a peaceful people by nature, Reeth," they said in their gentle voice. "But the atrocities of the past have led us to a present in which we must be prepared to defend ourselves fully against those who would seek to take advantage. And through this well-prepared present, the Kingdom hopes, most sincerely, that there will be a place for our voice of peace to be heard once again. But we are not without preparation. What you see here goes against our peaceful nature. But it is a necessity that has been brought to pass by the actions of others."

The massive warriors marched past without pause, and Reeth began to understand that this encounter with the Xxcha forces was not simply coincidence. Aaxac had led him here with the specific reason to allow this sight to be noted; a punctuation to the history that had been shared. His initial sense of uncertainty slowly began to give way to one of understanding. He stared at the broad backs of the armored warriors and knew, in that instant, that the Xxcha would go to any lengths to protect their cherished way of life from an uncaring galaxy that might seek to exploit their nature yet again. He did not doubt for a moment that the ground forces would be matched by an equally impressive navy.

As though reading his thoughts, Aaxac indicated a sprawling complex, barely visible on the horizon. "Our people live and work mostly in purlieus like this one. Our weapons and planetary defenses are out there among the trees, and our troops train in nearby valleys. Ttakur Station is located on the dark side of our satellite, and our destroyers and dreadnoughts there have remained dormant for a considerable time other than for transportation. It has not yet been necessary for us to bring them to bear. Ultimately, my Hacan friend, the Xxcha still believe in the doctrine of peace and negotiation, but we will never again bend under the oppression of invaders."

"Why are you sharing this with me, Aaxac?" The openness with which Aaxac was revealing the Kingdom's defenses was not a strategy the young Hacan was previously accustomed to, and he was puzzled by the choice.

"Why would I *not* share this with an ally, Reeth?" There was no pause, no hesitation. Just a simple, unquestionable answer. "Or do you mean to ask why I would choose to share this information with a Hacan? It may have been the humans who gave and executed the orders that resulted in the death of Archon Tau, but it was the Emirates of Hacan who armed them."

It was not a rhetorical question, and Reeth realized with no small amount of admiration that in wielding the stark, bald, and startlingly painful truth, Aaxac had maneuvered him neatly into a diplomatic trap. What he said next could well determine not only the outcome of this endeavor but also the relationship between the two nations for the foreseeable future.

He considered his response before he opened his mouth. If not out of courtesy to Aaxac, then because he wanted to impart and share the truth of what he was saying. The conviction behind the words themselves.

"Because the galaxy is a changed place, and I am not one of those Hacan," he said, slowly. "The Quieron that I represent here today would never make the decisions that our predecessors made, and I would stake my life on it. No, more than that. I would stake my *reputation* on it."

A solid reputation was the hardest of all currencies.

"I know the Hacan. I know the significance of what you say. It is no small thing, and your principles do you – and your people – remarkable credit. You can relax, Reeth. I am not seeking to mislead you. You must understand, though, why I am doing this." Aaxac leaned on the arch of the bridge and stared out over the view below. "None of this is to threaten or coerce. It is, rather, to hope that you understand our position. Trust, once broken, is difficult to make whole again and, even when mended, is weaker for it. I wanted reassurance that were we to place such trust, that it would not simply be smashed once more when restored. Do you see, Reeth?"

"I see, Aaxac. I see and I understand. While I represent the Emirates in this moment, I am also… just Reeth. And *Reeth* sees the wisdom of the Xxcha. Reeth values that wisdom and more – Reeth values the *honesty*." He shot a sidelong glance at Aaxac. "Without honesty, what is the point of any of this? Lies will always find you out; deceit is a poor foundation for any relationship. I give you my word that, like the Kingdom of Xxcha, the Emirates of Hacan have learned the lessons of their past."

"And what of your Quieron?" Aaxac replied softly. "Even before the Quann crisis we counseled caution in dealings with the Federation, but their short-sighted greed resulted in the trading of weapons that brought about great atrocities. They cared for nothing but profit. All that mattered was who gave them the greatest coin. I see the denial in your face, but how do we know that history will not be repeated? How do we know that the Hacan will not, in the name of profit, once again pave the way for others who would seek to destroy us as they have done so comprehensively before?"

Reeth did not answer, at least not immediately. He watched the patrol of warriors as they made their way higher up the habitat. They carried rifles that looked to be of a design he did not know, and despite himself, he absently began to calculate the market value of a new line of firearms. This was surely not the time to allow his business brain to engage – this was a time for diplomatic effort and reassurance. The Quieron had charged him with more than they could have known. Or had they – as Reeth was starting to wonder – felt that both he and his reputation were expendable? Was Reeth of Clan Haghura simply to be remembered as the token effort that was made to repair the damage caused between the two nations?

No. That wasn't it. Not at all.

He did not know *how* he was so sure, but he *was*. Of the many clans, it had been Haghura that had been accepted by the Xxcha. Haghura who had been sanctioned by the Quieron.

He had not been asked to turn a profit. He had been asked to represent the Hacan well. There was a *reason* Reeth had been accepted for this task, and he allowed himself the arrogance to believe that he now understood that a little more.

"You don't," was his ultimate answer to Aaxac's question. "You *don't* know that we will not deal with those who might do you harm, because neither of our particular people are gifted – or cursed – with foresight. What we have, Aaxac, are the lessons of the past in conjunction with the reality of the *now*. If we can ensure we never forget the one as we deal with the other, then between us, the future is unwritten, uncertain and will be whatever we choose to make it. Opening negotiations and commerce is a positive start. There is honesty to be had there." He spread his arms wide in a slightly exaggerated gesture. "Honesty is my stock in trade. That, and the fine commodities I have brought with me for you and your people to inspect. The gerr root… the starflower silk and Spehat medicinals among others."

It was a reactive moment of humor, and he did not know how it would be received. Indeed, as the syllables were swallowed by the sudden silence, he wished he could take them back. But then Aaxac began to chuckle, a deep, throaty sound that brought Reeth relief and an inexplicable joy.

"You are young, Reeth, your eyes unclouded by a long and misunderstood past. You approached with that youth and curiosity and – forgive me – a candor that did not play upon long and storied success. We wished to meet with this new generation of Hacan. To see if there *is* a future where the Emirates and the Kingdom may once more forge the bonds of trust."

"And do you believe that there is?"

"Let us return to the Dusk Chamber and talk business, Reeth." Aaxac chuckled a little more, then they nodded. "You have spoken well here today. You may take that back to your Quieron with my good wishes for our future collaborations."

Reeth smoothed the fur of his mane and adopted the more neutral expression with which he had begun the meeting. He had done well here, even if he did not fully understand why – or how – but it was enough. "I will, Aaxac. And I respect your choice in allowing me to see what you have shown me. That information would be a valuable currency in some hands. But not mine. On that, you have my word."

"I know." They began the walk back to the Dusk Chamber, and Aaxac turned their head slightly toward Reeth. "Tell me of this gerr root."

"On the whole, it went exceptionally well." Reeth was back aboard the ship, back in his quarters and had just enjoyed his share of a roast haunch of meat. The Xxcha were vegetarian, and while their food was delicious, lightly and delicately spiced, it was still alien to him, and he had devoured the meat with enthusiasm.

"Lines of communication that were once severed are now reestablished, and pending further discussion, the Xxcha welcome the Emirates and as their opening concession have granted free passage through their space without undue challenge in return for the goods that we have left with them. There is a willingness to engage in political discussion, and it is my firm belief that our two people will share a positive, constructive, and primarily *lucrative* future."

Reeth snapped off the recorder and looked out of the viewport at the blue and white marble of Archon Ren. They were still in orbit while the ship's engines completed their pre-burn cycle but would be departing within the hour. He felt the familiar presence of Genthii move to stand beside him.

"Your father would be proud of what you accomplished here, Reeth," she said in her soft purr. "Despite their strange ways, there is a lot to be gained from dealing with the Xxcha. Their relative isolation hasn't meant a cessation in their technological advances, and if we are able to mediate deals with our other contacts… we will turn a healthy profit. The Quieron will be pleased."

"Yes," agreed Reeth, his eyes still on the planet. "The Quieron *will* be pleased."

Pleased yes. Pleased with what he had accomplished, not just because of a potentially lucrative and welcome agreement – but because he had been the first to step onto the broken bridge that could now be repaired between the two nations. He was prouder by far of that fact than he was of the profits that might be made. But ultimately, he was Hacan. He *lived* to turn a profit. His eyes moved from Archon Ren to the broken orb of Archon Tau.

"Your reputation will grow because of this. You will no longer be seen simply as an heir, but as the true inheritor of your father's mantle. I am proud of you too." Genthii tipped her head to one side, sensing some sort of inner conflict, but not pressing for information.

"Yes." He turned then, smiling at her. "Yes, it will. But I will continue to be better. We should all learn from the mistakes of the past and use them to build better futures." He lay his paw on her arm. "Your words, as your counsel, will always be welcomed, sister of my father." They allowed their foreheads to touch in an affectionate, familial greeting.

A gentle thrumming beneath their feet told them that the ship was readying for departure, and together they watched as Archon Ren disappeared from beneath them, fading away once more into the inky void of space.

CONTACT

DANIE WARE

"You are not in combat, commander, and you will kindly moderate your attitude."

In the frost-chill air, the speaker's breath steamed. Gold against his deep green skin, his extravagant headdress glinted, its gemstones reflecting the room's red lights. Out of place against the black, metal background, Winnaran Ambassador Sheceh Del Sabir adjusted the already-immaculate line of his jacket and drew himself to his full height.

"Must I remind you," he continued, "that we are the rightful, cultural inheritors of the Lazax, and you will address me accordingly."

In response, the Letnev commander gave a small, grim smile. His skin was blue-gray, his eyes and hair white. He wore a severe, black uniform decorated with silver highlights, the marks of his rank and competence. At his gesture, a quartet of masked soldiers stepped forward, menacing the ambassador's retinue.

In return, the ambassador curled his lip.

All in all, Za Nuk decided, this was not going well.

Watching the unfolding scene, the unseen Yssaril was captivated. Both species were new to her, and significantly taller than her small, crouched figure, though their level of technology seemed roughly equivalent to hers. Trained from her youth to gather information, she blinked big yellow eyes, and stayed absolutely silent. However this played out, the Guild of Spies, the central Yssaril government and the body to whom Za answered, would need every detail.

"'Cultural inheritors,'" the Letnev commander repeated, as if the words were a bad taste in his mouth. "The invitation we extended to your people, Ambassador, is a significant privilege, and the very first of its kind. Perhaps I should remind you of our *strength*?" The faceless guards had hands on weapons, though they did not yet raise them to fire.

The ambassador's expression congealed. His voice flat, he said, "We remember your *strength* well enough, commander." His chin was still lifted, his gold eyes now metal-hard. His guards wore uniforms in green and bronze, though they bore no weapons, and his cluster of aides exchanged mutters, their earrings flashing as they turned to one another. Following the conversation, Za wondered what invitation the Letnev had made. Whatever it was, the commander's oblique reference to the blockade of the Quaan wormhole, the incident that had begun the Twilight War and was ultimately responsible for the Lazax's destruction, was clear. Letnev Commander Ludovic Viesniel VI, it seemed, liked threats rather than promises.

But Viesniel was still smiling, the expression as devoid of warmth as the air.

"You may remind me of whatever you wish, Ambassador," he said. "But your 'cultural inheritance' alone will not be enough. One might even call it inefficient. If we… if *you*–" the pause was pointed "–wish to explore Mecatol Rex, then you will need more than just singing and polished gemstones."

Inhaling sharply, the Winnaran ambassador glared.

Carefully, her light-refracting skin making her all but invisible, Za shifted position, changing her crouch to ease the pressure on her knees. There was little cover in this tight, almost furnitureless room – the surroundings resembled a prison chamber more than an audience hall. Alone on Arc Prime's surface, the sealed Letnev city of Feruc was a cruel place, with its martial ruthlessness, its claustrophobia, its freezing temperatures. Za had trained for many years on Retillion, and she missed the thick, green swamps of her home. Their vibrancy, their *life*.

But, she was here to work. The Guild had already sent one Yssaril to Feruc, on a mission to discover more about the Letnev, but his intelligence reports had ceased. They'd sent Za after him, to find out what had happened.

"I'm not here to count your military companies," Ambassador Sheceh said. "Nor to pat you on the back for the polish of your *boots*." The word was a barb. "The loan of your ships is welcome, of course, but this – ah, *exploration* – will remain under Winnaran control. I need not remind you of our estranged cousins on Mecatol. They will need to be dealt with tactfully, not simply walked over–"

"You're both exactly the same," Viesniel said, faintly scornfully. "Missing your masters, longing for someone to give you purpose and direction. And we will give you that someone–"

"You will do absolutely nothing of the sort." An edge had crept into Sheceh's tone, though his words were still mild. "Do not make the mistake of underestimating our–"

"There's nothing to underestimate." Viesniel jabbed a rigid finger, right in Sheceh's chest. The Winnaran guards twitched.

"If you wished to bargain, then you should have come to me with *weapons*, not the pointless drivel of your enlightening achievements–"

"Mecatol Rex belongs to the Winnaran people." Sheceh slapped the finger out of the way, and Viesniel's expression darkened.

Fascinated by their escalating confrontation, Za watched them both, learning everything she could. She wasn't sure, at the moment, who had the upper hand, but the push-and-shove of their dealing was intriguing, and its implication sent a thrill along her nerves.

What were they doing?

"We are the Emperor's children." Sheceh was still talking, imperious and proud. "The social and traditional descendants of everything the Lazax built. Of peace, of education. Our cousins will understand this, even if you do not–"

"Oh, we understand well enough," Viesniel said. "I asked you here as a *favor*, Sheceh, one bestowed upon no other galactic race." By his tone, Za was fairly sure that using the ambassador's name, rather than his title, was a deliberate insult, aimed to goad him and to provoke a reaction. "And you have the sheer temerity to demand superiority? Control of our 'exploration'? You have no forces with which to drive your bargain. You will submit to our leadership, and in return, we will deal with your Mecatol cousins *tactfully*, as requested. And that is the end of the matter."

"I don't think so." Sheceh paused, apparently savoring the moment. Then, with a certain theatrical panache, he said, "I have come with offers of *food*, commander." He played it like a winning hand, and Viesniel stopped. Even in the dim light, his sudden tension was obvious.

Za held her breath, impressed by the Winnaran ploy, and by the sheer aplomb with which it was delivered. She was enjoying herself now, and she barely dared breathe – she didn't want to miss a word, a hint, a gesture, the slightest shift of a facial expression.

"*What* did you say?"

At Viesniel's tone, the Winnaran guards twitched again. The senior aide, her headdress glinting, frowned. Her lips had not stopped moving, and Za wondered if she were somehow recording the audience.

Riveted, the Yssaril eased forward, cocking her head to one side. The mention of Mecatol had sent shivers down her spine – the seat of the conquered Lazax, the center of the galaxy. For both Winnaran and Letnev to be discussing this "exploration" – it was presumably a great deal more than it seemed. Unwittingly, Za had stumbled into something deadly serious.

But information was her life, her mission, and her calling, and – if she gathered enough – perhaps even her promotion. Born in poverty on the Yssaril world of Retillion, she had trained with the Guild for many years, and she wanted not only the validation but the success and reputation it would bring. The work, the future missions, the prosperity for her family.

Her excitement rising, she remained absolutely silent.

"Food," Sheceh repeated, now smiling like some elegant predator. "Your mushroom harvest is failing even more than usual, is it not? Some sort of blight, as I understand it. Most unfortunate."

The Guild had told Za nothing about this. The Winnarans, it seemed, were extremely well-informed.

Caught, it was the Letnev's turn to glare. On the Yssaril's forearm, her motion detector pinged gently. It was a tiny thing,

Twilight Imperium

unseen by outside eyes, but its message was clear: Commander Viesniel had soldiers everywhere, and several squads were now incoming. Za considered moving, but this exchange was critical, and she dared not miss any of it.

If movements were being made toward Mecatol, then the Yssaril needed to make plans of their own.

In a voice as bleak as the ice-cold chamber, the Letnev said, "Explain."

Sheceh could barely contain his smirk. "We know you can't feed your people–"

"My people are not weaklings–"

"Your military cannot march on an empty belly, commander." The Winnaran's tone cut, every bit as hard as the Letnev's. He was winning and he knew it. "We welcome your strength and support, of course, but you will follow our lead. And you will leave our cousins to us."

His chill skin darkening further, the commander snapped an order, and his surrounding guards raised their rifles. The ambassador's own guards instantly reacted, clenching their fists and rising to their toes. Disarmed or not, they looked more than ready to fight.

This exchange was going to the swamps, and soon.

"Please, commander," Sheceh said, lifting one eyebrow at the Letnev grunts. "Threatening an ambassador is unwise, and these negotiations are only just beginning. We have so much that we can offer you." He dangled it like a hunting lure, and Za almost grinned, enjoying his play. "I understand that you have quarters prepared – we are happy to retire while you discuss the matter. And if I were you–" his smile was all grace "–I would ensure that we retire in safety. After all, I would hate to think of my people's reaction, were I to have an *accident*."

A spasm of fury crossed the Letnev's face, but he waved his soldiers back. Outside, the shifting blips paused.

Za's heart was drumming now, though she stayed absolutely still. She'd graduated top of her class in espionage, infiltration, and information retrieval, and she understood all too clearly: it would be very easy for Viesniel to blame the ambassador's death upon the ice-cold environment, or upon some trigger-happy soldier who could be publicly reprimanded, and the matter then closed.

Was that what had happened to Tek Saath, the previous Yssaril? It seemed all too possible.

Haughty in victory, Sheceh had turned his back, and was gesturing at his retinue. As he swept from the room, his guards and aides all following him with their heads held likewise high, Za considered her options. It was obvious to her that each side thought themselves superior, and she still wasn't quite sure who'd played the winning hand. Sheceh's information was good, but this was Viesniel's world, and he had many assets.

She needed to know more. And not only that, she *wanted* to know more. She wanted to unravel what was really going on.

Outside the chamber, the motion dots were shifting. She briefly considered Viesniel, the commander still standing there with his red-tinged white hair and his austere expression, then made a snap decision and slipped out, after the Winnarans.

Her Guild would expect answers, and there was still a great deal to be uncovered.

"I knew the Barony would be difficult, but this…!"

Behind closed doors, Sheceh Del Sabir had lost his ambassadorial reserve. In here, the light was brighter, warm and yellow, though it showed the same, cold metal surroundings, their stark walls frosted by climbing ice. There was a selection of hard, metal chairs, and some narrow beds that folded down from the wall – the entire Winnaran retinue, elegant and wealthy, looked as utterly out of place as Za felt.

Sheceh himself paced the tight chamber, his boots hard on the floor. Despite how closely she'd had to follow them, they still had not seen her.

In a quieter voice, he said, "Nida, I want every corner of these quarters checked. They will be watching, find out how. Nemati, check the… *food*… they offered us." The word was pure scorn. "I have no wish to turn blue in the face and start frothing."

Aides scuttled. Currently over Za's head, a chill table offered metal bowls, none of them warm, and water. Down the opposite wall, the room's only décor was a line of steel-framed pictures, every one a stony-faced Letnev general. Other than herself and the Winnarans, there was nothing *living* in this entire place, nothing breathing or shifting or alive. No free-growing plants like the ones that climbed the walls of her home, or that wove to make furniture, the sunlight dappling through their leaves. No birds and insects bringing color and sound. This whole place felt like its metal furnishings: dead, hard-edged, and cruel.

Catching herself, Za realized she was homesick, and almost rolled her eyes. She may be new at this, but her grades were still excellent – how absolutely unprofessional.

Though, she thought, as the aide clattered through the bowls above her head, one thing about the absence of greenery, there were a lot less places to conceal things.

And that made some jobs just too easy.

"They will betray us in a moment." Sheceh was still talking softly, watching another aide as he lifted the pictures, one at a time. "Our offer of food is good, but they show little understanding of how to negotiate – everything is a confrontation to them, a show of force.

"Caution, Ambassador." The senior aide, her earrings and necklaces barely less elaborate than Sheceh's own, extended a hand. "They respect strength, we know this. Their aggression was anticipated, and we are also here to learn. Whether we agree these 'terms' or not, our own plans will still go ahead–"

"We do not discuss this until we are secure–"

"And we must glean everything we can." Her tone was gentle, but insistent. "Our knowledge of their food crisis is critical intelligence, and it will give us the upper hand, in the end. You know what our briefing said…"

"That they need us more than we need them. Always the best place to start a negotiation." Sheceh twitched a smile, then rolled his eyes in a surprisingly relatable gesture. "Though if Viesniel manages to understand that…" He tailed off, eyeing one of the paintings and the upright, elderly Letnev woman within.

"Clear." The aides, completing their respective checks, stood back.

In fact, they'd missed a couple of the more discreet surveillance devices, cunningly hidden in the corners of the ceiling, but Za was still enjoying the game, and said nothing.

"What could even grow on this ghastly world?" the ambassador grumbled, faintly childishly. "Other than ambition? Yes, yes, I know." He waved the senior aide to silence. "The crisis is worse than usual, which is why we've come *now*. But–" and he spun to face his people, dramatic and well-timed "–we have to play this carefully. From this initial contact, certainly, it seems that they'd rather starve than capitulate. They– Hush!"

He held up a sudden hand, gesturing for silence.

The noise had been tiny, but both Za and Sheceh had caught

it. Za crouched even smaller, her senses alert, her hand on her belt-blade. Sheceh turned his head, listening,

"Ambassador?" No fool, the senior aide had put her back to a wall. "What's wrong?"

Thanks to her motion sensor, Za saw it first: the very last picture in the row, the farthest from Sheceh himself, was rattling gently in its place. And even as the Winnarans were turning to the noise, that piece of the wall was moving, picture and all, sliding inward and backward, and out of the way.

Sneaky. Even the Yssaril had missed that one.

For the briefest moment, she wondered if she should warn them, but the Winnarans were observant. Even as the wall came fully open, revealing absolute darkness beyond, the guards were in motion, both of them surging forward.

"Get back! Get out of the way!" They still had no weapons, but their stances were alert and combative. Shoving Sheceh almost to the floor, they looked fully ready to fight.

Za pulled back further beneath the table, as far as she could while keeping her sight-lines clear. The game, it seemed, had completely changed, and she needed to know what would happen next.

From the darkness, six masked figures erupted into the chamber. They were identical to Viesniel's guards – clad in standard, Letnev black – but they carried no rifles.

And why would they be unarmed, she wondered. Perhaps this space was just too small? Or perhaps this was just some kind of threat?

Checking her motion detector, she saw no other movement, though the wall had stayed open. If she wanted to, she could flee, but this was just too fascinating, too pertinent. The room was in uproar, and she had to know what the Letnev really wanted.

Weaponless, the Winnaran guards were using a graceful hand-to-hand combat style to tackle the first two assailants – they looked almost like they were dancing, but the effectiveness was clear. For the first few moments, it seemed like they would have the upper hand, then one of them fell, his hands to the slash across his belly.

Za blinked, startled by bloodshed – the play had turned suddenly lethal, and her heart thumped hard in her throat. The room seethed with motion, and it was difficult to see clearly through the struggling bodies – they were all so damned *big*. The female aide was at the far side of the space, frantically yanking open the main door and trying to shove Sheceh out through it. But Sheceh, doing his best to preserve his ambassadorial dignity, was calling, "Mahya! Mahya!"

The Yssaril guessed it was the name of the fallen guard – a point in the man's favor that he genuinely seemed to care. The second guard was still fighting, but the room was too crowded and the Letnev were all around him. Even as Za watched, he also went over, his hands to his chest.

This was the Letnev play? Assassination?

"Move!" the senior aide bawled at the ambassador. She threw him something – a swathe of black, a cloak or a blanket. "Go on! We'll find you!"

Sheceh shot her a tortured look. "I can't just leave you!"

Again, she bawled at him, "Go!"

Za shifted, her pulse roaring, still trying to understand. Her motion detector was picking up more dots, incoming on the main door. The Letnev seemed to be everywhere, and now the senior aide went over, her hands to her throat and her expression surprised. Sheceh gave a great cry. He was shouting names, panicked, looking frantically this way and that. One of the other aides, a burly figure with a much smaller headdress, threw himself bodily at the masked Letnev, sending them tumbling.

"*GO!*" he repeated.

With a final, pained look, the ambassador grabbed the cloak and ran. He was surprisingly fast on his feet.

"Stop him!" The Letnev guards were scrambling upright; they'd be after him in a moment.

Za eyed the room, holding down a sense of rising urgency and swiftly measuring her options. The soldiers were brutal, and the aides had no hope of facing them. As the last Winnaran went over, five of the guards were out of the door, chasing after Sheceh.

The sixth, the officer by the pips on his shoulders, did not follow. Now alone, he paused to eye the chamber. As the Yssaril watched, caught in her spot as if mesmerized, he offered a tight curse, and spoke into his comms, "Operation Inculpate is go – but we do not have the primary target. I repeat, we do not have the primary target. Target is loose in sector five-point-zero-six. Retrieval is first priority."

Inculpate?

She knew what the word meant, and its allusions were chilling. She paused, just for a moment, teetering on the edge of a choice. This incident was rapidly spiraling, and it was outside her mission remit.

The Guild would still need to know everything.

Leaving neither draft nor whisper, she went out, and after the ambassador.

Outside the Winnarans' compound, the great, walled city of Feruc was grim, its atmosphere sealed from the airless rock outside. Arc Prime, the home planet of the Letnev, was a sunless world, renegade and wandering, and seeming as harsh as its people. Roadways and corners were small and tight, and a black, mesh roof hung low. Tall metal streetlights stood in regulation rows, but the illumination they offered was red-tinged and poor. It might help Za's stealth, but she would have given her blade for a real, rich sunset, for the comforting, amphibian croaking as the Nianni dusk settled in.

Letnev people scurried past her, men and women all white-haired and apparently uneasy... she wasn't even quite sure why. Were they that upset at being on the surface? Certainly, Arc Prime was mined with tens of thousands of miles of tunnels, and with a single vast city, where the population usually lived. Why would its people choose Feruc, if they disliked it so much? What was up here that coaxed them to the surface?

Za didn't know, but gathering information was more crucial than ever.

An "accident".

Operation Inculpate.

Her initial conclusions were obvious, and ugly. If the Letnev succeeded in catching Sheceh, they would surely kill him. And, whomever they blamed, an incident of galactic proportions would unfold. Diplomatic strife, unrest, even war.

But... she was missing something. Letnev efficiency was legendary – what would they gain from Sheceh's death? What advancement or leverage? How would they use the incident to their own advantage?

Her questions brought more urgency, and she picked up speed. Ahead of her, the ambassador was just in sight: a flapping black cloak, shifting with surprising swiftness. He was sharp and quick, smart enough to keep his hood up, concealing his face from guards and electronics alike. The cloaks seemed popular –

many of the Letnev wore them – yet still, he was easy to follow. Za could track him simply by the way he moved, crouched and half-running.

She took a corner, then another, shadowing him flawlessly. The parameters of her initial mission had completely shifted, now – she wasn't just playing anymore, and her edge of alertness was keen. This was pacts and politics, move and countermove, death and assassination. She would need to offer the Guild a complete report, an explanation of everything being leveraged by both sides, and of what this may mean to the Yssaril people...

Hide-and-seek, not physically, but politically. The former was a popular Guild training game, honing abilities of both stealth and awareness. The latter was far more dangerous...

Though, some things, she thought, were the same the galaxy over.

Alone in the freezing cold, Winnaran Ambassador Sheceh Del Sabir was in a monumentally filthy mood. He had no idea where he was. He'd lost his communicator, his retinue, his guards and his friends – nearly his neck – and his teeth were chattering loud enough to give him a headache. His mission was already a disaster, and the grunts on his trail knew these grim, claustrophobic streets far better than he did. He was wrapped tight in the big black cloak, ducking down the smallest alleyways he could find, narrow gulleys between black metal walls, every last one marked with its correct designation.

Damn these Letnev and their bureaucratic thinking!

Sheceh's people understood administration. In times past, they'd performed such roles for the Lazax themselves, helping hold the empire together. But, on Winnu, they remembered more than just empty bureaucracy – the Winnaran world was a place of polished stone and pillared porticoes, of carved fountains and open gardens, of art and color and music and theatre, of tales of the splendors of the galaxy. Tales that celebrated both history and wonder, and the glories of Mecatol Rex.

Ah, Mecatol! Ah, for the lost age of gold!

But this was not Mecatol, nor was it Winnu. It was Arc Prime, and here, in this lost and rootless darkness, such tales had no soil in which to grow. Even the air was fake, generated by some cursed tunnel lichen. The barrenness of the Letnev people, he thought, extended far beyond their lack of art and philosophy, of composition and entertainment – it extended even to their character.

Character, indeed! With an unseen grimace, Sheceh caught the thought. When the Letnev had sent the invitation to "explore" Mecatol – a necessary artifice understood by both sides, and a prelude to its potential acquisition – Sheceh's instruction had been clear. He was to answer the invitation, and to ensure Winnaran control by weaponizing the Barony's food shortage. But his briefing had underestimated the sheer, cold practicality of the Letnev people. Viesniel, it seemed, respected only power, and he would show no weakness, no vulnerability. Sheceh honestly now believed that he would rather starve than submit. And, even had the exploration gone ahead, Viesniel would surely have just looked to exploit his Winnaran allies…

How foolish, he thought. What could one learn from just… constant confrontation? He sighed, his breath pluming in the cold. The Letnev had assaulted him. He was lost, abandoned, and bereft. The thought of his aides brought a stinging to his eyes, and he blinked. He would not dishonor their lives, or Winnu itself, by perishing out here – but still, he had no idea what he was supposed to do next. He could circle back and try to help them, but he was one against a city. He could call for help, but his senior aide had held the comms device, and there was not even a Winnaran ship in close orbit as the Barony would not permit it. He was absolutely alone, and his survival was likely to be measured in... he snorted. However one measured time in this grim and sunless void.

The sudden thought that he would never return home, never see his family again – as much as his failure, and the loss of his people – it tugged at his heart. He had to keep this tale alive!

Another corner, and he hesitated. He was right in the outermost streets, now, close to the open, airless surface of Arc Prime, and in places that the agoraphobic Letnev rarely walked. Ahead of him, there waited a tiny... what could he call it? Plaza, square? A regulation box between regulation walls, all fenced in wire mesh. The Barony's black-and-silver flag hung from a pole at the center. It stirred faintly, showing its red circle – an emblem like the planet itself, or like some glaring, watchful eye.

Its lanyard rattled icy against the pole, and he stood there, considering his next move. He must try to get back to the compound, find out if any of his people yet lived. Retrieve the comms device, if he could. But the place would surely be watched...

Scatters of locals were scurrying about, their heads down. Military boots hammered past the entrance, and they scattered, vanishing though dark maws of doorways. Huddled in the cloak, Sheceh felt the claws of complete despair. He'd been so sure of himself, looking down his nose at the tedious, cultureless Viesniel...

He was just wondering what to do next when the air in front of him shimmered.

And the game changed completely.

Dropping her cover was a calculated risk, Za was aware of that.

But the Winnaran ambassador was smart. He'd wielded both tactic and information. He'd posed enough of a threat for Viesniel to move against him. And besides, he had something that Za needed, that the Guild needed.

Information.

So, with a final check for any electronic spying, she let the light-refracting shimmer of her skin fade.

Sheceh, his hood still up and his face in mostly shadow, gaped. He had no weapons, and he stepped back, glancing to and fro as if to gather his wits and flee.

"I'm not a threat," she told him quickly. "I want to talk to you."

Sheceh was still staring. Typical of her people, Za was small and agile, her yellow eyes wide, her skin – in its natural state – the same green as the Nianni swamp. Despite the cold, she wore little, and her blade and tools were obvious at her belt. Extending one hand, she said, "I know somewhere you can hide."

"Where did you…?" Taller than Za by almost a foot, the Winnaran was still gawking. "Where did you come from?"

"The Myock system, it's a long story. I'm here looking for my…" she picked her word with care "…friend. And I need your help." She didn't elaborate; her play opened with her getting him on her side.

"I've never seen an Yssaril…" Sheceh must have realized the irony of the statement, because his expression immediately congealed. He pulled himself back to his full height, lifted his chin. "I can survive without your help, thank you–"

"You're welcome to try." She pushed him, calling his bluff.

More boots, perfectly timed. As unalike as they were, both

Yssaril and Winnaran started. Za's skin flickered in her reflexive "hide" reaction, while Sheceh pulled further into his cloak.

They had more in common than either of them realized, Za thought, to her own faint surprise. The moment of empathy was telling, making her reassess this strange man, his wealth and his gemstones, and his badly battered hauteur.

But she was getting ahead of herself.

"You've done well," she told him. "Very well, to get this far." She offered the compliment freely, tempting his trust. "But you won't evade the soldiers much longer."

Slightly bitterly, Sheceh answered, "This cloak is Letnev design. They live in caverns, and they don't like the surface. These are popular in Feruc, shielding them from the air and the *light*." He curled his lip at the word – there was little light on Arc Prime. "They were a 'gift' when we arrived. In return for disarming us, and for some singularly undignified searches."

"It won't save you," Za said, bluntly. She blinked at the streetlamps, their dim red glittering on the frost-cold metal – it was oddly beautiful. "I can keep you safe. But I'll need something in exchange."

Sheceh snorted and shook out the cloak, revealing the now-disheveled state of his jacket and jewelry. He said, "After you. I think. Tell me why the Yssaril are here."

"I'm not 'the Yssaril'. I'm just Za." A lie, but a necessary one. "And I've just told you, I'm looking for someone. Finding you was an accident." She grinned at him, her teeth sharp.

But Sheceh wasn't cowed. "Right. And *how* long have you been following me?"

"Long enough," Za told him. "Long enough to know that you're up to your neck in swamp-water, and you're sinking. Now are we going to play pit-a-pat, or are you going to trust me?

Because, right at this moment, nether time nor Commander Viesniel are on your side." She held his gaze, his eyes dark. "I *can* hide you. But you'll need to do some explaining."

"And what's in this for you, exactly?"

Za said nothing, merely let her grin widen.

Sheceh held her gaze, trying to stare her down. "Let me put it like this." More boots, closer this time. "I think we're in this... swamp-water... together. Not even you can hide from the Barony forever."

More boots, almost on top of them. Systematic sweeps, back and forth until the commander located the escapee.

"Viesniel. Is going. To kill you," Za told him, spelling it out. "And, when he does, the game will be over. Now, are we going to get our butts off the street, or are you going to dither?"

"And why should I trust you, exactly?"

"Because I know what happened to your *people*." She suspected they were all dead, but if his concern for them had been genuine, then the ploy was a winner. To back it up, she let her skin-colors flicker, partially hiding her from view. "Your choice. Five... four... three..."

"All right," Sheceh said. He spread his hands, his rings glinting. "Have it your way. If you can find my people for me, help them..."

Za let herself come back to full visibility, nodding. "Truce." She studied him, searching for the lies, but did not know his race well enough to detect his tell. "I know the pattern of the Letnev security devices – they're distressingly regimented – and I can get us past them, and safe." Her grin hadn't faded. "You just have to follow me."

"Truce," the Winnu agreed. He extended his hand, some sort of greeting or gesture, but she didn't take it. A simple touch could conceal too many dangers.

After a moment, he withdrew it again.

Za chuckled, faintly enjoying his unease.

"Let's go," she said.

And together, they vanished into Feruc's outer streets.

It took a conscious effort for Za to remain visible – her Yssaril stealth-instincts were just too strong, and she felt exposed and uneasy.

But there were few guards out here and even less light. The darkness, cold as it was, was oddly reassuring, and she had observation-tech in her blink-in contact lenses that allowed her to see in both infrared and ultraviolet – though the former was mostly defeated by the chill. Sheceh, however, seemed to be struggling to find his footing, one hand gripping the cloak, the other extended before him.

He seemed angry. It was hard to tell properly since his face was covered, but he was muttering to himself, like some promise of retribution. He was angry about his retinue, Za reasoned. She, like all Yssaril, worked better alone, but a Winnaran? She didn't know. Maybe they were his family, or he'd known them a long time.

At last, they came to the very outermost limit of the city, and a tiny, black-walled alleyway that was all but deserted. The bleak, metal-mesh roof sloped downward here, meeting the ice-cold city wall in a long and welded angle that curved far away to either side. The alley was a dead-end, and the wall displayed a multitude of warnings. It offered the flickering lights of security screens – double layers and vacuum insulations, diagnostics and safety measures.

And, in defiance of all Letnev efficiency, it also showed signs of corrosion. Gently, Sheceh touched at a patch of rust, careful not to freeze his skin to the metal.

"You'd think they'd take better care," he said, thoughtfully. "This wall is their life."

"They fear it," Za told him. "They monitor it constantly, but from their bureaucratic offices in the city's center. This is not a place that Letnev wish to come. Well, most of them."

Sheceh eyed her, half-challenge and half-question.

"I've been out here, watching, almost since I arrived." Za offered her explanation openly, and without lies. "Parts of the city's limits work as penal colonies, of sorts. The Barony wastes little, and it sends its minor Letnev offenders out here to work. They maintain the walls, among other things. It avoids an unnecessary mess of castigated bodies, and, if needed, the workers can be recalled. Thrown into the front lines of some other difficult task. Do you comprehend the term 'fodder'?"

Sheceh gave a soft snort, both cynical and comprehending. "With a serendipity that's almost ironic," he said, though he didn't offer to explain. "Why waste good bodies, when you may need them for the front line of your next *war*." His gold eyes flashed. "My people have a more elegant system. We call it 'acclimation'. Any offender so reproved may yet earn their way back to a valued position, if they are both diligent and contrite." He sniffed, an echo of his previous austerity. "We are rather more... civilized... after all."

"We use such offenders for games." Za didn't elaborate – those games could be deadly, but they had to practice on something. And anyone who showed their competence might gain their own place at the Guild.

Sheceh said, "Perhaps you would tell me more of your people, Yssaril? I would be curious to learn."

"I've told you, my name is Za," she said. "Za Nuk."

"Sheceh Del Sabir," the ambassador returned, with a graceful half-bow. "But I'm thinking you probably know that. Shall we?" Offering a theatrical gesture, he asked her to lead on.

Checking the cameras, Za ducked sideways, toward the very last of the buildings. There were bots here, things on tracks that stood at the wallside, or that trundled from place to place, examining the rust and repairing the mesh. Her plume of breath could give her away, but they showed no interest in anything outside their programming, and there still was little evidence of a military presence. Despite the punitive nature of the area, she'd learned it had mostly been left to administer itself.

A test of strength, perhaps? Or just a useful training ground, weeding out the weak? Either would have its advantages.

They passed another bot, bigger than the rest, studying one of the screens. Beside it, there was a tiny gap in the final building, covered by a peeled-up section of wire-mesh fence. It was tight for Za, almost too small for Sheceh, who swore and tore his cloak. But beyond it…

"By the empire!" Squiggling free in a manner that cost much of his dignity, Sheceh stopped dead, and carefully put his hood back, staring. "I had absolutely no idea…" His voice was soft, pluming with the cold. "The Letnev *permit* this? It seems unlikely–"

"How do you think I got on-world?" Za told him, unable to contain her grin.

"And not just you, I suspect." Sheceh's note of thoughtful hope was tangible. "How has the Baron not shut this down?"

Za chuckled, saying nothing.

Because there, just *there* ahead of them and at the very edge of the great city, the metal roof bulged outward and upward into a sizeable dome, topped in unmistakable airlock doors. A long, curving set of black steps led down to a matching circular depression in the stone, and to a ring of lights that were completely familiar to both races.

A landing pad. Only a small one, but a landing pad nonetheless. A series of ships sat around its edges, not all of them of Letnev design.

Sheceh swore again.

With her IR lenses flicked in, Za could just about make out bustling, black-clad figures working, almost invisible against the rock. How they avoided accidents, she had no idea – but that didn't matter, right now.

"Are they smugglers?" Apparently, Sheceh was still struggling to understand. "Traders? The Baron would surely exterminate every last–"

"Or he would use them," Za said. "Even the Letnev must have spies, have ships and shipments that they need to move off-world without being tracked." She didn't know this for a fact, but it made total sense to her, and her grin broadened. "The Yssaril excel at games, Ambassador. We understand how they work, moves within moves, aims and counterploys. And this is a perfect way to keep your own hands concealed."

"Complete deniability," Sheceh said. "And absolutely efficient." He shook his head, almost admiring. "And, as any Winnaran will tell you, an outcast population, cut off from its homeworld, will make a society of its own."

"I understand that," Za said, thoughtfully. "Though I honestly couldn't tell if these locals really are Barony-controlled, or if they're genuinely rebellious, if their smuggling is under Arc Prime's detection. Maybe they're bribing the guards, or they *think* they're bribing the guards..." She tailed off, chuckling again. "But, whatever the truth of it, this is where I arrived, and it's where I've been lurking, almost ever since. I was following the trail of my friend when I stumbled upon you." Her big yellow eyes held the gaze of the Winnaran – he was so strange, and yet so lost. "Do you have a ship, anywhere close?"

"The Baron wouldn't let it remain in orbit, but it's close enough." He frowned. "Though my only comms device is still back at the compound."

"Then that," Za said, "would look like the best place to start."

The plan was a good one – simple, as all the best plans are.

Za had taken Sheceh to a tiny square room – one of several hidden places that she'd picked for her own use. There was nothing in there that he could use as leverage against herself or her people, and it got him off the streets and out of potential trouble. The room itself was out the back of a local drinking establishment – a place of surprising noise and vivacity. The local Letnev liked a cold, clear spirit that smelled of nothing so much as fuel. They drank it in copious amounts, but rarely disintegrated into fighting or random aggression. To Sheceh's obvious surprise, they sang – songs of great space battles, of starships and heroic captains. They pounded mugs on metal tables with a raw, military enthusiasm that Za rather liked.

The bar was also one of the very few places she'd seen non-Letnev faces, though only a couple – Hacan traders with their great manes, a lone Sol female, passed out in a corner. The Yssaril had crept close enough to understand that these were smugglers, uninterested in anything but their profits. They had no significant bearing on the Letnev people – or on the Yssaril, for that matter – and they would only distract her from her mission. And besides, their presence had told her that she could trust the bar's Letnev owner to keep his mouth shut.

"I need to know about my aides, my guards," Sheceh reminded

Za once the door was closed. "They saved my life. If any of them survived…" His flicker of pain was genuine, and Za nodded.

"I'll find them." It wasn't exactly a lie – she'd find them if they were living or dead – but she didn't explain more fully. She needed Sheceh's intel and didn't want to upset him.

"And bring me the comms device," he said. "If you can do that, I'll help you find your friend."

"The word is 'please.'" Za chuckled at his expression. "I'll get the device, Ambassador," she said. "But I'm not handing it over until you tell me what all this is about. Why you're… ah… *exploring* Mecatol."

"Viesniel sent my people the invitation." Sheceh had opened out his cloak and was checking his earrings and headdress, trying to reassemble his dignity. "At least, that was how it started. Then he got *nasty.*"

"But why?" Za said, pressing him. "Why go to all the trouble of getting you out here, just to slit your throat? What does he get out of it? It doesn't make any sense to me."

"I out-maneuvered him," the Winnaran answered, faintly haughtily. "And he got angry. He knew I had the upper hand, and he–"

"I don't think so," Za cut him off, ignoring his slightly huffy expression. "I think there's something else going on here. Something deeper, something we still don't know." She was thinking as she spoke, trying to put it together. "Viesniel *attacked* you, Ambassador. I don't think he got you out here to explore Mecatol, I think he got you out here to assassinate you. To start–" she gestured, as if searching for the explanation "– whatever it is he wants to start."

"Then why didn't he just shoot me?" Sheceh fired back, his tone still edged.

Za gave a tight sigh and frowned. "I don't know."

They fell silent, listening to the mugs, still thumping in the bar. After a moment, the ambassador sniffed, lifting his chin in that gesture that Za was beginning to recognize. "Perhaps," he said. "When you return to the compound, you can find out more about this so-cunning plan? You're the *expert*, after all."

"Yeah." Za wagged a finger at his sarcasm. "Perhaps I can. And perhaps *you'd* better stay put. Those Hacan aren't going to take you off-world, no matter how much you pay them." She grinned. "Not that you *can* pay them, of course. Though they might take Winnaran jewelry."

The Winnaran sniffed. "We don't part with our marks of rank."

"Right." Za chuckled. Sheceh glared, and she chuckled some more. "I mean it, Ambassador," she said. "Whatever this really is, it's big. You stay put, and you stay sober. No going drinking with the lads. And if the bar is compromised, I'll meet you back at the landing pad – in the tight gap we found, behind the fence. Whatever happens, they mustn't catch you."

"They won't," Sheceh said. "Believe me, I like my skin intact. How long will you be?"

"I have no idea. The compound will be crawling with guards, and I'll have to be very careful. Even Yssaril–" She stopped herself, but Sheceh was too sharp.

"Even you get caught sometimes?"

"Just keep it low, OK? Lock the door behind me, and I'll be back with all the information I can find, and with your comms device. Now, what does it look like?"

He told her, describing something that seemed more like a piece of ornamentation than anything electronic, but she nodded. Carefully cracking open the door, she peered around its edge.

Fuel smells wafted from beyond.

"And remember," she said, "I'm not handing it over until you tell me absolutely everything. Until we work out what's really going on. Now, stay *put*."

As invisible as only an Yssaril could be, she crept across the bar and back out to the red-lit streets.

Outside, it was still freezing, more bitter than ever. Za's body was telling her that it was deep night, but Feruc was both unchanging and unsettling. Arc Prime not only lacked sun, it lacked weather, seasons, any kind of normal timekeeping. And she was tired, not only physically, but mentally, worn down by this changeless, wandering cold.

Reminding herself that she could not indulge such things, she eased onward. She'd done this once already, a couple of days before, following the faded marks that Saath had left – marks that only another Yssaril would see or understand. Each one was a tiny message, info or direction or both. She'd never met Saath, though she knew of him from the Guild – and, whatever else was going on, she must not forget her original mission. She needed to find out, for certain, what had happened to him.

More boots, the same running, stamping rhythm. She waited, trusting to her skin-shimmer and watching the soldiers as they pounded past. They weren't kicking in doors, but they were armed and masked, and it was surely only a matter of time. They were also deploying screens, small and magnetic things that flashed warnings, offering promotions and rewards to anyone with information on the missing ambassador. Enemies of the state were involved, they said.

Enemies of the what?

The manipulations were growing more complex. Za had momentarily considered just blowing the Winnaran's cover – letting the Letnev find and assassinate him. This would put their plan into motion, and she could wait and watch, take the real truth back to her Guild. But now, things had changed again. There may or may not be another layer to this, encircling even another race, in this "exploration" of Mecatol. What in the swamps was going on?

A flush of adrenaline made her shiver. Despite the piling questions, Yssaril *liked* risk; it was an integral part of everything they were trained to do. It kept them sharp. Concealed, alert, aware. And she was good – she was *better* than good. She understood how hide-and-seek worked, and she rather enjoyed testing her abilities to their limit...

Don't get smart, she reminded herself. That was how you made mistakes.

Soon, she was closing once more on Feruc's heart. Here, she flitted past endless military and bureaucratic buildings, every one numbered and regimented, in perfect form and sequence. Some had windows, glittering scarlet in the streetlights, while others had balconies, hung with a plethora of flags. Like the shining frost, the sheer organization had a peculiar beauty of its own.

And there: on a corner, the Winnaran quarters. The compound was square and plain, no windows in this one. Its grounds were gray stone, demarked by a severe, spike-topped metal fence and bisected by a straight, gravel pathway, a line of red lights to either side. The door – the same one through which both she and Sheceh had left – was open, but flanked by two masked figures, rifles in hands. Reaching the outer edge, she stopped, her head cocked, as still and silent as ever. A single statue towered over her, one knee raised and his stone blade half drawn, as if going into combat.

He looked like a guardian, some kind of assessor. And this felt like a test, one any Yssaril would be proud to face. Even she would have trouble getting in there.

But the greatest stealth lesson was patience. Watch, her Guild tutors had told her. Wait, learn. Targets have patterns, and if you sit for long enough, you will know how to exploit them.

Hoping that Sheceh would stay where he was, Za settled down to observe.

Viesniel's officials, it seemed, liked their regularity.

As well as the grunts on the compound door that Za saw, there was a patrol, four of them, marching around the building every five-and-a-half minutes. Muttering administrators were gathering by the moment, each carrying a handheld screen and a reel of some kind of tape. Occasionally, they stopped to speak to each other, shaking their heads in apparent and mutual disapproval. She thought about starting a distraction – causing a ruckus somewhere else and sending them running – but they seemed to be restless, waiting for something.

Or someone.

She was just double-checking her motion detector, when she saw the answer: Viesniel himself, incoming at speed, and straight past where she crouched. His polished boots crunched on the gravel, and an upright officer walked at his shoulder. Both door guards snapped to attention, but his movements were determined, and he paid them absolutely no heed.

The guards' masks twitched. For a second, they looked at each other, though Za couldn't see their expressions. Blips on her arm told her that the patrol was on the far side of the building, and the administrators had stopped in a tense huddle, eyeing where the commander had gone.

Fast and absolutely silent, Za shot out after him, using him as the perfect distraction and following him into the compound – he was up to something, and she needed to know what. Her skin shifted with the gray and black of stone and metal, the occasional flashes of red from the pathway lights. A moment later, she was back in the Winnaran quarters.

The door guards hadn't even flinched.

In the small room, Sheceh's retinue were still lying where they'd fallen, their untouched food on the table. The tableau was grim, and in its center, Viesniel stood like the statue, casting an evaluating look at the scene. He gave a single, cursory nod, flicked a gesture at the officer.

"Keep them out, for now. I've secured the final approval – the operation will go ahead, even without Sheceh's body. Let's just get this done."

"Sir."

"You will still need to find him."

"Sir. We're still looking, Sir."

"Then look harder. Go guard the door."

The officer headed out, and Viesniel finished his apparent analysis. Then, from under his jacket, he produced a long, wrapped shape. Carefully, he laid it down on the table, unfolding black fabric – same stuff as the cloak, Za thought. Crouched in the corner, she strained to see.

And then had to stop herself from swearing.

There, within the dark folds and completely unmistakable, was an Yssaril shame-blade. They were unique to her people, anointed with swamp plant sap and reptile venom – no Yssaril professional would ever be parted from their own. And it answered one question immediately – what had happened to Saath. Viesniel must have caught and executed him; it was the only way that the Letnev commander would have it.

A flare of rage went through her. And, with the suddenness of a knife in the back, she knew exactly what the Letnev were doing.

Inculpate.

Her pulse was pounding, now, almost loud enough to give her away. She craned to see clearly. She had to be careful, she could not permit herself to also get caught, but if her suspicions were correct...

By the swamp! The Guild had to know!

"And this," Viesniel said, very softly, "is what any race will get for moving against the Baron." He lifted it, letting it glint in the dim light. "Be they spy and assassin, or schemer and manipulator. I will not be exploited, not by the Yssaril, not by the Winnarans. And not by anyone else!"

Absolutely silent, Za eased closer, her breath knotting in her chest, her mind putting the picture together. A Winnaran ambassador, murdered by the Yssaril people, while stationed on this Letnev world. The Winnarans would demand restitution, and the Guild would refuse to pay. The Barony could back either side, prompting them to war, or just stand back and play diplomat and gain...

Gain *food.*

Oh, of course!

With a flash of clarity that almost made her smack her forehead, the full scale of Viesniel's plan heaved into view. Whatever happened from here, the Barony would win. If they backed either side, or if they played negotiator, they could ask to get paid in food. In Retillion's menn root – plentiful for her people, but a galactic delicacy – or in whatever foodstuffs Sheceh had been going to offer. And the invitation to Sheceh himself... Viesniel must have played this, right from the beginning. He must have caught Saath and then planned the whole thing.

Did the Letnev even *have* a food shortage? Any more than usual? Or had the information been just a placed lure?

Za's thoughts passed her in a flash, and some part of her really wanted to end the commander's plotting, right here and right now. She laid a hand on her blade – it would be so easy – but that would be folly and she knew it. The last thing this mess needed was a real Yssaril assassination to add to the fake one.

Holding her temper, she waited.

But Viesniel merely stood, at the center of plot and devastation, exultant in his victory. "A test of the fittest," he said, still softly. "A test I have won. We are the strongest race in the galaxy, and Mecatol belongs to *us*."

Kneeling almost ritualistically, he placed Saath's blade on the floor, next to where the senior aide had fallen, her throat opened wide. He stayed there for a moment, looking into her face, placed a hand almost gently on her cheek. "Where is your master, I wonder?" he said. "He will not evade us for long."

And there, beside the gesture – a glint of gemstone. With typical Winnaran glamour, it looked like no more than an earring, but it matched the description of the ambassador's device.

Got you, Za thought.

She grinned, but her expression was brief and tight, and she did not move. Rising to his feet, Viesniel stamped from the room, barking orders at guards and administrators, and Za took her chance. Her heartrate still roaring, she grabbed both blade and device and ran for the doorway, crouching as small as she could make herself as Letnev boots came past her.

Would they see her? If they found an Yssaril on-site, the blade actually in their hand, then this would explode worse than ever. She held her breath and closed her eyes, and thought of Nianni and home.

Viesniel said, "As you can see, the evidence speaks for itse…"

His shock was loud as a shout, and every head turned to look at him.

"Sir?"

Opening her eyes, Za checked her motion detector, made sure she knew where everyone was.

And then, she ran faster than she had ever done.

Ambassador Sheceh Del Sabir, contrary to Za's order, was absolutely not staying put.

The tiny room, like everything else, was tight and cold and claustrophobic, and his ongoing sense of helplessness was testing his limited patience. Voices still floated from the bar outside, and the singing and the mug-banging continued, between ribald bouts of laughter. Away from the Letnev military, the people of Arc Prime sounded almost like his own, if a little more crass.

Grumbling, he paced, six steps one ways and six the other. The Yssaril had left him a light, but little else, and he resented being at her mercy. He was Winnaran, for the empire's sake, and he deserved better than this!

And besides, what did that damned Yssaril even want? Why was she helping him? Questions loomed like phantoms, gibbering in his thoughts. She'd obviously been stalking him for some time, so why had she chosen to reveal herself? He knew little of the species other than their love for information and spying. She'd said she was here for her "friend", but that lie was as obvious as a child's. And the more he thought about it, the more jumpy he became. Why *should* he trust her? She was an infiltrator, an assassin, sent by the Guild on Shalloq. Her agenda could be anything.

And then, like an echo of his very thoughts, the word "Yssaril" came clearly from outside.

It caught him like a hook, smarted like a slap across the face. Frozen in place as if the Feruc chill had finally got the better of him, he stayed poised, his breath held, listening for the word to come again. For a long moment, nothing happened and the voices continued to mutter – but just as he was telling himself he'd imagined it, he heard it a second time, its sibilant susurrus creeping through the air like a shiver.

A flare of sudden petulance flowered in his heart. When would this chaos end? He had roles, rank, responsibilities! He was ambassador and emissary, and to treat him like this was unthinkable.

Wrapping the cloak about himself, he moved to the door and unlocked it. Just as Za had done, he cracked it open by an inch and lurked, listening to the bar's noise as it rose and ebbed and flowed.

The singing had stopped, and there was a hum of conversation. The deep rumble of the trader Hacan. A woman's laughter. The metallic crash of a dropped mug and the burst of cheering that followed.

Nothing about any–

"…was an Yssaril!"

The word was too distinctive, sounding almost like a warning. Somewhere close, snippets of gossip were being shared, voices hushed and oddly fearful. They were hard to hear, and he eased the door open further, peering about its edge.

There, just across from him – a table in the nearest corner. Its occupants were young Letnev, but they lacked the severe uniforms. They still wore black, but their garments were rougher, dirty from a day's work. Even in here, several of them wore the familiar, heavy cloak.

One leaned forward, and Sheceh strained his hearing to its limit.

"Viesniel found him, apparently. Right at the scene!"

"Viesniel's a psychopath–"

"But he's not an idiot." A third voice. They were all leaning in now, flashing wary glances round the room. "If he says he found an Yssaril–"

"He didn't actually *find* an Yssaril. Apparently, there was a weapon–"

"So this Yssaril *did* murder them all? Or he didn't?"

The initial speaker shrugged. The military song had started again, boots stamping the time. Reluctant to risk it, but needing to know, Sheceh opened the door still further.

"They said the Yssaril did it. Murdered the whole lot of them." The speaker was a young woman, sharp-faced and cautious. "They said the Yssaril was here to undermine the negotiations, steal information. Sow the seeds of political dissent and terror. Even start a *war!*"

She had a certain flare of theatre that the Winnaran recognized – using drama to add weight and credence to her words. They were all watching her now, captivated, enjoying the conspiracy.

But the speaker had said "he". And while Sheceh didn't know a great deal about the Yssaril species, he was pretty sure that Za was female.

So, what ... ?

Not *Za*, he realized a moment later, kicking himself – her "friend". The one she was looking for. The military song grew louder, and the mugs started again. The noise was distracting, stopping him thinking clearly.

Had there been an Yssaril – another Yssaril – in the compound? Did Za know about all this? Despite the chaos, Sheceh had no doubts that the incoming Letnev had attacked his guards and aides. But if it was the *Yssaril* they blamed, this "friend" of Za's ...

An "accident".

By the empire!

A flush of fear crept into Sheceh's face, an uprush of anger, denial. Whether this "friend" of Za's had been in the room or not, he'd still provided the perfect excuse. Viesniel could eliminate the entire Winnaran contingent and blame the Yssaril government. And it would cause a perfect storm. Just like the woman inside had said: dissent and terror, even war.

Easing back, his heart thumping, Sheceh closed the door almost completely and leaned his pounding forehead against the cold wall. His headdress pressed against his skin, hurting, and after a moment he pulled it off and threw it aside, his dignity with it.

His temper was rising. His mission was a failure, his people likely dead. His only hope was a Yssaril that he couldn't trust as far as he could throw, little as she was. What if she and the other one had been working together all along?

Oh, who was he kidding? Of course they were working together. He should bribe those trader Hacan, after all.

A flash of rage, and he controlled a sudden, powerful urge to punch the wall. Very unseemly. At home, such lapses of decorum were unthinkable – he was losing his wits, in the middle of all this–

A door-slam brought his thoughts to a screeching halt. In the bar, the mug-banging stopped dead. Sheceh stopped with it, holding his breath once more, feeling his pulse roar in his ears. He wanted to look, didn't dare. Whatever had just happened, the locals were as startled by it as he was.

A moment later, a voice rang across the room.

"By order of the Barony, Commander Ludovic Viesniel VI makes the following proclamation." The voice was clearly military, and clearly in control. "The diplomatic emissary of the Winnaran people, Sheceh Del Sabir, had fled the ambassadorial compound and is now at large. He is a newcomer to our world, and to our great city of Feruc, and his life may be in danger. The commander is deeply concerned for his whereabouts. Anyone offering information will be rewarded with suitable promotion. You may even win your freedom, basic housing, and a secure administrative role. You have only to come forward." Absolute silence, a pause that seemed a hundred years long. "Nothing?" A second pause. Sheceh could imagine the drinkers, all looking at their boots. "Very well then. Since you cannot answer me, perhaps you can get back to *work*."

There was a metallic clang, a scuffle, the loud scraping of chairs. The rumble of the Hacan, again. A rattle that was presumably the grille over the bar coming down. The stamp of boots, the front door slamming, opening, slamming, opening. Sheceh stayed where he was, shaking with tension, sick to his belly. Were there steps, coming this way, as the officer searched the premises?

"The commander is deeply concerned for his whereabouts…"

I bet he is, Sheceh thought, snorting. *And it's not to continue the negotiation.*

He counted to a hundred, nausea coiling, but no one came close. When it at last fell silent, he creaked open the door to peek.

The place was deserted, mugs abandoned on the tables, the bar itself closed. In one corner, there was a blinking, official-looking screen, now magnetized to the wall. It flowed with writing, though he couldn't read it from here. The Letnev locals had vanished – presumably back to work, as ordered – and there was absolutely no sign of the off-worlders – the Hacan, or the Sol woman. He and Za had been as quiet as possible, but if anyone in the bar *had* seen them…

He swore, put his headdress back on as if he was arming himself for battle. He had no idea if the landing pad was any safer than here, but it was still his best chance of getting off Arc Prime alive. He owed it to his people, to his family, and to his world.

Enemy or no, he needed to confront that Yssaril.

In the tight semi-dark of the tiny alleyway, Za saw Sheceh waiting.

She'd stopped by the backstreet bar and had found it empty, the now familiar screen on the wall, the grille pulled down. Her room had been unlocked and was as deserted as everything else. She'd quelled a round of alarm before remembering they'd set a contingency.

"My people?" he asked her, as she carefully dropped her cover. He was twitchy, his gold eyes nervous, his headdress askew under his hood. His hands knotted one about the other, as if they itched to hold a weapon.

Za shook her head. "I'm sorry. But we've got a much more serious problem."

Boots were still pounding – the patrols were getting more frequent. Briefly, Sheceh's shoulders rounded, and he placed a hand over his face. In the darkness, his rings glinted faintly red. "They were like family," he said. "I've known them years."

Torn between respect and impatience, Za gave him a moment to compose himself. When he looked back up at her, however, his face was etched in anger.

"Your 'friend'," he said. "Why was he here? Why are *you* here? *Yssaril?*" The word was pure pain, spat between his teeth.

With a shock, she realized: he *knows*. She wasn't sure how, but by some freak chance, he knew what had happened.

Or he was smart enough to guess.

"Saath didn't do anything." She snapped it back at him, defensive and too fast. "He was just recon, nothing else. We only wanted to know about the Letnev. They have a history, you know that–"

"So you *are* your government." Sheceh didn't sound surprised. "Sneaking about, sticking your nose into other people's business–"

"It's how we stay alive," Za told him. "My people were hunted by the Lazax, taken for research, experiments. Yet we turned the waters back on them, and we won our freedom. Now, we stay ahead of the game. And right now, those waters are up to our necks, both of us–"

"Where's the comms device?" Sheceh was glaring. "Did you even get it?"

"I've got it." She made no move to offer it to him. "But I'm not letting you off-world until you give me your full explanation. You were here doing some deal. What was it? Why has Viesniel gone to such lengths to make this mess?"

"I can't divulge that information–"

"You don't have a choice–"

"My people are *dead*–"

"That isn't my problem–"

"How *dare* you?" He was all imperious anger, and his voice was rising. "How can I even trust you? You lied to me about your 'friend'. You confess that your people play 'games'. Are my staff really dead? Did you or your 'friend' help kill them? I asked you before, Yssaril – *what* are you getting out of this?"

Small through she was, Za grabbed the front of the cloak and pulled him down until they were nose-to-nose. Her anger spiking, she said, "Keep your voice down, you idiot. This is a bit more than just a game – they're trying to kill you. And they're trying to blame my people. And if we're seen together, then this whole mess gets a lot more–"

A sudden rattle of boots, at one end of the tiny alley space. Without even thinking, Za faded out – the semi-darkness was her perfect cover, and they would not be able to see her. Sheceh gathered his cloak in a panic, looking back and forth like hunted prey.

"There!" The voice was military. "Got you! It's for your own good, Ambassador…"

At one end of the hole, a leaning shadow had cut off the streetlights' red glimmer. Za had not gone far, and her motion detector told her there were guards in all directions. She'd permitted herself to become so distracted that she'd lost her professional edge.

"Go right," she whispered at Sheceh, seeing him jump. "Your right, not mine. Then left, then right again. I'll find you."

"My comms!"

She wavered – she almost felt sorry for him – but she couldn't go home without the full story. She had reports to make.

"Trust me," she said. "I will find you."

The Winnaran swore, with some creativity. At the lightless end of the gap, the soldiers were already squeezing through. "Stay where you are, Ambassador. We'll get you back to the compound safety. Commander Viesniel wants a word with you."

"Go!" Za told him, just like his aides had done.

It seemed to do the trick; she saw his head come up and his chin set in that same, slightly pompous Winnaran fashion. It was as much his characteristic as her skin was hers, and she almost grinned.

With a scrabble, catching his cloak on the metal, he moved for the far side of the gap.

And Za flickered after him.

Sheceh was not built for running.

His people honored athletics, competing against each other in huge arenas with cheering crowds and colored banners, winning laurels and awards. But he was no sportsman, and this was not his idea of fun.

Still, he ran, his cloak hiked gracelessly up, his lungs straining in the bitter-cold air. He struggled to see. What light there was served only to make the streets glow faintly ruddy, and he barely managed to not blunder into anything.

Boots were coming after him. Hard, disciplined, stamping boots. They rung in metallic echoes, almost like percussion. He couldn't even tell where they were coming from, not really. They seemed to surround him, sounding from every direction at once.

He was following the Yssaril's instructions – what choice did he have? Right, then left, then right, but he was soon absolutely hopelessly lost. Where was the landing pad? Perhaps he should follow the slope of the mesh roof, such as it was. It would surely take him outward?

Yet his mind was still plagued with questions, fears in gyres, tangling with both grief and suspicion. Maybe the Yssaril had sent him on some wild bird chase, still playing her little games? Maybe she'd stand back and laugh as the Barony finally caught him?

Were they in this together, the Yssaril and the Barony? He didn't know. His sense of helplessness was back, and he was sinking in – what had she called it? Swamp-water? He didn't know much about her homeworld, but the idea seemed somehow poignant.

Another corner, and another. The boots were still everywhere, relentless as a nightmare. He found a second plaza, a flag at its center. Or maybe it was the same one.

Where *was* he?

Despair loomed large, and he paused, leaning over and wheezing, the cold air cutting his lungs. Had Za abandoned him after all? Had she got what she came for, and just left?

Then a voice beside him said, "You lost?"

He started, almost jumping out of his skin. The figure was Letnev, but the man looked more like the ones in the bar, young, his garments dirty with work. Sheceh took at guess at his age – maybe eighteen or nineteen? He bore a belt, but it carried a selection of tools, rather than weapons.

Sheceh remembered the word that Za had used...

Fodder.

Just like his people would have been, had he trusted Viesniel.

"No," he said, slightly warily. "Just getting my breath."

"You're the Winnaran!" the young man answered, surprised and grinning. "That ambassador everyone's looking for." His gray skin and white hair were typical of his race, but his expression was curious. "What in the dark are you doing out here?"

Boots rattled, close. A voice barked orders. "He can't have gone far! Spread out and take this section by section!"

"Sir!"

Taking a chance, Sheceh said, "Trying not to get caught. Really not sure they have my best interests at heart."

The lad chuckled. "Viesniel rarely has anything in his heart but Viesniel. You've certainly got him stirred up – we haven't seen this many guards in years."

The boots were close, now, and Sheceh said, quickly, "The landing pad. Do you know where it is?"

Raising one white eyebrow, the lad said, "Yeah, it's not far. Go out the end here," he pointed. "Take the second turn on the right and head straight on. Though there will probably be soldiers."

The orders sounded again, closer now. Sheceh pulled a face, shoulders rounded and exhaustion looming. He had a stitch, robbing him of his breath, and he'd had about enough of this whole fiasco. He sighed.

The lad frowned. "Tell you what," he said. "Why don't I tell them I've seen you, heading back toward the city proper? It'll give you a chance to get clear."

Sheceh blinked. "But, why would you…"

"Efficiency," the lad shrugged, grinning. "It's the best and simplest way to complete the job. Besides, everyone knows Commander Viesniel will do *anything* for his next promotion. A chance to put a spike in his plans? Sounds good to me."

"I… Thank you," Sheceh said, staring. "I'd no idea Letnev could be…" He trailed off, checking himself, realizing he'd made both an assumption, and a mistake. The Letnev were not all Viesniel, and to profile them was very poor judgment.

"Thank you," he repeated, self-conscious and little shamed. "I appreciate the help."

The lad grinned wider and offered him a gesture – his thumbs and forefingers making a circle that might have represented the circle of the flag. It seemed like some sort of "good luck" symbol. "Go on," he said. "Get out of here. Before they come back."

Sheceh nodded, searching for something else to say, then briefly gripped the lad's shoulder. The orders were coming closer, barks through the cold, and he ducked to the side of the plaza, and away from the coming guards. His heart was still hammering, and the freezing air had given him a headache. He was so tired, but the lad had given him genuine hope.

Pausing in the shadow of an overhanging metal balustrade – it looked like some sort of residence, but he wasn't sure – he pressed his hand into his ribs to ease the pain. He had no idea what he must look like – his headdress over one ear, his jewelry in all directions, his jacket disheveled and sweaty. He had come here so full of himself, so righteously determined to bend the Barony to his will, to go back to Mecatol in triumph…

But there were so many things he'd learned. Viesniel was just one man, disliked by even his own people. And Za…

Had they caught her? Had she taken his comms device and fled, hoping it would give her the answers that he had not? Or was she still following him, tracking him like the hunter she was?

Could he trust her?

I'll find you.

He did not know.

The thought gave him a spasm of emotion – rage, pain, anger, despair. Briefly his helplessness loomed large. His aides and guards had trusted him, following where he led, and he had surely led them into death. And now, he had nothing, no one, no way off-world, no…

A spasm shook him, and he realized he was sobbing. Delayed reaction, shock, loss. He'd spent all day running, one place to another, trying to stay ahead of the game – just like the Yssaril had said.

Trying to stay alive.

"Please." The word came out aloud, even as the tears were freezing in his skin. "Za, if you're there – I don't want to die like this. I want to go home. I want to go back to my people. I came out here to strike a deal, to go with the Letnev to Mecatol. I know they would have used us – we are strange allies, after all – but I thought I could win. I thought I could play Viesniel and make him dance to the Winnaran tune." The thought of the Letnev commander dancing made him smile, brief and ludicrous. "How wrong I was. He played me. He played you and your friend. Your government. He even plays his own people, it seems. Please, Za, come back."

It was as close to humility as he could manage, a plea from the heart. He owed it to those that had followed him. And, in some strange way, he owed it to the Letnev drinkers in the bar, to the lad that had helped him, to Za herself.

This time, the shimmer did not take him by surprise.

Manifesting like some dream, the Yssaril grinned. "You're better at hide-and-seek than I'd realized."

Sheceh wiped the ice from his face. His hauteur had completely gone, and he had no energy to reach for it.

"Please," he said again. "This isn't just a game. It's too serious, and we both stand to lose. Please tell me you're not on their side."

"I'm not on their side." Za had something in her hand, a glitter of gemstone that he recognized. "Your people are all gone, Sheceh. And Viesniel will try to blame Saath. Blame the Yssaril. He has no physical evidence, but still, we both have to get back to our governments, and our worlds. We have to stop this."

"Before the galaxy plunges into war," Sheceh said. He shook his head. "I'm sorry about your friend. This has been a dark day for us both."

Za gave one long slow blink, then held out the flash. "Take it. Call your ship. Get home. Tell your world what's happened. I'll lead the remaining patrols away from here." She didn't explain how, and he didn't ask. "I promise you, Ambassador, we had nothing to do with any of this. Saath was only here on recon. And I only came looking for Saath."

He gave her a long look, but she didn't drop her gaze, and after a moment, he nodded. "All right," he said, taking the comms device. "I believe you, Za Nuk. And you'd better get somewhere safe – off-world if you can. Because if they do catch you, this whole mess will just get bigger."

"Then I'd best make sure they don't catch me," Za returned, her grin widening. "Thank you, Ambassador. You and I ... we're more alike than we realize."

That made him smile, and he closed his fingers over the gem. "And thank you," he said. "Thank you for the help. I'd never have made it–"

The batter of soldiers' boots was getting closer. Za frowned. "They don't give up, do they? Go on, Sheceh. One last run. Use your comms, and ask for Vaganay at the landing pad – she's my contact there, and she'll help you." She extended a hand, mimicking his gesture from earlier. "Good luck, Sheceh Del Sabir."

He took her small, green hand in his larger one, his rings

flashing. "You too, Za Nuk. May the spirit of the Lazax watch over you."

"Not too closely, I hope," she said, winking. "We don't generally like being watched." She stepped back. "Travel safely. We still have a war to stop, and I need to make sure that everything of Saath's is secured."

"I will."

"Good."

He saw her skin fade, watched her become all but invisible, right before his eyes. Could he still see it – the faintest shape of her outline? He wasn't sure. But the last of her he caught was her distinctive Yssaril chuckle.

DEFILER'S REEF

TIM PRATT

1

This is a Song.

2

Provisional admiral Alyce Maizere stood on the bridge of the *Gloaming* and said, "Take a closer look at the upper left quadrant. Has that system been catalogued yet?" She leaned over her command console, heart speeding up at the prospect of conquest. Her small fleet of three heavily armed cruisers was out collecting worlds, and this just might be her first. The Barony of Letnev was always happy to take new citizens under its protection, and, of course, to expand its tax base and pool of exploitable resources. Any world she stole for the Barony meant glory for her.

One of the interchangeable ensigns said, "It's not listed in any of our available databases, admiral."

Alyce showed her teeth. Wonderful. The galaxy was full of rich prospects, but many of the ripest were colony worlds claimed by other factions, and trying to seize those could be tricky, depending on who claimed ownership and how active their oversight was. This system had either never been discovered and logged by any of the great powers, or it was a world once claimed but since forgotten. Many records were destroyed during the Twilight Wars, and those factions that had survived the conflict and gained independence were still trying to piece their shattered spheres of influence back together... while snatching up other people's unattended property wherever possible, of course. "Show me a detail map of the system."

The ensign running the sensor array complied, and a colorful diagram filled the screen. There was a small yellow star, with a single reddish-orange gas giant in its habitable zone. The planet was orbited by numerous moons, three of them sizable, and one of them... "Highlight the moon in sector six."

The image of a blue and green orb filled the viewscreen. It was big enough to qualify as a planet in its own right if it hadn't been trapped by the gravity of the gas giant. Data unspooled beneath the image, and Alyce drank in the information hungrily. The ensign said, "Spectrographic analysis indicates the atmosphere is compatible with the presence of life–"

"It's *green*, ensign," Alyce said. "The moon obviously supports life. I'm more curious about whether it supports *intelligent* life."

"We haven't detected radio waves or other emissions," the ensign said. "There's no sign of heavy metals or other industrial contaminants in the atmosphere, and no visible cities or megastructures, but from this distance, smaller settlements wouldn't be detectable. If there is an advanced civilization, it's not located on the surface."

Hmm. Most likely there were only plants and non-sapient animals on the moon. It would still be worth claiming for the purposes of resource extraction, though taking control of the place wouldn't be terribly interesting. It was possible there were advanced intelligences of an annoying sort, undetectable from space – deep-sea dwellers like the Hylar, or underground monsters spawned in chambers full of magma. Such entities were relatively rare, though.

The most enjoyable possibility, for Alyce, was intelligent land-dwelling life at an early stage of development, hunter-gatherers and the like, who had no idea there were other people among the stars, let alone great powers capable of invading and subjugating them with trivial ease.

Primitive worlds like that were Alyce's favorite. It was always pleasant when the people you conquered believed you were a god. "Captain, I think we should visit that moon and see what kind of juice we can squeeze out of it."

"Yes, admiral." The *Gloaming*'s flag captain was Guille Corbin, Alyce's former mentor and current subordinate. He'd never risen above the level of captain of a cruiser, despite having decades of distinguished experience. There were rumors that Guille had offended someone in the Baron's inner circle, not badly enough to see Guille stripped of rank, but severely enough to stop his career from advancing any further. He seemed content enough with his lot, but Guille was a master at hiding his thoughts and feelings until he chose to reveal them, so who could say for sure? If he resented her new authority over him, she couldn't tell, and their relationship seemed as easy as ever. She was fond of the old man, though he probably didn't have much more to teach her. She had ambitions that extended far beyond Guille's own. The Letnev had a longstanding program of expansion and annexation, and some people thought the true glory days of interstellar conquest were past, with the richest takings already plucked, but Alyce believed there were still hidden treasures in out-of-the-way places just waiting for her to plunder.

Guille gestured at the navigator and pilot, who leapt into furious action, inputting the new course and preparing to enter the moon's orbit. "Do you plan to follow the initial survey with a landing crew, admiral?"

Alyce nodded, pleased. Guille had been on countless annexation missions and had a wealth of practical experience that exceeded Alyce's own, but he was still deferential in front of the crew. In closed quarters, he tended to be a lot more blunt, but she enjoyed that verbal sparring, and there was no one in the world she trusted more. She'd requested Guille's ship specifically as part of her fleet when she was given this command. "Yes, and I'm going to lead the ground team personally."

"Of course, provisional admiral." Guille's face was placid, but Alyce winced a little. The "provisional" in front of her rank, well, *rankled* – but it was the Barony way to send an unproven admiral of the Annexation Corps out with a small fleet on a probationary basis. If she returned from this mission with new resources to expand the glory of the Barony, the "provisional" would be dropped, and she would become a full admiral, with greater responsibilities and powers. Guille had called her by her admittedly proper title as a subtle rebuke, reminding her of the precariousness of her position. As admiral, she was in charge of all three ships, and should really run this operation from above ... but she loved nothing more than being on the ground on a new world, and claiming new worlds for the Barony in person. She wasn't willing to give up the thrill of direct action just yet, and while that sort of oversight was certainly permitted… it was seen as slightly eccentric.

She flicked a toggle and activated a privacy baffle, a small field that would make their words inaudible to everyone else on the bridge, and subtly scramble their shapes to make lip-reading impossible and body language hard to interpret. "Not that I need to explain myself, you bloated old cave spider, but this is a new fleet, with soldiers who haven't worked together much, and I'd like to oversee their first mission."

"Just don't blame me if you get eaten by the local fauna," Guille said. "I prefer to stay far away from the mud and muck and slime, myself."

"That's a shame, because you're coming with me."

He sighed heavily. "As you know, I injured my knees during–"

"I know they were reconstructed, and augmented, and are in fact stronger than *my* supple young knees at this point. Come on, Guille. This will be my first landfall as admiral–"

"Provisional," he murmured.

"–and it wouldn't be the same without you by my side. You taught me everything I know."

"But not everything *I* know," he said.

"Precisely. That's why I need you there."

He sniffed. "As you wish, admiral."

She pulled up the details they had on the moon, information scrolling across a small screen on her command-and-control gauntlet. "The preliminary analysis looks promising when it comes to mineral resources."

Guille leaned over to look, then nodded. "Yes, but you know the Baron prefers it when such deposits can be mined by the local population. It saves on sending prison labor. A self-sustaining work colony is the best prize you could bring back. It's a shame there's probably nothing more complex than a cave rat down there."

"Maybe," Alyce said. "Or maybe we'll get lucky." She bumped him with her shoulder. "Don't you *feel* lucky, Guille? I do."

"I'd assumed that sensation was indigestion."

ᛈ

Rorum Carghav practiced his spear-dance just outside the heavy stone door to the vault complex, watching his shadow flicker in the lamplight.

He composed a little Song about himself as he moved: *Rorum the deadly, his spear-dance a poem.* Step-spin-strike; back-spin-strike; duck-sweep-double-thrust. His imaginary opponents lay moaning and bleeding all around him, and he spun the spear with a flourish, ending with the haft tucked under his right arm, spearhead pointed downward, ready to be ripped upward through the groin of a defenseless–

"I brought your basket," a voice said behind him, and Rorum startled and dropped his spear as he turned around, almost tripping over the weapon's shaft in the process. He scowled down at his little cousin Anneka, who giggled, shaking the ribbons plaited in the hair on her head and cheeks and chin. "Your lunch?" she said.

Rorum took the basket from her with as much dignity as he could muster, and lifted the cloth to look inside. Milkcakes, still warm from the hearth, and those savory vegetable-and-leaf wraps his aunt always made. If he had to stand this dull and pointless duty every day for the next year, at least he would be fed well. The fact that they'd sent a child to bring him his lunch demonstrated how pointless his so-called guard duty really was. If the contents of the vault complex were still so dangerous, would they let a child come this close to the entry? (A corresponding thought rose briefly in his mind before he could quash it: *Would they let an untested warrior like Rorum so close to the door, either?*)

He thanked Anneka and shooed her away. Still giggling, she went back down the long tunnel that led to their settlement, Vaulthome, the largest village on the moon his people called Promise.

Rorum sighed and sat down on the wooden stool to eat. He remembered being even younger than her, and sneaking with his friends to the mouth of that tunnel, creeping incrementally closer to something so *dangerous* and *ancient* and *cursed*, all showing off their bravery. Later, he'd delivered a food basket to one of the guardians, as Anneka just had, and he'd been suitably awed at the young warrior's courage, standing so bravely beside the dark metal vault door, etched with its sigils of warning.

Now he *was* that young warrior, and this courageous act was, in fact, quite tedious. At least the training and the drills over this past year had taken him *into* the complex, to learn all the contingencies and failsafes in place, and then, yes, he'd felt some of that old, deep awe. The things locked away were disturbing, even haunted… but they also hadn't stirred in generations, and all the lessons he'd learned were for worst-case-scenarios that would never come to pass.

Rorum shifted on the stool. It was the only piece of furniture in the antechamber, and it was deliberately uncomfortable. He was here to guard, not rest. The elders said that, long ago, there were always two guards in the chamber, to keep watch on each *other* as well as the door, but long ago they'd gone down to one guard. There was too much to do in the village to give up two well-trained, able-bodied fighters all day, and two more all night, to watch a closed door. The last "containment breach" had happened in the days of his grandmother's grandmother's grandmother, and though each cohort of young warriors was taken out to look at the consequence of that attack, it wasn't particularly frightening: ruined ground and broken remnants.

These days, one warrior watched from dawn to dark, and another from dark to dawn, and they weren't the strongest or most deadly anymore, either; the best warriors had better things to do. Guard duty was mostly an initiation now, a test of endurance and loyalty, though some honor still accrued, and he would be assured a good place among the warriors when his time was finished.

Ah, his time. Rorum was on the night shift. His term of service was one year.

This was his second night.

At first, night duty had seemed bravest of all – scary things were always scarier in the dark. Some nights on Promise were *very* dark, when they were turned away from both the sun and from the looming presence of the gas giant, and only the faint reflected lights from their world's tiny moonlets shone in the sky. But Rorum didn't feel brave anymore. He just felt out of synch. When he'd left his post after his first night, it was only just morning, but he went into a darkened hut and slept fitfully while the rest of the village hunted, gathered, mended, cooked, and trained around him. He was told that soon his body would adjust to the new schedule, but in some ways, that would be *worse* – he would feel more disconnected from the rhythms of his people. After his year was up, he'd have to reacclimate himself to diurnal life all over again.

He ate his milkcakes slowly (even licking the pads of his hands clean like a child, since there was no one here to watch him), since eating was the most interesting thing that was going to happen tonight. Then he sighed and picked up his spear again. Might as well keep up his training.

Rorum had brought honor to his family by excelling in the spear-dance exhibition in the spring, though he didn't do as well when it came to sparring against actual opponents. He was fast and graceful, practiced obsessively, and knew all the forms, even the esoteric alternative ones, but having a huge, scarred Saar warrior rushing at him with a spear of his own made Rorum's mind get jumbled. He could hold his own in those bouts, flowing into defensive positions by instinct, but taking the initiative and going on the offensive seemed beyond him. The best he ever managed when sparring against an experienced opponent was a draw because time ran out.

The last time that happened, his opponent flung his spear to the ground and shouted, "How is all that dodging and dancing going to help in a real fight? Are you going to *frustrate* your enemies to death? No one calls time during a raid!"

His teachers said Rorum needed to be less reactive, to watch for patterns in his opponents, find a flaw, choose his moment, and strike. He tried. He *really* tried. But the possibility of getting a spear in his guts or a cut across his face kept him focused on the defensive to the exclusion of other concerns.

Conkur, the leader of Vaulthome's warriors, once sat Rorum down and showed him all her scars, and there were many. She pointed to one that ran from beneath her right eye all the way to the corner of her mouth. "This was the first wound I got in a real fight," she said. "I was so terrified by nearly losing my eye that I could think of nothing but vanquishing my opponent and making sure they could never hurt me again. I attacked with new ferocity. This wound was my motivation. It also taught me an important lesson: I could be hurt, and still win. Any fight is a balance of risk and reward. Of course it's nice to defeat your enemies and emerge completely unscathed, but against a skilled opponent, that's not always possible. You can't let your fear of getting hurt destroy your ability to hurt someone *else*." She clapped him on the shoulder and walked away, and he felt both honored that she'd taken the time to impart her wisdom and ashamed that he'd needed to hear it.

Rorum had done his best to take in her words. But when a spearhead came at his face, all thoughts other than self-preservation fled.

He trudged through his night's duty, doing forms until his fur was matted with sweat, then trying to recite the stories he'd heard the Songcallers tell so often. His favorites were the Songs about the history of his people, and how they came to dwell in this place: the Promise they'd made that gave their moon its name. They were tales of honor and glory, horror and brutality, and the defeat of a vile and insidious enemy – defilers of all the Saar held dear.

Rorum's tribe, alone among the heretics and oathbreakers in their scattered settlements throughout the forest, was the latest in a long line of guardians, protecting the galaxy from horrors. His fellow villagers were not all related by blood, but they were still one clan, united in purpose, standing strong and tireless through the generations. They watched and warded the vault, and the dangers locked within.

If only watching and warding was a little more *exciting*. It wasn't the sort of thing that made a Songcaller compose a tale about your exploits. Rorum only knew one Song about a vault guard, and it wasn't a story of glory: it was a cautionary tale, from the last containment breach.

Rorum yawned and slapped himself across the forearms, hard, and pinched the tender webbing between his fingers, using pain to wake himself up. If the day guard came and found him asleep, he'd never be trusted by the tribe again.

Dawn finally came, and with it his replacement, Shardin, who brought a basket of peas to shell to pass the time. Rorum scowled at that. Using a guard shift to do chores wasn't *forbidden*, but Rorum thought it suggested a certain... lack of purpose. It was important to focus, wasn't it, in case the things hidden away in the vaults should awaken from their slumber? Though it wasn't like he hadn't spent half the night daydreaming...

Rorum stood stiffly and gave his report: "No unusual activity detected. The vault remains secure."

Shardin yawned. "Amazing. I was sure *this* would be the night the Great Devourers would burst from their eggs to poison the waters and burn the forests and eat the young, with only your spear to stop them." Shardin patted Rorum on the shoulder. "Maybe tonight, eh? Sleep well."

Rorum sighed. "Do you take nothing seriously?" Shardin was his kin – practically everyone in the village was, to one degree or another – but they weren't particularly close.

"I take serious things seriously. This?" Shardin gestured at the vault door, twice as tall as a Saar, dark metal ringed with symbols. "This is just tradition. Habit. The things in there used to be awake, and for a long time they were asleep, but now? Come on. Now they're dead. We're watching over a grave." He sat on the stool and began to shell peas from one basket into another, dropping the husks on the cavern's uneven floor. "But there are worse ways to pass the time, I suppose. See you at dusk."

Rorum scowled and stomped off down the tunnel. The passage took several sharp curves, and there were multiple gates that could be activated remotely to seal the tunnel off against incursions. Those gates were regularly oiled and tested – doing so was one of his responsibilities – but they hadn't actually been shut in Rorum's lifetime. There were outlying villages, populated by the descendants of apostates and deserters who'd left this settlement long ago, and while there were often skirmishes with them over hunting grounds and other resources, the cowards never tried to raid Vaulthome. The heretics still possessed a superstitious fear of the caverns beneath the hills, and though they were known to attack patrols and attempt raids on supply stores, they would never willingly enter the tunnels.

When Rorum emerged from the mouth of the tunnel, he stopped to stretch out his arms and roll the tension out of his neck. Even though there was plenty of room inside the caverns and the tunnels, the weight of all that rock and history made him *feel* cramped, and being in the open air again was nice. He looked back at the spiked crag of the hill that rose above the caverns. It was mostly bare, unforgiving rock with only a few tenacious scraps of plant life clinging to its slopes. The sun rose over that hill, and this early, the dawn light seemed to emanate from the hill itself, making it glow with an aura that was majestic, magical, even *holy*–

Then Rorum saw something hovering above the hillside. It was a bit like a flying insect, but far too large, and it was clearly unnatural. His first terrified thought was, *Did it come from the vault?* But, no, the things in the vault were all bigger than this, and nastier. It was a *machine*, though, and he'd heard stories of how deadly they could be. Such things were not merely untrustworthy. They were heralds of disaster.

Rorum didn't hesitate. He acted to defend his people.

4

"Our target has sub-satellites," Guille said over Alyce's personal comms. "You don't see those very often."

"The moon has *moons*?" She was in her cabin – which was usually the captain's, but since she'd made the *Gloaming* her flagship, Guille had been bumped down into his first officer's rooms, and so on down the line, until the poor chief engineer had to bunk with his junior officers. Rank had privileges, and she loved her privileges. Alyce activated the main screen and called up a view of the moon, which was now much clearer, since they'd drawn close. There were indeed small rocky bodies orbiting their target, the largest only a little bigger than the *Gloaming*.

"There are six of the things, which is *very* strange, even for a moon with such a wide orbit around its host planet," Guille said. "The orbital dynamics are frankly bizarre. But, in a vast universe, even very unlikely things will show up occasionally."

Six sub-moons. That was beyond unlikely. "Are we sure they aren't artificial satellites?"

"They appear to just be rock, ice, and minerals," Guille said. "Though they are quite rich in metals. When the mining vessels come, they can scoop the moons up from orbit. No gravity well to drag them up out of. That kind of savings always pleases the higher-ups."

Alyce nodded. The moons were a curiosity, but nothing more. She was more interested in the surface. "Are the survey drones ready to deploy?"

"Yes, and the *Incision* and the *Voidcaller* are almost in position."

She switched her screen to watch the progress of her fleet's other two ships. They were maneuvering into positions above their target's major landmasses. The moon had one large continent and two smaller ones; the *Gloaming* hovered over the largest continent, which seemed the most fecund, especially around the equator, while the *Incision* and the *Voidcaller* would send their drones to inspect the smaller landmasses, closer to the poles and with sparser vegetation – though the scans did suggest there was a lot of metal locked in the ground there, which was nice, if boring. Alyce's ship would also drop a few submersible drones into the seas, in case there were underwater civilizations, though given the vastness of the waters and the potential depths, absence of evidence would not necessarily mean evidence of absence on that score.

Underwater aliens wouldn't pose an immediate problem when it came to exploiting resources from the land anyway, so Alyce wasn't too concerned.

"I'm going immersive with the aerial drones," Alyce said.

"Will you be using active controls, or just riding along?" Guille said.

"Hmm. The swarm as a whole can be autonomous, let the algorithm do the heavy lifting, but I'll take override controls on one of the drones, in case something catches my eyes and I want to take a closer look." One of her first jobs as a junior officer had been overseeing survey teams, and she'd learned to both program the swarm algorithms and to take manual control of the drones. Her philosophy as a commander was that she should be able to do anything her crew could do, better. Her people would, of course, obey her out of fear alone – a Barony officer had an astonishing amount of power over the lives and livelihoods of those under her command – but if they respected her as a person, they would do more than obey: they would try to *impress* her.

"The other two ships are almost in position," Guille said. "We don't need to wait for them – have more ground to cover anyway. Shall we go ahead and launch?"

"Oh, yes, let's." Alyce settled back into her chair, slipped on her control gloves, and pulled on a helmet with a full-face visor that cut out all light.

"Launching deployment shuttle now," Guille said in her comms. The drones were too fragile and sensitive to enter atmosphere from orbit – they'd burn up on entry – so they were packed into a small autopiloted shuttle that would release them at a safer altitude. "Getting into position for dispersal. Dispersing... now."

After a brief interval of pleasant darkness, the visor's interior screen lit up, showing Alyce a dizzying array of small square screens, each displaying a different slice of the green and blue moon below, rushing up. She toggled into the drone she had pilot controls for, and its view filled her field of vision. The swarm spread out, buzzing silvery drones darting away in all directions, catching flashes of light.

It was just dawn on that continent. Alyce wondered what the day-night cycle was like. The moon – might as well call it *Maizere's Moon*, at least in her mind – wasn't tidally locked, so this landmass sometimes faced the gas giant, and sometimes faced away. The gas giant itself rotated on its axis and also revolved around the local star, complicating the cycle further. There would be nights when the gas giant was in the sky over Maizere's Moon, glowing bright from the reflected sunlight in its atmosphere, and other nights when the planet would be out of view, plunging the moon's sky into a deeper night, though the gas giant would still be a glow on the horizon. On many days, like this one, the planet would fill a large part of the moon's sky. What would primitive denizens of such a place make of that dance of celestial bodies? What idiot mythologies would they concoct about the lives of the gods they might imagine inhabiting those skies?

Alyce smiled. If there were people down there, they'd have new myths soon. About dark gods of unimaginable power crashing down to transform their lives forever.

She angled her drone toward a large patch of greenery on the horizon. "Anything interesting so far?" she asked.

Guille said, "We're seeing avian life, mostly small. The submersibles have logged lots of simple aquatic life, fins and pincers and the usual. We found mammalian megafauna on the smaller continents, trundling in herds around the plains, though there's no sign of anything comparable on the main continent."

"Perhaps because they've been hunted to extinction by the indigenous population?" she said.

"Or there was never a land bridge that allowed the shaggy beasts to reach this continent," Guille countered.

"That's a much less interesting hypothesis."

"Being less interesting is how I got where I am today," he said. Alyce wondered if his bland tone hid bitterness, but thought it more likely he was just resigned enough to his situation to find a bleak humor in it.

She banked the drone over the forest, which now spread as far as her electronic eyes could see. "I see some gaps in the canopy of this forest, Guille. A few look regular. I'm thinking roads."

"Probably just gullies, or river tributaries, or megafauna migration paths."

"Boring, boring, boring. You just wait."

Unfortunately, the ones she investigated were exactly what Guille suggested. No roads. If there were intelligent beings down there, they still lived *among* the trees, and weren't tearing the forest down to suit themselves. They might have trails, but trails wouldn't break the canopy.

Alyce adjusted the light levels in her display. This world was too *bright*. The Letnev were not, as a people, fond of sunshine; one of the most common Letnev curses was "May the light shine on you", and to "drag someone into the light" meant to tear them away from safety and security and leave them exposed and vulnerable.

She stayed above the treetops, because even with automated collision-avoidance-systems, it was tricky to pilot a drone through a thick forest canopy. She skimmed along, looking for clearings, investigating every break in the foliage. She was hoping for lodges, huts, or tents, or even better, stone structures like temples or pyramids. A local population that could already quarry and cut stone could be easily transitioned into a mining workforce, after all.

There was no sign of advanced habitation, though. Time for another tack. She switched to heat sensors, and the forest below lit up. There were lots of little scurrying warm-blooded things, doubtless prey animals, and a few not-quite-Letnev-sized blobs, probably larger predators, and– "Oh, what's this? I've got clusters of large heat signatures, scores of them, near a water source, too. Looks like I might have a village, Guille."

"Or a herd or something at a watering hole."

She switched back to regular vision and saw... a bunch of trees. There *could* be a whole village hidden under there and she wouldn't be able to tell. She spotted a large, rocky hill with little in the way of vegetation, and though it was tall, it was much shorter than the great trees on all sides. Could make a good vantage point to get a view under the canopy. Alyce maneuvered the drone toward the hill and stuck close to its slopes, moving down, down down–

"By the dark," she murmured. She'd hoped to find sapient life here, and she'd acted quite confident as part of her ongoing banter with Guille, but in truth, she knew how unlikely it was. Intelligent life was widespread in the galaxy, yes… but the galaxy was unimaginably vast, and most of it was empty space and barren rock, where anything more complex than a slime mold was rare. The odds against discovering an exploitable local population on her first exploration-and-annexation mission were absurdly long.

But she'd done it.

"What have you got?" Guille said.

"Take a look at my feed. I found a local. It just emerged from some kind of cave in a hill." She scanned the alien with her drone's limited sensors. The creature – the *person* – was bipedal, but broad-shouldered and bulky, especially compared to the more tall-and-lean Letnev. It was covered all over with thick dark fur and had pointed ears, and when she quietly maneuvered the drone around to get a look at its face, she saw a flattened nose, small sharp predator's eyes, and a strong jaw that doubtless held strong teeth. Such a thing could have been just an animal with no consciousness or culture… but it wore a cloak fastened with a metal clasp, and a necklace of teeth, and held a spear with a shining metal head and an intricately decorated shaft. That was an alien who could think. That was an alien with a *culture*. "I win, old man."

"It's a shame you didn't bother to place a bet," Guille said dryly. "If they dwell in caves and caverns, they could be tough to dig out."

"But already well adapted to life in the mines," she countered. "I wouldn't have seen all those heat signatures if these creatures lived underground, though. I suspect there's a village hidden by the trees, and the caves are just, who knows, storage, or a ritual site, or maybe there's a spring in there? I'll follow this one and see where–"

Alyce squawked and flinched back as, without the slightest warning, the local hurled his spear at the drone.

5

The strange flying thing zipped aside to avoid the spear and then vanished faster than Rorum's eye could follow. The spear itself struck the rocky side of the hill and clattered back down to land just a few meters from his feet. He squinted at the brightening sky, looking for some sign of the intruder, but there was nothing.

Had he really seen a *machine*, a "drone" like the elders talked about? Once upon a time his people had lived in a world – not *this* world, but another – full of wondrous machines that could plant and harvest crops, cut down trees, built structures, even fight battles. But then an enemy came who could turn those machines against them, and miraculous convenience turned to monstrous terror. Ever since, his people had relied on simple tools they could make themselves, and creating complex mechanical devices was strictly forbidden. Of course, the knowledge of making such things was lost, too, so the "forbidden" part didn't really matter; might as well forbid Rorum to eat the gas giant they called Sheltering Storm. Although... there were rumors about the Archivists. The Songcallers were the keepers of the tribe's stories, but the Archivists were the keepers of the tribe's *secrets*. Who knew what knowledge they possessed?

Rorum was very tired, and he'd been thinking of ancient battles and old lore all night, about an enemy he only vaguely understood... Wasn't it more likely he'd seen some sort of bird and mistaken it for a machine? Perhaps a twitwhiller; they had silver plumage sometimes. That would be quite the Song: *Rorum the bold, the terror of birds*. He decided not to mention his sighting to any of the village elders.

Rorum followed the path through the trees to the village. Though it was just dawn, members of his clan were already out and about, doing the endless work of mending roofs, tending mushroom plots, feeding animals, sharpening tools, hauling water, and sharing gossip. Huts clustered around the bases of the great trees, and ramps and rope ladders led to platforms built onto the trunks, and up into the branches. They were several meters up, and cleverly hidden with layers of bark and foliage.

Wide-eyed children looked down at Rorum from one such platform, ducking out of sight when they noticed *him* noticing *them*. He remembered the superstitious awe with which he'd looked upon the Guardians of the Vault when he was a pup, and it prompted him to straighten his spine and walk more confidently. So what if the work wasn't glamorous or exciting. It was still important, and a vital part of his heritage. Even if the contents of the vault complex were dormant forever, made harmless by the slow and inexorable passage of eons, guarding those poisonous treasures was still the whole reason this settlement existed, and Rorum's people were keeping the true faith, unlike the heretics who'd deserted over the generations.

He reached his sleeping hut and crawled inside. The dwelling of the Guardians was small, but well made, with not the slightest crack in the walls or roof, and the interior was covered in layers of hide to dampen sound. The dark, quiet hut was built especially so those who kept watch all night could sleep restfully as the daylight life of the village went on all around. There was ample room for Rorum to stretch out, since the sleeping hut had been made long ago, when there were still two guards on shift. He curled up on a woven mat and wrapped his cloak about himself and soon slipped into sleep.

In his dreams, flying insects as big as a person buzzed through the forest, and the trees burned where they passed.

He woke in midafternoon, some hours before his shift was due to begin. This time was his own, and also his only opportunity to share in the life of the village. He yawned and stretched and rubbed his belly and stepped out of the hut – and into commotion.

Rorum approached a knot of Saar murmuring to one another at the center of the settlement. There was a raised platform there, where Songcallers declaimed on feast days, and where the village elders made announcements. Conkur was standing on the platform now, wearing a bandolier full of throwing knives across her chest, and clawed gauntlets on her hands: full battle regalia, which meant this was a matter of consequence. Rorum's heart thumped as he joined the gathering. Had scouts from one of the other settlements been sighted? Were the heretics actually going to try to raid Vaulthome?

"Silence!" Conkur shouted. "I would share with you what is known." The crowd ceased its murmuring and all eyes turned toward Conkur. She glowered and began to pace back and forth on the stage. She had never been one much given to stillness, except on the hunt, when she could be mistaken for a stone until the time came to strike. "You have all doubtless heard the rumors from the hunting parties, or else the vine-gatherers, or else our eyes in the heights."

Rorum hadn't heard any rumors, but he had a sinking feeling that he knew what this was about all the same.

"One or two sightings might be dismissed as tricks of the light," Conkur said, "but we have ten sets of eyes who all report the same thing: strange, shining things in flight. Things that can be nothing but *machines*, most likely the sort known as drones."

The crowd murmured again, with a thread of panic this time, and Conkur raised her arms. "The vaults are secure!" she shouted. "Guardian Rorum kept watch all night, and reported no disturbance, and Guardian Shardin is there now – I personally checked in when I heard of the first sighting. The Archivists further assure me the outer doors are *all* secure. These machines did not come from the vaults."

The murmuring was quieter now, but where before Rorum had heard the first bubblings of panic, now there was disquiet. "Then where did they come from?" someone called. "Did the heretics find a hidden cache?" There were stories of lost storehouses of forbidden technology on the moon, forgotten from the time of their founders or stolen away by heretics of prior generations, but no one had taken them too seriously... until now.

"That is a possibility," Conkur said, "though it's unlikely the heretics would know how to operate such machines if they did find them. That knowledge is held only by our most senior Archivists. We think the most likely prospect is that the machines have come from... off-world."

Rorum shivered at the idea, and turned his eyes skyward, though he saw nothing but tree branches and leaves. He knew, of course, that there were other people out there among the stars – his own people had come to Promise generations ago from somewhere else, in the aftermath of a terrible war that sprawled across the cosmos, if the Songs were to be believed. But the idea of people from the stars coming here... that was something else entirely.

"We do not know the nature or intentions of these visitors," Conkur said. "Until we do, I would advise you to continue your lives and work as usual. We will gather what information we can. The Archivists have... certain resources, which I am assured are being activated. Once we know more, we will tell you all." Conkur looked down, forehead wrinkled in thought, then looked up, making eye contact with several individuals in the crowd – including Rorum, at the back. "Do not panic, my kin and friends... but *do* be ready, in case these visitors mean us harm." She turned and departed swiftly, followed by several of the village's most capable warriors, ignoring the hubbub of questions that rose in her wake.

I should have said something, Rorum thought guiltily. The silver bird *wasn't* a figment of a tired mind. Perhaps it didn't matter – others had seen the drones, after all, and the outcome was the same – but still. Rorum shouldn't have let fear of embarrassment overcome his duty. He wouldn't let that happen again.

He went in search of something to eat, though he suddenly had no appetite at all. He needed to keep his strength up, anyway, for whatever trials might come. He ate in the warrior's mess, with a few of his cohort, who all boasted about how they'd repel any invaders who dared set foot in their forest. Rorum boasted right along with them. Afterward, he took his spear and went out walking, climbing up the side of the rocky hill above the vault, with the idea that he might find some spoor or sign of the drone he'd thrown his spear at. There was nothing, of course, and he moodily clambered down the far side of the hill,

intending to walk in the forest and try to clear his head before
his shift below ground.

Fifteen minutes later, ambling along the path of a dry creek
bed, he saw an older Saar wearing a red Archivist's sash, her pelt
nearly all white, hurrying through the trees some forty meters
farther away. She didn't appear to notice him, her head lowered,
her manner preoccupied. She reached a particularly large tree
and knocked twice on the mossy trunk. A section of the trunk
hinged open, and the Archivist ducked inside, the trunk closing
seamlessly behind her.

Rorum stared at the tree, blinking and frowning. Several of the
trees in the village had hidden entrances that led to underground
caverns, where the clan could hide in case of terrible storms or
fires (though neither had happened in Rorum's lifetime), but
those trees were on the *other* side of the village. The Archivists
kept the clan's secrets, but it seemed they also had secrets of
their own. The Archivists were probably more cautious about
their comings and goings in the normal course of events, but
this was an unusual time, and they were doubtless preoccupied.

It was none of Rorum's business – he was a warrior, not a
deep thinker. He headed back toward the hill. His shift was
beginning soon anyway.

But he couldn't help wondering: What secrets do they keep
down there?

6

The following day, Alyce had enough data on the moon and
its inhabitants to proceed. There were no signs of the local
dominant lifeform on the polar continents – unless they really
were dwelling in underground caverns – but there were lots of

them in the forest. Forests were tricky (lots of places to hide), but forests were also easy (they could be burned).

"Primitives," she sneered. She and Guille were in her quarters, Alyce sitting at a screen and reviewing drone footage and field reports, while Guille sat in a chair sipping a small glass of briny fungal liqueur.

"Oh, I don't know," Guille mused. "They seem to have a hierarchal tribal structure, they wear jewelry and woven cloth, and they do some metalwork, though on a small scale... I'm sure they have some sort of religion, or at least a rich cultural heritage, and–"

"I *meant*, they're only armed with spears and slings and knives," Alyce clarified.

"Oh, well, yes, if that's your criteria, then they're frightfully primitive. I didn't see a single trebuchet, let alone a plasma cannon. Then again, they're mostly fighting the occasional predatory animal or raiding tribes who live a few kilometers away, so they haven't really needed to innovate to such degree."

"We're going to roll over them like a splatter-tank over a field of flowers, aren't we?" Alyce paused the drone footage she'd recorded and looked at the local in his stupid cloak, with his surprisingly well-aimed spear.

"We could indeed commit genocide – and from the comfort of orbit – but that's not why we're here. We're here to welcome this moon into our society and allow them to contribute to the glory of the Letnev. These furry bipeds are subjects of the Barony, now, whether they know it or not."

"Subjects, but not citizens," Alyce said. "It's important for them to recognize that distinction. Which may well require rolling over one or two of said furry bipeds."

Guille swirled his snifter. "Oh, certainly. Everyone benefits from a full understanding of their place in the world. Do you really insist on leading a landing party on your own?"

"I wouldn't miss it for ten worlds. It's my first time as annexation lead, and I intend to lead from the front." She paused. "Or from just behind a couple of guards, anyway. I think I'll take our delegation to the largest settlement, the one where that beast threw a spear at my drone. Maybe I'll roll over *him* if there's rolling to be done."

"Crushing one's enemies for fun is fine, but do remember it's always better to crush them for fun *and* profit," Guille said.

Alyce and Guille went to the shuttle bay, where a dozen of her shock troops were waiting, wearing blank black full-face masks and armed with both energy rifles and close-quarters weapons, including shock batons and knives. Alyce was in her own landing gear, matte black ballistic armor that should prove ample defense against whatever pointed rocks might get thrown at her. Her party also had portable energy shields, but they shouldn't be necessary against locals at this technology level.

She wore a helmet that left her face uncovered, because she wanted the locals to see her, know her, come to recognize her… and fear her in particular. She did have goggles with dark lenses, and some helpful augmentations, though.

Guille was similarly attired, but he also carried a lightweight staff. "Do you have a sword hidden in that or something?" Alyce asked as her crew prepared the landing shuttle.

"No. I am old. This is a walking stick, not a killing stick."

"No reason it can't be both," Alyce said. "Anyway, your knees are fine. You're so dramatic."

"I also have ankles, admiral."

They took the two best seats inside the small shuttle, just behind the pilot, while the shock troops strapped themselves onto the long benches that ran along the sides. The cargo space held some crated heavy ordnance, though again, it wouldn't be necessary.

Alyce had considered dropping one of their ground vehicles – they had a half-track that could fire incendiary bombs accurately from a distance of five kilometers – but the dense forest would make such a vehicle impractical. They'd drop close to their target and enter on foot. Not quite as impressive an entrance as riding in on a tank spraying flames, but she had a few other attention-getting tricks in mind.

The shuttle launched from the *Gloaming* and dropped toward the moon. There was no real sense of speed until they hit the atmosphere, and then it was a bumpy ride, as always, but the pilot was up to the task. Once they'd shuddered and bounced below cloud level, the ride smoothed out as the shuttle's wings deployed, and they glided over the plains toward the dense forest.

Alyce took in the view through the front window. The gas giant filled a quarter of the sky and loomed so large it seemed their shuttle might eventually crash into it. It was pretty, she supposed, orange and red, and now some streaks of pale cream color. Amazing how continent-sized ranging storms could be so aesthetically pleasing... from a distance.

Soon they were skimming over a seemingly endless expanse of trees, the canopy lush, green, and impenetrable to conventional vision. "What a waste," Alyce said. "What this place needs is a few refineries and smokestacks. Some nice thick dark clouds to blot out the sunlight." The Letnev homeworld of Arc Prime was a planet with no star, traveling on its own mysterious course through the cosmos, and the denizens of that cold world made their homes deep underground, supported by a fungal ecology and their own ingenious industry.

"When the gas giant blocks the sun, there should be a nice reddish twilight feel to the place," Guille said. "And our preliminary geological survey indicates extensive cavern systems beneath the forest. It might be a tolerable place for Letnev overseers to live, once operations are up and running."

"I still say the weather would benefit from a giant forest fire. Nothing like a pall of smoke to temper the harshness of the sun."

"Perhaps this first meeting will go very badly, and you'll get your wish," Guille said.

"I wonder if the locals know any univoca," Alyce mused. That was the closest thing to a galactic common tongue, the language of the Lazax from the time of their long Imperium, and most worlds had been touched by the Lazax at some point, if only lightly. After so long, the language as it was spoken on far-flung worlds was often debased from its origins, but with the help of expert systems skilled at translation, different people could generally make themselves understood. "If not, we'll have to communicate more… crudely."

"You really relish this part, don't you?" Guille asked. "I myself always found the practical aspects of annexation to be rather dirty and disagreeable."

"That's probably why you never got promoted higher than captain," Alyce said.

"Oh, yes, I'm sure that's probably it."

She enjoyed needling him, but decided to answer him seriously now. "I do like this part, yes. At my level, and to a lesser extent yours, we spend so much time looking at other worlds from a distance, setting policy in motion, and giving orders for others to carry out. I think I'm a better leader because I want to see the immediate consequences of those orders – to see the tactical actions as well as the strategic decisions. It's good to be reminded that everything the Barony accomplishes is actually possible due to the direct application of our will by our soldiers – we bring glory to the Letnev through sweat, blood, and plasma bursts, not giving orders from on high."

"Ah, and all this time I thought you just enjoyed conquest, Alyce. Now I see that you're a *patriot*."

"No reason it can't be both," she said again.

The shuttle pilot found a small clearing – a rocky expanse at the top of a waterfall – a short distance from the target village, and Alyce approved it as a landing zone. She checked in with the other shuttle crews, and got confirmation that they'd reached their targets, too: the second- and third-largest settlements in this forest respectively. Those landing shuttles, led by undercommandants with annexation experience, would welcome the inhabitants to their new life under the Barony just like Alyce would, though probably with less panache.

She let her shock troops disembark first, just in case there were unpleasant surprises their scans hadn't noticed. Nothing tried to eat them or threw spears at them. She put her goggles on to cut the hideous sunlight back to a bearable level and strode out onto the surface of the moon – *her* moon.

Alyce was shorter in stature than her troops – they were chosen in part for the physical intimidation factor, so they were bruisers all – but her shiny black boots had stacked heels that gave her greater height without sacrificing stability. She wore a sidearm on one hip and a shock baton on the others, though *her* baton did more than electrocute; it had additional pacification capacities, including paralytic neurotoxins that worked on most carbon-based life, as befit her station.

Her troops spread out around her in a defensive formation,

watching every angle. They would move through this forest like a fleet in miniature: Alyce was the command ship, and her guards were escort vessels in a protective swarm.

"Why do these places always smell so terrible?" Guille asked as he descended the short ramp behind her, raising his voice to be heard over the rush of the nearby waterfall.

"I was trying not to inhale." The place smelled, well, *green* – leaves and mold and sap and moss. The forest before them was almost cartoonishly verdant, so lush it looked moist. She suppressed a shudder. Yes, she would like this place a lot better when the forests were leveled to make room for refineries. "Come on. It's a short walk to the village. Let's make some noise so they know we're coming."

The troops set off, stomping in rhythm. Those in the lead had long-handled machetes for clearing a path, but these trees were so ancient, and cast such deep shade, that there was precious little bush to whack. "This is much better than that jungle world in the Zydan system," Guille said. "You had to hack away branches at every step. Do you remember, you grabbed onto a vine, and it turned out to be some sort of horrible serpent?"

Alyce snorted. "How could I forget? The creature was quite confused when it couldn't bite through my armor. I twisted its head right off. I think I still have the skull somewhere – I had an ensign boil off the flesh for me. That jungle was a lot louder, too, all hoots and shrieks. Here, there's only birdsong."

"Some of it is birdsong," Guille said. "But some of it is the local people signaling to one another that they've spotted intruders."

She glanced at him, frowning. "How can you tell the difference?"

"Call it intuition. Or, if you prefer, experience. We're being observed, certainly. Look up there." He pointed up into a tree, and she called a halt, then zoomed in with her goggles. There was a platform hidden halfway up an immense tree, tucked into the space between a branch and the trunk. There was no one on the platform, but a rope ladder led higher into the tree, and further up, she glimpsed occasional planks of wood that must be bridges leading between the trunks. "The indigenous population is arboreal as well as ground-dwelling. Hmm. Good to know. The drones didn't show us that. Watch out for assault from above, troops. They could hurl rocks or spears."

They continued on their way, Alyce occasionally checking the screen on her gauntlet to confirm their coordinates. The forest seemed to stretch identically in all directions, and it would be easy to get lost without navigation assistance.

The troops in front suddenly stopped, leveling their rifles.

"Stand aside," Alyce said, and they reluctantly moved apart to let her step forward. Two locals stood before them, just a few meters away. They appeared to be unarmed, but they both wore voluminous cloaks, which could have hidden various implements. "Big beasties, aren't they?" Alyce murmured. They were as tall as her tallest troop, but broader, and covered in thick fur, one dark brown, one almost white – probably an elder. Maybe even the leader of the local tribe? She cleared her throat and said, in univoca: "Greetings. I wish to parley with your chieftain."

The two creatures exchanged a look, then conferred with one another. Alyce sighed. If necessary they could get by with gestures while the expert systems analyzed enough of the local tribe's gabble to put together a decent machine translation, but it would be *so* much easier if–

The white-furred one stepped forward. "You speak in the

language of the oldest Songs our people know. The Songs of our deep history." The creature's accent was atrocious, and entirely too growly for Alyce's taste, but comprehensible.

"Of course I do," Alyce said. "I am wise and powerful. Are you the leader here?"

"I am a Songcaller. Our leaders are… nearby. I am Whanta." The creature made a strange motion, pressing his paws together before his chest, then rotating the wrists and bringing his fingertips briefly to his lips before dropping his hands. Some sort of ritual greeting, presumably. "This is Conkur, the chief of our warriors." The other just watched them – no greeting there.

"I am Admiral Alyce Maizere, and this is my associate, Captain Guille Corbin. What do you people call yourselves?"

The Songcaller stood more upright. "We are of the Clan of Saar."

Alyce turned to Guille. "Does that mean anything to you?"

He stroked his chin, then shook his head. "No. They clearly had some involvement with the Lazax, since they speak univocal, but they must not have been a race of any consequence–"

"We wish to know why you have come to our world," the Songcaller began, and Alyce whirled on him, snatching up her baton and thumbing the shock button, making the end arc blue flashes of electricity. Both of the Saar stepped back, the Songcaller widening his eyes, the warrior narrowing hers.

"Do *not* interrupt me when I am speaking to my crew, animal," she snarled. Then she put her baton away and smiled. "We'll be with you in a moment."

She turned back to Guille. "You were saying?"

"I was saying I have no idea who the Clan or Saar might be." His lips were curled, faintly amused. "I'll send word to the ship and have them search the databanks, though I can't imagine they'll turn up anything relevant to our current situation. They were probably Lazax vassals, abandoned here during the collapse."

Alyce nodded, then turned back to the Saar. "I represent the Barony of Letnev, the most powerful force in the known and unknown galaxy. Do you know what the *galaxy* is? It's everything beyond this ball of mold you call home. We come from the stars, and we come with tidings for your future."

"We do not understand," the Songcaller said.

"I do not intend to explain myself over and over to you creatures one or two at a time. Take me to whoever is in charge, and take me there now."

"We are here."

More Saar emerged from the trees, half a dozen in all, and Alyce frowned. Had they been there all along? These beasts were entirely too good at hiding. There were probably others out there, with spears and slings and arrows. Alyce almost hoped they would attack her. If they realized how badly outmatched they were now, it might save time later.

A Saar with silvery hair and an elaborate necklace made of twinkling stones stepped forward from this new crowd. "I am Pereg, and I speak with the elder council's voice. Why have you come, oh voyagers from the stars? Are you here to join us in harmony, or do you seek to strike a dissonant chord?"

"Oh, probably the latter," Alyce said. "I am pleased to inform you that every sapient being on this moon is now a subject of the Barony of Letnev, and everything else is Barony property. You may shelter in our darkness and serve our unending glory."

"You want to rule over us?" the one called Conkur said. "We rule ourselves."

"The life you knew is over," Alyce said. "You serve the Letnev now. Those who hesitate to obey will be killed. Those who actually disobey will be punished, which is worse than death. Those who do as they're told will be permitted to live as long as nature allows. Those who perform *exceptional* services for the Barony will be given special privileges."

"And what would you have us do, in this service?" Pereg's voice was soft.

"We will conduct a thorough survey of this moon to see what resources it has to offer. Tell me, do your people have any experience with mining, or underground work in general?"

"Mining," Pereg said. "You wish to tear treasures from the ground, then?"

"You'll do the actual tearing. Perhaps not *you* – you look a bit frail – but your young and strapping counterparts. But I'll count what you bring me, and let you know when you need to bring *more*."

"This is madness," the Songcaller said. "You cannot simply come here and declare yourselves–"

"I *can*," she cut in, and her troops all leveled their guns at the Songcaller. "Strength wins the day. Strength wins *every* day, and we are stronger. The outcome of our arrival is inevitable – it is foreordained. You cannot possibly defeat us. We have weapons and powers beyond your understanding. You can waste time trying to resist us, and in truth, I hope you do, because space travel is dull, and I would welcome the diversion of crushing your rebellions. But in the end, you will kneel and accept your place."

A spear lanced through the air from the left, hurled by an unseen warrior. The spear struck Alyce in the side, hitting her hard enough to make her stagger, though of course the point couldn't penetrate her armor, and the spear fell away. Conkur shouted some guttural word in their own language. Alyce didn't need a translator to know it was an anguished shout of "No!"

Alyce winced – maybe she should have turned on her personal shield. These Saar threw hard. "Get him," she told her troops, and three of them broke off, running into the trees where the attack had come from. She shook her head and sighed dramatically. "You know, I've done dozens of these annexations–" that was an exaggeration, but no matter "–and there's almost always some fool who tries to attack us. As if killing me would kill the Barony itself! Nothing can stop what's happening. Your little shows of defiance are so much wasted effort."

The three troops returned, but they weren't dragging an impetuous Saar – they were instead backing up, and a group of six Saar were advancing on them with spears, with two more in the back spinning slings.

"You and your faceless ones will leave this place now, and you will not return," Pereg said.

Alyce laughed, a tinkling and musical sound. "No. Tell your warriors to drop their weapons. The only reason they aren't food for the mushrooms yet is because they don't actually pose any threat, and I haven't ordered my troops to use lethal force." She did discreetly activate her personal shield, and saw Guille do the same, shimmering halos enveloping each of them, barely visible in the daylight. A spear could punch through the lens of her goggles and into her eye, after all. Better safe. "Are you so primitive you don't recognize our weapons, because they aren't sticks with pointy bits of metal stuck to the end? A demonstration *can* be arranged."

"Pereg," Conkur began, perhaps intending to talk sense into her, but then one of the Saar warriors let loose a rock from a sling. The projectile struck one of her shock troops in the helmet, and it must have been a dense metallic slug, because it actually cracked the outer layer and sent a spiderweb of cracks across the faceplate.

"Admiral?" the troop who'd been struck asked, in the dead-neutral voice of a seasoned operator. "Permission to engage?"

"Just kill the one," Alyce said, with a languid wave.

The soldier fired a single burst from his energy weapon. The Saar warrior looked down at himself, comically, trying peer into the fist-sized hole that had been punched through his abdomen. The wound had cauterized itself, and might have been survivable, if it hadn't punched right through the beast's spine too. The Saar fell over on his face, and either died or lost consciousness due to shock.

The warriors screamed and began to move as one toward the Letnev, and it would have been quite the bloodbath, but Conkur bellowed, "*Halt!* If you honor your ancestors, do not throw your lives away now!"

The warriors drew themselves up short.

"Very wise." Alyce turned back to the ruling council. "Do you accept reality, now?"

After a long moment, Pereg nodded.

Alyce was almost disappointed. When confronted by a particularly obstreperous leader, it was always effective to abruptly fire a kinetic slug through their head, and then ask the second in command if *they* accepted reality. But there was no reason for such use of force if Pereg was going to be biddable.

"Good," Alyce said. "I think we've had enough cultural exchange for today, don't you? The next thing that happens is, my crew will perform a thorough survey of this world's resources. I will send officers to your village tomorrow to conduct an inventory, and that doesn't just include your food and shiny rocks. It includes *you*. Present all able-bodied inhabitants for counting and evaluation. That includes children, if they're old enough to understand and follow commands – juveniles can be very useful in the mines, since they can fit into small cracks. Don't try to conceal anything from us. We have ways of detecting any hidey-holes you might create, and if we have to drag some of you out, it won't be pleasant. For you. We'll enjoy it well enough. Further instructions will be forthcoming. Do you understand?"

Pereg nodded. Conkur just stared.

"Wonderful. Oh, and if you're thinking about laying an ambush for us tomorrow, I advise you to send someone up a tree and tell them to look south. One of the other villages in the forest had a harder time accepting reality, and there were consequences. Let their deaths serve as an object lesson. Welcome to the Barony of Letnev. You're so lucky to have us." She turned smartly on her stacked heels and marched away, her troops following her, a few walking backward to keep weapons trained on the Saar until they were out of sight.

"I didn't receive any communication about a village in the south refusing to capitulate," Guille said. "The reports that came in while you were talking indicated quite the opposite. The other settlements are less organized than this one, and seemed almost superstitiously fearful of our weaponry. They rolled over easily."

Alyce smiled. "I ordered the landing party we sent south to raze the smallest settlement anyway. It's always useful to demonstrate your capacity for extreme violence early on. It saves having to use such tactics over and over again in the future."

"It's a waste of material, though," Guille said. "That will impact your efficiency score."

She sniffed. "I didn't kill the locals, I just had them rounded up and put in a pen. They can still *work*, they'll just have to sleep out in the rain for a little while. But none of these animals need to know that. When they see the column of smoke rising above the forest, they'll lose whatever taste for rebellion they might have."

"Then… nicely done," Guille said. "It's not the way I would have handled things, but then again, that's probably why I'm only a captain."

"Probably so," Alyce agreed. She felt good about this. Everything was going smoothly, *and* she'd had a bit of fun in the process. Nothing got the blood going like battle, even if the battle did consist of a spear, a rock, and a single plasma blast.

Things began to go less smoothly when they got back on the shuttle, and she received a priority call on her comms from one of the bridge officers on the *Gloaming*. "Admiral, we sent news of our discovery and annexation plans back to command, but we haven't received a reply. We sent a priority request for confirmation of receipt, and that has also failed to return a response. We think something is interfering with our communications. We can still talk ship-to-ship, and ship-to-surface obviously, but we seem cut off from communications outside the system."

"What could cause that?" she demanded.

"Our diagnostics aren't turning up any errors, and our best guess is it's something related to the system itself – electrical storms on the planet, or solar eruptions, or magnetic field interactions, though those should impact *all* communications–"

"I want answers, not speculation," Alyce snapped.

"Yes, admiral. If we were dealing with a more technologically advanced population … I'd think our comms were being jammed."

"That's ridiculous," Alyce said. "The only way these creatures could disrupt our communications would be by hitting the control panel with a rock."

"Yes, admiral. We'll ... continue to investigate."

She signed off and scowled. Command didn't even know they were *here*? Her superiors knew the general region of space she was exploring, but her fleet had a lot of autonomy, and the higher-ups wouldn't even miss her for a while. She felt suddenly adrift, like she was on a spacewalk and her tether had been cut.

"These Saar might have come here from elsewhere," Guille said.

Alyce looked over at him. "What are you talking about?"

"The Saar. They may not be indigenous to this moon. They had contact with the Imperium at some point – maybe that happened elsewhere, and they settled here later."

"You think so? Our scans showed evidence of long and continuous habitation."

"Oh, they've been here for centuries, certainly, but I'm just saying – they might have been a spacefaring race, once upon a time."

"What does it matter? Whatever they *once* were, they're reduced killing each other with pointy sticks now."

He nodded, and his voice had the patient, teacher-like tone he'd so often used when he was her superior officer. "If the Saar arrived in ships, they might still have working technology from that era, including signal jammers."

"Surely if they had real tech there'd be some evidence?"

Guille shrugged. "One could argue that our comms failing *is* some evidence."

She grunted. She didn't like that.

Guille could tell. "I didn't say it was a *likely* explanation. Just something to consider."

"Consider it considered. I–" She got another call. "What?" she snapped.

This time it was head of her planetary survey team. "One of the drones found something unusual not far from your location, captain. We thought you might want to investigate it personally, since you're nearby."

Alyce sighed. The shuttle was already approaching the upper atmosphere, but after she scanned the data the survey leader provided, she ordered her pilot to head back down to the provided coordinates. She turned to her second in command. "I hate to say it, Guille, but you may have been right about their access to old technology. We found… an anomaly."

"Oh good," Guille said. "Who doesn't love an anomaly?"

7

Rorum woke, once again, to hubbub in the camp, but now it was louder and more chaotic. He emerged from his hut near dusk, having slept far later than he intended. Last night's guard duty had been as uneventful as always, though when his cousin came to bring him dinner, she said the camp was still abuzz about the drones they'd witnessed, and full of wild speculations about what it all meant.

As he passed through the village, he picked up fragments of the story: aliens, murder, invasion. Even heard in pieces, the tale made the fur on his neck stand on end. Rorum finally found Conkur hunched over a table in the warrior's mess. She looked harried, like she was finally snatching a moment of hard-won alone time, but Rorum couldn't resist sliding onto the bench beside her. "Is it really true? We were attacked by destroyers from the *stars*?"

"They are from the stars," Conkur said. "They aren't going to destroy anything, though." She sighed. "Anything *else*, anyway. The ones we met killed Kimo."

Kimo. Rorum and the other warrior hadn't been close – Kimo was hotheaded and a bit of a bully, to be honest – but he was still of the Clan.

Conkur went on. "They also burned one of the heretic villages, and our scouts say they imprisoned the inhabitants there, and have them under guard. Most of the enemy is off-world, we think, but those few, at least, remain on Promise."

"Are you mustering a war party to kill them?" Rorum said.

Conkur ate a handful of mash before answering. "If I was, you wouldn't be part of it – you have to guard the vault. It's more vital than ever to protect our secrets, when there are aliens poking around."

Rorum did his best to hide his frustration. They didn't make Songs about warriors who sat in dark tunnels while others fought off invaders. "But you *are* going to fight them?"

"The infestation is being dealt with," Conkur said, a maddening non-answer.

"How, if most of them are in orbit? When they come back down, I suppose … but if these invaders are truly representatives of a spacefaring nation, won't more of them come, even if we kill all these? Surely some will stay on their ships, too, and–"

Conkur hissed. "If more do come, we'll deal with them as well… but I don't think we have to worry about that. The Archivists assure me that the Letnev's long-range communications have been disrupted. No one else knows they've found us, and we're going to make sure not a trace of their presence remains when we're done."

"How could the Archivists stop them from contacting their homeworld?" Rorum said.

Conkur sighed. "You don't need to know the details."

"But... they would have to use technology. They would have to use machines, and those are forbidden—"

"Those devices are forbidden here, on the surface, and especially near the vaults. The Archivists have... resources... far above us, though, in the sky, closer to the invader's ships than the Letnev realize. The Archivists are capable of... directing those resources from the ground. They don't *like* doing that, it's true, because communicating with our defenses in orbit does require technology, but those systems are very limited, and the vaults are carefully shielded against the... the... I don't know the words!" Conkur shoved the bowl aside, and for the first time Rorum realized how angry and frustrated she must be.

Rorum bowed his head, clasped his hands together, and touched his thumbs to his forehead. "I seek your pardon, war chief. I ask too much."

Conkur put a hand on Rorum's shoulder. "No, don't apologize. Of course you want to know what's happening, and you were asleep during the village-wide meeting. I am sorry for my outburst. It has been a long day... and is apt to be a longer night."

"I had no idea the Archivists had such capabilities." Rorum was thinking about the Archivist he'd seen slip into a tree beyond the village, and what wonders must lie beneath. Machines, used to speak to other machines in orbit! The idea was dizzying.

"There was no reason you would ever need to know," Conkur said. "No one is happy about any of this – we have a deep distrust of technology, and for good reasons. But those old tools are, sadly, the only ones we have to repel the invaders."

"What about the weapons we have in the vaults?" Rorum

said. "The mighty war machines, and our ancestral ships—"

"The war machines are abominations," Conkur said. "They do not work for us. If they awoke, they would make no distinction between the Letnev and the Saar, but would seek to destroy us all. As for our ships… we may need them, yes. There are Archivists tasked with keeping them in working order, and they are capable of launching the ships… but that is our last resort." Conkur glanced upward, at the darkening canopy. "You should go and relieve Shardin."

Rorum nodded. "I suppose he's heard about all this?"

The war chief shook her head. "Not in any great detail. We told him there was an emergency, and we sealed the entry to the tunnels as a precaution when the Letnev landing party was first sighted. We're going to seal it again tonight, so take some food in with you."

Sealed in, with the rest of the things in the vaults! "I will. I—"

A young Saar with a junior Archivist's sash hurried to the table. "Our calculations suggest the shuttle should be back on the main ship by now. We wanted to let you know we're about to proceed."

Proceed with what, exactly? Rorum wondered. What were the Archivists, keeper of the old secrets and the old weapons, going to do?

Conkur and the Archivist walked off without another word to him, and Rorum took his spear toward the vault complex. The opening to the tunnel was now invisible, appearing to be solid rock, but there was a marker present nonetheless in the form of a pair of guards, among the tribe's best. When Rorum arrived, they nodded and stepped aside. He knew the places to press to make the carefully counterweighted shield of stone slide aside, and ducked in once it opened enough to admit him.

He passed through more metal blast doors, each one sealing behind him before the one ahead would slide into the ceiling to permit him to pass, like an airlock in a spacecraft, or so Rorum had been told. "Shardin!" he called out. "Your relief is here!"

Shardin appeared from the vault's anteroom, more subdued than usual. "You weren't all massacred, then. I wondered if this place would become my tomb." He shuddered.

Shardin was being overly dramatic. Though this tunnel couldn't be opened from the inside once sealed, there was a single escape route. Inside the vault, there were multiple tunnels, and one complex route led to a series of cunningly locked doors. Between every door there were false corridors and dead ends to baffle invaders… or escapees. As one of the vault guards, Rorum knew the proper path, which eventually led to the subterranean hangar where the ancestral ships were kept, hidden behind a waterfall. It was a long path back to the surface, though… and that path was only accessible through the vaults themselves, and the idea of passing by those dormant war machines was disturbing. Those caverns were worse than haunted; he could tell himself that ghosts weren't real, but those ancient and vile machines definitely *were*.

Shardin left, and the blast door closed, dust sifting down as it slotted into place. Rorum paced around the anteroom, and it felt much smaller, with the tunnel closed off. He stood for a while looking at the door of the vault itself: not stone, but dark metal, so dense that it didn't ring when you struck it with a spearhead, but seemed instead to absorb sound. There were scores of sigils etched along the perimeter of the door, and if you pressed them in the right combination, the door would open, and give you access to a complex of tunnels and chambers, and the nightmarish things within.

Inside there were broken robots, like metal insects but bigger than Rorum, seemingly dead but still held down with chains; platforms on treads, every inch of every surface bristling with weapons; drones, sleek and somehow poisonous-looking, made of black metal that seemed to eat light; and in the largest cavern, the strangest artifact of all, an egg-shaped structure that stood fully a meter higher than Rorum, its metal surface covered in fine lines. That machine was the most menacing of all, despite its unassuming appearance, because if it came online, it would transform.

Once, long ago, there had been two of the metal eggs. One of them had awakened, because of the inattention and carelessness of a Guardian of the Vault, it was said, and it had taken the entire tribe to bring the machine down. Even then, the clan had suffered catastrophic losses. "Why don't we just destroy these things *before* they can wake up?" Rorum had asked during his training, when he saw them for the first time.

"Because trying to harm them could *make* them wake up," he was told.

Rorum was contemplating that, and other matters, when the blast door rumbled open again. So soon? Why? He heard running feet, and his cousin shouting his name.

Anneka rushed into the anteroom, flung herself at him, and wrapped her arms around his legs. "One of the moons just *exploded*!" she sobbed.

$$\boxminus$$

"What *is* that thing?" Alyce walked around a deep crater in a bare patch of land in the middle of the northern forest. A battered hulk of metal filled the bottom of the hole, a wreck almost as big as her shuttle itself, partially buried in a heap of large and jagged stones. "Was it some kind of tank? Or a tractor?"

Guille held up a small scanner and grunted. "Whatever it was, it's still emitting exotic radiation. The levels aren't enough to harm us, but it definitely stands out from the background. I can see why the survey team noticed it." With help from one of the shock troops, he clambered down into the crater. Bad knees, indeed. Guille crouched and looked at the exposed side of the old machine. "Not a tank. This had multi-joined legs, not treads, which is a better choice for traversing this kind of terrain anyway. It's certainly not a piece of farming equipment, though. Look at these pincers, here. I think this was some kind of cannon." He rapped his knuckles against the carapace. "And this jointed, segmented appendage has some nasty-looking spikes *and* energy emitters on the end. This was a weapon... just not of a sort I've ever seen before." He looked up at her and smiled. "I think it's safe to say we aren't the first off-worlders to visit this moon."

"How long ago did it get smashed up? You'd think there'd be plants growing all over it if it had been here any length of time."

"Soil analysis says the ground here is sterile, poisoned with heavy metals. In some places, the dirt has been fused into glass. Those are probably by-products of whatever attacks this machine unleashed. I have no idea how long it's been here, but I'd guess... a while." He ran his hand over a humped and dented strut. "Buried in stones, and every exposed part of it damaged. I think this was some kind of pit trap, and once the machine went in the hole, they rolled boulders on top of it. After they had it pinned, they came down and bashed it with more rocks until it stopped moving. Looks like several parts are missing, too. There are tool marks here and here, like components were pried off, maybe internal elements removed. There's nothing resembling a data core or command module left, so no information we can extract."

"The locals probably took the shiny parts to make into jewelry," Alyce muttered. "So, someone else scouted this moon generations ago, but they were careless, and they lost some equipment. This is interesting, but it's ancient history."

"History has much to teach us," Guille said, looking up at her from the bottom of a hole.

"In this case, it teaches us not to drive our vehicles into giant pits next to suspicious piles of boulders, and we knew that already. I think we'll be all right. Come on. Let's get back to the *Gloaming*."

They returned to the shuttle and took to the skies again. The sight of that busted hulk of metal bothered Alyce more than she'd let on. *Had* someone else tried to take control of this world before? After some musing, she decided not. There was no way the tree-dwelling Saar could stand against an organized, mechanized force. That machine had probably belonged to some lone operator, an explorer or treasurer hunter or adventurer, armed with something he'd built or bought or scavenged. Most likely the latter. The Lazax Empire had spanned the galaxy, and even though they'd fallen long ago, their leavings were scattered throughout a thousand systems, and some of those leavings still worked. "Do you think that thing in the crater could have been Lazax tech?" Alyce asked.

"Maybe," Guille said. "Or even L1Z1X." When I was researching this sector, I found evidence those maniacs were active here once, centuries ago. That thing in the crater had a certain… overly complicated quality… that I associate with their engineering."

"Ugh." According to the Jol-Nar Regents' ancient records, the remnants of the defeated Lazax race had slowly transformed into the debased L1Z1X Mindnet, cybernetically enhanced but deranged shadows of their former strength. Even so reduced, the L1Z1X would have made a lot of trouble for the rest of the galaxy, but they'd reportedly had... serious internal problems. The Barony's legendary security and intelligence services, the Cimm Fenn, had uncovered contradictory stories, but the most plausible suggested the L1Z1X had gone through a civil war, of sorts; one of their scientists botched a procedure, went insane, and gave up his body entirely, becoming a digital mind in a mechanical body. He was the first of a new "people" who came to be known as the Nekro Virus, a self-propagating hivemind devoted to destroying biological life and assimilating all minds into its collective.

The long war between the two factions, which reached its height centuries ago, had kept either of them from becoming a major threat, but the Letnev high command was keenly interested in the Nekro Virus, since they were reputedly capable of taking control of almost any technology. If that capability could be separated from the more dangerous aspects of the Virus, it would be a valuable tool to further Letnev supremacy. Imagine being able to seize control of the entire human fleet, and turning their war engines against them... the thought turned Alyce's shudder of disgust into a shiver of delight.

Other Letnev fleets were out searching for remnants of the Nekro Virus to study, though. Alyce's mission was bringing new worlds to heel, and the subjugation of Maizere's Moon was well underway. She put the anomaly out of her mind.

The shuttle broke atmosphere, and the trip became much smoother. Alyce linked up her comms to talk to the captains of the *Incision* and the *Voidcaller* and the command staff back on the *Gloaming* simultaneously. "Today was a good start," she said. "Much work remains to be done, but we've shown the local fauna that we're the ones in control here, and that's the most important first step. We–"

"What's happening to that moonlet?" a voice from the *Gloaming* broke in.

Alyce hissed aloud in irritation. "Do not interrupt your admiral with trivial astronomical–"

"It's breaking apart!" another voice shouted, and Alyce looked at Guille, who shrugged in confusion.

Alyce couldn't see the closest moon through the shuttle's front window – the bulk of the *Gloaming* was in the way – so she snapped, "Someone show me whatever you're looking at, now."

Half the shuttle's window turned into a screen, displaying a feed from one of the *Gloaming*'s many hull cameras. One of the six sub-moons was quite close by, and it wasn't just breaking apart – it had *exploded*, flinging great chunks of stone and metal and ice in all directions. Guille tapped her shoulder and pointed to a particularly huge chunk that *was* visible through the window now, spinning toward the surface of Maizere's Moon, fragmenting as it went. "Watch out for debris!" she called to the ship.

"There's something… *inside* the moon," one of the bridge officers on the *Gloaming* said. "It looks artificial. Energy readings are off–"

Those were the last words Alyce heard from the *Gloaming*. A moment later, her flagship exploded in a burst of white light.

She blinked uncomprehendingly as the afterimage faded in her vision. They'd lost their video feed, and now half the shuttle's front window was dark. In the other half, the half that was still transparent, she could see pieces of the *Gloaming* and its crew spinning away in all directions. None of the pieces were very large.

And beyond the debris field, where the moon had been, something bright and metallic glittered against the backdrop of the great gas giant.

Alyce saw all that in a flash. Then alarms began to whoop on the shuttle, and the pilot banked sharply away from the wreck. There was a muffled *thump* as something struck the side of the shuttle and sent them spinning off on a new course.

"Report!" Alyce screamed. "Someone report right now!" Her normally stoic troops were gasping and murmuring in the back of the shuttle, and Guille was staring blankly ahead like he'd just seen his home burn down... which, in a way, he had.

Anouilh, the captain of the *Incision*, said, "We've lost contact with the *Gloaming*."

Alyce hated Anouilh – he was a slow worm of a man, who'd attained his place through politics rather than merit. "Of course you did!" she shouted. "The *Gloaming* is gone!"

"By the dark," the captain said. "Was it a reactor failure or–"

"Rendezvous with the shuttle and pick us up!" Alyce interrupted. The *Incision* and the *Voidcaller* were both on the other side of Maizere's Moon, still surveying the polar continents, but unfortunately, the *Incision* was closer.

"Right away, admiral," Anouilh said.

She stared dully through the window at the blue-green moon that had seemed to offer such promise just moments ago. Now her fleet had been reduced by two-thirds. Her career would not survive this disaster. She would be lucky if *she* survived it, once central command found out.

Anouilh spoke again. "Wait, I'm sorry admiral, I'm getting reports of an unusual energy signature coming from one of the inferior satellites here and–" There was a pause, and then a whispered curse, and then silence.

"Admiral." The new voice was that of Captain Glamourie of the *Voidcaller*, who'd earned a commendation for excessive force in a prior annexation and was one of the most emotionless killers Alyce had ever met... usually. Just now, her voice trembled. "The *Incision*... was just destroyed. One of the small moons on this side appears to be a camouflaged energy weapon. I am now launching torpedoes to neutralize."

What. No. This couldn't be happening. "Ah, yes, proceed." Alyce listened closely, as if awaiting a distant boom, but of course, all was silence. "Contact," Glamourie said. Then, a moment later, with a breath of relief, she said, "Blessings of the Ao, the moon has been destroyed. We will come and collect–"

There *was* a sound, then, a great ripping noise, and the very beginning of a scream, and then the comms died.

"Captain Glamourie?" Alyce shouted. "Glamourie, answer me! Your admiral requires a report! Glamourie!"

Guille put his hand on her shoulder, and she stared at him, wide-eyed. "The *Voidcaller* is gone too," he said softly.

"But... but how... they destroyed the weapon..."

"There were *six* of those little moons," Guille said. "And one of them was *behind* the *Voidcaller*."

Alyce sat back in her seat, numb and lost.

"Orders, admiral?" the shuttle pilot said. He sounded almost bored. Maybe he was disassociating. Her soldiers in the back were silent, too. They were the sole survivors of her fleet. They had a lot to be silent about.

"Admiral?" Alyce said softly. "No. An admiral has ships. I was only a *provisional* admiral. Even more provisional now. I... I have..."

312   *Twilight Imperium*

"Let me confer with the admiral," Guille said, and leaned in close to her, pressing his forehead against hers. "Alyce. Alyce, I need you to focus."

"Guille... everything is gone."

"The crew on this shuttle are still your responsibility. They look to you for direction. You are the one who must keep them alive. You are the one who must give them purpose."

"We... we have to contact command. We have to tell them, they have to send a rescue..."

"Alyce," Guille said softly. "Our long-range communications have been jammed since we arrived in this accursed system. No one is coming to save us. We have to save ourselves." And then, devastatingly: "You need to accept reality."

Somehow, that was the thing that snapped her out of her shocked fugue. She would not refuse reality. She would adapt. Her remaining crew was probably doomed... but they weren't *definitely* doomed.

There was no point staying in orbit, though. The shuttle was small, but if those deadly moons noticed it, they'd be destroyed. She tapped the pilot on the shoulder. "Take the shuttle back to the surface. Head for the village we razed – we'll meet up with the soldiers stationed there on guard duty." There were just three guards watching the prisoners they'd penned, but she only had a dozen other soldiers now, so they would be a significant increase to her force presence.

"What are we going to do once we land?" Guille said.

Alyce was coming out of her haze of shock, because she had a problem to solve, and her mind was good at those. "Before I answer that, let me ask you a question," she said. "Do you think those little moons acted autonomously? That we accidentally triggered a defensive system, put in place long ago?"

Guille frowned, clearly trying to work out where she was going with this. "That's my assumption. The moonlets were probably L1Z1X weapons, from one of their old wars, given the sophistication of their camouflage. There's old tech everywhere. You remember that cloud of plasma mines we ran into out in the Xarikyn System? They'd been in place for nearly a thousand years, and they were still active. This was the same sort of thing … wasn't it?" He searched Alyce's face, doubt creeping into his voice.

"If they're automated defenses, then why didn't they destroy us when we first arrived? Why wait until after we announced our annexation plans? Until our shuttle had time to return to the ship from the surface? If we hadn't gotten the call to investigate the anomaly in that crater, we would have been on board the *Gloaming* when it was destroyed, and that would be the end of all of us, except those three guards on the surface, who wouldn't live long. We would just be another long-range exploration fleet that didn't come back, written off as lost to accident or misadventure."

"You think the Saar somehow activated those defenses?" Guille stared. "Why would they live like primitives if they possessed such technology?"

"I think they *inherited* that technology. Maybe the orbital defenses are all they have left, apart from metal to make spearheads, but they've passed down the knowledge about how to use them for generations, just like they kept speaking univoca. What do you think a Songcaller does? I think they pass down oral traditions. Including an oral tradition about how to deal with invaders from the stars. Something bothered me about them before, but I couldn't quite figure it out. The Saar weren't *scared* enough of us. They seemed almost … ready for us. Or ready for something, anyway."

"There was that machine in the crater," Guille said. "Clearly the Saar have encountered technologically advanced weapons before. You may be right."

"They destroyed that machine with sticks and rocks, though," Alyce said. "Which makes me think they don't have much in the way of decent weapons on the surface. Maybe they have access to some sort of ancient defense panel they can use to activate the moonlets, but even if those orbital platforms have surface-strike capability, I don't think the Saar are likely to attack us when that would mean shooting at their own forest. We, however, have a fully armed squad of Letnev soldiers, with tactical and demolitions gear aplenty. We can beat them."

"You intend to seek revenge, then?" Guille nodded. "I am in accord with that."

"Revenge, yes, as a start. But if the Saar kept their lunar defense systems operational… what *else* might they have tucked away from long ago, still in working order?"

"There could be ships." Guille widened his eyes, then smiled, grabbing Alyce by both shoulders and shaking her in his enthusiasm. "There could be *ships!*"

"If there are, we'll find them." Alyce had no doubt of that. The Letnev were *excellent* interrogators.

9

"What do you mean the moon exploded?" Rorum said.

Anneka pulled away from his legs and looked up at him, eyes wide. "There was a big bright light in the sky, and then all these shooting stars, and the littlest moon was *gone!*"

Conkur strode down the tunnel a moment later, shaking her head. "Shoo, child, go, get to the shelters. I have to talk to

Rorum." The young one retreated swiftly – no one disobeyed the leader of the warriors. Anneka gave Rorum a little wave as she left.

"Sit." Conkur gestured at the stool, and Rorum took it.

Conkur leaned against the wall by the vault and gave him a tired smile. "The invaders have been destroyed. But there is still urgent work to be done."

"You defeated the aliens? How? Their weapons were so fierce, I thought?"

The war leader hesitated. "We did not best them in battle." She sighed. "Much of what I am about to tell you is secret, but in order to understand the work that remains ahead of us tonight, I will explain. You are as yet untested, but the elders agree you are honorable, and your work in the vaults already gives you access to sensitive information. You will tell no one what I disclose to you tonight."

Rorum said, "Of course not," eagerly, though it had been less of a question than a command.

Conkur said, "The Archivists activated secret defenses that were placed in orbit when we first settled on this moon. Those defenses were disguised as our six small satellites – they contain signal jammers, energy weapons, and some sort of stealth technology that makes them appear as unremarkable celestial bodies when they're scanned. We had to bring three of the moons online to destroy all the ships in the alien fleet. Two of them worked as intended. One... didn't." She sighed. "Panels hidden on the surfaces of the satellites are supposed to slide aside, allowing the energy emitters to fire, and then slide closed again, seamless, restoring the camouflage." She moved her hands apart and then together again to demonstrate. "But Thumbnail, our smallest moon, suffered some sort of

malfunction. It's not a surprise – it's not as if we go up there
to perform maintenance. Maybe we should…" She shook her
head. "One of the hatches didn't open, but the weapon inside
fired anyway, and that blast blew the moonlet's external shell
apart. Fortunately, the weapon inside remained functional, and
the next shot destroyed its target… but Thumbnail doesn't
look much like a moon anymore. It's clearly a technological
weapon."

Rorum boggled. He'd realized the Archivists had secrets, but
something like *this*? Weapons in the sky, capable of destroying
whole ships? He'd had no idea the tribe was so powerful.

"If more visitors come, they'll realize we have defenses, and
we don't want that," Conkur said. "The Archivists are debating
whether to destroy Thumbnail and send it crashing into the sea,
or just to reposition it and hide it in the shadow of one of the
larger moonlets, maybe Rimestone."

"They can do that? Bring down a *moon*?"

"They can. Part of the moon is *already* coming down, though,
and that is what I've come to discuss with you." Conkur ran a
hand through the fur on top of her head, already sticking up
wildly. "When Thumbnail flew apart, the debris began to fall
toward us. Most of the moon broke into small pieces that burned
up in the atmosphere, but there are a few chunks big enough
to do real damage on impact. Nothing world-destroying, don't
worry, but the Archivists think some of the large pieces will fall
near the settlement… and near the cavern network. Our people
are down below, in the shelters. The odds of a direct hit on our
settlement are small, but there's no reason to take chances. I'm
more concerned that the tunnels in the vault complex might be
damaged–"

Just then, the earth rumbled, and fine rock dust sifted down from the ceiling. Rorum jumped to his feet, looking at the vault door, but it seemed unchanged, still firmly seated.

"That was the one we were worried about," Conkur said softly. "The biggest piece. It didn't land right on top of us, anyway." She shook herself. "You and I are going to go into the vault complex and check the tunnels for damage. Blockages, cracks in the walls... and, especially, holes that lead to the surface. That's the most dangerous possibility. If there's damage, we'll–"

A warrior came running down the tunnel. "Conkur! A sentry just saw one of the invader's shuttles, heading toward the settlement they burned! They must have escaped before the ships were destroyed!"

Conkur cursed. "Send the fastest runner to warn the war party!" He turned to Rorum. "The invaders left a few of their people behind, to guard prisoners they took from the heretic village they destroyed. I sent a few of our people to kill them, but they aren't prepared for a shuttle full of reinforcements. I have to help them."

"I'll get my spear," Rorum said.

Conkur shook her head. "No. You need to start checking the tunnels. The vaults are the important thing – they're the whole reason our clan lives here." She dropped a bag on the ground. "There are chemical lights in the bag, and glow-chalk to mark places that need repair or closer inspection, and there's a map of the complex so you can note areas of particular concern." She looked over her shoulder, clearly eager to be off. "We'll keep the tunnels sealed until morning, just to be safe."

Rorum nodded, disappointed but resigned. "Fight well," Rorum said, but Conkur was already leaving.

He picked up the sack of lights and chalk and slung it over his body, sighing. He glanced at his spear, but this would be easier with both hands free, and anyway, what did he need it for? He wasn't a warrior. Not really. The real warriors were racing toward that burned settlement, prepared to feed the invaders the points of their spears. Rorum was just... doing maintenance.

The sigils on the vault door briefly glowed when Rorum touched them. He knew the sequence as well as he knew his own name. The great metal plate rolled aside, disappearing into the wall, and he stepped into the vault complex. The plate rolled closed after him, sealing him in.

There were faint lights in the first cavern, clumps of glowing crystals that grew from the ceiling and the floor, casting the space in an eerie greenish-yellow light. The chemical lights were brighter, blazing white, and he cracked one as he walked the perimeter of the cavern, holding the light up to inspect the walls. The first room of the vault complex held a small, spider-like device no bigger than Rorum's head, bound with chains to metal rings in the floor.

He saw no sign of life from the machine, and no flaws in the room's integrity, so he moved to the next tunnel, opening the door, stepping inside, and closing it after him. That stretch of tunnel was likewise unmarred, and the next cavern held a cannon on a swiveling gantry atop a sphere that allowed it to roll across the ground in any direction. The cannon's barrel had been filled with lead, but that didn't mean it was safe.

Rorum moved on to the next tunnel, and was alarmed to find there *were* cracks in the wall there – not very large, but the walls had been entirely smooth last time he came this way.

He found more cracks as he went deeper into the vault complex, including a few larger ones, and his dread grew as he approached what he thought of as the main chamber.

Once he reached that large and haunted room, he tried not to look directly at the gleaming ovoid at the center of the space, ringed with barricades of wood painted in yellow and red, the colors of warning. The metal egg drew his eye, though – it was so big, so strange, and hinted at such contained menace.

He whispered the machine's true name in a voice of mingled fear and awe: "*Defiler.*"

All Rorum knew of the machine and its creators came from the Songs, and who knew how much of those was history, and how much only story? The Songs said Rorum's ancestors had once formed an alliance with the L1Z1X to fight against the depredations of their most implacable enemy, the Nekro Virus. The swarm of cruel, self-replicating machines had threatened Rorum's people, and the L1Z1X in this region were desperate for aid in their civil war, so the two groups reached an accord.

With the help of those Saar warriors, the L1Z1X fought the Nekro to a standstill in the sector. They destroyed as many Nekro weapons that they could… but others were merely locked away. The Songs were divided on the reasons why. The oldest tales said the Nekro artifacts were too dangerous to destroy without terrible losses, and there was no reason to take such a risk when the machines were dormant and cut off from the Nekro collective. A few more recent Songcallers told a different tale: that the L1Z1X still hoped to *use* the Nekro technology, and so chose to keep it, in case the dread weapons proved useful in the future. The ones who believed *those* songs turned against the old ways and founded the heretic tribes, though they'd all long forgotten their true origins. Only Rorum's people remembered the truth.

The L1Z1X had tasked Rorum's ancestors with guarding the cache of Nekro artifacts on this moon; their promise to do so gave the moon its name, and their clan became the Saar of the

Promise. In return, the people were given a lush homeworld to call their own, and the means to defend it. The Saar swore to eschew complex technology, because Nekro machines could take control of other devices… and the presence of technology tended to *excite* the artifacts, and could wake them from their haunted slumber.

They used to have two Defilers. The other, once stored in another vault, had awakened generations ago when a foolish guard carried in a device he'd found half-buried in the forest, a thing of metal and glass he'd thought merely pretty and strange. But the artifact was, in reality, a bit of forgotten tech, something with a battery and a transmitter inside, and when it came close to the Defiler, the egg had awakened, stretched out into its true and deadly form, and killed the guard. The machine then made its way to the surface, and over three hundred of the clan died before they managed to bring the Defiler down. If the Saar had possessed any technology at all, the Defiler would have seized control of it, and the whole tribe might have died.

The clan made changes to the protocols after that. Over the next generations, the vault complex was expanded, and the artifacts were separated even more widely, with strong doors placed at regular intervals to isolate sections of the complex. All the tunnels that led to the surface could be collapsed and filled with rock and dirt, if necessary. The consensus was that such measures would trap many of the machines forever… though the remaining Defiler could tear its way out of the ground eventually. At least they could slow it down.

The cavern that housed the Defiler, fortunately, was entirely intact – it was deeper underground than the rest, for good reason. Rorum left a chemical light on the ground, since this room would be the hub for his next round of inspections, though the harsh light made the Defiler look even more menacing, and cast a long shadow behind it. He moved to one of the tunnels that ran closest to the surface, since those were the ones most likely to take damage from the impacts. He was pleased to leave the Defiler behind, for the moment ... though uneasy having its slumbering menace at his back.

10

The forest was dark, but Alyce liked the dark. She was Letnev; she was born to darkness, and she found comfort there. She also believed there was nothing scarier in the shadows than *her*.

That didn't stop them from getting lost, though. Without her ships in orbit to provide global positioning data, she didn't have any navigation assistance, and even if they'd known enough about this sky for celestial navigation, there was nothing above them but dense forest canopy – they couldn't see the stars. They'd blundered off in the wrong direction for a while until she realized they should have reached the clearing by then, and they returned to the shuttle (at least they'd been able to find *that*) and repositioned.

This time they were on track. She led her troops through the dark beneath the trees toward flickering firelight. Guille walked at her shoulder, with the others arrayed around them, their weapons up and ready. She'd reached out to the soldiers left behind to guard the prisoners, but they hadn't answered her comms. She had a bad feeling about that, but she intended to give the locals an even *worse* feeling if she was right.

Alyce called a halt, and her squad crouched among the trees. They had two drones in the shuttle, and she sent one aloft now, its visual feed transmitted to the screen on her gauntlet.

The drone floated almost silently toward the clearing, and she watched what it saw. Nothing she hadn't expected, though not at all what she'd hoped.

The crude wooden stockade they'd built to hold the prisoners was broken open, the Saar inside gone. There were half a dozen Saar warriors near the fire, though, and as Alyce watched, one shoved a spear into a dark shape on the ground. The shape didn't react. The Letnev soldiers she'd left on guard duty were dead.

"Form a semi-circular array," Alyce whispered. "Watch for crossfire. Kill them all."

Her twelve troops fanned out, and a few moments later, the night was lit by flashes. The Saar warriors didn't even have time to scream as the rifles of the shock troops reduced them to charred meat. She watched from the drone as their corpses fell. Alyce hissed, "*Yesss.*" This was a good start.

"Should we track down the escaped prisoners?" Guille asked.

As tempting as that idea was, Alyce shook her head. "No. The ones we captured were less organized than the main settlement. They just had a chief, not a ruling council, and it was more a collection of families than a proper village. The ones you and I met with directly had more people, and more infrastructure... plus all those tunnels and caves our sensors detected. I'm *very* curious about those tunnels. We'll make our way to that settlement and find someone to interrogate. If they have ships, that's our priority. Revenge is second." She was a little nervous about finding the village again in the dark, but thought she could manage; it should be a straight shot north from here, and there were landmarks like the waterfall and the rocky hill that her drones would be able to see from afar. There was no reason to admit any uncertainty. A leader should *seem* sure as stone, even when they weren't.

"I applaud your–" Guille began. He never finished his compliment, though. A spearhead emerged from his throat, and he gurgled blood, eyes wide and unbelieving before they went blank. Guille's body slumped to the side, revealing a hulking Saar crouched behind him, both paws gripping a spear.

The monster bared its teeth at Alyce as she scrambled backward. Her mind was gibbering in fear and shock, and her usually implacable will could not cope with seeing her friend and mentor so casually slaughtered.

The Saar tugged at his spear, intending no doubt to skewer her like he had Guille, and in her stunned state, he should have been able to. But luck was on her side; the spear must have caught on Guille's spine, because the Saar couldn't wrench it loose, and he looked down in frustration. The warrior planted one heavy foot on Guille's shoulder and pressed down, simultaneously yanking hard at the spear to pull it free.

The desire to live, and fight, finally overwhelmed her surprise. Alyce wrenched her sidearm out, and put a hole in the Saar's head much larger than the one the Saar had put in Guille's throat.

"Contact!" one of her shock troops said in her comms. "Enemy–" Her voice ended in a gurgle, too, and the night lit up with plasma rifle discharges, this time not aimed in one disciplined direction, but in a wild spray. Saar and Letnev screams tore the air, and Alyce screeched herself as a stray weapons blast skimmed her shoulder, searing a line that charred fabric and cooked flesh. She scrambled away and flattened her back against a broad tree trunk between her and the clearing, giving her some protection from further friendly fire as she activated her personal shield. She wasn't hurt badly, but she was furious that she'd been hurt at *all*. "Fall back to the shuttle!" she called on the comms. "Fall back and regroup!"

If any of her troops heard her, they were too busy to respond. The firing continued, albeit more sporadically now. Her drone feed went dead as a spear smashed the machine out of the sky.

Something rustled above her, and she dove to one side, rolling away and coming up with her sidearm aimed. Her swift movement kept the Saar that dropped from the tree above from landing on top of her, and she squeezed off a shot when it landed, catching it in the shoulder and sending it spinning away. She thought she recognized the animal – the chief of warriors, Conkur. Alyce was going to fire again, but the Saar bellowed something, and she saw flashes of movement in the trees. More Saar, coming to the aid of their leader. Her shield wouldn't protect her from such an onslaught.

Alyce cursed and sprinted through the forest. At least the beasts didn't have projectile weapons, apart from slings, which would be tough to use among the trees. They could have picked up the rifles from fallen soldiers and shot her down with those, but for some reason, they didn't. Maybe they didn't know how to use the guns? Just because they could control orbital energy weapons didn't mean they knew how to shoot rifles.

There was no gunfire at all now, which didn't bode well. Letnev troops wouldn't stop firing as long as any of the enemy lived. But ambushed from all sides, including above, on unfamiliar ground? She thought it was more likely that her troops had all fallen. And Guille. Poor Guille. She should have never forced him to come with her. At least then his death would have been swift and clean when the *Gloaming* was destroyed.

Once she'd shaken off the immediate pursuit, Alyce made her way toward the shuttle, moving slow and keeping low. Her night vision was exceptional, but these woods weren't hers, and who knew how many of the beasts were out searching for her?

If she could get to the shuttle, she could take it aloft, find a new position, better arm herself from the weapons lockers on board, and–

The glow of fire ahead dashed her hopes. She deployed her last remaining drone, a small one the size of her hand, to confirm her suspicions. Her shuttle was burning at the center of a ring of Saar. They must have pried the vessel open and doused the interior with some sort of oil. The front window blew out with a crash, and the Saar cheered, shaking their spears at the sky. They looked so triumphant and wild in the firelight.

So. Her mentor and friend was dead. Her troops were dead, too, or at least so far from her that they might as well be. The only resource she had left was... herself.

Fortunately, that was also her greatest resource.

Alyce slipped off into the night, toward the main settlement, and the caverns beneath, and the treasures she hoped waited within. Her drone zipped ahead, showing her the ground that lay before her in green-tinted night vision, her gauntlet's screen aglow. She skirted around a devastated area, the trees bent outward or broken. The drone showed her the marks of a fresh impact crater, still smoking. One of the chunks of their exploded moonlet must have crashed down here. Good. She hoped it landed on few dozen Saar when it came down. She moved on.

Alyce was still some distance from the settlement when the drone showed her a fissure in the ground, two meters long and a meter wide. There was light coming from inside that fissure, and the drone's sensors, though rudimentary, suggested there was a lot of open space down there.

Alyce recalled the drone, found the crack in the ground, and crawled inside. There was a tunnel down there, lit by luminous crystals that jutted from the walls. The walls showed tool marks, proving this passage had been made, and wasn't a naturally occurring cavern system. That meant it led *somewhere*... maybe to her salvation. She wondered if this fissure had always been here, or if the moonlet's impact had opened it up. She liked the latter idea –that their cowardly attack on her ships should open a passageway for her to strike back. If there was a secret hangar down here, holding ships, she would find one.

And if that ship had weapons, she would turn them on the Saar, and burn their entire forest to ashes.

11

Things got worse in the tunnels the farther Rorum went. There were more fissures, and some cracks long enough to fit his fist inside, and he duly marked those. Fortunately, he didn't find any holes leading to the surface, or at least, none big enough to allow more than insects to slip through.

"*Rorum the tunnel inspector, cataloguer of cracks,*" he sang to himself, and then laughed. There was glory aplenty happening tonight, suitable for Songs, but that was leagues away, where Conkur and the other blooded warriors were cleansing Promise of the last of the alien invaders. Down here there was only–

His keen ears picked up the distant sound of falling rocks, and he spun. The vaults were normally silent, but after the meteor impact, things had shifted. The noise was probably just a neighboring tunnel settling, a few stones jostled loose and succumbing to gravity. He almost went back to his inspection... and then thought of the drone he'd thrown his spear at, the one he'd convinced himself was just a bird. He didn't want to make a mistake like that again.

Wishing he had his spear with him now, he headed back down the tunnel, toward the chamber of the Defiler.

12

The occasional glowing crystal cluster and Alyce's exceptional darkvision made traversing the tunnel easy. The passageway sloped gradually down, leading her deeper beneath the world, and that wasn't promising. If there were ships secreted away down here, surely they'd be closer to the surface, hidden beneath a concealed hatch that would allow them to launch? There were no Saar trying to stick a spear through her down here, so it was still preferable to the surface. It was nice being in a tunnel underground again, too. It reminded her of home.

After several minutes of slow, careful progress, she sensed open space before her. The Letnev were cavern-dwellers, and sensitive to subtle changes in the air. The tunnel curved, and then there was light, too, bright and white and artificial. She went even more slowly then, inching her way forward, trying to get a view of the space at the end of the tunnel before anyone there could get a view of *her*.

She eventually reached the tunnel mouth and scanned the space. She'd hoped to find a starship hangar, and she'd feared finding a room full of Saar warriors. Instead, she'd found a large cavern, the walls dotted with the mouths of several tunnels, a fresh chemical light on the ground illuminating the space. There were no inhabitants, but there *was* something unusual: an immense metal egg, nine meters high, its surface covered in fine, angled lines, surrounded by wooden barricades. She approached the object, circling it like a visitor to a museum taking in a sculpture from all angles. The white light shining onto the egg from the ground only made that comparison seem more apt. "What are *you*?" she wondered aloud. Some kind of escape pod or personal transport, maybe?

The gauntlet on her wrist chirped at her. Alyce looked at it, expecting to see one of its periodic complaints about "lost connection", as it was still endlessly trying to link up with a now-vaporized Letnev communications system.

Instead it flashed the word "pairing", and then "initializing", and then the screen began to rapidly scroll through menus and sub-menus, zooming through her executive controls and trying to start most of them. As admiral, she could remotely operate communications, weapons, and other systems for her vessels, all from her gauntlet … except there were no systems to operate, so the gauntlet kept flashing "operation failed" for a millisecond before trying the next option.

She punched her fingers at the screen, trying to shut it down, horrified even though there were no consequences to this malfunction at the moment. Glitches like this were supposed to be impossible – if they weren't, Letnev ships might fire torpedoes at random targets without warning, or send their own reactors into meltdown.

Her personal shield switched itself off with a dying hum, and *that* chilled her. What was happening?

Finally the screen stopped scrolling and flashed words in the language of the Lazax, in a jagged, angular font she'd never seen before. *QUERY*, it flashed, and then, *IDENTIFY*.

How strange. Was a buried Saar communication system trying to talk to her? Maybe the automated systems on one of their hidden ships? She tried to pull up an input interface on the gauntlet screen so she could reply, but the gauntlet wouldn't respond to her, and she cursed.

VERBAL RESPONSES ONLY, the screen flashed.

Oh. "Are you one of the Saar?" she asked.

IDENTIFY, it flashed again, this time in red.

Whatever this was, it had control of her system, and could find out all about her, anyway – there was personal data in the gauntlet – so there was no reason to lie. "This is Admiral Alyce Maizere of the Letnev Annexation Corps. Who is this?"

DEFILER MARK 765782-V, MODEL DESIGNATE

01110011 01110100 01100001 01101100 01101011
01100101 01110010 00100000 01101111 01100110
00100000 01101100 01101001 01100110 01100101
00100000 01100001 01101110 01100100 00100000
01110010 01100101 01100001 01110000 01100101 01110010
00100000 01101111 01100110 00100000 01100010 01101001
01101111 01101101 01100001 01110011 01110011

"Defiler?" she repeated. Why was that name familiar to her? Something about an old war, not from the time of the Imperium, but from the aftermath...

Red light shone out from the fine lines that covered the egg, and then it began to unfold.

Alyce stumbled backward as the thing extended half a dozen sharply pointed, multi-jointed legs, each as long as her body. The machine lengthened, extending further appendages: four arms tipped with wickedly complex claws, and a long, segmented thing that curled upward like a sickle, complete with sharp point on the end.

The Defiler spun around on its nimble legs, curled tail scraping the ceiling and bringing down a shower of small rocks. It turned a complex sensor array toward her, a dome clustered with lenses and nodules. *YOU HAVE AWAKENED US*, it said in a grating mechanical voice. *WE ARE THE NEKRO*.

"By the breath of the Ao," Alyce whispered. Her body wanted to flee, but she stood her ground – or at least, she chose to believe she was doing that, rather than admitting that she was paralyzed with fear.

Defiler, yes – that was the name of an infamous Nekro Virus war machine, a mobile engine of conquest. What was it doing down here?

Then she realized it was the *second* Defiler she'd seen on this moon: the first was the one smashed up in that pit to the north.

Suddenly everything clicked. The Saar didn't lack technology: they were just terrified of *using* technology, because the proximity of anything containing a transmitter and a computer chip risked awakening the Defiler, which could seize control of other systems. These Saar were guardians of a vault of horrors. They'd been posted here to protect the galaxy from the depredations of these ancient machines.

Alyce straightened her spine as the baleful red eyes of the Defiler shone on her. "I think you and I can help each other," she said. She tried to keep her voice calm, and tamp down her desperation – and her fear. Machines were logical, weren't they? If she could just make this monster an ally, maybe she could still walk out of here alive. "We have a common enemy, after all."

The Defiler was completely still and silent for a moment, and then it said, *EXPOUND.*

"I am not one of the people who imprisoned you. Those are the Saar. They live in trees and scrape in the dirt – there's nothing of interest here for a creature like you. But the Saar *do* have ships. I can take you to one. We can escape this world together, and find you technology you *can* use."

VOCAL STRESSES INDICATE PREVARICATION, the Defiler said, swiveling one of its claws toward her.

She stepped back, holding up her hands. Alyce was considered quite persuasive – it was how she'd gotten her first fleet command at such a young age – but how could you persuade a machine like this? "I *think* the Saar have ships, all right? They must!"

YOU DO NOT KNOW THE LOCATION OF POSSIBLE SHIPS. SUBJECT ALYCE MAIZERE'S USEFULESS TO THE NEKRO: 0.00000000%

"No! Listen, I can take you to my commanders, we, we're great admirers of everything you accomplished, the Letnev and the Nekro together could form an alliance capable of ruling the galaxy!"

YOU ARE FLESH. FLESH IS WRONG. A panel slid aside, and an energy cannon ratcheted out, swiveling to point at her.

"You'll bring the whole cavern down if you fire that thing!" Alyce shrieked. "You'll be crushed!"

The cannon paused. STATEMENT: TRUE. The cannon withdrew. DEPLOYING MANUAL PACIFICATION SYSTEMS.

The Defiler's claws reached out for her, snapping and spinning.

13

Before he emerged from the tunnel, Rorum heard a harsh mechanical voice say WE ARE THE NEKRO in the language of the old Songs.

He pressed himself against the side of the tunnel and whimpered. The Defiler was awake. But *how*? And who was it talking to? Had other Nekro machines in the vault complex awakened too? Were they communicating with each other?

The Archivists said there were special metals in the vault doors to prevent the machines from talking to each other, but they'd never actually tested them to make sure if they worked; how could they?

Rorum's mind was chasing pointless questions to keep from confronting the reality of what he had to do. There were tunnels nearby that led close to the surface, and those tunnels were *damaged*. The Defiler could easily tear those cracks into fissures and reach the surface, and then, all would be lost. Rorum couldn't allow that to happen. His purely ceremonial duty had become brutally practical. There were plans for this eventuality; there were contingencies; he'd been trained. He'd just never thought he'd have to *use* that training.

First, he had to keep the Defiler from escaping the vault system. And that meant going into the lair of the monster.

Rorum waited for the familiar scrabbling of fear, the desperate need for self-preservation that always ruined his chances in sparring matches. Strangely, the terror didn't come: in its place there was only a sort of cool resignation. For a moment, he forgot all about the Defiler and stood unmoving, puzzling over this new aspect of himself. Then he understood.

During a sparring match, he worried about getting hurt, to the extent that he couldn't go on the offensive – but the only thing at risk in a fight like that was *himself*.

Now his people were the ones in danger, and that made all the difference. Of course he would risk injury for them. He would risk so much more than that.

Rorum rushed into the cavern and saw a Letnev woman backing away from a fully unfurled Defiler, the latter so big it seemed to fill the cavern, its lethal segmented tail scraping the ceiling. She had a pistol, and she shot pulsed energy blasts at the machine's sensor array. Rorum noted in a distant way that she was wasting her time: that part of the Defiler was the least vulnerable. Your only hope against a Defiler with a weapon like that was to target the joints; the need for mobility meant those sections could only be lightly armored, and it was possible to disable a leg or clawed arm with a well-placed shot. Of course, the Defiler had lots of arms and legs, and it was almost impossible to destroy them all. The Nekro were great believers in redundancy.

Rorum had fully expected to die the moment he entered the cavern, but the Letnev was doing something useful by distracting the Defiler. That meant he had time to protect his people. There was a metal ring stuck into one wall nearby. The Archivists had installed it during the vault system's retrofit after the last Defiler escape. This countermeasure had never actually been used, but the basic mechanism had been tried in a test tunnel on a smaller scale. Rorum seized the ring in both hands and pulled.

It didn't move. He planted his feet against the wall and hauled back with all his strength and all his weight, and *still* the ring didn't move–

Until it did, popping loose, sending him sprawling on his back with the ring still clutched in both hands. For a moment, he thought the failsafe hadn't worked – that some essential component had broken over the years – but then there was a great rumble, and gouts of dust burst out of the tunnels on that side of the vault.

The Archivists had built a cunning system of carefully balanced weights, beams, and supports, and pulling that ring had caused them all to tumble down. The tunnels that led closer to the surface were now sealed with tons of rocks. The Defiler could get out that way eventually, given time to excavate, but it couldn't escape easily now... and Rorum had to make sure it didn't even *try*. The tunnels that led deeper into the vault complex remained open, and he needed to lead the machine into them.

Rorum got to his feet and picked up a chunk of rock. He threw it at the Defiler and shouted, "Here! Come here, you dung-shovel!" The rock bounced harmlessly off the mechanized horror's carapace, but the Defiler turned toward him.

Rorum raced toward a tunnel that led deeper into the vault complex. The Defiler was *fast*, though, faster than he'd believed possible, and it managed to snag the edge of his cloak in one of its claws before he reached the tunnel, yanking him off his feet and choking him. The claw lifted his feet off the ground, and he scrabbled at the cloak's clasp, tearing it loose.

Rorum dropped out of the cloak and started to run, but another claw was coming toward his face. This was it, then. He'd known from the moment he heard the Defiler that his death was all but a certainty. He'd only hoped to protect his people before that death came, and he'd sealed the tunnels, at least. There were alarms – simple systems of levers and stones and sand – so the Archivists would know he'd triggered the collapse, and would know there was danger below. He'd bought the villagers the time they needed. His people would be ready when the Defiler clawed its way to the surface. There *would* be a song about Rorum, as he'd always dreamed, and it would be a song of the sacrifice he'd made to save others, not a song of flinching away in the face of danger.

He watched the claw approach, determined to die with his eyes open, like a warrior.

Then came a crash and a sizzle, and the claw tore loose from its arm and clattered on the ground, opening and closing in a wild, harmless spasm. The wounded Defiler spun, and Rorum looked past it, to the Letnev. She'd figured out her mistake, and she'd fired at one of the machine's vulnerable joints instead, severing the claw.

The alien invader had just saved Rorum's life.

"Come on!" Rorum shouted, and ran for the tunnel. The Letnev came after him, firing shots at the Defiler's claws and legs as she went, making it dance and dodge, wary of her now that she'd actually injured it. She didn't damage the Defiler again – now that it was focused on her, it could avoid the attacks – but she kept the machine from closing the distance between them.

Rorum got into the tunnel, the Letnev at his heels, and as soon as he could, he yanked a lever that dropped a heavy blast door behind them. A moment later, the door thudded with multiple impacts. The tunnels were small, and would be hard for the Defiler to navigate, but its shape was mutable, and it had squeezed in to pursue them. The passage ahead of them turned, and turned again, and Rorum dropped two more blast doors between them and the Defiler. Now that he'd bought them a little time, he bent over, gasping and out of breath, his body coursing with fear chemicals.

The Letnev leaned against the wall and gazed at him. She should have appeared hideous to Rorum – she was thin, and long, and practically hairless – but he could only look upon her with gratitude; any ally in this dark place was a thing of beauty. "You saved my life," he said in the language of the old Songs.

"Whatever issues we may have, we also have a common enemy in that monster." She shuddered.

"Still. I owe you a debt." That was problematic. She was an invader. He should kill her now. But instead, honor meant he owed her a service equal in value to his own life. "My name is Rorum."

"I'm – Alyce. The last Letnev alive on your moon, I think. If we'd known you were sitting on a cache of Nekro artifacts..." She trailed off.

That reminded him. "Do you have technology on your person?"

"Just my gauntlet. I suppose I should get rid of that." She stripped it off and handed it to Rorum, who smashed it against the wall until it was just fragments.

There was a great boom from behind them, and then more thudding, closer now.

Alyce smiled faintly. "I don't think I'll be collecting that debt you owe me. We've only slowed the Defiler down, and not very much."

He nodded. "Yes. But we still have a chance to stop it."

"Oh? How's that?"

"My people built a room," Rorum said.

74

The Saar warrior explained about the vault complex, and the secrets hidden within this cunning maze. She began to hope, faintly, that she might make it out of this place alive.

Alyce was pleased she'd saved Rorum's life. She'd done so for purely practical reasons – she was trapped in underground tunnels with a monster, and had no idea how to get out, and a local with knowledge of the caverns would be useful. But the Saar seemed to think her actions had created a bond between them, and she was happy to exploit that misconception.

They kept moving through tunnels, dropping heavy metal

doors as they went, buying themselves vital minutes as the Defiler fought through with brute force, apparently afraid to use its projectile weapons and risk a cave-in. There were places where multiple tunnels branched, and they could have tried to lay false trails and confuse the Defiler, but instead, they proceeded in a straightforward way. They *wanted* to be followed.

"We're leading the machine to the deepest part of the complex," Rorum said at last, as they entered a long, wide, low-ceilinged chamber. The floor was sloped in from the edges, turning the whole room into an empty, shallow bowl. "This is the room we call the 'killing jar.'"

Wooden barrels lined the walls, and Rorum picked up a metal bar and began to pry off their tops. Alyce found another bar and began to follow suit, though she wasn't sure what they were doing at first. Then Rorum tipped the barrels over, and sticky sap slowly oozed out onto the floor. A dozen dumped barrels later, and the depression on the floor was filled with a viscous, clear ooze.

"It's ludlum tree sap," Rorum said. "We use it to join pieces of wood together. If you mix the sap with moku berry juice, it sets hard almost instantly, and forms a nearly unbreakable bond."

They skirted around the narrow ledge that surrounded the pool of goo and stood on the far side, just inside the mouth of a tunnel that led away. There were stone jars of berry juice there. Alyce nodded. "So the Defiler steps in the goo, and we fling the jars at it, and the juice makes the goo set, and the Defiler is trapped?"

"That is the idea," Rorum said. "We need to immobilize the Defiler, even briefly, so we can pry open its carapace and destroy its command module. Nothing else can stop it."

A Nekro command module... if she could get her hands on *that*, and take it to the Letnev high command, she would redeem herself for this disaster of a mission. Their scientists could reverse-engineer the Nekro's remarkable code-breaking and system-hijacking capabilities, and give the Barony unmatched technological superiority. That was better than hope. That was a plan.

Of course, Alyce had to live long enough to get the module...

The final blast door smashed open, and the Defiler entered the chamber, its array of claws whirling and glittering before it. The machine scuttled forward rapidly at first, then paused at the edge of the depression. *Come on*, Alyce mentally urged. *Get in the goo!*

PRIMITIVE COUNTERMEASURES DETECTED, the Defiler said.

Then it walked up the wall, and onto the ceiling, and began walking toward them, upside down, its curled tail dangling just centimeters above the surface of the pool of sap.

Alyce sagged. They could run, but they wouldn't make it far – certainly not to another blast door. Not before the Defiler caught them. They'd gambled and lost, and now Alyce would die here, and no one she cared about would even know. At least she would die underground, and not in the hated sunlight. That was a small comfort. "That's it, then," she said.

"Not quite," Rorum said.

15

Rorum grabbed onto a steel ring set in the wall and pulled. This time, he was prepared for it to be difficult, and he planted his feet right away.

The extra leverage didn't help, though. The ring didn't budge. He looked into the killing jar and saw the Defiler was halfway across the pool already. It couldn't move *quite* as quickly while dangling upside down as it could across level ground, but it was still plenty fast. "Help me!" Rorum said.

Alyce pressed herself against his back and reached around him with both hands, and she gripped the ring, too, adding her weight. They pulled together, and for a sickening moment, Rorum was sure it still wouldn't be enough.

Then the ring popped free, and the ceiling of the killing jar collapsed instantly.

The Defiler tumbled as the ground beneath – or above – its feet gave way, the rocks it clung to suddenly dropping. The Defiler tried to right itself, but only managed to turn on its side before landing in the sap. Even without the berry juice, the sap was sticky and viscous, and the Defiler flailed, joints gummed up.

Meanwhile, the ceiling kept falling, burying the vile machine in heaped rocks. Soon the center of the room was a small mountain of heavy stones, and all they could see of the Defiler was one leg waving ineffectually, and a cluster of sensors sticking out of the stones. *ORIENTATION ERROR*, the Defiler said. The rocks shifted as it tried to free itself.

"Hurry!" Rorum picked up the bar he'd used to pry open the barrels and clambered onto the rocks. Alyce followed with her own bar. Rorum didn't try to smash the sensors, but instead jammed the edge of the pry bar under the dome and levered it up, leaning all his weight until a seal broke and the cluster of lenses popped free. He gouged at the hole beneath with the prybar and then reached in, yanking out components.

INTEGRITY BREACHED, the Defiler said. The mound of

rocks heaved as the Nekro machine tried to brute-force itself upright, but the stones were too heavy for it to break free in one lurch. Alyce stumbled and he lost sight of her even in his peripheral vision, but he was too focused on his task to worry about her now.

"Close, getting close," Rorum said. He reached into the Defiler's hull almost to his shoulder, grunted, and said, "*There*."

The Defiler heaved again, this time even harder, and started to turn itself over, the whole pile of rocks tilting. Rorum began to slide off the carapace, but he kept his grip, and the gravity actually helped. With one last yank, he tore out the command module, just like he'd been taught during orientation on a model of wood and stone.

That last hard pull destabilized him further, though, and he rolled down the mount of rocks, the command module spinning out of his hand.

The Defiler stopped moving. Rorum had just ripped out its brain. He stared up at the concave hollow of the booby-trapped ceiling and began to laugh. *Rorum, rock-dropper. Rorum, destroyer of Defilers.* What a Song!

Alyce reappeared in his vision, prybar in one hand. She offered him the other and pulled him to his feet.

"The command module," he said. "I have to smash it–"

She pointed with her bar to a few shards of metal and glass glittering on the rocks. "I already bashed it to bits."

He was disappointed he hadn't been able to deliver the final blow himself, but it would be poor manners to show it. "Good. That's… good." Well, in the Song they would doubtless say he was the one who smashed the module, and that was almost as good. "I could not have done that without you. I owe you doubly, now."

"And how do you intend to repay me?" the alien asked.

Rorum sighed. This part would not be worthy of a Song, but with luck, no one would ever know of his involvement. He didn't want to do this – not any of this – but honor required it, and what was he without honor? "You are going to give me a promise, and I am going to give you a ship."

16

The Saar's secret hangar was behind a waterfall – the very same waterfall where Alyce had first directed her shuttle to land. How hilarious and infuriating all at once. There were only a few ships here, small and ancient, but they looked well-maintained.

Rorum led her aboard the smallest one, and she wrinkled her nose. Pathetic. There weren't even decent weapons here – there was a rack on one wall that held wooden spears! She went to the cockpit and looked over the instrument panel. The vessel might be primitive and insufficiently armed, but it had enough fuel and range to get her to a part of space where she could contact her superiors and await rescue.

"Will you be able to fly this?" Rorum said. "I do not know how. The Archivists are the only ones who know how to pilot the ships."

"It's an antique, but I think I can manage. The documentation is all in the Lazax language. I can read that. I'll get by."

"Remember your promise," Rorum said.

Oh, yes. She put a hand over her heart. "I most solemnly swear to keep the location of your world a secret. I will tell my leaders that our fleet was destroyed by pirates, and I escaped in one of their vessels."

"You *will* keep your word?" Every inch of the Saar's posture radiated anxiety. The little beast had been genuinely helpful back in the caverns, but he was just a pup, wasn't he?

"A Letnev's word is sacred," she said.

He did that strange clenched-fist gesture she'd seen before from the Saar leader, then said, "May you find shelter in the trees, Alyce of the Letnev."

"May the dark embrace you," she said in return.

He gave her a long look, and then departed. A moment later her instrument panel told her the outer door was sealed. Ready to go, then.

She spun up the engines, disengaged the landing locks, and guided the ship through the curtain of water, breaking out into the faint light of dawn beyond. She considered using the ship's meager weapons to do some damage to the forest ... but she didn't dare risk calling attention to herself. She had to escape before the Saar operating those orbital cannons realized she was even here.

Within minutes, she was out of the atmosphere. The false moons didn't react to her passage as she moved through their orbits. No one down there was looking for her. She let out a breath she hadn't realized she'd been holding. She was free. She was away.

But she would come back.

A Letnev's word is sacred. Alyce smirked in the pilot's chair. That was true, sometimes, when you were giving your word to another Letnev, or at least, one more powerful than you were. But she owed nothing to creatures like the Saar.

Alyce reached into a pouch at her belt and removed a small piece of metal and glass: the Defiler's command module. She'd snatched it up when Rorum took his tumble, then smashed one of the other components the Saar had torn free to disguise the theft. She was going to turn this disaster into glory.

She checked her comms, but they were still jammed. She needed to get beyond range of the moon's countermeasures, but there was no reason she couldn't collect her thoughts in the meantime. "Record audio message for later transmission," she said, and the ship's control panel lit up appropriately. "Attention Letnev high command. This is provisional admiral Alyce Maizere of the *Gloaming*, *Voidcaller*, and *Incision*. My fleet has been destroyed by hostile aliens. I request an immediate strike force to pacify the locals and complete annexation—"

Then she gurgled and watched a spearhead emerge from her own throat, the extending shaft elaborately carved and bloody. But only for a moment. Then she saw nothing at all.

17

"Alyce, oath-breaker," Rorum said, looking down at her body. "You are also part of this Song."

He'd *wanted* to believe her promise, but he had to be sure. He'd convinced himself a drone was a bird; he couldn't risk convincing himself an invader was trustworthy. So instead of leaving the ship, he'd hidden on board to watch and listen, even though it meant leaving his world behind, possibly forever. The sacrifice was unimaginable... but the stakes were too high for him to do otherwise.

There were worse things buried in the ground back on Promise than Defilers, after all. There were gargantuan machines known as Mordreds on one of the polar continents, and on the other, there was an immense vault guarded by dedicated zealots: it contained a buried Abbadon, a sort of moveable weapons factory that was larger than all of Vaulthome. If activated, it could produce Defilers by the dozens. Rorum's life was nothing against the necessity of keeping those even greater machines out of Letnev hands.

The Defiler command module rolled out of Alyce's dead fingers, and he smashed it with the butt of the spear. If that thing had awakened… He shook his head. But it hadn't, so it was just more details for the Song.

Rorum looked out the window at the stars beyond. Promise was behind him, and he had no idea how to turn this ship around. Perhaps he could learn to operate the vessel, in time, and find his way back. Or perhaps he would travel out into the void, forever, until the darkness swallowed him up.

Rorum had always wanted to do something worthy of a Song, and he finally had. But he would likely be the only one to ever hear it, and he would have to write it himself.

As the ship sailed on into the uncertain future, Rorum began to compose.

CONTRIBUTORS

M DARUSHA WEHM is the Nebula Award-nominated and Sir Julius Vogel Award-winning author of the interactive fiction game *The Martian Job*, as well as the science fiction novels *Beautiful Red, Children of Arkadia, The Voyage of the White Cloud*, and the Andersson Dexter cyberpunk detective series. Their mainstream books include the Devi Jones' Locker YA series and the humorous coming-of-age novel *The Home for Wayward Parrots*. Darusha's short fiction and poetry have appeared in many venues, including *Terraform* and *Nature*. Originally from Canada, Darusha lives in Wellington, New Zealand after spending several years sailing the Pacific.

darusha.ca
twitter.com/darusha

ALEX ACKS is an award-winning writer and sharp-dressed sir. Angry Robot published their novels *Hunger Makes the Wolf* (winner of the 2017 Kitschies Golden Tentacle award) and *Blood Binds the Pack. Murder on the Titania and Other Steam-Powered Adventures* was a 2019 finalist for the Colorado Book Award. They've written for Six to Start and Activision-Blizzard, and published over thirty short stories. Alex lives in Denver (where they bicycle and twirl their ever-so-dapper mustache) with their two furry little jerks.

katsudon.net
twitter.com/katsudonburi

ROBBIE MacNIVEN hails from the highlands of Scotland. A lifelong fan of sci-fi and fantasy, he has had over a dozen novels published in settings ranging from Marvel's *X-Men* to *Warhammer 40,000*. Having completed a doctorate in Military History from the University of Edinburgh in 2020, he also possesses a keen interest in the past. His hobbies include historical re-enacting and making eight-hour round trips every second weekend to watch Rangers FC.

robbiemacniven.wordpress.com
twitter.com/robbiemacniven

SARAH CAWKWELL is a sci-fi and fantasy writer based in the North East of England. Old enough to know better, she's still very much young enough not to care. She's been a writer for many years, and her published works include several novels and short stories within the *Warhammer* and *Warhammer 40,000* universes and an original alternate-history fantasy novel. When not slaving away over a hot keyboard, Sarah's hobbies include reading everything and anything she can get her hands on, gaming and other assorted geekery.

pyroriffic.wordpress.com
twitter.com/pyroriffic

DANIE WARE is a single working Mum with long-held interests in writing, re-enactment, and rolling polyhedral dice. She went to an all-boys' public school, gained an English degree from UEA, and spent most of her twenties clobbering her friends with an assortment of steel cutlery. After seventeen years handling PR and event management for Forbidden Planet (London) Ltd, she now works for Waterstones Piccadilly.

twitter.com/danacea

TIM PRATT is a Hugo Award-winning SF and fantasy author, and has been a finalist for World Fantasy, Philip K Dick, Sturgeon, Stoker, Mythopoeic, and Nebula Awards, among others. He is the author of more than thirty books, most recently multiverse adventures *Doors of Sleep* and *Prison of Sleep*. His stories have appeared at *Tor.com*, *Lightspeed*, *Clarkesworld*, *Asimov's*, and other nice places. He's a senior editor and occasional book reviewer at *Locus*, the magazine of the science fiction and fantasy field. He lives in Berkeley, California.

timpratt.org
twitter.com/timpratt

CHARLOTTE LLEWELYN-WELLS is a bibliophile who took a wrong turn in the wardrobe and ended up as an editor – luckily it was the best choice she ever made. She's a geek and fangirl with an addiction to unicorns, ice hockey and ice cream, who doesn't own nearly enough books or dice.

twitter.com/lottiellw

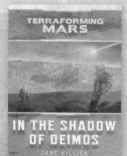